BETTER you THAN ME

☆Maya☆

Also by **Jessica Brody**

Addie Bell's Shortcut to Growing Up

BETTER *you* THAN ME

JESSICA BRODY

A YEARLING BOOK

Text copyright © 2018 by Jessica Brody Entertainment, LLC
Cover art copyright © 2018 by Alyssa Nassner

All rights reserved. Published in the United States by Yearling, an imprint of Random House Children's Books, a division of Penguin Random House LLC, New York. Originally published in hardcover in the United States by Delacorte Press, an imprint of Random House Children's Books, a division of Penguin Random House LLC, New York, in 2018.

Yearling and the jumping horse design are registered trademarks of Penguin Random House LLC.

rhcbooks.com

Educators and librarians, for a variety of teaching tools, visit us at RHTeachersLibrarians.com

The Library of Congress has cataloged the hardcover edition of this work as follows:
Names: Brody, Jessica, author.
Title: Better you than me / Jessica Brody.
Description: New York : Delacorte Press, [2018] | Summary: When two twelve-year-old girls—one a famous TV star, the other an obsessive fan—switch bodies the results are nothing but disastrous.
Identifiers: LCCN 2017041744 | ISBN 978-1-5247-6971-0 (hc) |
ISBN 978-1-5247-6973-4 (ebook)
Subjects: | CYAC: Celebrities—Fiction. | Fans (Persons)—Fiction.
Classification: LCC PZ7.B786157 Be 2018 | DDC [Fic]—dc23

ISBN 978-1-5247-6974-1 (pbk.)

Printed in the United States of America
10 9 8 7 6 5 4 3 2 1
First Yearling Edition 2020

To Joanne, Brad, and Benny
for the endless conversation and inspiration

BLAH, BLAH, BLAH . . . GENIE

The magic lamp shimmers in the hot red sand. A diamond in the rough. A jewel in the desert. I wipe the sweat from my brow—evidence of walking through miles and miles of scalding-hot nothingness. With trembling fingers, I reach for the ancient relic, my breath catching in my throat as soon as I make contact.

"This is it!" I tell Miles, my travel companion and best friend. The violent desert winds have wreaked havoc on his perfect hair.

"Are you sure?" he asks.

I nod. "This is the one from my dream."

I sink to my knees, my silk caftan immediately filling with rough grains of sand. I rest one shaking hand against the side of the lamp, hold my breath, close my eyes, and rub. And then . . .

Nothing.

I fall back into the sand, hopeless, defeated. Miles sinks down next to me. "I'm sorry, Ruby."

He puts a hand on my arm and we sit in silence for a moment. Then I tilt my head back and call into the cloudless sky, "Where are you? Why can't I find you?" The words are cheesy. But I say them anyway. Because I have no choice.

Just then, the golden lamp I'm still clutching begins to shudder. Gently at first, like a shiver on a cool day, then more violently, until I have to squeeze it between my knees to keep it from shaking out of my hands.

I fight not to roll my eyes. It's a bit much.

Then, in a puff of blue smoke that looks more like glittery pixie dust than genie smoke, a man appears before me. An ancient, powerful genie with blue skin and golden eyes that sparkle in the desert sun. From my seated place in the sand, he looks gigantic. Towering above Miles and me in gold harem pants that flap in the breeze and a red jewel-encrusted turban covering his hair.

He folds his arms over his bare blue chest and glares down at me, his gilded eyes cruel and cold. "Who awakens me from my long and peaceful slumber, and for what purpose?" he says in a deep, booming voice.

I look up at him, eyes wide, mouth agape, struggling to keep a straight face. But I just can't do it. With the blue-tinted skin, and the yellow contacts, and the BeDazzled turban, it's too much. I try to speak, but instead of words coming out, I break into uncontrollable laughter.

"Cut!" says a voice from the darkness beyond the desert. "Cut! Cut! Cut!"

The lights come on and the giant warehouse-size building is illuminated around me, making this little patch of fake sand and green background look even more ridiculous than it feels. I know the background won't really be green. It's just temporary. In post-production, when the editors splice the episode together, they'll insert rolling hills of sand dunes behind me so it'll look like I'm actually outside in the Sahara Desert and not inside a soundstage in Burbank, California, at three o'clock on a Wednesday afternoon. Three *hours* past schedule, I might add, because Barry Berkowitz, the show's executive producer and creator, didn't like the look of the first three batches of sand.

"What was that?" Barry demands, stepping out from behind the bank of cameras and viewing monitors. "We're one line away from the end of the scene!" I secretly call him Barry *Bark*owitz—or some variation of that—because he seems to bark everything he says.

"Nice job, Ruby," Ryder sneers, pushing himself up from his seated place in the fake sand. The sarcasm is rich in his voice. I stick out my tongue in reply. Ryder Vance, my costar, has played Miles on the show for the past four years. He's like a brother to me. A very annoying, obnoxious, way-too-obsessed-with-his-hair brother. "Now we have to reset the whole shot." He stomps off set toward the food table, smoothing his windblown hair with one hand while he grabs a chocolate doughnut with the other and shoves half of it in his mouth. He turns to me and taunts me by chewing dramatically. He knows I can't have chocolate doughnuts because I've basically been on a flavor-free diet since I was eight, and he loves to rub it in my face.

I roll my eyes and turn away from him, my gaze landing once again on the actor playing the ancient genie. And then I lose it all over again, laughing uncontrollably. I feel bad for the guy, I really do. This—blue skin dye and harem pants—is probably his big break into Hollywood.

Barry Barkhead stalks menacingly toward me, wiping sweat from his bald head. "Do you find my writing humorous?"

No, I think. *I find it ridiculous.*

But I don't dare say that aloud. The whole stupid show is over-the-top. I mean, seriously, a school for genies with classes like Wish Granting and Carpet Driver's Ed and Yoga for Lamp Dwellers? It's like Barry just sat down one day, made a list of the cheesiest genie-related things, and poof! Here's a hit TV show for you.

"They have twenty more minutes," Russ reminds Barry. He's the show's production assistant, recognizable by the clipboard that's practically glued to his hand, and the way he seems to shake in his shoes whenever he's around Barry.

Barry waves Russ away with a rough hand, nearly swatting him in the face. Fortunately, Russ ducks just in time before running away. Of all the people on set who are afraid of Barry—which is pretty much everyone—Russ is probably the most terrified. And I can't blame him. If he's not getting nearly smacked by Barry's wild gestures, he's getting spit on by Barry's saliva-heavy rants.

But Russ is just doing his job, reminding Barry that Ryder and I have only twenty more minutes until they

4

have to let us go home. It's California state law. Because we're only twelve, we can only work for five hours at a time, and can only be on set for nine and a half hours total, including makeup, hair, and meals. Thank goodness for that law, or Barkhead would make me stay here all night.

Frustrated, Barry jams his fingertips into his temples. "Do you know the line, Ruby?" he asks me through gritted teeth.

"'I'm looking for my mother,'" I recite dutifully.

"Yes!" Barry shouts with mock enthusiasm, as if I've just announced I've discovered the cure for some mysterious disease. "Yes! That's the line. 'I'm looking for my mother.' The last line of the episode leading up to the epic season finale. This is a moment the viewers have been waiting for, for *four* seasons. It's a significant line. It's a *dramatic* line. What it is *not* is a laughing line."

"I—" I start to respond, but I'm quickly cut off by my mother, who's suddenly standing next to Barry, looking like she just got a blowout and a makeover, despite the fact that we've been on this soundstage since six in the morning. That's because she spends almost all her time between takes in the makeup trailer, refreshing her perfectly drawn cat eyes and her plum lipstick.

"Of course it's not a laughing matter," she says soothingly, placing her hand on Barry's arm in a way that makes my insides squirm. "It's a wonderful line. A Shakespearean line."

I cringe. *Shakespearean? Really?*

The only way my mom would ever like Shakespeare is if they somehow managed to turn it into a reality show with people running around in swimsuits on an island.

"Thank you," Barry says, flashing her a smile. "I'm glad someone around here appreciates creative talent."

Mom gives Barry's arm a friendly squeeze, her three-inch red acrylic nails practically digging into his shirt. My eyes immediately drift to the huge sparkling Tiffany diamond on her ring finger. It's new. Not from a guy, of course. She bought it as a present for herself for managing to finish two weeks of the Paleo Diet. Mom says you should never reward yourself with food. Always jewelry. When she finished the Werewolf Diet—fasting on every full and new moon (yes, it's a thing)—she bought herself a fifty-four-carat diamond choker, which I thought was fitting for the Werewolf Diet because it kind of looked like a bejeweled dog collar.

Mom turns to me. "Why don't you try the line again, sweetie," she says in a tender voice that's supposed to fool every single crew and cast member on this soundstage. But it doesn't fool me. I see the real message in her eyes.

Don't screw this up, Ruby. It's contract negotiation time.

I silently calculate how many of Barry's cheesy, clichéd lines I've had to recite to pay for that diamond ring. Three hundred? Three thousand?

Just say the stupid line and get it over with, I tell myself. The last thing I want is to have to come back here tomorrow and do the scene all over again. Put on this cheesy silk caftan, trudge through the fake sand dunes, and listen to Ryder gripe about what the wind machine is doing to his hair.

After this you'll be one step closer to the end of the episode and the end of the season.

I force a smile onto my face. "Sorry, Barry. I'll get it right this time."

He returns my smile, although his is probably faker than mine. "Good." Then he calls out to the rest of the crew. "Reset! Let's do this! We have eighteen minutes and counting!"

Russ repeats the command into the headset of his walkie-talkie, relaying it to all the other crew on set. Sierra, the costume designer, adjusts my silk caftan, straightening it around my hips. Cami, the makeup artist, touches up my powder before spraying my forehead with artificial sweat. And Gina, the hairstylist, poufs my high ponytail, adjusting the gold cuff around the base and finishing it off with a spritz of extra-hold hair spray.

Jericho, the prop guy, runs over, takes the gold genie lamp from my hand, and reburies it in the sand. Then he switches the wind machine back on, causing sand to swirl around my feet.

"Places!" Barry calls.

I return to my position and Ryder runs over to stand next to me. "Let's see if you can manage to do this without royally messing it up again," he says, flashing me a goading grin. His teeth are stained with chocolate glaze and I'm tempted not to say anything and just let him make a complete fool of himself, but Cami catches every-thing. She runs over with a cloth and rubs his teeth until they're shiny white again. The blue genie man steps off camera, leaving Ryder and me alone again in the middle of the green-screen desert.

"And, action!" Barry barks.

The soundstage falls silent; the giant stage lights blaze overhead. All eyes and cameras are pointed directly at us. Ryder's face instantly takes on the caring, dutiful ex-pression of a boy in love with his best friend. And then I, Ruby Rivera, magically transform myself back into a twelve-year-old genie, on a four-season quest to find her mother.

FALLEN IDOL

Skylar

It's just breathing, I tell myself. *It's easy. You do it every day. You just inhale. Then exhale. Inhale. Then—*

HUUUGHHUUP!

My whole body spasms as I let out another loud and out-of-control hiccup.

Oh gosh. This is not happening. This is not *happening.*

I can't get the hiccups now. Not now. I'm up next! This is my one and only chance to prove to these people that I'm not the weird, shy kid who smells like cabbages. Okay, to be honest, I'm not sure where they got the cabbage thing. I shower every day. I even made my mom buy me the same body wash that all the Ellas use. (I overheard them talking about it at lunch once. Apparently, it's supposed to smell like roses after a rainstorm. I don't get any of that when I smell it, but I admit it smells pretty good.)

But anyway, this is my shot. My one opportunity to make friends in this place. If I can just get on that stage, perform the monologue I've been practicing nonstop for the past week, and get a role in the film club's new movie, then this nightmare will all be over. The kids at Fairview

Middle School will finally see that I'm normal. That I fit in somewhere. That I'm just as cool as those Ellas.

Okay, well, no one is as cool as the Ellas, but at least I'll show them I'm cool enough to be someone's friend. *Anyone's* friend. Honestly, right now I'd settle for being friends with the cafeteria ladies.

I wish Leah were here. She's my best friend back in Amherst, Massachusetts. That's where my dad lives, too. I live with my mom, in Irvine, California. It's temporary, though. At least, that's what Mom and Dad keep telling me. Mom's only here because she got a visiting professor job at UC–Irvine. One school year, tops, they promised me. But I'm not sure I believe them. I mean, I believed them when they promised me they would never get divorced, and look how that turned out.

It's Wednesday afternoon. School is out, and I'm standing in the wings of the auditorium, peering around the edge of the curtain, watching Daniella finish up her audition. She'll definitely get a role in the movie. And not just because she's the leader of the Ellas, but because she's really good. Like Ruby Rivera good.

Daniella finishes her monologue with a dramatic bow and everyone in the auditorium goes wild. Mr. Katz, the film club advisor, who also happens to be my Language Arts teacher, is clapping right along with everyone else.

Yup, she's definitely getting a part.

I sigh, wondering if I made a mistake signing up to audition. It doesn't really help that Mr. Katz kind of hates me. He's always ragging on me in class for not reading the assigned books. What makes me think he's going to cast me in this movie?

I don't need to be the lead or anything. I'd settle for being a random extra. I just want to be part of something. I just want to join something and be able to say—

HUUUGHHUUP!

And there's my problem. Every time I get nervous I get the hiccups. And not just regular hiccups. The wildest, loudest, most violent hiccups ever. I mean, they're pretty much equivalent to an earthquake in a small country.

As I stand in the wings, I close my eyes and try to take deep breaths. And yes, I know what you're going to say. You're going to tell me the best way to cure hiccups is to hold your breath/drink water/eat hot sauce/get someone to scare you/swallow a spoonful of sugar/guzzle vinegar/breathe into a paper bag.

I've heard just about every supposed hiccup cure there is, but none of them actually works. I just have to wait it out and pray that by the time they call my name—

"Skylar Welshman!" Mr. Katz's voice booms from the stage.

My whole body freezes. I can feel blood rushing from my head to my toes and I'm pretty sure blood isn't supposed to rush that way. My toes don't need that blood. My brain needs that blood! I sway slightly and grab on to a nearby chair for balance.

You can do this, I tell myself. *You're ready. You've practiced this.*

As I fight the wave of dizziness that passes over me, I think about what Ruby Rivera would do. She's my all-time favorite celebrity. Not only is she the star of the best show in the world—*Ruby of the Lamp*—she's also the best *singer* in the world. She wouldn't let a little bout of hiccups stop her.

In fact, the monologue I prepared for today is from one of my favorite episodes of her show: season 1, episode 22. It's called "Dream a Little Dream," and it's the one where Ruby discovers (through a magic dream) that her mother (who she thought died when she was a little girl) has actually been trapped inside a genie lamp for the past ten years. I've seen the episode at least twenty times and I still cry every time.

Just pretend you're her, I tell myself. *Be Ruby. Channel Ruby.*

I stand up straight and push my shoulders back, ready to walk onto that stage with confidence, and poise, and—

HUUUGHHUUP!

I sigh again. I wonder if Ruby Rivera ever gets the hiccups. Probably not. Rich and famous people probably have a secret cure for the hiccups that we normal people don't know about.

I take one step toward the stage but am stopped when I hear the high-pitched voice of Daniella call out behind me. I turn to see her approaching. She must have left the stage through the other wing and come around the back of the curtain.

"Nice outfit," she says, giving me the once-over. I don't have to be an award-winning English literature professor like my mother to figure out she's not complimenting me.

The non-compliment compliment is followed by a chorus of giggles, and I turn around to see the other two Ellas walking toward me. Actually, "walk" is the wrong word. The Ellas don't walk. They swagger. They strut. They sashay. All hips and highlighted blond hair and attitude. Okay, well, Gabriella's actually a brunette, but she still has the attitude. And she always has this bitter, just-swallowed-a-bug look on her face.

"No offense, but where did you get *that*?" Daniella asks, scowling at my clothes. "The Salvation Army?"

"Probably like a Halloween costume discount store," Isabella guesses.

"Yeah," Gabriella chimes in. "A discount store for Halloween costumes."

Gabriella is the least original of the three Ellas. She usually just finds a way to reword what one of the other Ellas says, and it's never very creative.

I bite my lip, fighting the urge to tell them my outfit— fuchsia leggings, a black chiffon leopard-print skirt, and a sequined top—is actually inspired by something Ruby wore in her music video for "Living Out Loud" (my favorite Ruby Rivera song), but I know that won't help. The Ellas think Ruby Rivera is lame. Something they made a point of telling me on my first day at Fairview Middle, when I showed up to math class with a Ruby Rivera binder.

"So, what are you going to do for your audition?" Daniella asks, like she genuinely wants to know, even though I know she doesn't.

"She's going to get up there and just stare awkwardly at people like she always does," Isabella says. "That's her real talent."

"Yeah, she's really talented at staring," Gabriella agrees, before getting a weird look from her friends and quickly adding, "Awkwardly."

"I—" I start, wanting to tell them that I'm not just going to get up there and stare at people, that I'm going to do the monologue I rehearsed relentlessly for the past week. But I feel another hiccup coming on, so I quickly close my mouth.

"You?" Daniella prompts, looking eager to hear what I have to say. When I don't continue, she turns to the other Ellas and laughs. "Wow. That's the most I've ever heard her say."

"Skylar Welshman?" Mr. Katz's voice repeats from the stage. "Are you here? You're up!"

I have to go. I have to get out there and prove to these people that I'm not who they think I am. Everything will change after this moment. I'm sure of it. Everything will get better.

Daniella crosses her arms and stares at me, as if to say *Go ahead. Show us what you got.*

I put on my best Ruby Rivera smile, turn on my heels, and glide out of the wings. I position myself in the center of the stage and wait for Mr. Katz to signal me to begin.

"Action!" comes the cue.

I take a deep breath and open my mouth to say the first lines of my monologue.

"Mom! I know it was you. I saw you. I thought you were dead!"

I know the words. I've known the words since I was eight years old, when the episode first aired. But when I open my mouth now, it's not those words that come out.

It's the loudest, most obnoxious hiccup I've ever heard in my life.

HUUUGHHUUP!

Except, in the middle of the dead-quiet auditorium, it doesn't sound like a hiccup. It sounds like a giant burp.

·····················

I can't do this.

Not today. Not any more days. I have to tell her. I have to walk right up to her and tell her that this is my last season. I'm not renewing my contract. I'm not returning to *Ruby of the Lamp* for a fifth season. They'll just have to do the show without me. They can call it . . . just . . . *Of the Lamp*. Or even *Miles of the Lamp*. I know Ryder would jump at the chance to have the show named after his character.

Yes. This is it. This is the day I tell my mom that I'm done.

I'll wait until she's had her second latte. And her cookies. She's on the Cookie Diet this week. Or was that last week? Anyway, I'll wait until she's properly caffeinated and fed and then I'll tell her.

I glance at the clock on the wall of the "classroom." It's seven a.m. on Thursday and Ryder and I are in "school." Of course, it's not a real school. It's a closet that's been ⌐d into a tiny windowless classroom on the Xoom!

Studios lot. I haven't set foot in a real classroom since I was eight years old.

I often wonder what my life would have been like if I had never walked into the audition for *Ruby of the Lamp*. If Mom had never decided to move to Hollywood to try to break her daughter into show business. If we had never left Texas.

Based on our old address, I already know that I'd be a seventh grader at Woodlands Middle School, just outside Dallas. I found it on Google Maps once. It's right up the street from our old house. I'd probably walk to school every day. I'd have a green backpack because green is my favorite color, and it would be filled with books and textbooks and my notes on every subject under the sun. I'd have tons of friends. We'd hang out after school every day and study together in the library and spend the weekends having slumber parties and sleeping late.

I never get to sleep late.

Maybe there would be a cute boy in my Language Arts class. Someone who looks nothing like Ryder Vance. Someone sweet and innocent and kind of nerdy. Maybe we would be assigned a special project together where we'd have to hang out after school. Maybe we would laugh about our conflicting interpretations of *To Kill a Mockingbird* and then we'd accidentally brush hands and . . .

"Hey!" Ryder interrupts my thoughts. I turn to find he's shoving his phone in my face so I can see the screen. "Check it out."

Ryder has pulled up the *Star Beat* magazine website and is pointing to his own picture on the top of the page. It's another one of his signature "smolder" looks, as he calls it, where his head is cocked and he's looking at the camera with one eyebrow raised, like he's about to tell you a juicy secret. Ryder thinks the pose makes him look hot. I think it makes him look constipated.

Underneath the picture there's a caption that says "Hottest Tween Actor."

He nods arrogantly. "Four months in a row, baby."

I groan and turn back to the online course I'm taking on my phone. This is pretty much how we spend most days at "school." Greg, the on-set tutor, sits at the front of the closet-classroom, flipping through a magazine, while Ryder and I *supposedly* read from some textbook. We never really do. Both of us are always on our phones. Ryder is usually looking at pictures of himself on celebrity news websites, and I'm usually watching a lecture from the Learning Space, my favorite online course site. I discovered a long time ago that if you want to get a good education around here, you have to give it to yourself.

"Oh, and look who's at the top of the actress list," Ryder says, trying to get my attention again. But I don't turn. I can see who he's pointing to out of the corner of my eye. It's Carey Divine, the twelve-year-old star of Xoom! Channel's other hit show, *Story of My Lives*. And my so-called BFF.

I know exactly which picture it is, too. It's the one of her in that sleeveless top and cutoff shorts, with her knees pulled up to her chest and her elbows resting atop them. Her long, silky blond hair is spread out over her arms like a blanket. She's not smiling; she never smiles in photos. She thinks it makes her look more sophisticated. Mom says it makes her look too mature for her age.

"It's stars like Carey who fizzle out before they're even fifteen," Mom likes to say. "They try to grow up too fast. They try to look older than they are. And then before you know it, their reputations are ruined and the only jobs they can get are acne cream commercials."

When the clock finally strikes nine, I leap from my seat and race out of the classroom. I have an hour before I have to be on set. I give myself a mental pep talk the whole way back to my trailer.

You can do this. Just march in there and tell her you're done. It's over. No more Ruby of the Lamp. *You're old enough to make your own decisions about your life.*

But just before I reach the trailer, my phone rings and I see it's Lesley, my agent, calling.

Oh, thank goodness.

Lesley will give me the courage I need to go through with this. Lesley always knows the right thing to say.

"Hello?"

"What on earth do you think you're doing?" Lesley thunders into my ear.

I cringe and quickly duck behind the makeup trailer for some privacy. "I know. I *know*."

"I have Barry Barky McBarkerson and his Barky network of lawyers barking down my neck every single day,

19

wanting to know what's taking so long with these contracts. Ruby, I can't stall them for much longer."

Lesley is the only person who knows about my secret nickname for Barry. I once told her, during a lunch, that I called him Barkowitz. She laughed so hard, and she and I have been calling him variations of it ever since. Of course, only to each other.

"I'm sorry," I say. "I'm going to tell her. Today."

There's a long pause on the other end of the phone, during which I check the screen twice to make sure the call is still connected. *"Today?"* she screeches after her long pause. "You mean you haven't even *talked* to her yet? I thought you were going to do it yesterday!"

"I know! I'm sorry! I got scared! You know how she gets!"

Lesley chuckles darkly. "Oh, I know."

"Well, what am I going to do?" I whine into the phone. "I can't do another season of the show. I can't. I can't rub one more lamp or fly on one more magic carpet or recite one more cheesy genie spell!"

"Okay, okay," Lesley says quickly, switching to her supportive voice. "Calm down. It'll be fine. You'll talk to Eva today and I'll put the studio off until . . . Oh gosh. I can't put them off all weekend. I need to give them an answer before the Tween Choice Awards on Saturday night. If you don't talk to your mother by end of day tomorrow, I'm afraid you're going to be stuck rubbing lamps and flying on magic carpets for another year."

"But what should I say?" I ask, desperate for any guidance I can get.

"Just say . . ." And then there's about two seconds of static, followed by what sounds like Lesley's every fifth word. "Your decision . . . Genie . . . right . . . sad . . . but . . . more to life . . . blue skin . . . do it."

"You're breaking up!" I tell her. Then the line goes dead.

Great.

I guess I'm on my own.

When I reach my trailer, I stop and attempt to give myself another pep talk. *You can do this,* I tell myself again. *Just say it and get it over with.* I want to quit the show. *See? It's easy.*

I stare at the door to my trailer. Then I take a deep breath, open it, and step inside, finally ready to take control of my own future.

Skylar

I can't do this.

I can't go back to that place. I can't face the Ellas or anyone else at Fairview. Not after what happened yesterday. I burped! I burped onstage. It echoed everywhere. It shook walls. I didn't even get a chance to say one line of my monologue. Once I heard the Ellas laughing from the wings, I just bolted. I ran offstage, out of the auditorium, and all the way to the bus stop. I'm never going to live this down. Never.

"Morning, my bird!" Mom says, coming into my room on Thursday morning and opening my Ruby Rivera–themed curtains. She calls me her bird because I was named after her favorite Percy Bysshe Shelley poem, "To a Skylark."

Mom turns around from the window, her eyes immediately falling on the stack of library books on my desk. No doubt she's detecting that they look untouched, and in the exact same order and alignment as yesterday. And the day before that.

She clears her throat. "I noticed you fell asleep in front

of the TV again," she says. I can tell she's trying to keep her voice light and non-accusatory, but I hear the disappointment there. She doesn't like that I watch TV. If it were up to her, we wouldn't even have one in the house. In fact, my parents told me they didn't even own one until I was old enough to ask for one.

"Yeah," I mutter. "Sorry, I must have dozed off."

Mom nods like she understands. Like she's ever sat through an entire television show in her life. She walks over to the stack of books and picks up the hardcover on top, giving it a thorough inspection, as though she's fascinated by the contents. "This one looks funny," she says, pointing to the surprised-looking girl on the cover. "It's about a twelve-year-old girl who makes a wish to be sixteen and wakes up to find her life has been fast-forwarded four years."

I shrug and yawn.

She picks up the next book in the stack. "And this one is about a young girl who's a genie. Just like in your show."

Every week, she comes home with another stack of books, convinced that in *this* pile there'll be one I like. One that will finally turn her only child into the little reader she's always wanted. But stories in books just don't interest me. They're not as exciting as the stories on TV. Besides, it would take me weeks to get through one book, when I can watch an entire episode of *Ruby of the Lamp*—with a beginning, middle, and end—in twenty-two minutes (if I fast-forward through the commercials).

Mom sighs and puts the books down. "Fine. I'll take them back to the library today. But did you at least read your assigned book for English? Mr. Katz called me. . . ."

I wince as I flash back to yesterday. Not only did I burp onstage, I also totally bombed my oral presentation in Language Arts. I hadn't exactly read the book. I *tried* to read it, but it was so incredibly boring, with absolutely no plot. Who wants to read a book about mice and men? I don't have any interest in either of those topics. So I just skimmed through an online summary before the presentation. Then, when I got up in front of the class to talk about the story, I completely choked. I started mumbling something about farmers and rabbits and . . . well, let's just say it ended pretty much the same as the auditions. With peals of laughter echoing around me.

"He said he'd give you a chance to redo the presentation tomorrow," Mom continues. "Otherwise, he's going to fail you."

My stomach clenches. *Fail me? As in an F?*

"You can't just read the online summary, Skylar. Reading is not just about summarizing the plot. It's about *living* the plot. Befriending the characters. Getting inside their heads."

I fight not to roll my eyes. Here we go again. Mom's big speech about how reading is life's greatest gift and how much I'm missing out on by choosing to watch TV instead of burying myself in a life-changing book.

"The problem with reading a summary," Mom goes on, oblivious to my frustration, "is you're unable to insert any of yourself into the story. That's the whole joy of reading. *Interpreting*. Letting your own experiences shape and color the material. You can't do that with a summary."

"Okay, I'll read it," I promise her, even though we both know I probably won't. But thankfully, Mom finally decides to drop the issue.

"Well, you better get up or you'll be late for school."

School. I can feel my eyes prick with tears at the very thought of the place.

"Mom?" I say.

"Hmm?" she replies absently, straightening the stack of unread books on my desk like a meticulous librarian.

"Is it okay if I stay home today?"

She looks over at me, tilting her head. "Why?"

I shrug and stare at the ceiling, hoping she won't see the moisture in my eyes. "I just don't feel like going."

"Oh, my bird." She comes and sits on my bed. "Are those Elmo girls giving you trouble again?"

I roll my eyes, wishing I'd never told her about them in the first place. "They're called the *Ellas*, Mom."

Mom snorts at this. "I don't care what they're called. Ellas. Bellas. Bobs. Boingos. Scared, insecure little girls is what they are."

She really doesn't understand anything, does she?

"The Ellas are *not* insecure, Mom."

"Of course they are. Any woman—or girl—who is mean to another member of her own sex is covering for a deep-rooted insecurity, buried beneath a wardrobe of trendy clothes and a face full of fancy makeup. It's the same whether you're twelve or forty. It's all a facade to hide the fact that they have nothing else to offer."

And this is what it's like to live with a college professor. You never get any practical advice. It probably doesn't help that my mom spent exactly two weeks in seventh grade when she was my age, before the teachers determined she was too smart for their classes and promptly moved her up two whole grades to the high school. She loves telling the stories about how adorable all the teenagers thought she was. The little bespectacled brainiac in their advanced classes.

Yeah, well, life isn't that easy for the rest of us.

I sigh. "You just don't get it, Mom."

"I get it!" she insists. "Believe me, I get it. Their lives *look* perfect, right? But that's just from the outside. If you want to see someone's real life, you have to look beyond appearances. Everyone has problems underneath."

I know there's no use arguing with her, so I just smile and say, "Thanks, Mom."

She pats my leg. "You're welcome. Now get up and show those Ellas that you *do* have something more to offer. That you're a strong, accomplished woman. And that you won't be intimidated by them just because they're intimidated by *you*."

I almost want to laugh. The Ellas, intimidated by me? Yeah, right. The Ellas aren't intimidated by anyone. But I really don't want another lecture. Mom can save those for her students. So I get up. I say good morning to the life-size Ruby Rivera cardboard cutout that stands guard in front of my closet. Then I make my Ruby Rivera–themed bed (complete with the extra Genie decorative pillow) and head to the bathroom to shower. Afterward, I comb out my long, dirty-blond hair, which would probably look less flat and dull if I could use a little styling product. If only Mom would let me buy some. She doesn't believe in styling product. She thinks it's just corporate America pushing its antifeminist agenda on the consumer, trying to make women feel bad about themselves so they'll buy useless beautification products.

Of course, Mom doesn't need any styling product. Her hair is a gorgeous shade of strawberry blond that shimmers naturally in any light. Too bad she always keeps it tucked back in that ponytail. What a waste.

After my hair is brushed, I stand in front of the mirror, staring at my reflection. My pale skin looks almost ghostly in this light. Mom and I live in faculty housing on the UC–Irvine campus. It's a small, two-bedroom apartment with horrible lighting. Not that good lighting would help my skin situation. I've always been pale. I wish I had Ruby Rivera's skin. Her mom is from Mexico and her dad is from El Salvador, so she has this beautiful light brown skin that always looks flawless.

I sigh and shut off the light. There's only one bathroom in the apartment, so Mom and I have to share. It's in the hallway between our two bedrooms. As I walk back to my room, I can hear Mom in the kitchen. She's talking in that hushed angry voice again. The one she uses only with Dad. It's a new voice. I'd never heard it until a few months before they told me they were getting a divorce and then Mom *coincidentally* got this guest professor job shortly after. She didn't even *try* to stick around and work things out with Dad. She just gave up. Packed up our stuff and shipped us both to California. And did I get any say in it? No. Because apparently *my* feelings on the subject don't matter.

"Don't patronize me, Jared," Mom is saying. "I'm not one of your doting little students." There's a pause and then she says, "Yeah, well, a lot of things you do used to be charming but aren't anymore."

I run to my room and close the door.

It doesn't matter, I reassure myself. This is temporary. Just like us being in California. As soon as we get back to Amherst, they'll both admit that they've been stupid and they've missed each other and they want to get back together. Absence makes the heart grow fonder. Everyone knows that.

Plus, I just don't have the time or energy to deal with my parents fighting. I have other stressful problems to tackle right now. Like my closet.

I can't stop thinking about how the Ellas made fun of my clothes yesterday. That was one of my favorite outfits. I would ask my mom to take me shopping for new clothes, but she'd probably just lecture me about how I don't need new clothes to impress the people at my new school. I just have to be my brilliant self.

The problem is, I *can't* be myself. I can't show these people who I really am, because I keep getting in my own way. It was easier in Amherst, when I had a built-in best friend I'd known since preschool. I never had to think about how to act around Leah; I just acted normal. And she acted normal, and that was that.

Leah says when you pick out clothes, you should think about a cute boy and then pick out an outfit you think *he* would like. So of course, I think about Ryder Vance. He's the only boy for me. He plays Ruby's longtime crush, Miles, on *Ruby of the Lamp*. And he's everything you'd ever want a cute boy to be. He has long, light brown hair that swoops across his forehead like he's trapped in a constant breeze. And he does this dreamy, pensive thing with his eyes whenever he looks at Ruby on the show, like he's thinking really hard about how much he secretly likes her. He's obviously a very deep and introspective person in real life. I mean, no one can act *that* well.

I wonder if Ruby thinks about Ryder when *she* gets dressed in the morning.

Mom says you should never dress to impress a boy. Boys should fall in love with your brains, not your looks; that's what makes a lasting relationship. She always said that's how it worked with Dad. He fell in love with her opinions about Sylvia Plath, the famous poet. But now Mom and Dad are getting divorced, so that strategy didn't work out too well. I wonder if it has anything to do with the fact that Sylvia Plath killed herself. Maybe if they'd fallen in love over someone less dramatic, like, say, Shel Silverstein or Dr. Seuss, I might still be in Amherst with Leah.

I finally settle on an orange dress with orange tights and white ankle boots. It's similar to something Ruby wore in the premiere episode of season 3, after she heard that her crush, Miles, liked the color orange. I figure if *I* can't dress to impress a boy, I can at least channel Ruby dressing to impress one.

After getting dressed, I head into the kitchen, where Mom is thankfully off her call. She's packing up her school bag between hurried bites of cereal. She's always been really good at multitasking, a skill I must get from her, because I manage to eat breakfast, pack my lunch, *and* watch a YouTube video of Ruby at a movie premiere the other night all at the same time.

I close the lid on my container of leftover brown butter and thyme gnocchi and put it in my backpack. I made it last night in an effort to distract myself from the burp incident. That's what I do when I'm stressed out: I cook. It takes my mind off things. I'm actually really good at it. It was a skill acquired of necessity. When you grow up with two busy professor parents who value knowledge more than the quality of the food they eat, you learn to follow recipes pretty quick. Unless you want to spend the rest of your life eating takeout and cardboard-flavored mac and cheese.

With bags and lunches packed, we're off. The school bus doesn't make stops at the university faculty housing, so my mom drives me to school each day. Then I take the public bus home. It's the one reprieve I get. I've heard the middle school bus is even worse than the middle school hallways.

When Mom pulls up to the student drop-off zone in front of the school, she must notice the look of total panic on my face, because she says, "Don't worry. I'm sure today will be better."

I wish I could believe her. I wish I could know with absolute certainty that everything will be okay. That no one will even remember what happened yesterday.

But this is middle school.

Everyone remembers everything.

"And hey," Mom says, her voice sounding extra peppy. "The weekend is just around the corner, and then it's the big day!"

Okay, I admit that the reminder of the weekend does cheer me up a little. Ruby Rivera is doing an autographing session at the South Coast Plaza mall in Costa Mesa, which is only a short drive from Irvine, and Mom promised to take me. It'll be the first time I've ever seen her up close. I mean, I've seen her in concert in Boston three times, but we had terrible seats, so she was like the size of an ant.

"And afterward," Mom goes on, "maybe I can show you around campus a little."

I grimace. Mom has been trying to get me to come to UC–Irvine to see her office ever since we moved here. But I don't really understand the point when it's just a temporary position. Pretty soon she'll be back at Amherst College and back with my dad, where she belongs.

"That's okay," I say, trying to sound breezy. "I think I'll skip that part."

Mom smiles, although I can tell she's holding back disappointment. I feel a twinge of guilt but quickly push it away. *She's* the one who insisted we come out here. *She's* the one who walked out on Dad and our whole life in Amherst. She can get used to disappointment. I have.

Well, almost.

I pull on the door handle and kick the door open with my foot.

"Have fun!" Mom calls after me.

"I'll try," I mutter before closing the door and threading my arms through the straps of my backpack.

Okay, I tell myself, walking slowly toward the front doors of the school. *You can do this. You can—*

But as soon as I enter the building, I know for certain that I *can't* do this. Coming to school today was a huge mistake. I should have just faked sick, refused to get out of bed, told my mom I had the plague. Because the moment I step into that hallway, every single person turns to look at me.

I duck my head and continue down the main hallway toward my locker. I try to tell myself it's just my imagination. No one is looking at me. No one even knows who I am in this school! But then a group of guys passes by me and one of them lets out a disgustingly loud burp that seems to shake the very floor I'm standing on. The other guys break into hoots of laughter as they all nudge and high-five each other.

"Nice going, Belchman!" one of them shouts.

I run to my locker and quickly dial in the combination, trying to keep my head down.

"I guess you haven't seen it yet," a voice says to me, and I look up to see a boy from my science class standing next to my locker. His name is Ethan. We were paired together for a project at the beginning of the year so we hung out in the library together a few times. He's sort of cute, with shaggy blond hair, a small nose, and a super-pointy chin. He plays lacrosse. I only know that because he told me once and I didn't know what lacrosse was and had to look it up. Right now he's probably the only one in this hallway *not* laughing at me.

"Seen what?" I ask, dread coating my throat.

He sighs and pulls out his phone. "Daniella posted it this morning," he explains, looking sympathetic. "It's kind of gone viral."

He turns the screen toward me and suddenly everything makes sense. The titters. The stares. The attention. My hand flies to my mouth as I realize what I'm looking at. All the blood seems to freeze in my veins.

"Oh my gosh!" I utter, horrified. "Oh my gosh!"

Ethan looks like he's about to say something—maybe he's going to start laughing at me, too—but I don't wait around to hear what it is. Without even bothering to close my locker door, I turn and run as fast as I can out of the school.

THE (UN) REAL WORLD

Mom is standing in the mini kitchen of the trailer, pouring blueberries from a carton into a tiny white bowl that looks like it was stolen from a dollhouse.

"Hi!" She greets me with a beaming smile when I step inside. "How was school?"

I groan. "The same as always. Ryder was annoying and I took a Learning Space course."

She shakes her head. "Why do you bother with those online courses?"

I shrug. "They're interesting. And maybe they'll help me get into a good college."

Mom chuckles. "Sweetie, people only go to college to get a good career. You already have one of those."

"And to learn stuff," I remind her.

She looks confused for a moment, like she's not following my logic. I know it's no use trying to explain it to her. Her idea of higher education is keeping up to date on which actress wore which designer to the latest awards show.

I nod toward the tiny bowl of blueberries. "What are you doing?"

Mom glances down. "Oh, I'm starting a new diet! That darn Cookie Diet didn't work. I gained five pounds on it. FIVE pounds."

I want to say, *What do you expect, eating nothing but cookies for a week?* But obviously I don't.

"So I'm starting something new," she goes on. "My nutritionist says it's all the rage right now. It's called the Bowl Diet."

"The Bowl Diet?" I repeat incredulously.

"Yup. You can eat anything that you can fit into this." She picks up the tiny bowl and brandishes it toward me like a game show hostess.

Seventy-three wisecracks float into my mind at once but I push them all back. "Sounds logical," I say with a smile.

Mom beams. "I know, right?"

This is good. Mom is always in a good mood when she starts a new diet. She gets super optimistic about life.

I set my phone down on the table in the trailer's living room and take a deep breath. "Mom, can I talk to you about something?"

Mom pops a single blueberry into her mouth and flashes me a warm smile. "Of course, sweetie. You can talk to me about anything."

I fight not to roll my eyes. She always says that. Mom fancies herself one of those "cool" stage moms whose daughter thinks of her as more of a BFF than a mom.

"I was thinking about—"

I'm interrupted by a knock on the trailer door. It's Stan, the catering manager, coming to deliver my morning meal. It consists of exactly one hard-boiled egg, two pieces of tasteless skinless chicken breast, three carrot sticks, and twelve green peas. It's been my staple meal for the past four years, and the sight of it makes me want to gag, particularly today, when my stomach is already a wreck in anticipation of this conversation with my mom.

"Thanks, Stan," Mom says brightly, setting the plate down on the table and gesturing toward it. "Eat. You need your calories for the next scene."

I slide into the bench seat and poke at the hard-boiled egg with my finger. It feels like rubber.

Mom pops another blueberry into her mouth. "So, what were you saying?"

I pick up a carrot stick and play hockey with the green peas on my plate, using the two chicken pieces as goals. "Right. So . . . I was just talking to Lesley, and—"

Mom's eyes go wide at the mention of my agent's name. "What did she say?" she asks, instantly turning defensive. "What are those lowlifes trying to pull on us this time? They're holding their ground on the pay raise, aren't they? Those ungrateful little—"

"Mom," I quickly interrupt before she gets herself too worked up. "No. We didn't talk about the contract negotiations."

Mom visibly sags in relief. "Oh. Okay. Good. Then what were you talking about?"

"I was just . . ."

Spit it out, Ruby!

". . . well, *wondering* . . . what would happen if . . . you know . . . maybe . . ."

But before I can finish the sentence, Mom's phone rings and her attention whips away from me like a dog who's just spotted a squirrel. "Sorry. It's Peter. I have to take this. I've been waiting for him to call me back." She clicks a button on her Bluetooth headset. "Hello?"

I sigh and continue to play with my food. Peter is our money manager. He handles all the things I'm apparently too young to understand. And it's true. I don't really understand how any of that works. All I know is Mom used to be a poor single mother living in a tiny house in Texas, and now she's a rich single mother living in a mansion in the Hollywood Hills. All because of me.

"What?" Mom says into the phone, looking aggravated. "What do you mean there's not enough? I thought you said we were fine. I thought you said not to worry about it. Weren't those your exact words to me, Peter? 'Eva, don't worry about it'?"

I feel all my hopes get sucked right out the window of the trailer. There goes Mom's good mood. This doesn't sound promising at all. If we're having money problems, then I can't tell her I want to leave the show *now*. I'm the breadwinner of the family. *Ruby of the Lamp* pays for everything—the house, the car, the clothes, Mom's ridiculous jewelry budget. If I tell her I want to quit, what will she say?

She'll call me irresponsible. She'll call me selfish. She'll tell me I'm just as bad as my father.

All my life I've listened to her tell stories of what a horrible person my father was, leaving a pregnant woman alone to fend for herself. Abandoning his family in their time of need.

How is that any different from what I'm trying to do right now?

My breathing starts to grow heavy and erratic. I tell myself to calm down. Take deep breaths. Relax. Maybe I'm just stressed. I always get stressed around the end of the season. I mean, my job isn't *that* bad, right? I have my own trailer and three months off between seasons—although Mom usually makes me shoot a TV movie or record a new album during that time—but maybe one more season won't be so terrible. Maybe I should just call Lesley and tell her to close the deal.

"You need to handle this," Mom is telling Peter in her stern take-control voice. "I'm counting on you. We all are."

As she says this, I can almost hear her saying the same thing to me. *I'm counting on you, Ruby. We all are.*

Mom ends the call and closes her eyes for a moment, as though she's trying to maintain her composure. When she opens her eyes, she flashes me a smile. "Sorry, sweetie. Okay, what did you want to talk to me about?"

I swallow hard. "Nothing. I . . . It doesn't matter."

"Are you sure?" Mom asks, and before I can respond there's another knock at the door. This time it's Russ, the production assistant. When he steps inside, he looks even more anxious than usual, and I soon realize why when he extends a single sheet of paper toward me and says, "Barry made a few changes to the next scene."

I go to take the page but Mom beats me to it. "What kind of changes?" she asks brusquely, skimming the script. Mom is always suspicious of Barry's last-minute changes. She thinks he's trying to pull one over on her.

"No," Mom says, crumpling up the paper. "Tell Barry she's not doing this. We had a deal."

What is she talking about? What deal?

I think back to the scene we're supposed to shoot this afternoon. It's the final scene of the episode where Miles and Ruby get back to the Jinn Academy after their trip to the Sahara Desert to find Ruby's mother, which led to another dead end. In the scene, everyone has already dispersed into their respective classrooms, leaving Ruby and Miles alone in the hallway. Miles tells Ruby that they won't give up. They'll keep trying to find Ruby's mother, as long as it takes.

Then Miles grabs Ruby's hand and squeezes it. It's supposed to be some huge romantic moment. The two characters have been best friends since the start of the show, but all the fans have apparently been waiting for something more to happen between them. (Their shipping name, by the way, is Muby—pronounced *Moo-bee*.)

"You know what?" Mom says, tossing the balled-up page onto the table. "Never mind. I'll tell Barry myself." Then she storms out of the trailer, with Russ following at her heels.

As soon as she's gone, I grab the piece of paper and smooth it out.

```
INT. JINN ACADEMY HALLWAY — DAY
Ruby and Miles stand by the lockers. Miles won't
meet Ruby's eye.

                    RUBY
          What did you want to say?

                    MILES
          I just wanted to say that we'll find
          her. I promise. I'm not giving up
          and neither should you.

For a moment, Ruby looks disappointed by his
answer.

                    RUBY
          Is that all you wanted to say?

                    MILES
               (uncomfortably)
          Yes . . . no . . . um . . . well,
          actually . . .

But Ruby doesn't let him finish. She leans in
and silences his nervous rambles with her lips.
```

Bile starts to rise up in my stomach as I read the scene again. I flip the page over to see if there's anything written on the back, but this is it. The last page of the script. The last scene of the episode. Barry is ending the fourth season of the show with this!

Which means sometime today, I'm going to have kiss Ryder Vance.

THE BUS TO EVERYTHING

··

Skylar

I can hear the first-period bell ringing in the distance as I run all the way down the block until I've reached the bus stop. I plop down on the bench and dig out my phone. I click on Daniella's feed.

And there it is. It wasn't a dream. It's real.

There I am, standing on the stage during my botched film club audition, with my fuchsia leggings and leopard-print skirt and I'm hiccupping into the dark auditorium. But of course, it doesn't sound or look like a hiccup. It sounds and looks like a burp. The clip is obviously set to loop because it plays over and over and over. The Ellas filmed my most embarrassing moment ever and posted it online for the entire world to see.

My watery eyes scan down to the read the caption.

Welshman or Belchman?

Oh my gosh, what am I going to do? I can't ever go back inside that school again! I can't walk down those hallways and sit in those classrooms and eat in that cafeteria while the entire student body laughs in my face.

No. No way. I'm not going back there. I'm going straight home and hiding in my mom's closet until this school year is over and we can go back to cold, gray Amherst, where I belong.

I used to do that when I was little. I would hide in my mom's closet when I was scared or after I'd had a fight with Leah. It always felt safe in there. Like I was protected by a fortress of clothes and shoes and comforting smells. The rest of the world couldn't reach me in there.

But I'm older now. I know that's not true. Viral videos still exist within the walls of my mom's closet. The mean Ellas don't stop being mean just because I'm crouched under a rack of shirts.

HUUUGHHUUP!

Great. And now my hiccups are back. The very thing that got me into this mess.

After the horrifying burp clip replays for the twentieth time, I finally gain some sense and switch over to Ruby Rivera's feed instead. In Ruby's world, there are no mean girls. There's just glitz and glamour and red carpets and movie premieres and the adorable face of her costar, Ryder Vance. Ruby is one of the most talented actresses in Hollywood. She's won like seven Tween Choice Awards in every category. Well, except Best Actress, but that's only because that annoying, talentless Carey Divine keeps stealing it from her every year. But don't get me started on *her*.

Ruby's profile says she's up to eleven million followers now.

That's like a whole other level of popular that the Ellas can only aspire to. Daniella has three hundred followers, and I'm pretty sure almost all of them go to our school.

I scroll through Ruby's latest posts. There's a picture of her from the set of her show yesterday. She's wearing an exotic-looking tunic dress and flashing a thumbs-up to the camera. The caption says, "Filming the second-to-last episode of the season! Are you guys as excited as I am?" The pictures from the set are my favorite. Ruby always looks so thrilled to be there. And why wouldn't she be? She has the perfect job and the perfect life. The picture already has over three hundred thousand likes, and the comments are all sweet and enthusiastic. I've never seen a single mean comment on her feed.

Ruby, you are the cutest! I <3 YOU!
Love the outfit, Ruby!
OMG! I CAN'T WAIT FOR THIS EPISODE!!!

I sigh and look away from my phone. My life will never be that amazing. I'll never have eleven million followers. At the rate I'm going, I doubt I'll have eleven, period.

As I wait for the bus—the one that goes to the UC–Irvine faculty housing—I decide to distract myself with one of my favorite *Ruby of the Lamp* episodes, "Hearts and Crafts," the finale of season 3.

It's the one where Miles is hiding in the art supplies closet, trying to escape Headmistress Mancha after he accidentally crashes his magic carpet into a tree. Then Ruby goes in there looking for more string for the genie beads she's making as a gift for her grandmother, who raised her after her mother mysteriously disappeared. Anyway, the two bump into each other in the dark and almost accidentally kiss! Their lips come *this* close to touching. It was the most romantic episode ever.

I stick my earbuds in and press play. The "Be Your Genie" theme song comes on. Although it does nothing to cure my annoying hiccups, the familiar sound of Ruby's voice calms my pounding heart. After the song, I fast-forward to the closet scene. It's toward the end.

I remember the first time I saw this episode. Leah and I watched it together in the basement of my Amherst house. I remember how we both squealed and clasped hands when Ruby walked into that closet, certain this would be the moment we'd been waiting for: Ruby and Miles's first kiss.

Then, just when their lips were about to touch, Mrs. Mancha turned on the light in the supply closet, and Miles and Ruby jumped apart. Leah and I both shouted "NO!" at the same time and stared numbly at the TV.

I hear a bus rumbling up to the curb right as the episode comes to an end on my phone. I glance up and see it's the number 72. I stand up and am about to shut off my phone when something on the screen catches my eye. It's the last line of the closing credits of the show. I know

I've seen it before—thousands of times—but this time it seems to have more meaning than ever.

FILMED ON LOCATION IN BURBANK, CALIFORNIA.

Burbank, California.

Isn't that just north of here? When Mom first told me about her visiting professor job at UC–Irvine, she mentioned we'd be living less than two hours from the Xoom! Studios and promised me she'd take me on the studio lot tour so we could see where the show is filmed. Although we still haven't been.

The number 72 bus pulls to a stop and the doors hiss open in front of me. My heart is suddenly pounding again.

Can I do it?

No. Mom would kill me.

Maybe I can go and come back before she finds out.

No. It's crazy. I'd definitely get in trouble.

But it's Ruby Rivera . . . and Ryder Vance . . . and the Jinn Academy! It's everything!

"Are you getting on, sweetie?" the friendly female driver asks me from behind the wheel. It's then I realize I'm just standing there, staring into the bus with my mouth hanging open.

Then, before I can second-guess myself, I ask, "Is there a bus that goes to Burbank?"

She nods. "Number fifteen, transfer in Hollywood to the number eight."

I repeat the directions in my mind over and over, like a

spell. The doors close and I watch bus 72 pull away from the curb. I stand there in a trance for ten minutes, the bus driver's words still echoing in my head.

Number fifteen. Hollywood. Number eight.

When the number 15 bus pulls up to the curb and the doors open, I feel like my heart is going to beat right out of my chest.

I'm doing this. I'm actually doing this. I'm going to see Ruby Rivera!

I dig my transit pass out of my pocket and, with another loud *HUUUGHHUUP,* I step uncertainly onto the bus.

RUBY VS. RYDER

When I walk into the hair-and-makeup trailer with *Life of Pi* tucked under one arm, Ryder is already seated in his chair, his perfect light brown hair being blow-dried into its famous silky soft swoop. I almost want to laugh every time I see him in one of these chairs, being made up like a doll in a five-year-old's make-believe beauty parlor. If only his millions of screaming fangirls could see him now.

"Hey, Rubes," he says in a low, husky voice. It's the voice he puts on when he's talking to one of his doting fans. He thinks it makes him sound suave. I think it makes him sound like he has the flu. "Did you see the rewrite yet?"

He catches my gaze in the mirror and closes his eyes, miming a tender, romantic kiss. He looks like a monkey making kissy faces to the people at the zoo.

I shudder and try to fight back the wave of nausea that rolls over me as I plop down into the chair next to him.

"I know how long you've been waiting for this day," Ryder teases.

I groan. "Gross. No."

"Come on, Ruby. How could you not want to make out with this?" He takes out the latest issue of *Star Beat* magazine, which of course has *his* face on the cover, and shoves it toward me. I pretend to gag and throw up on it. He turns it back around and puckers his lips, like he's actually going to kiss it himself. "Every girl in America wants to be in your shoes right now."

"Every girl in America can have my shoes," I tell him sullenly.

Gina finishes styling his hair, spritzing it with shine spray. "You're all set." Then she moves over to my chair, covers my jeans and T-shirt with a plastic cape, and begins combing out my hair. It's all part of my normal morning routine. Gina sets my hair in obnoxious giant rollers; then Cami spends approximately an hour making up my face, after which Gina takes out the rollers and spends another half hour teasing my hair until I get my signature chocolate-brown wave. Then Sierra dresses me in whatever Mom-and-Barry-approved outfit has been selected.

Ryder hops out of his chair and heads toward the door of the trailer, but not before making another round of obnoxious kissing noises. I try to lean forward to slug him in the arm, but he moves away too quickly and I start to fall toward him. Fortunately—or unfortunately—Gina has hold of a giant chunk of my hair, which she's preparing to wrap around a roller, and it keeps me from falling into Ryder. But it also feels like it's being ripped out of my scalp.

"Ow!" I scream, sitting upright and rubbing the aching spot on my head.

"Well, sit still," Gina says with an impatient sigh, giving my hair another firm tug.

"He started it," I cry, pointing at Ryder.

"Hey! I can't help that she's *so* in love with me she simply can't stay away."

"Yeah, right. In your dreams."

"No," Ryder says, catching my gaze again in the mirror and licking his lips. "In less than an hour." And with that, he struts out of the trailer, leaving me to fume in my chair.

"Don't let him get to you," Gina says, her voice softening. "He's just another boy who got too famous too young. Sadly, it's what happens."

Gina secures the roller in my hair with a clip and lets out a heavy sigh. I have a feeling when she signed up to be a hairstylist in Hollywood, she didn't envision having to babysit preteens all day.

An hour and a half later, once my makeup is done and Gina is just putting the finishing touches on my waves, Mom bursts into the trailer, looking like she's come back from battle. And in a way, she has. She's been arguing with Barry about the kiss scene for the past hour. I glance up from my book to hear what compromise has been reached. I'm half wishing she'll tell me she's gotten me fired from the show, but so far, that wish has never come true.

"You're still doing the kiss," Mom says, "but it's going

to be two seconds instead of five, and they're rewriting the scene so *he* kisses *you* instead of you kissing him."

Gina continues to fluff my hair in silence. She's smart not to get involved.

"Great job, Mom," I commend her with a smile, knowing it will calm her down. Even though what I really want to say is *What difference does it make who kisses who?*

Mom lets out an exhausted sigh and collapses into Ryder's vacant chair. "Thanks." She turns toward her reflection in the mirror and starts fussing with her own hair. "And you'll thank me later when you still have an acting career at age twenty."

I close my eyes for a brief moment as my breath catches. *Please don't let me still be doing this at age twenty.*

But I realize that's exactly where I'm heading. Unless I can get the guts to talk to my mom and tell her how I feel, I'll be doing this job that I hate for the rest of my life.

"All done!" Gina announces cheerfully, pulling the protective plastic cape from my clothes.

Russ peeks his head in the trailer and gestures to his all-mighty clipboard. "They're just rewriting the scene now and changing a few camera setups. Barry says to tell you it'll be another hour until the first shot is up."

He glances uneasily at my mom, presumably waiting for her to explode again, but she just flashes him a smile in the mirror, clearly in a good mood now. "Thanks, Russ! You've been super helpful in all this."

I close my book and head for the door of the trailer.

"Where are you going?" Mom asks, looking suddenly

worried. Like I'm going out there to kiss Ryder Vance right this second, just for the fun of it.

"I'm just going to get some air," I tell her.

It's a total lie, but it comes out easily. I've been hiding the truth from my mother since I was eight years old. It's one of the small perks of being an actress on a hit TV show. You learn how to fool just about *everyone*.

I'm not going to get fresh air. I'm going to the one place where I know I can be alone. Where no one ever thinks to look for me. Where I can sit in silence, read my book, and think about what I'm going to do. How I'm going to fix this.

When I was younger, before we moved to Los Angeles and my whole life imploded, my secret hiding place used to be in my mom's closet. There was this little corner in the back between her long, hanging dresses and her hamper where I could just barely fit and be unseen by the rest of the world. That's where I felt the safest. The most guarded. The most invisible.

Now it's impossible for me to *ever* be invisible.

I step out of the trailer just as one of the studio lot tour trams rounds the corner and starts heading toward me. I quickly duck into the soundstage to avoid being spotted. The tourists are technically not allowed to take photos on the tour—the studio confiscates their phones and cameras before they leave the visitor center—but someone inevitably manages to smuggle a camera on the tram, and then I inevitably end up in a tabloid magazine two weeks later.

Inside the soundstage, the school hallway set is being

lit for our first shot—the big kiss scene—which just happens to be the last scene of the final episode of the season. Nothing is ever filmed in order in Hollywood. As always, Barry is barking orders at the crew. Right now he's telling them how to stage the shot so they get the best possible angle on Ryder's lips touching mine.

I shudder at the thought of those greasy, pouty lips anywhere near mine and then keep walking down a long corridor into the back areas of the soundstage, past the writers' room, the wardrobe closet, and the production office, before finally reaching the prop room.

The door is slightly ajar, and I smile. Jericho is the only person who knows I like to come in here. He always leaves it open for me.

Checking that no one is watching, I slip inside and make sure to leave the door propped open a sliver so I don't get locked in. Then I head to the back, past the shelves of genie paraphernalia: Lamps. Rings. Old dusty books. Swaths of gold fabric. I slide down the wall until I'm sitting on the cool tile floor. I flip open my book and try to focus on the words, but I can't stop thinking about what I saw back there. Ten people setting up my first kiss, making sure the lighting is perfect, the cameras are angled right, the blocking is optimal.

My first kiss was supposed to be special. It was supposed to be romantic and spontaneous and memorable. It wasn't supposed to be in the middle of a fake school hallway, with fake lockers in the background and a bunch of cameras pointed at my face while a red-faced bald man tells me how much to tilt my head and exactly when to close my eyes.

Well, I guess the memorable part will be true enough.

I sigh and rest my head back against the wall. I have to find a way out of this. I have to find a way to tell Mom I'm not going to sign next year's contract. I *have* to. Otherwise, I'm going to spend the rest of my life hiding in prop rooms. Because sure, right now it's just "one more year," but what happens next year when this starts all over again? Or what happens when Barry writes some horrible spin-off show—*Ruby, the College Years* or *Ruby in the Workplace*—and I'll be expected to sign up for that, too? When does it end?

Never. It never ends.

Unless *I* end it.

If only I had the nerve to do it.

THE REBEL WITHIN

Skylar

"And on your right is our Cities of the World set. A single block of nondescript buildings that can be decorated to look like almost any city on earth, in almost any time period. . . ." Luanne, our Xoom! Studios tour guide, yammers on in a thick Southern accent, pointing out landmarks. Meanwhile, I've been bouncing in the last row of the tour tram for the past twenty minutes, just waiting for a sign of *Ruby of the Lamp*. To my frustration, Luanne hasn't mentioned it once. We've passed the famous yellow cottage where they film the kids' show *Little House on the Big Lane* and the soundstage where they're currently filming *Hot Diggety Dog 2,* the sequel to one of Xoom! Channel's most successful TV movies last year (which, I have to admit, I was pretty excited to see because I really liked that movie), and we got to see a stuntwoman fall from a roof and land on something that looked like a giant blow-up bouncy house. Apparently, she was filming a scene for some new show called *Me, Myself, and Spy,* about a teenage girl who thinks she's caught up in an international espionage plot, but it could just be her wild imagination.

"On your left, you'll see soundstage six, where they film the wildly popular show *Story of My Lives* starring Carey Divine, about a girl who, thanks to a rip in the space-time continuum, lives two different versions of the same life."

Carey Divine is *so* overrated. Some people think she's talented, but I just don't see it. Sure, she plays two different versions of herself on her show, but that shouldn't be enough to beat out Ruby Rivera for Best Actress on the Tween Choice Awards *three* years in a row. Also, I've seen interviews with her and she seems so fake and pretentious. I have no idea why Ruby is best friends with her. That's Ruby's only flaw, in my opinion. Apparently, the friendship started a year ago, after they shot that TV movie *Lemonade Stand-Off* together. Ruby was, of course, awesome in it. Carey was just annoying.

I'm just starting to lose hope that we'll ever see anything relating to Ruby Rivera when I hear the tour guide say, "And coming up is soundstage eleven, where they film the übersuccessful *Ruby of the Lamp,* the show that launched Ruby Rivera into tween stardom."

Luanne slows to a stop a few feet away from the giant warehouse-size building and launches into the story about how Ruby Rivera rose to stardom, but I've stopped listening. Mostly because I already know the whole story by heart. She moved from Dallas to Los Angeles with her mom, Eva Rivera, when she was eight years old to follow her dream of becoming a star. She was soon cast on *Ruby of the Lamp* and the show was an instant success, kicking off her acting and singing career.

I don't need a rehash of Ruby's life story. I need to *see* her. With my own eyes. I need to witness just a tiny glimpse of her perfect life. I need to believe that there's still hope for someone my age to survive in this world.

But through the hustle and bustle of people, clothing racks, golf carts, and filming equipment, I don't see a single person I recognize. Not Ryder Vance. Not Ruby Rivera. Not even that freakishly tall woman who plays Headmistress Mancha.

"And now we'll continue on to the Costume Department, where you'll be able to see the actual dress worn by the fabulous Lennon Harper in the music video for her hit song 'Small-Town Heart'!"

The tram slowly starts to move again and I feel panic bloom in my stomach like butterflies emerging from a cocoon.

That's it? No!

We can't leave yet! We just got here! And I haven't seen Ruby! I came all this way—on two crowded and smelly buses—just to see her face! I can't go back to that awful school with those awful giggles following me around wherever I go. Not without seeing her first. I need her strength. I need her courage. I need to get off this tram!

My gaze darts toward the tour guide. Her back is turned to us as she points out a sculpture that was used in some old TV show I've never heard of.

She's not looking. She probably wouldn't even notice.

Do it! A voice inside me shouts. It's the same voice that told me to run from the school hallway. The same voice that kept me from boarding the number 72 bus. The same voice that led me all the way here. That fished out the emergency credit card from my wallet and handed it over to the girl behind the counter at the Xoom! Studios Lot visitor center to pay for this ridiculously expensive tour.

It's the voice of some side of myself I didn't even know I had. A rebellious Skylar. A school-ditching Skylar. A rule-breaking Skylar.

Do it now or you'll regret it for the rest of your life!

While everyone on the tour is focused on the sculpture, I leap from the moving tram. It's not going very fast, so it's not like it's some impressive stunt. I land on both feet and quickly duck behind a nearby trailer. I peer around the corner to watch as the tram glides down the cement pathway, disappearing behind another massive soundstage.

I turn back to the looming building in front of me. On the wall is a gold plaque that reads "Stage 11," and underneath that is a list of all the shows that have been filmed inside. The one on top makes my stomach do a double-twisting backflip.

RUBY OF THE LAMP

I can't believe I just did that. I can't believe I'm about to sneak onto the set of *Ruby of the Lamp*!

Next to the sign, there's a giant garage-size door that's wide open. People are running in and out, carrying things like food, clothes, cords, and fancy lights. I need to get in there. That's definitely where Ruby will be. She's probably in the middle of filming a scene right this minute. Oh gosh, what if she's filming a scene *with* Ryder Vance? What if I get to see both of them at the same time?

I take a deep breath, stand up a bit straighter, and walk toward the open door.

Just pretend you're supposed to be here, I tell myself. *Try to blend in.*

I nearly snort aloud. Yeah, right. I've never blended in in my life. Just ask the Ellas.

But it soon becomes evident that I don't even need to try, because everyone is so busy with their various tasks, no one even seems to notice me. A short, dark-haired girl pushing a giant rolling rack full of clothes brushes past, yelling something about skirt options. A squirrely-looking guy with a mop of hair and glasses runs past me with a clipboard, calling, "Where's Barry? Has anyone seen Barry? I need Barry to approve these script changes!" I wonder if he's talking about Barry Berkowitz, the creator of the show. I always see his name in the credits.

As soon as I step inside the soundstage, my jaw immediately drops and I think I let out some kind of squeaking noise, but I can't be sure because I'm having trouble hearing with the sound of rushing water in my ears.

No way.

No freaking way!

It's . . . it's . . .

EVERYTHING!

Ruby's entire world is laid out right in front of me: Her dorm room. Her Enchanted Objects classroom. The Jinn 'n' Juice shop, where all the students hang out after school. The Jinn Academy's main hallway. Rogue Raymond's Junkyard and Bazaar (which I thought was outside but appears to actually be *inside*). Even the art studio where Ruby and Miles almost kissed! It's all here. It's kind of weird, though. All the rooms are clumped together in seemingly random order. The Enchanted Objects classroom is next door to the Jinn 'n' Juice shop, even though the shop is supposed to be on the other side of town. And Rogue Raymond's Junkyard and Bazaar backs up to the Wish Granting classroom, even though it's nowhere near the school. Plus, all the rooms only have three walls and no ceilings. Like someone forgot to finish building them.

I watch in absolute fascination as a crew begins setting up cameras around the school hallway, right where the missing wall would be.

Eek! They must be getting ready to film a scene in the hallway!

Tons of great scenes take place in front of Ruby's and Miles's lockers. They're right next to each other, so Ruby and Miles are always hanging out there. Nothing exciting *ever* happens in front of *my* locker. Well, unless you count that horrible video Ethan showed me this morning.

"Excuse me, miss. Are you supposed to be here?"

I startle and look up at a man in a navy-blue uniform

wearing a badge that says "Studio Security." He gives me a once-over, zeroing in on the little red sticker still stuck to the front of my orange dress.

I glance down at it and mentally kick myself.

It says "Studio Lot Tour." I forgot to take it off when I jumped. How could I be so careless? Now I'm busted for sure.

"Um . . . ," I say, scratching my chin while trying to casually hide the sticker, but it looks more like I'm massaging my chest with my elbow. "Um . . . ," I say again.

Think, Skylar! Think!

Just then, a man holding a giant tray full of various flavors of smoothies comes teetering toward us, looking like he's about to fall over and splatter everyone in the vicinity with berry and banana goo. The security guard glances away from me for a moment, reaching out to help the man. I seize the moment and run, turning and bolting down the first hallway I come to.

I can hear footsteps echoing behind me and then a voice says, "Hey! Stop! Come back here!"

Breathlessly, I keep running, my white ankle boots clacking obnoxiously against the tile floor. I round another corner and try the first door handle I come to, hoping I can slip inside and hide until the security guard passes, but the door is locked. I try the next door. Also locked. Every single door in this hallway is locked!

I'm about to give up and just turn myself in, when I find the last door on the left is open. I bolt inside and pull it quietly closed behind me. I try to catch my breath and calm my thundering heart as I slip to the back corner of the room, slide down the wall, and pull my knees up to my chest.

But the moment I hit the ground, something else kicks my pulse back into overdrive and I feel like I might actually vomit right then and there.

Because sitting against the opposite wall, not five feet away from me, in almost the exact same position, is none other than Ruby Rivera.

LESSONS IN CRAZY

The moment the girl bursts into the prop room and sinks to the floor across from me, all I can think is:

Fantastic.

Just what I need right now. Another stalker fan who's managed to sneak past the security guards. And there's no way that's not what this girl is. I can tell by the look on her face. They all have the same look: Those bugged-out eyes. That open mouth. That scream that's bubbling up inside of them. Sometimes when fans recognize me, it looks more like they've just seen a horrible four-headed monster than someone on TV.

It's been four years and I still haven't quite gotten used to that look. I don't understand people's reaction to celebrities. I'm just a person. Same as them. In fact, this girl looks my age. And yet she's staring at me like I just sprouted out of a piece of broccoli.

It appears as though crazy stalker girl is about to say something, but when she opens her mouth all that comes out is the loudest hiccup I've ever heard in my life. It actually sounds more like a really obnoxious burp that shakes her entire body. Her hand flies to her mouth, as though she's trying to pull the hideous sound back in, but it's way too late for that. That thing was epic. It seemed to echo through the entire prop room. I would have burst out laughing had I not been more concerned with checking the shelves to make sure nothing was going to fall on my head.

She buries her head in her hands, and a moment later her body starts to shake and I hear soft sobs coming from the other side of the room.

And that would be my cue to leave.

It wouldn't be my first time dealing with a crying fan, and I've learned over the years that the blubbering types are the craziest of them all. They seem harmless at first, so overcome with emotion, but then the tears slowly turn into hysterics and before you know it, they're chasing you around a mall food court, swearing that they're your BFF and they're going to sneak into your bedroom tonight so you can have a slumber party.

Yes, it happened.

I push myself to my feet, tuck my book under my arm, and move slowly and quietly toward the door.

Crazy Stalker Fan Lesson #1: Don't make any sudden movements.

She must hear my footsteps, because her head jerks up and I can see the streaks of tears running down her cheeks. She watches me with fascination as I ease my way to the door.

Crazy Stalker Fan Lesson #2: Be nice but firm.

I flash her a fake hurried smile as I reach for the door handle. "Thanks for watching the show," I say brightly. "I have to get back to set now." I gently turn the handle and pull on the door.

Except it doesn't open.

And that's when I notice that it's not propped ajar like I left it. It's shut. Locked. The crazy hiccupping girl must have closed it behind her when she came in here. I jiggle the door handle and yank on it with all my strength. It doesn't even budge.

I turn back toward the girl, keeping my back pressed against the door. She's still just sitting there watching me, like I'm a caged animal at the zoo. Tears continue to stream down her face and she sniffles and wipes her nose on the sleeve of her dress, which is probably the ugliest shade of orange I've ever seen.

I reach into my pocket, feeling for my phone, before remembering I left it in my trailer. I immediately start gnawing on my fingernail. Mom hates it when I bite my nails but I don't care. Desperate times call for desperate measures.

I glance around the room, searching for something that can serve as a weapon in case she decides to charge. My gaze lands on a marble sculpture of a genie head. It's from the episode where Ruby goes to the Jinn History Museum to research her ancestry in hopes of getting information about her mother's whereabouts. I could smash it over the girl's head, but I know the thing isn't real marble. It's probably made of some special lightweight plastic. It would be like hitting her over the head with a tissue box. As I continue to scan the shelves, it suddenly occurs to me just how tiny this room is. There's nowhere to run. Nowhere to hide.

I'm trapped in here with a crazy hiccupping girl.

Just then, as if reading my mind, she opens her mouth and says,

HUUUGHHUUP!

LESSONS IN HUMILIATION

....

Skylar

STOP HICCUPPING!

Oh gosh. I'm so humiliated, I'm going to die. I finally meet my favorite celebrity of all time, and not only am I incapable of saying a single word to her, I can't open my mouth without sounding like a squirrel choking on an oversize acorn.

HUUUGHHUUP!

Ruby Rivera, who's already made it very clear she wants to get as far away from me as possible, turns back toward the door and starts banging on it with her fists, shouting at the top of her lungs, "Help! I'm locked in here! Russ! Jericho! Mom! Anyone!"

I feel another sob rising, and I drop my head in my hands and start crying again. This tour was supposed to cheer me up after the whole humiliating video. I came all the way here to try to make myself feel better, and what do I end up doing? Crying and hiccupping myself to even *more* embarrassment.

I'm hopeless! I'm a lost cause. I may as well just ask

Mom to homeschool me so I can lock myself in my room and never see another living person again.

"Excuse me," comes a small, timid voice, and I glance up to see that Ruby Rivera is looking at me now, her head bent at a slight angle, her expression cautious, like she's afraid I might leap forward and bite her. "Yes, hi. Um . . . so we seem to be . . . um, locked inside here and I was . . . um, wondering if I could . . . borrow your phone."

My heart literally stops beating.

Ruby Rivera is talking to me! She's asking to borrow my phone! MY phone!

I leap to my feet, a sudden movement that causes Ruby to jump backward, her hand clutching the door handle. She looks so small standing there. Smaller than I thought she'd be, actually. I mean, I know we're the exact same height (four eleven), but for some reason I thought she'd look . . . I don't know . . . bigger somehow. I'm surprised to see she looks like a normal twelve-year-old girl. Well, apart from the totally awesome hair and makeup, of course.

Keeping my movements small and slow so I don't scare her again, I reach behind my back, searching for my backpack before remembering that it's in a locker in the visitor center. Along *with* my phone.

"Uh . . . ," I say nervously, commanding myself not to hiccup. "I—I don't have it."

Ruby slumps, looking disappointed. She glances around the room and I wonder if she's searching for something to pick the lock with. I do the same, my gaze soon landing on a silver falcon-shaped hair comb. My eyes light up as I scurry over to grab it from the shelf.

"Here!" I say excitedly, extending my arm to hand her the comb. She takes a tentative step away from me and stares at the object in my hand as though I'm brandishing a weapon.

"To pick the lock," I explain, but she doesn't seem to understand. "Remember?" I prompt, my confidence building with each word. "You used this in season two, episode seven, when you and Miles got locked inside Headmistress Mancha's office. You were wearing this comb in your hair and you used the teeth to—"

"That wasn't a real lock," Ruby says, as though this is the most obvious statement in the world.

I suddenly feel incredibly stupid. Of course she doesn't *really* know how to pick locks. That was just a story line in a show. And she's not a real genie. She's an actress. Otherwise, she could just poof us out of here.

I drop the falcon comb back on the shelf. The *clank* sound it makes against the metal echoes in the endless silence between us.

Say something, I urge myself. *Talk to her.*

After all, when will I ever get the chance to talk to Ruby Rivera again? It's not every day you get locked inside a prop room with your all-time favorite celebrity! Maybe if I strike up a conversation and act normal, she'll see I'm not just some strange hiccupping/crying crazy girl and we'll become friends! Maybe even best friends! We'll hang out in her mansion in Hollywood and she'll invite me to come to all the big movie premieres and awards shows with her and we'll pose on the red carpet together in gorgeous evening gowns. She won't need that annoying Carey Divine once she has *me*!

I peer over at her. She's still pressed against the door, her gaze narrowed distrustfully at me. I need to break the ice. I need to find something to talk about that won't send me into a nervous, stammering tailspin.

"I'm Skylar," I say, hoping if she knows my name she won't look so terrified. But she doesn't even respond.

Well, duh. Of course she wouldn't respond. What would she say? *Hi, I'm Ruby*? Obviously I know her name. I know the name of her mom, her grandmother, and even the pet fish she got for her fifth birthday. It was called Murray. It died a week later.

I glance around the room again, searching frantically for a conversation starter. Then I spot a gold genie lamp with a jewel-encrusted handle and my mind sparks with an idea.

Of course! I should talk about her show! It's the one topic I can always rely on. I walk over to the shelf and pick up the gold lamp. "Hey!" I say, trying to sound upbeat. "This is the lamp you used for that April Fool's episode when you tricked Miles into believing he'd lost all his genie powers."

Ruby Rivera just stares at me like she has no idea what I'm talking about. Maybe she doesn't remember the episode. I mean, it was a few seasons back. Maybe she just needs a little reminder.

"You know," I say, trying to jog her memory. "You found it in Rogue Raymond's Junkyard and Bazaar and he told you it had no magic left in it. But then *you* swapped it out for Miles's lamp in Wish Granting class and . . ." My voice trails off because Ruby Rivera is no longer staring at me like she doesn't know what I'm talking about. She's now staring at me like I'm certifiably insane.

Did I mess up the story line?

Maybe I should try something else. I set the lamp back down and pick up a masquerade-style mask. "Oh! This is the mask you wore when you and Miles snuck into the neighboring wizard school to crash their dance!" I snort out a laugh, remembering how Miles drank all that punch, not knowing one of the wizards had spiked it with truth serum. "Remember you had to drag Miles home because he nearly got beat up for telling that one wizard he thought his face looked like a donkey? That was so funny!" Then, suddenly, the rest of the episode comes flooding back to me. "Oh my gosh!" I exclaim. "That was the episode when Miles admitted he had a crush on you! Because of the truth serum in the punch! But you had already put your headphones on and you couldn't hear it! I felt so bad for him."

I watch Ruby Rivera's reaction carefully. Her eyes are darting around the room and her grip on the door handle seems to tighten.

She thinks I'm crazy. She thinks I'm a stalker.

"Sorry," I say, although I doubt she can hear me because it comes out like a mumble. I set the mask back

71

on the shelf. "I'm not very good at talking to people. I get nervous. And when I get nervous I get the hiccups. The only thing I can really talk about is your show, but I guess you don't want to hear about that. I get it. No one at my school wants to hear about it, either. They all think I'm a giant loser for watching it. Actually, they just think I'm a giant loser, period. I don't think my TV preferences have anything to do with it. That's probably why I have no friends."

I wring my hands together, wishing I had my phone to play with. I grab a random object from a nearby shelf, just to have something to do with my hands. It's another beautiful gold genie lamp, this one with a pattern of swirling sapphires around the base. It looks vaguely familiar, but I can't remember what episode it's from. I clutch it in my hands, tears welling up in my eyes again. I can't do anything right. I stink at everything: Middle school. Life. And let's face it, they're pretty much the same thing.

And now Ruby Rivera thinks I'm a psycho.

I walk back to the wall and sit down again. "I just . . . ," I say, sniffling. "Have you ever felt like you don't belong anywhere?" I let out a dark laugh and wipe my cheeks with the back of my hand. "That was a stupid question. Sorry. Of course you've never felt that way. You're famous. Everyone loves you. You probably fit in everywhere you go."

I stare down at the lamp in my hand. The gold band looks worn and aged, but the sapphires are dazzling.

Such a deep shade of shimmering blue. And the handle is curved up like a cat's tail.

Where have I seen this lamp before?

I rack my brain, trying to place it in the show. But the memory is just out of reach. I lift my head to ask Ruby what episode this is from, but the words evaporate when I see that she's no longer standing next to the door.

She's standing right in front of me, seemingly towering over me. Then, before I can utter—or, rather, stammer—a single word, she sits down next to me. She leans against the same wall. She's so close, the sleeve of her T-shirt brushes against my arm.

I could reach out and touch her right now. But obviously I won't. I don't. I stay statue-still, staring straight in front of me, careful not to make any sudden movements in fear that she might go scuttling back to the door.

Then she tips her head back against the wall with a heavy sigh and says, "Every. Single. Day."

I flinch, startled by her response. And so confused. What is she talking about? Is she speaking in some kind of secret celebrity code?

Then, just as I'm about to ask her what she means, she closes her eyes and whispers, "Every single day I feel like I don't belong anywhere."

JUST ANOTHER PROP

So it turns out the strange hiccupping girl—Skylar—is *not* a crazy stalker fan. I mean, she does seem to know a frightening amount of information about the show, and she did manage to sneak into our soundstage, but all in all, she seems pretty harmless. I think she's just sad. And a little pathetic.

Kind of like me.

Which is why I somehow feel the need to sit next to her. Seeing as neither of us is going anywhere anytime soon. The set is already dressed for the day. It could be hours before Jericho needs anything from the prop room. Eventually, they'll be ready for me on set, and when they don't find me in my trailer, they'll come looking for me. But who knows how long it'll take for them to figure out I'm stuck in here.

Plus, there's something about this girl. The way her sadness kind of weighs her down. The way she talks about not fitting in. About not having any friends. I feel like she and I are not so different. Both lonely. Both trapped.

And I don't just mean in a prop room.

"Every single day I feel like I don't belong anywhere," I tell her, and out of the corner of my eye I see her gaze slide to me. I can tell by the way she's gawking right now that she doesn't believe me. I'm not surprised. I'm sure she follows me on all my social media sites. She sees the way my life is presented to the world. All the glamorous clothes and red-carpet premieres and autograph sessions. But that's not my life. I'm not even sure *whose* life that is. Some fake, made-up person invented by Barry Barkowitz.

Just once, I want to tell someone that the girl in the pictures and the videos and the interviews is not me.

And just once, I want someone to believe that.

But by the way this girl is still staring at me with her mouth hanging slightly open and her eyes looking like they're going to pop right out of her head, I don't think *she's* going to be that someone.

"B-b-but," she stammers, and then hiccups again. "But you're Ruby Rivera."

I have to laugh at this. At the fact that she thinks this is a valid argument, when in reality it's the problem.

I scoff. "Yeah, and I'll tell you, it's no picnic. Everyone telling you what to say, what to wear, what to eat. It's like your own life doesn't even belong to you. It belongs to the Xoom! Channel. You're just a . . . a . . ." I gesture to the shelves full of fake objects made to look real. "A prop. A product on the shelf."

I'm honestly not sure why I'm telling her all this, when I've never really told *anyone* this. But after what happened earlier with my mom, I feel like I have to tell someone. If I don't, I think I might burst.

Skylar snorts. "Yeah, well, I'll take that over being in middle school *any* day."

I turn to her, shock on my face. "Are you kidding? I would *love* to go to middle school. I would love to go to a regular school with regular kids and have a regular life."

"No," she says adamantly, and hiccups again. "No, you wouldn't. Regular kids are mean. And middle school is the worst."

"This place is the worst," I say, starting to get frustrated. I'm so tired of everyone making fame out to be this giant amusement park. I'm sick of being told I'm lucky and I should be grateful for my life. I don't *have* a life!

She sputters. "But your life is so amazing!"

"Trust me, it's *not,*" I tell her.

"Of course it is! You have everything!"

"No I don't. I have no freedom. I have no friends. No fun."

She shakes her head, like she refuses to believe me. "But you're famous and pretty and talented and you live in a mansion with a closet full of designer clothes."

"That my *mom* picked out."

Skylar lets out a noise that sounds like *pushah.* "At least your mother cares about clothes. All my mom cares about is her stupid books."

"That sounds like a dream."

She stares at the ceiling. "Well, it's not."

I'm about to argue with her more, but then I notice

something in her eyes that stops me short. Hurt. Pain. I've hit a sore spot.

She strokes the gold lamp she still has clutched in her hands. "Maybe if my mom cared less about those stupid books, I wouldn't be here right now."

I scrunch my forehead. She's not making any sense. But I don't want to press the issue because there are tears welling up in her eyes again.

"Sorry," she says, sniffling. "My parents are getting a divorce. And it's all my mom's fault. If she had just stayed around and *tried* to work things out, they probably could have. I *know* they could have. But instead, she decided to move us all the way across the country for some lame job. I mean, she couldn't have picked a place farther away from Massachusetts." She sighs. "And now I only get to see my father during holidays."

I glance at my feet. "At least you get to see him at all."

Skylar's hand flies to her mouth, like she's trying to shove her words back in. "Oh my gosh. I'm sorry. I'm so sorry. I know your dad left when you were little."

"Before I was born," I correct her. "He left the minute my mom told him she was pregnant. That's how excited he was about having a kid."

"But your Wikipedia page says he left when—"

"The publicity people at Xoom! Channel thought it would make a better story if he left when I was a kid. More tragic, I guess. Most of what you read about me isn't true. It's a string of lies carefully woven together to tell a good story. Just like an episode of a hit TV show."

77

There's a heavy silence next to me, and I know Skylar is processing everything I've just said. Although it's probably unfair of me to burst her bubble like this, I feel surprisingly good. Weightless. Like a heavy burden has been lifted from my shoulders.

"I'm sorry about your dad," she says after a long moment.

I bite my lip. I've never cried over my father. Probably because I never knew him. But right now, right here, being stuck in this prop room with this stranger, I feel a stirring of tears.

Or maybe that's just all the other things that are wrong with my life piling on top of each other. The contracts. The upcoming kiss scene. My mother.

"Thanks," I manage to say, blinking away the moisture. "And I'm sorry about your parents."

"Thanks." She's quiet, like she's thinking really hard about something. Then she says, "So your *entire* Wikipedia page is fake?"

I chuckle. "Pretty much."

"What about the part that says that you and Carey Divine are best friends?"

I bark out a laugh. "Ha! Yeah, no. That's not true. I can't stand that girl."

"I knew it!" she says excitedly. "I knew you wouldn't be friends with her. She's so . . ."

"Annoying," we both say at once, and then giggle.

"*So* annoying," Skylar confirms.

I wrinkle my nose. "And I hate how she pronounces her name. De-*veeeeen*. So pretentious."

She snorts. "Totally! And she has no talent."

"Thank you!" I say appreciatively. "Finally, someone with *taste*."

Skylar grins, tucking her knees under her and turning to face me. "So why does she keep winning Best Actress every single year?"

I shake my head. "I have *no* idea."

She opens her mouth to say something, but then a thought seems to strike her. "Wait. If you don't like her, why are you always acting like you're friends?"

I roll my eyes. "That was the Channel's idea, too. They invented the friendship to help promote the TV movie Carey and I did together."

"*Lemonade Stand-Off*," Skylar says, jumping in like she's a contestant on a trivia game show.

Wow. This girl really does know everything about me. I'm actually a tiny *bit impressed.*

"Yeah. That one. And then the media seemed to love the whole BFF thing so much, the Channel decided they wanted to keep it up."

"So you have no say in it?"

"Nope."

"That's lame." Skylar continues to fidget with the genie lamp in her lap, and for the first time, I notice which one she's holding. It seems like such a bizarre coincidence that of all the lamps in this room, she'd pick up that one.

My mother's lamp.

And I don't mean my mother, as in Eva Rivera. I mean my mother from the show. The one who's been missing since Ruby was a little girl. She's supposedly trapped inside that lamp.

Skylar seems to notice me staring at it and stiffens. "Sorry!" She quickly returns it to the shelf behind her. "I forgot I was even holding it. I'm probably not supposed to touch the props."

"No, that's okay," I say, grabbing the lamp from behind her. I've always loved this prop. Maybe that's because the one scene it appears in is the only scene in the entire show that I'm proud of. The only scene where I felt like I was really able to *act*. Not just recite another one of Barry's cheesy lines.

Skylar studies me for a moment, like she's trying to figure out something. And then suddenly she blurts out, "Season one, episode twenty-two. 'Dream a Little Dream'!" She falls back against the shelf with relief. "Thank goodness. That was going to bug me all day."

I laugh. "You really like our show, don't you?"

She looks at me like she's wondering if I'm joking. "Um. Yeah. It's only the best show on TV."

"Why?" I ask. "Why do you like it?"

"Because Ruby is so cool!" she exclaims. "She's brave and she speaks her mind and she goes after what she wants and she doesn't let people push her around." She lets out a deep sigh. "Sometimes I wish I could be like that. Just be someone else, you know? Someone cooler.

Someone braver. Someone who doesn't get the hiccups every time they try to talk." She pauses and turns to look at me. "Someone like you."

I laugh. "Yeah, well, you can take my life any day."

She laughs, too. "Same here."

"Are you kidding? I would take it in a heartbeat! You get to eat and wear whatever you want. You can leave your house each day without the fear of ending up on the cover of a tabloid magazine with a bad headline." In my excitement, I accidentally lose my grip on the lamp and it goes tumbling to the floor between us.

"Believe me," I say as I reach for the lamp. "I *wish* I had your life."

"And I wish I had yours," she says, reaching for it at the exact same time.

For a brief moment, our fingers brush and I feel a small chill.

"Oh, sorry!" Skylar says, quickly letting go of the lamp.

I stand and place it back on the shelf. "Wouldn't that be nice? If we could just magically—"

But I'm never able to finish the sentence, because just then, the floor starts to tremble violently. Like the earth itself is having a bad dream.

SHAKING THINGS UP

Skylar

Earthquake!

I can't believe it! My first real Southern California earthquake!

Of course, I've heard people talk about the earthquakes out here. And obviously I've seen plenty of disaster movies about them. Oh, and just before I moved to California, Leah made me watch all these "what to do in the event of an earthquake" safety videos on YouTube so I'd be prepared.

But it turns out nothing can really prepare you for the real thing, because as soon as the room starts to shake, my entire brain empties and I can't think of a single piece of advice from those videos.

Thankfully, Ruby Rivera seems more on top of the situation. I watch her scurry to the front of the room and duck under a table full of props.

"Get under that table!" she yells at me, and I snap to attention.

Right! Tables!

You're supposed to find a table or doorway to hide in so nothing falls on your head.

I spot the table she's talking about on the other side of the prop room, hidden behind a row of shelves. The ground continues to quiver beneath my feet, making it hard to walk, but I manage to reach the table and crawl underneath it.

The noise is so loud. It sounds like a team of giants is playing tackle football above our heads. The props on the shelves are clattering against each other. The walls are squeaking. I swear I see flecks of debris falling from the ceiling.

Then the lights go out.

Oh gosh, I don't like this. I really don't like this.

HUUUGHHUUP!

And now my hiccups are back. Perfect. Just when I thought I'd gotten them under control. At least Ruby probably can't hear them over all the rumbling noise.

Then, without warning, the shaking just stops. It's like someone pulled the plug on a really bad carnival ride. The lights still haven't come back on, so I still can't see anything because there are no windows in this room, but I'm relieved that the earthquake seems to be over.

"Ruby?" I call out, startled by how different my voice sounds. Deeper, and almost raspy. It must be the nerves. I'm shaking like a leaf.

"Yeah?" comes a response a moment later, but it doesn't sound like her. Her voice sounds higher. Squeakier. Strangely, more like mine. She must be scared, too.

"Are you okay?"

"Yeah." She clears her throat. "You?"

I nod, even though I know she can't see me. She's all the way on the other side of the dark room. "Yeah. That was scary. What do we do now?"

But Ruby never gets a chance to answer because just then, the door opens, casting a welcome shaft of light across the floor.

"There you are!" a displeased male voice says, and I freeze. "I've been looking all over this soundstage for you. You're in huge trouble."

Oh no. It's that security guard. He's found me!

"C'mon. Enough playing around. Let's go."

I hesitantly crawl out from under the table and stumble toward the source of the light.

It's strange, though. I could have sworn the door was on the other side of the room, to my right, but apparently the earthquake got me all turned around.

When I step out of the prop room into the hallway, I expect to see the same security guard who chased me down here, but it's not him. It's some other guy, wearing jeans, a polo shirt, and a headset that's wired into a walkie-talkie clipped to his belt. "I've got her," he says into the microphone.

"It's about time!" a voice booms back through the earpiece. It's so loud, even I can hear it.

This is bad. This is very bad.

There's more than one person looking for me? Luanne, our tour guide, must have noticed I wasn't on the tram and radioed for backup.

"I'm sorry!" I rush to say as the man grabs me by the sleeve and ushers me down the hallway. "I got locked in the prop room and then there was the earthquake."

"Right, right. The earthquake," the guy repeats with a strange inflection. It almost sounds like he doesn't believe me. Like he thinks I'm making the whole story up. Didn't he feel it? I can't exactly lie about an earthquake.

"I'm really sorry," I try again.

"I would save your apologies for your mother," the guy says.

My mother?

She's here? They already called her? How did she manage to get here so fast? How long were we locked in there?

"She's livid," the man says.

I cringe. My mom doesn't get mad very often, but when she does, she goes all out. It's like she saves it all up for the really important things. Like ditching school, riding a bus to a whole other county, and then using my emergency credit card to buy a studio tour ticket.

We emerge back into the main area of the soundstage. The Jinn Academy hallway is all lit up with fancy lights, and there are about twenty people milling around it, looking bored. Then a large man with almost no hair left on his head comes barreling toward me. "Where have you been?" he thunders.

It takes me a moment, but I soon recognize him as Barry Berkowitz, the creator of the show! They always interview him on all the behind-the-scenes stuff. Wow, even *he's* mad at me? I wouldn't think the creator of the show would care about random tourists sneaking into their set. This is even worse than I thought.

I try to apologize to the big booming bald man, who is literally turning red in front of me, but he's so scary looking, all that comes out is another hiccup.

"And you're not dressed!" he rants, looking me up and down. He turns to a dark-haired girl standing behind him, whom I recognize as the same girl I saw pushing the rack of clothes earlier. "She's not dressed! Why is she not dressed?"

Dressed? What is he talking about? Of course I'm dressed. I'm not naked.

I glance down at my clothes and suddenly feel a wave of confusion.

Huh. I don't remember putting on jeans and a T-shirt today. I could have sworn I put on my favorite orange dress today. Or was that yesterday?

Suddenly, my thoughts feel fuzzy and far away. Did that earthquake rattle my brain? Am I not remembering things correctly?

Maybe it's just because I'm hungry.

As soon as the thought enters my mind, my stomach grumbles. Geez, when was the last time I ate? I'm *starving*!

"I'm sorry," the woman says to Barry, clearly terrified of him. "I couldn't find her."

"Get her dressed now!" he commands. "We're almost an hour behind schedule, and we only have Ryder for another two hours."

The breath hitches in my chest.

Did he just say "Ryder"? As in Ryder VANCE?

Is he here? My eyes dart around the busy soundstage, searching for that beautiful head of light brown hair, but I can't find him. I feel a tug on my elbow and I turn back to the dark-haired girl, who's guiding me away from the set. Before I can even start to figure out what on earth is going on, I'm being hustled through a nearby door. The girl closes it behind me. "Let's be quick about this."

That's when I turn and take in my surroundings.

That's when my mouth falls open and my knees start to wobble.

That's when I realize I must be dreaming. Because this is better than Disney World. Better than the mall. Better than anything.

I let out the tiniest of shrieks, and then words start gushing from my mouth like soda from a shaken-up bottle. "What *is* this place?"

TANGERINE DREAMS

I can't believe we're having *another* earthquake. That's the second one this year. This is going to put Mom and Barry in an extra-bad mood. I'm sure they're already going out of their mind looking for me, and now that the power is out, it's going to push production back even longer. I should have just stayed in my trailer, where I belong.

The shaking finally ends, but I stay under my table, just in case there are aftershocks.

"Ruby?" Skylar calls to me. She sounds different, although I can't put my finger on why. Her voice is still meek and lacking any confidence whatsoever, but there's something about the tone that's changed. It sounds much lower and throatier. Almost like *my* voice, which is really weird. She's probably just terrified. I get the feeling this was her first earthquake. No one ever forgets their first.

"Yeah?" I say, and strangely enough, *I* sound different, too.

"Are you okay?" she asks.

"Yeah," I repeat, startling at the sound of my own voice.

What's up with that? Why is it all high and squeaky? I clear my throat. "You?"

She doesn't answer right away, and for a moment, I worry that she might be injured. But then I hear her say, "Yeah. That was scary. What do we do now?"

I'm about to tell her to just stay put. Maybe wait for the lights to come back on, but just then, the door creaks open, letting in a shaft of light from the hallway.

There's light in the hallway?

Did the earthquake only cut the power to this one room? That seems unlikely.

"There you are!" comes a voice I instantly recognize. "I've been looking all over this soundstage for you. You're in huge trouble." It's Jericho, the prop guy. If *he's* out looking for me, that's not good. That means Russ failed to find me and Barry sent reinforcements. I squint toward the light, just making out Jericho's face in the doorway. But I soon realize something is off. The door is in the wrong place. It should be on the other side of the room.

Did I get turned around during the earthquake?

I'm just about to climb out from under my table when I realize that Jericho isn't talking to me. He's talking to Skylar.

Why is he looking for her?

"C'mon," Jericho says sternly. "Enough playing around. Let's go."

Oh, I think with sudden realization. *She must have snuck onto the set. Of course. How else would she have gotten back here to the prop room?*

I cringe, knowing exactly what's going to happen to her. Jericho is going to hand her over to studio security. They're going to use that code word they always use for obsessive fans who sneak onto the set: "raccoon." Her wrists are going to get bound with zip ties and she's going to get escorted off the studio lot by a security guard in a golf cart. At least, that's what happened to the last fan who snuck in here. Hopefully this girl is at least smart enough not to try to run.

As soon as she disappears into the hallway, I consider continuing to hide out in here. Jericho didn't appear to even notice me. They might not know I'm in here. Which means I could linger a little longer, but I already know I'm in trouble, so I might as well face the music. Plus, I don't want to risk getting locked in here again. So I jump up and catch the door just before it swings closed. Then I peer into the hallway, looking for Barry or Russ or Cami or anyone else who might be looking for me. The hallway is empty.

I breathe a sigh.

Maybe I got lucky. Maybe the earthquake sent everyone into a frenzy and they completely forgot I was missing. Maybe the script changes are taking longer than anticipated and no one even noticed I was gone!

Leaving the prop room door slightly ajar, I creep down the hallway toward the soundstage. I can see that the first shot of the day is already up. The Jinn Academy hallway is lit, the cameras are set, and everyone seems to be just hanging out, waiting on something.

I catch sight of Barry looking at his watch and I swallow hard.

They're waiting on me.

Thankfully, I don't see my mother anywhere. She's probably been banned to the trailer after her fight with Barry. That was likely part of the negotiations.

I take a deep, courageous breath and approach the monitor bay, where Barry is pacing. "Sorry," I say, "I'm so sorry. I got locked in the prop room!"

Barry gives me a quick once-over, his face contorted like he's sizing up a cockroach that just crawled out of his kitchen wall.

"Russ!" he calls out. Then he turns his back to me and continues to pace.

I roll my eyes. He can be so dramatic sometimes.

"Barry," I say, stepping in front of him. "I'm here. I'm ready. Where's Sierra? I just need to change into . . ." My voice trails off when I glance down at my clothes.

On my gosh. What on earth am I wearing?

I look like a tangerine. I'm wearing a bright orange dress with white ankle boots. They look eerily familiar. Where have I seen this outfit before? Wait a minute—isn't this what that Skylar girl was wearing? What happened to my jeans and T-shirt? Did something fall on my head during the earthquake? Because I'm all sorts of confused now.

"Uh," I mumble, staring down at my dress. "Is this what Sierra picked out for the scene? Is this what you want me to wear when I kiss Ryder?"

I can't imagine Sierra picking out anything like this, or Barry approving it. It's not an incredibly flattering dress. It's kind of tent shaped and made from a very cheap-feeling material.

"RUSS!" Barry calls out again, and a second later Russ appears next to us, looking as harried and terrified as usual. I feel bad that I'm getting him in trouble.

"I'm sorry, Russ," I begin to say, but Barry doesn't let me finish.

"Russ, get this person back into the holding room. We don't need any extras until the next setup."

Extras?

"But I'm not an extra," I say, totally baffled now. Am I dreaming? Am I lying unconscious in the prop room right now with a giant welt on my head?

Russ grabs me by the arm and begins to pull me away from the soundstage. "What are you doing?" I complain. "Russ? It's me! Ruby."

Russ stops walking and stares at me intensely for a long moment. I widen my eyes, waiting for him to realize his mistake. I mean, I know this dress is hideous, but I can't see how he wouldn't recognize me.

His expression finally softens and I exhale in relief. I know he's going to feel incredibly stupid and probably start apologizing incessantly. It was an honest mistake, though. Everyone gets a little stressed out when working with Barry.

"Russ," I say gently, "it's fine. Don't worry about it. It was just a misunder . . ."

I stop talking when I notice Russ's hand is on the walkie-talkie clipped to his belt. He's pressing a button and, without taking his eyes (or his hands) off me, he speaks very slowly and clearly into the microphone on his headset. "Security. Please come to soundstage eleven. We have a raccoon. I repeat, a raccoon, on soundstage eleven."

THE PALACE OF CLOTHES

Skylar

The room is filled to the brim with clothes. And not just any clothes. Ruby Rivera's clothes. All of them. Every single thing she's ever worn on the show is hanging right before my very eyes. My mouth goes dry as my gaze zeroes in on a gorgeous sparkling purple dress.

It's the dress Ruby wore to the Jinn Ball at the end of season 2!

That's my favorite dress in the entire world. I searched everywhere online for that dress but they don't sell it. It was custom made for the show. I take a step toward the dress, just wanting to touch it, but I'm roughly pulled back by that girl who brought me in here. And before I can argue, she's undressing me! Like actually taking off my clothes.

"C'mon," the girl urges me, pointing at my jeans. "We need to get you changed quick. Everyone is waiting."

Everyone is waiting for me?

Why would they be waiting for me?

"Um . . ." I hesitate, trying to find my voice. "What's going on here?"

The girl sighs like she doesn't have time for my questions. "What's going on is that you're forty-five minutes late to set and the shot is already up and the entire crew is on the clock."

Set? Shot? Crew?

"What shot?" I ask.

She rolls her eyes. "The most important scene of the episode! Barry will go ballistic if you mess this up."

I stare at her with my face scrunched up. What is she talking ab—

Oh!!!!

Suddenly, I understand exactly what's going on here. They must be confusing me for someone on the show. Maybe an extra or some small guest role. They probably think I'm supposed to be in the scene.

I nearly sag in relief. I'm not in trouble! This isn't about me ditching the studio tour! This is about me appearing on an episode of *Ruby of the Lamp*!

My pulse starts to race. I'm going to be on TV! This is too cool!

Of course, I'm not the person they're looking for, but they don't seem to know that. And I'm certainly not going to tell them.

I wonder what the role is. Most of the time extras just hang out in the school hallway or sit in one of the classrooms. Every once in a while they have a small line, like "Do you know what time it is?" or "Has anyone seen my lamp?" I can handle that. No problem. Maybe I'll even get to stand next to Ryder Vance!

"Hello!" The girl's voice breaks into my thoughts and she gestures to my jeans again. I leap into action, unbuttoning, unzipping, and yanking off. She quickly helps me step into a cute flowery skirt and zips it up. Then she slides a blue tank top over my head and tucks it into my skirt, finishing off the whole look with a thin white belt. She takes a step back and examines the outfit before nodding and placing a pair of ballet flats in front of my feet. I step into them.

Wow, they fit. How did they even know my size?

"Well, it's not perfect, but we don't have time for perfect. Plus, no one is going to be looking at your *clothes*." She gives me a conspiratorial wink. I have no idea why. Maybe it's some secret Hollywood code. I wink back just in case.

"Okay!" she says, clapping her hands together and reaching for the door handle. "Are you ready for your big kiss scene?"

I nod and start for the door, until her words finally settle into my brain.

Wait—what, now?

KISS SCENE?

"Uh . . . ," I falter, my feet literally freezing in place like they're trapped in blocks of ice. "*Who* am I kissing?"

She slaps her forehead. "Oh, right. Sorry. I forgot. They changed that in the script."

Phew!

I feel my feet slowly start to unfreeze and my breathing return to normal.

That is, until she says, "Technically, Ryder Vance is kissing *you*."

CHASE SCENE

"Is this some kind of joke?" I yell at Russ. I usually try not to raise my voice at him because he gets enough of that from Barry, but I'm sorry, this has gone on too long. What kind of stupid prank is this? People acting like they don't recognize me? I'm the star of the show. My *name* is in the title.

I glance desperately around the soundstage, searching for my mother. She'll put an end to this. For once, I actually *want* to see her rip into Barry. But she's nowhere to be seen. I do, however, spot Ryder standing by the Craft Services table, stuffing his face with doughnuts.

I break free from Russ's grip and dash over to him. "Ryder!" I exclaim, trying my best to paint a breezy smile on my face. "What's going on around here? Why is Russ acting like he doesn't know me? He just called security on me!" I let out a nervous laugh, hoping he'll join in. He doesn't join in. He drops the doughnut in his hand into the trash and slowly backs away from me, like I'm a grizzly bear in the woods. Not the costar he's shared stages and red carpets, not to mention *billboards,* with for the past four years.

I roll my eyes. "Ryder? What are you doing?"

But he just continues to back away, his eyes wide and alert, like I might pounce at any moment.

"RYDER!" I screech.

And that's when I feel someone behind me. Someone large. I turn and find myself face to face (or rather, face to chest) with Garrett, a former WWA wrestling champion *and* the head of security at Xoom! Studios. I know he's head of security because he's protected me from more than a few crazy fans.

Except now he's looking at me like *I'm* crazy.

"I'm not crazy!" I shout, tears of frustration welling in my eyes. "I'm Ruby Rivera!"

"Okay, *Ruby Rivera,*" Garrett says, his tone dripping with sarcasm. "Time to come with me."

"No!" I yell, and then I turn and bolt. I need to find my mother. I need her to tell these loons who I am, because clearly they've all lost their minds. I figure she must still be in the hair-and-makeup trailer. That's where she spends most of her time on set. But to make it there, I have to get to the other end of the soundstage *and* out the doors, all without Garrett catching me.

Fortunately, after working here for four years, I know a shortcut.

I run toward the set of Rogue Raymond's Junkyard and Bazaar, my pulse starting to pound in my ears. I can feel Garrett's heavy frame shadowing me the whole time.

He's actually *chasing* me. Like I'm some criminal. What is wrong with everyone today? Did Stan, the catering manager, secretly switch the coffee to decaf?

As I run through the junkyard set, I duck between cars and old scraps of machinery, but Garrett stays close on my tail, bounding over car hoods and tossing aside junk like he's whacking through bushes in the jungle. I run from the junkyard into the adjoining set—the Wish Granting classroom—and have to scramble over the desks to avoid getting snatched up by Garrett, who is still close behind me.

A moment later, I burst out of the giant building of soundstage 11. The hair-and-makeup trailer is straight ahead of me, and I can just see my mom through a window. She's exactly where I thought she'd be: sitting in one of the chairs, facing the mirror, staring down at something in her lap. That would be her iPad. She's scouring the internet for negative comments about me. It's what she does for fun.

"Mom!" I call out breathlessly, but she doesn't hear me because the window is closed. She takes a bite of yogurt from another impossibly tiny bowl.

I run for the trailer, darting up the steps and lunging for the door handle.

But I never make it inside.

Garrett's hand clamps down hard on my shoulder.

"MOM!" I shout, and this time, I'm certain she must hear me because her head lifts and she glances around, searching for the source of the sound. "Over here!" I yell.

I start to wave my arms around, trying to get her attention, but my hands are soon yanked behind my back while Garrett fastens zip ties around my wrists.

As Garrett ushers me back down the steps and away from the trailer, I call out for my mom again, this time, using her first name. "EVA!"

She stands up and peers through the window of the trailer. For a brief moment, I swear she sees me. I swear our eyes lock. But I must be wrong, because a second later, she shakes her head and returns to her seat, glancing at herself in the mirror and fluffing her hair.

FIRST KISSES AND LAST LINES

Skylar

WHAT IS HAPPENING RIGHT NOW?

Why am I standing in the middle of the Jinn Academy hallway with a row of gold lockers behind me while a girl fiddles with my hair? Why are there like a zillion lights and cameras pointing right at my face? And why is—

OH. MY. GOSH.

I gasp as he steps out of the darkness and onto the set like he's stepping out of a dream. *My* dream. I've had this exact dream. That I'm standing in the Jinn Academy hallway and Ryder Vance walks up to me and says . . .

"What's up, nerd?"

Okay, that's not what he says to me in the dream.

But that's what he's saying to me now! The real Ryder Vance. In the flesh. Right in front of me. But why is he calling me a nerd? He doesn't even know me! Or is it just that obvious? Is it written all over my face? Is that how the Ellas just *knew* on the first day of school that I didn't fit in?

My knees start to wobble. My head goes a little woozy. Ryder bumps my shoulder with his. "You ready for all this magic?" he asks, making circling gestures around his lips.

His lips!

Is he honestly going to kiss me? Or was that lady in the clothing closet just joking around? Is this some kind of strange hazing ritual for extras? Make them think they're supposed to do a kissing scene with Ryder Vance?

A girl with purple hair approaches Ryder and starts dusting his face with white powder. He closes his eyes and, for a moment, I'm just able to stare at him. He's so gorgeous. And his hair is even better in person than it is on TV!

There's no way he's supposed to kiss me.

My life just isn't that perfect.

But then a voice booms out from the darkness beyond the cameras, rendering me utterly speechless, paralyzed, numb, dizzy, and feeling like I might actually pass out. Or throw up. Or both.

"Kiss scene, take one!"

And the next thing I know, Barry Berkowitz is standing right in front of me. Actually, it's more like he's towering over me, looking down at me like I'm a bug he wants to squash. "Okay!" he spits. Like *literally* spits. I feel specks of moisture hit my nose. "We can't afford any more delays. All you have to do is stand there and *pretend* to be in love with Ryder. Do you think you can handle that?"

I almost snort at how ridiculous that question is.

Like I have to *pretend*.

"Y-y-yes," I stammer.

Barry throws his hands in the air. "Hallelujah!"

I smile, feeling pretty proud of myself, until I realize he's being sarcastic.

"So," he says, making intense eye contact with me. "Just so we're clear. You don't say anything. You just stand there and let Ryder kiss you, okay?"

I blink up at him and nod. My very first kiss ever is going to be with Ryder Vance! Just *wait* until the Ellas find out about this. They'll fall all over themselves.

"Great," he snaps, then turns and strides off set, calling out to no one in particular. "Places!"

Everyone springs into action, like Barry Berkowitz is some kind of king, giving orders to the courtiers buzzing around his throne. The girl with purple hair—the makeup girl, I assume—turns to me and starts brushing gloss onto my lips. I'm glad she's on it, because I never would have thought of glossing up my lips before a kiss. But I suppose that makes sense. You don't want yucky chapped lips before kissing Ryder Vance.

Ryder walks slowly toward me and I feel my stomach clench. He reaches out like he's going to punch me in the face, but instead he rests his hand against the locker behind my head, like he's trying to make sure I won't run away.

Trust me, there's no need for that. I'm not going *anywhere*.

But then suddenly, a thought pops into my head.

Why is Miles kissing some random extra? Shouldn't

he be kissing Ruby? That's what all the fans have been waiting for. Including me!

Maybe this is just a ruse. A side plot to make us *think* Ruby and Miles are never going to get together. Or maybe it's one of Ruby's vivid dreams. Right after Ryder and I kiss, they're going to cut to Ruby waking up in her bed, sweaty and breathing heavy.

Come to think of it, where *is* Ruby?

I never saw her come out of the prop room. Did the door lock behind her again? Is she still in there? Should I tell someone?

I glance around for someone to tell, but the set has emptied again. It's just me and Ryder alone in the brightly lit hallway, surrounded by darkness.

He's really close now. Like touchable close. No . . .

Kissable close.

All the air in my lungs evaporates in an instant.

This can't be happening. This can't be—

"And, action!"

Ryder looks me in the eye like he's looking deep into my soul. That magical gaze that I've always loved so much is now pointed directly at me. ME!

"I just wanted to say . . . ," he says, his voice soft, compassionate. Nothing like the voice he used to call me a nerd just a second ago. ". . . that we'll find her. I promise. I'm not giving up and neither should you."

It's a good thing I don't have any lines, because I'm not sure my mouth would be able to form words right now. I'm completely speechless. All I can do is stare back into those gorgeous blue eyes while my entire body turns to a puddle of goo.

Then Ryder is leaning in to me. His lips are moving toward me. He has that dreamy half grin on his face that every single girl in this country has fallen in love with. His eyes start to drift closed and . . .

Oh my gosh. This is really happening. He's going to do it. He's going to kiss me. I'm going to . . .

HUUUGHHUUP!

And yeah. That's what I do. Because that's me. Skylar Welshman, professional screwup.

"Cut!" calls someone from the darkness. I'm pretty sure it's Barry. He's got one of those voices that you only need to hear once to remember. It's kind of thunderous and terrifying. Like an angry dog's bark.

"What in the name of all that is holy was *that*?" he asks.

"I—I," I stammer, and then break into a series of multiple hiccups that come so fast, they even surprise me. I glance over at Ryder Vance, who's not even looking at me. He's typing something into a phone. He's probably so grossed out right now. That was even worse than hiccupping on the stage of Fairview Middle School and having it broadcast all over the internet!

"Come here, please," Barry says from the darkness, and I can tell he's trying really hard to keep his temper in check.

I bite my lip to try to get my hiccups under control and walk toward the sound of his voice. As soon as I leave the hallway set, I can see that Barry is sitting in a small booth with three flat screens. They're all showing different angles of the Jinn Academy hallway. They must correspond to the various cameras. On all three, I can see Ryder now standing alone by the lockers, on his phone. One screen shows his back, one shows his left side, and the last one shows his face.

His beautiful, beautiful face.

That I just hiccupped on.

Ugh.

"I'd like you to watch this playback and tell me what's wrong with it."

I swallow. I know what's wrong with it. *I'm* wrong with it. But I have a feeling you don't argue with Barry Berkowitz. So I just nod meekly and turn my attention toward the screens.

"Roll playback, please!" Barry shouts to someone, and a second later, the image on the screen flickers and now there are two people in the shot. Ryder and . . .

Huh. That's weird.

The person with Ryder in the hallway looks exactly like Ruby Rivera. Is he showing me footage from another scene? Except she's wearing the same outfit as me. The flowery skirt, blue tank top, and white belt.

Why is Ruby in another scene wearing the same outfit as an extra?

"Action!" comes a voice from off screen, and then I watch as Ryder says, "I just wanted to say that we'll find her. I promise. I'm not giving up and neither should you."

Then he starts to lean in toward her. She looks panicked. She looks like a deer caught in headlights. She looks like she might—

"Do you notice anything *wrong* here?" Barry asks me, and I want to scream, "Yes! It's all wrong! Everything is wrong! That's not me!" But all I can do is swivel my head from screen to screen, trying to find an angle where this makes sense.

"Well," Barry prompts, clearly growing agitated. "Do you, Ruby?"

Ruby?

Then I watch the center screen in total shock and disbelief as Ruby Rivera lets out a loud, obnoxious hiccup right in Ryder's face.

And that's when I really do pass out.

SO NOT MY MOTHER

Garrett puts me on a golf cart and drives away from the soundstage. It doesn't take me long to figure out where he's taking me. To the visitor center. The only rational explanation floating around in my head is that maybe they've confused me with someone on one of the tours. Maybe Cami did something strange with my makeup today and I don't look like myself.

"We've called your mother," Garrett says after parking the golf cart in front of the large one-story brick building. "She's on her way here."

"Good!" I spit back, thinking about my mom sitting in that trailer with her iPad, getting the message that I've been escorted to the visitor center by security.

"She's going to have your head on a platter!" I say, and then quickly amend my statement. "Okay, well, technically this week, she's going to have your head in a tiny bowl, but still. She's probably already called our lawyer."

Garrett ignores me and escorts me into the visitor center and down a hallway toward the Xoom! Studios security office.

"Looks like your mother has already arrived." Garrett nods toward a set of glass doors and I see a woman standing in the office. She's tall and willowy with strawberry-blond hair pulled back into a ponytail and tortoiseshell-rimmed glasses.

I snort. "That is *so* not my mother."

That woman is clearly the very opposite of my mother. First of all, my mother would never be caught dead wearing her hair in a ponytail in public, not to mention wearing glasses. And don't get me started on her clothes. She's dressed head to toe in a blah shade of gray. I don't think my mother owns even a single gray item.

The woman turns just then and sees me. Her entire face lights up and she rushes through the glass doors into the hallway. "Oh! Thank goodness!" she wails, and then pulls me into a hug.

And my mother *never* hugs.

She's too worried it'll wrinkle her clothes. *And* mine.

I stand very stiff and still while this lady—this stranger—embraces me, wondering what bad dream I'm stuck in and when I'm going to wake up.

"Skylar!" she says, pulling back and looking me up and down as though she's checking a car for scratches after an accident. "I was so worried! What were you thinking?"

Skylar?

Garrett comes up behind me and releases me from the zip ties. Meanwhile, the strange woman continues to study me. She reaches out and lovingly touches a strand of my hair. I'm about to pull away when I notice something out of the corner of my eye.

That's weird.

My hair is not black.

It's dark blond.

And it's not thick and wavy.

It's stick-straight and limp. Like overcooked spaghetti.

"Skylar," the woman repeats, a sudden sharpness to her voice. "I asked you a question. Your principal called and told me you weren't in class. I ran home from work and you weren't in the apartment. I was about to call the police until the studio called, saying you'd jumped off the tram during a tour and snuck into a soundstage?"

Principal? Class? Apartment? Those are not words that in any way relate to my life.

"Uh . . ." I hesitate, unsure of what to say. I glance desperately down the hallway, searching for some type of escape from this woman's pinning gaze. I spot the restrooms behind me and hastily announce, "I have to go to the bathroom!" Then I dart through the door and stand in front of the sinks with my eyes closed.

I can't look.

I already know I'm not going to like what I see.

"This isn't happening," I whisper. "You're dreaming, Ruby. WAKE UP!"

My eyes pop open and I come face to face with the reflection in the mirror.

Then I let out a scream that echoes across the entire city of Burbank.

THE FACE IN THE MIRROR

···

Skylar

I wake to the sound of a phone ringing. I want to open my eyes but they feel so heavy. And my head hurts. And I'm *starving*. Why am I so hungry? When was the last time I ate? It feels like I haven't eaten since Christmas.

The phone continues to ring, but it's not mine. It's a generic ringtone I don't recognize. I have "A Little Bit of Magic" by Ruby Rivera programmed as my ringtone.

Ruby Rivera . . .

Oh my gosh, I had this strange dream that *I* was Ruby Rivera. I was on the set of *Ruby of the Lamp* and I was filming a scene with Ryder Vance and I was—

"Are you going to answer that?" an unfamiliar male voice says.

"I don't recognize the number," another voice says. This one is female. "Let it go to voice mail."

Eventually, the phone stops ringing and I try to pull my eyes open.

"She's coming to," the man says.

"Is she going to be all right?" the woman asks. She sounds panicked. "I can't believe this happened."

"She's going to be fine," says the man. "It's probably just stress."

The woman sighs. "I told Barry she wasn't ready for that kiss scene. But does he listen? No. And now look what's happened."

Kiss scene?

"It also wouldn't hurt her to eat a little more," the man says. "I have some crackers in my bag."

Ooh. I want crackers.

I finally manage to drag my eyes open to see that I'm lying on a bed and there's a man and woman hovering over me. I've never seen the man in my life, but I definitely know that woman. She's petite, with wavy brown hair, the most perfectly sculpted eyebrows I've ever seen, and tons of makeup.

"Oh, baby," she says, reaching out and brushing hair from my forehead. "Thank heavens you're okay."

And that's when I know I must still be dreaming, because I'm almost certain that I'm staring at Eva Rivera, Ruby Rivera's mother and manager.

"What happened?" she asks, her eyebrows knitting in concern.

I sit up and take in my surroundings. I'm inside some kind of long, rectangular room. A trailer? In front of me, there's a tiny kitchen with a fridge, microwave, sink, and even a tiny oven and stove. Across from the kitchen is a small living room with a dark brown leather couch and a flat-screen TV.

The woman who looks like Eva Rivera sits down next

to me on the bed and presses a cool hand against my forehead.

The man, who has been rifling through a nearby black bag, returns, holding a bag of crackers. I nearly cry out in relief. Food! I go to reach for them but the Eva Rivera look-alike grabs them first. "Thanks, Doctor."

Doctor? Why is there a doctor here?

I hear a knock and Eva calls "Come in!"

A door next to the tiny kitchen opens and in walks that tall, skinny guy with the clipboard.

"What?" Eva barks, clearly not happy to see him.

He doesn't even look her in the eye when he speaks. "Barry wants to know when she'll be ready to come back to set."

"Come back?" Eva screeches, and I cringe at the sound. "She fainted! Does he not understand that? She fainted and it's his fault." She turns to the doctor. "Tell him she's not ready. Tell him she needs to take the rest of the day off."

"Well," the doctor says, squirming slightly. "If she's feeling up to it, then—" But Eva shoots him a very scary look and he quickly changes his answer. "She probably *could* benefit from some extra rest."

"You see?" Eva says to the man still cowering in the doorway. "I'm taking her home. Doctor's orders. And maybe that'll give Barry time to think about his decisions today."

The nervous-looking guy nods, still refusing to meet her gaze, then leaves and closes the door softly behind him.

The doctor clears his throat. "Well, I guess I'll be

going." He turns and gives me a gentle smile. "Take it easy."

After he leaves, Eva turns back to me and sighs. "My poor baby. Let's get you home and into bed so you can rest. Do you want some water?"

I nod, and she hops up from the bed and scurries over to the kitchen. When she opens the fridge, I see it's fully stocked with bottles of water, juice, and diet soda. It reminds me of a minibar in a fancy hotel room.

"Is that apple juice?" I ask, squinting at the shelves. "Can I have one of those?"

Eva Rivera lets out a tinkling little laugh as she grabs a bottle of water. "Don't be silly," she says. "You know how many grams of sugar are in that?"

I squint in confusion. "But it's fruit."

She hands me the water. "Exactly."

I unscrew the cap and take a long swig. "Not too much," she says in a warning tone. "Or you'll look bloated."

I stare at the water bottle in my hand.

Bloated?

The phone rings again—that same generic ringtone—and I watch Eva Rivera grab it from a nearby nightstand and frown at the screen. "Who keeps calling from a four-one-three area code? I hope your number didn't get leaked again. I don't want to have to change it a third time."

Four-one-three?

That's the area code in Amherst. Is Leah calling me?

Eva drops the phone on the bed, and I immediately scoop it up and stare at the caller ID in confusion.

Wait a minute. That's *my* phone number. Who's calling from my phone? I swipe to answer the call and press the phone hesitantly to my ear. "Hello?"

"Skylar?"

"Yeah?"

"It's me! Ruby!"

My eyes nearly pop out of my head. "What?" I shout, causing the scary lady to give me a strange look.

I cover the phone with my hand. "Uh . . . sorry. I just have to take this really quick." I scoot off the bed and wander into the first door I see. It's a tiny bathroom. I hastily shut the door. It's pitch-dark in here, but I can't find the light switch, so I just feel around until I find the toilet and sit on the closed lid.

"Ruby Rivera?" I whisper into the phone.

"Yes."

I'm still not following. "What are you doing calling from my phone?"

There's a long pause and I worry we've been disconnected. "I think something happened during that earthquake. Something really strange."

Memories come flooding back to me. I remember leaving the prop room. I remember that woman dressing me in that big room full of clothes. I remember standing under hot lights while Ryder Vance leaned in to kiss me. I remember hiccupping in his face. That *was* a dream, wasn't it? A really weird, horrifying dream.

"What do you mean?" I ask warily.

"Have you looked in a mirror yet?" Ruby says.

"No," I reply, my voice shaking.

"Find a mirror," she says, and there's something in her voice that really freaks me out. It's not just that she doesn't sound like the Ruby Rivera I've watched on TV for the past four years. It's that she sounds terrified.

I feel around the wall until I finally locate the light panel and flip on the switch. It takes a moment for the lights in the tiny bathroom to flicker on, but once they do, I find it difficult to breathe.

I'm looking into a mirror, but not at my face. The girl in the reflection is staring back at me wide-eyed, with a phone pressed to her ear, but it's not me. It's . . . it's . . .

"It's you," I whisper into the phone.

She lets out a sigh, like this somehow makes her feel better, although I can't imagine why. "I know. And when I look into a mirror, I see you."

I blink. The girl in the mirror blinks, too. "You do?" I screech.

There's a knock on the door. "Ruby? Is everything okay?"

I leap at the sound and rush to lock the door. "Yes! I'm fine!"

"Is that my mom?" Ruby asks.

"Yeah," I whisper. "I think I'm in your trailer."

I continue to stare into the mirror, touching my face and watching as the girl in the reflection—Ruby Rivera!—touches her face, too. "Um, so, what is happening?"

She huffs out a breath. "I don't know. It's like . . . it's like we . . ."

But I realize she can't say it. Not aloud. Because it would sound crazy. It sounds crazy in my head. But someone has to say it.

"Switched bodies?" I ask.

Yup, definitely crazy.

"Yeah!" she says, sounding relieved that I'm the one who was brave enough to utter the words.

"But how?" I ask. I touch my nose. Ruby's perfect, dainty, adorable nose.

"Skylar?" I hear a distant voice call through the phone. "Are you all right in there?"

"Uh . . . ," Ruby says hesitantly, her voice slightly muffled. "Yeah! I just . . . um, have a little stomachache."

"Was that *my* mom?" I ask, dropping my hand from my face.

"Yeah."

"What are you doing with my mom!"

"She picked me up from the studio. She thinks I'm you! Then we drove for more than an hour. I think I'm in your apartment. I don't know. The first thing I did when we got here was find a bathroom and lock myself inside."

Ruby Rivera is in my bathroom?

I glance at my reflection in the mirror again and shake my head. No. Ruby Rivera is in this mirror. Then who's on the phone?

This is weird.

"Your mom is really mad at me," the girl on the phone

says, and then quickly corrects herself. "Or at you, I guess."

I cringe. "How mad?"

Ruby lets out a low whistle. "Pretty mad. She lectured me the entire drive here. Did you really ditch school, take a bus to Burbank, use her credit card to buy a studio tour, and then jump off the tram?"

"I . . . um . . . sort of had a bad day." I touch my face again, running my fingers over that perfectly shaped chin. "How do you think it happened?"

"I don't know!" Ruby cries.

"Did it have something to do with the earthquake?" I wonder aloud.

"Maybe," Ruby says.

"But when I came out of the prop room, no one else seemed to be fazed by it."

Ruby scoffs. "Well, this *is* Southern California. Earthquakes are more common than rain here. Let's retrace our steps. When was the last time you were"—she falters—"well . . . *you*?"

I bite my lip. "I don't know. I thought I was . . . um . . . me when I came out of the prop room, but now I'm not sure."

"I definitely wasn't me when I came out of the prop room," Ruby says. "No one recognized me when I walked back to the soundstage, and then I got chased by security and hauled off to the visitor center."

"Oh! Security was chasing *me* when I first ran into the prop room."

"So something happened in that prop room," Ruby concludes.

"Hmm." I watch Ruby's mouth twist in concentration in the mirror. This is so strange. I'm talking to her on the phone and looking at her in the mirror at the same time, except it's not really her on the phone and it's not really her in the mirror.

Or is it the other way around? I'm so confused!

I turn my back to the reflection so I can think. I struggle to remember everything that happened in that prop room. The memories are fuzzy, but they slowly start to come back to me. I remember trying to make conversation about the props. Then I gave up and burst into tears. Ruby sat down next to me and we started to talk. Eventually, I said I wished I had Ruby's life and she said she wished she had mine.

Yes! I remember! It was right after I found the . . .

Oh my gosh.

My whole body freezes.

Ruby must be on the exact same train of thought as me, because a moment later, we both shout the same thing at the same time.

"The lamp!"

THE REAL DEAL

"You were holding it when you said you wished you could have my life!" I say with sudden realization.

"So were you!" Skylar exclaims.

"So the lamp actually granted our wish?" I confirm, feeling ridiculous even saying it. How could a stupid fake prop from a stupid fake show grant wishes?

I stick my thumbnail in my mouth. I know Mom would disapprove of me chewing on my nails, but technically it's not really *me* chewing it. It's not even my nail! The strange girl in the mirror is chewing *her* nail. And it's really freaking me out.

I can't look at her anymore.

I turn my back to the mirror and sit on the toilet lid to think.

"Is it possible the lamp is like . . ." Skylar's voice trails off. I can tell she's having as much trouble wrapping her head around this as I am. ". . . the real deal?"

The real deal.

As soon as she says it, I get a flash of memory. It's faint and hazy. From a few years ago.

"This one. This one right here. This is the real deal. I found it in a heap of junk at the Santa Clarita flea market."

It was Jericho who said this. He was so proud of that lamp when he brought it to the set. He said he immediately knew it was special. It's only appeared in one episode. Ruby had a dream about her mother being trapped in that lamp. She's been looking for it ever since.

But it can't *actually* be real. Genies aren't real! Therefore, magic lamps that grant wishes aren't real!

"Hello?" comes Skylar's voice, breaking into my thoughts.

"Yeah, sorry. I'm here."

"So," Skylar prompts. "Do you think the lamp is real?"

No, I think automatically. *I don't think anything from that show is real.*

But that reflection in the mirror is telling me otherwise.

"We should check it out," I finally say.

"Check it out?" she repeats, sounding confused. "How?"

I rack my brain, trying to come up with options. I sigh. "You need to get back to that prop room."

Skylar

"Don't worry," Ruby Rivera tells me. "I'll walk you through the soundstage. Just keep me on the phone."

"Okay," I say, sounding much less confident than she does.

I ease open the bathroom door to find Eva Rivera standing there scowling at me, with her hands on her hips.

"What was that about?" she demands.

Unsure how to respond, I press the phone tighter against my ear, waiting for Ruby to tell me what to say. Eva's gaze flicks to the device. "Who are you on the phone with?"

"Tell her it's Carey Divine," Ruby Rivera whispers urgently in my ear.

"It's Carey Divine," I say quickly, gesturing to the phone.

Eva softens. "Oh? Why was she calling from a four-one-three area code?"

"She had to borrow a PA's phone," Ruby prompts me.

I repeat the explanation, having no idea what it means.

"What are you two talking about?" Eva asks, and I can tell she's suspicious of something.

"The Tween Choice Awards," Ruby says.

"The Tween Choice Awards," I repeat.

Eva's mouth turns to a hard line. "She better not be wearing Cynthia Rowley. Did you tell her we already claimed Rowley?"

Ruby groans in my ear. "Shut up, Mom."

I open my mouth to repeat that but Ruby catches me before I do. "No, don't say that! Just tell her to stop worrying."

"Ruby Rivera says to stop worrying," I say.

"What?" Ruby and her mom say at once.

"I mean, stop worrying," I fumble.

Eva pins me with another inquisitive stare. "We really need to get you home. You're obviously not feeling well. Russ cleared your shooting schedule for the day and rescheduled all your scenes for tomorrow."

"They're sending you home?" Ruby asks.

"Yeah," I reply. "I fainted after the kiss scene with Ryder Vance."

Ruby barks out a laugh, which really doesn't help my confidence. A moment later she clears her throat. "Actually, this is good. It buys us some time to sort this out. First we need to get you out of the trailer." Her tone is suddenly very commanding, and I'm glad she's taking charge of the situation, because I haven't the slightest clue what I'm doing. "Tell my mom you left something on set and you're just going back to get it before you leave."

"Um . . . ," I say, trying not to make eye contact with Eva. "I just need to run back to set to get something before we leave."

"Oh, no," Eva says, stalking up to me. "You shouldn't be running around in your condition. I'll call Russ to go get it."

"No!" Ruby shouts in my ear.

"No!" I shout with just as much enthusiasm. Eva startles and stops in her tracks, shooting me a funny look. I take it down a notch. "I need to get it myself. I'll be back in a second."

"Good," Ruby commends. "Now get out of there fast before she can argue."

Eva opens her mouth to say something and I bolt for the door. As soon as I'm outside, I let out a sigh of relief. "Your mom is really . . ." I search for the right word, but I can't quite come up with it.

Ruby seems to understand anyway. "I know."

I glance around the studio, once again taking in the massive building in front of me and the gold plaque that reads "Ruby of the Lamp." I get another jolt of adrenaline. I still can't believe I'm here. On the set of my favorite show!

I keep the phone pressed to my ear as Ruby guides me through the soundstage and down the hallway to the prop room. I'm relieved to find that the door is propped open. I slip inside and Ruby warns me not to close it behind me this time.

"Now," she says, "we need to find that lamp. Do you remember what it looks like?"

125

"Yes," I reply, heading toward the back, where Ruby and I sat before the earthquake . . . or whatever that was. Thankfully, the lights are back on.

I spot the lamp on the floor. We must have dropped it when the room started to shake. I race over and scoop it up. "Got it!"

"Put me on video," Ruby commands.

"Okay. Hold on." I press a button on Ruby's phone and a moment later, a face appears on the screen.

My face!

I startle and nearly drop the phone.

"Whoa. This is so weird." I squint at the screen. My stomach swoops as I take in *my* pale blue eyes, *my* dirty-blond hair, *my* wide nose.

"Totally!" my face says.

"It's like I'm talking to myself."

My face giggles. "You kind of are. Okay, hold up the lamp to the camera."

I do what Ruby says, turning the lamp this way and that, examining it from all angles, while she does the same. The problem is, I don't know what we're looking for.

"Hmm," Ruby says, sounding disappointed. "I was kind of hoping it would be obvious."

"You were hoping *what* would be obvious?" I ask.

"How to switch us back!" she says, sounding slightly exasperated.

"Oh, right." I immediately feel a splash of disappointment. Of course she'd want to switch back. She doesn't *really* want my life. She was just saying that. She was just venting. Now that she's gotten a glimpse of how flawed it is, she wants to go back to her perfect life. I don't blame her.

"Try making the wish again," Ruby suggests. "I mean, the opposite wish."

"Okay." Even though I really don't *want* it to work, I know it's the rational thing to do. Obviously I can't *be* Ruby Rivera. And she can't be me. That's ridiculous.

I set the phone on a nearby shelf with the screen facing me. I close my eyes so I don't have to see my own face watching me. It's too strange. I take a deep breath and clutch the lamp with both hands. "I wish Ruby Rivera and I could switch back."

I wait with my eyes shut tight. I don't know what I expected—some kind of tingling sensation, swirling pink smoke like on the show, maybe another earthquake—but nothing happens. When I open my eyes again, I'm still in the prop room, and Ruby Rivera—or rather, Ruby Rivera with *my* face—is still on the screen.

I can't help feeling just the slight twinge of relief. "It didn't work," I say.

"Really?" Ruby replies sarcastically. "I hadn't noticed."

Her comment stings a little, but I try not to let it show. I watch my face on the screen pull into a frustrated scowl. "Okay," she says, chewing on her thumbnail. *My* thumbnail. "It must only work if we touch the lamp at the same time. Like we did before. Which means I need to get back there."

"But how?" I ask. "My mom is never going to drive you all the way back."

She continues to gnaw on my nail. "You're right. She was still really mad when we got here. But there has to be a way. I can't miss another day of filming tomorrow. We're finishing the season finale! I can't *not* be there. I still have to shoot that stupid kiss scene with Ryder Vance. Not to mention *all* the other scenes of the episode."

The reminder of Ryder Vance sends a wave of giddiness through me, followed by cold humiliation. I still can't believe I hiccuped in his face.

"Well, you're lucky," I say with a sigh as the reality of my life comes crashing back to me. "Kissing Ryder Vance sounds like a dream compared to what *I* have planned for tomorrow. I have to give an oral presentation on *Of Mice and Men* at school. Otherwise, I'll fail Language Arts."

"*Of Mice and Men*?" Ruby asks, raising a single eyebrow. I don't know how she's able to do that on my face. I could never manage to raise just one eyebrow.

"Yeah," I reply. "Why?"

She shakes her head. "Nothing, it's just . . . that's one of my favorite books."

I snort. "Well, my Language Arts teacher would *loooove* you."

Ruby is quiet for a long time.

"What?" I ask, the endless stretch of silence starting to grate on my nerves.

"Did you say you live in Irvine?" Ruby asks.

"Yeah, why?"

She continues to gnaw at my thumbnail like she's been left stranded on a deserted island and it's her only source of food. "That's close to Costa Mesa, right?"

I have no idea where she's going with this. "Yeah. It's only like ten minutes away. I know because my mom said she would take me to South Coast Plaza on Sunday afternoon to see . . ." My voice trails off.

To see Ruby Rivera.

A chill runs down my arms. "What are you thinking?"

She finally pulls her thumb from her mouth, her eyes lighting up like she's just made the scientific discovery of the century. "I might have a plan."

WELCOME TO MY LIFE

Three days.

That's all.

Three days to live in another girl's shoes. To experience something new. To be *normal*.

The thought fills me with so much joy and adrenaline, I nearly drop the phone. I stand up from the toilet seat and start pacing the tiny apartment bathroom. And it really *is* tiny. It's barely bigger than my trailer bathroom. Plus, judging from the two toothbrushes in the holder, it's the only bathroom in the house.

So this is how normal people live.

They share bathrooms.

They probably have nice, long, *normal* conversations while brushing their teeth side by side. That sounds pretty nice.

"Are you pacing my bathroom?" Skylar interrupts my thoughts.

I stop pacing and stare at the camera. On the screen my own face stares anxiously back at me.

It could work.

It really could.

And it kind of has to, because I'm not sure we have any other choice.

I suck in a breath and quickly blow it out. "Be me," I tell her. "Just until Sunday. And I'll be you. And then we'll meet up at the mall and switch back."

My dark brown eyes stare back at me in disbelief. "What?"

"It'll be fun!" I insist. "I'll go to school for you tomorrow and do your oral presentation. I've read *Of Mice and Men* like five times! And you can memorize a few scenes, right? It's not like the kind of acting I do is *hard*. Then on Saturday you can go to the Tween Choice Awards. You can get all dressed up and walk the red carpet and meet celebrities. And I'll do whatever you have planned."

"I don't have anything planned," Skylar says glumly, looking embarrassed.

"Even better!" I exclaim. "I can sleep in for the first time in four years!"

I watch Skylar's reaction carefully. There's shock etched into her face. *My* face. It's actually a better reaction than I think I've ever done on the show. And then, just to sweeten the deal, I quickly add, "You'll get to kiss Ryder Vance!"

"Y-y-you want me to just *be* you?"

I nod vigorously. "Yes! Isn't that what you said you wanted?"

She blinks. "Well, yeah, but—"

I cut her off. "But what? It'll be great. You'll get to be

131

a TV star for the weekend, and I'll get to be a normal kid. Just take the lamp with you now so you don't forget, and bring it to the mall on Sunday. No one will even notice it's gone."

"Be you," she repeats numbly, like she's trying on the words, waiting to see how they feel. "Be Ruby Rivera."

"It'll be like a mini vacation from our lives. And we can help each other out. I can save your Language Arts grade, and you can save me from having to kiss Ryder."

Skylar's face twists in confusion. "Wait, why don't you want to kiss Ryder?"

I fight the revulsion that passes over me. I could tell her the truth—that he's an obnoxious, self-centered, narcissistic jerk—but I don't think that's going to help convince her to go along with my plan. So I just tell her a half truth. "Because he's like a brother to me."

She looks contemplative for a moment before her eyes (*my* eyes) light up like someone just flipped a switch. "Okay! Let's do it!"

I grin. "Awesome! Okay, so you'll need to memorize scenes five, seven, nine, fifteen, and twenty in the script."

Panic flashes in her eyes as she glances around the prop room. "Should I be writing this down?"

I shake my head. "It's fine. It'll all be in the call sheet."

"Call sheet?"

"You'll get it emailed to you tonight. It's basically a shooting schedule." She nods like she's following, but I can tell she's already feeling overwhelmed by my life. "Don't worry. Just follow everyone's lead and you'll be fine. Mom will drive you to the studio; then Russ will lead you to the hair-and-makeup trailer—he's the one who's always holding a clipboard, you can't miss him. Cami will do your makeup and Gina will do your hair. Then Sierra will get you dressed before you go to set. Make sure you memorize your lines tonight or Barry will yell at you. Actually, he'll probably yell at you anyway. He yells at everyone, but he'll yell at you *less* if you're prepared. You can find a copy of the final episode script in my trailer. Or my mom always has a copy on her."

"Final episode?" she asks, the panic quickly replaced with excitement. "You mean, I get to find out what happens in the season finale before everyone else?"

I smile. "Yup."

"Oh my gosh, that is *too* cool!"

"So do you think you can handle all that?"

She nods. "Definitely. I won't let you down."

"Okay, what do I need to know about *your* life?"

She bites her lip, thinking. "Um, well, my mom is a professor of literature at UC–Irvine."

I think my heart just stopped. "Are you serious?"

She rolls her eyes. "I know, super boring, right?"

"Super *amazing,*" I correct her.

She shrugs. "Well, good. Have fun with that, then."

"What else?" I ask. "Like, what about school?"

"Oh, okay. Well, my class schedule is on my phone. Language Arts is first period, so be ready for the presentation first thing. My locker number is seven ninety-two and my combination is one, fifteen, twenty-nine."

"One, fifteen, twenty-nine," I repeat. "Seven ninety-two. Got it."

She blinks. "Really? Just like that?"

I laugh. "I've been memorizing lines since I was eight years old."

"Oh, right. Okay. So Mom takes me to school, but I take the number seventy-two bus home. It's a public bus."

My stomach knots. She takes the public bus all by herself? At twelve? Mom won't let me do anything by myself except bathe. And even then she sometimes barges in on me in the bath to remind me to scrub my face with the extra-strength acne wash. Not just soap.

"Get off at California Avenue," Skylar continues. "Oh! And I almost forgot. Watch out for the Ellas."

"The Ellas," I echo curiously. "Is that like a disease you get from riding the public bus?"

She giggles. "No! The Ellas are a group of girls at my school. Daniella is the leader, and then there's Isabella and Gabriella. You can't miss them. They're the prettiest girls in school, but they can be kind of mean."

"Okay. Ellas. Mean. Got it."

She shakes her head. "No, you don't understand. They . . . they're . . ." She pauses, like she's searching for the right words but can't find them.

"Did these girls do something to you?" I ask.

She turns away from the screen, like I've hit a sore spot, but then a moment later she shakes her head and says, "No. Just . . . be careful."

I nod. "Okay."

Just then, there's a knock on the door and I nearly jump. "Are you sure you're okay? I'm getting worried." It's Skylar's mom again.

"I'm fine!" I call, and then turn back to the screen. "I better go before your mom calls an ambulance or something."

Skylar nods. "Okay. Well, good luck! Call me if you need me." Then she giggles. "I guess you know the number."

I giggle, too. The anticipation of stepping outside that bathroom door is making my whole body tingly. "Yeah, I guess I do. And good luck to you, too! I'll see you on Sunday."

I end the call and set the phone down on the counter. I give my new, unfamiliar reflection another long, hard stare, taking in Skylar's dark blond hair and pale blue eyes and pasty skin. She's cute, in a sort of childish way. I mean, she wouldn't be getting any auditions for the Xoom! Channel, but to me she has the most beautiful face in the world.

A *normal* face.

And just outside this bathroom door is her life. The life I've always wanted for myself. A life she *clearly* does not appreciate.

"Are you hungry?" comes the voice of Skylar's mom again. "Do you want some dinner?"

A life I'm about to devour whole.

I want to call back that I'm starving. Famished. That I've been hungry for the past four years. But I don't. Instead, I turn away from the mirror, I open the door wide, and with a huge smile on my face, I say, "Yes, I'm ready."

135

MESSAGE IN A BOTTLE

Skylar

Be Ruby Rivera?

It's like a dream come true. I mean, it *literally* is a dream come true. I get this awesome glamorous life and she's going to take my blah life in exchange? I definitely got the better end of this deal. She really has no idea what she's in for tomorrow.

I stare down at the phone still clutched in my hands. *Ruby's* phone. On the outside it looks like mine, but on the inside . . .

I open the Contacts app and nearly drop the phone in shock.

WHOA!

She has like every celebrity *ever* in here! I quickly scroll through the names, my mouth stretching wider and wider as I see people like Ryder Vance, Lennon Harper, Audrina McCoy, and . . .

"Berrin James?" I screech, covering my gaping mouth with my hand.

As in *the* Berrin James from my favorite boy band, Summer Crush? No way. No freaking way! I click on the contact, and there, displayed right on the screen in front of me, is Berrin James's personal phone number. At my fingertips.

If I texted him right now, would he text back? What would he say? What would *I* say? Maybe I'll tell him how much I liked Summer Crush's last album.

No. Too obvious.

How about "OMG! BERRIN JAMES I'VE BEEN IN LOVE WITH YOU SINCE FIFTH GRADE!"

Definitely *not*.

I know—I'll just ask him what he's up to.

With shaky hands, I click on the Message app and type:

Hey Berrin! It's Ruby! What's up?

I press send and hold my breath. A moment later, a text message pops up on the screen of the phone, causing me to scream.

WHERE ARE YOU???

Sadly, it's *not* from Berrin James. It's from Ruby's mom. I laugh aloud.

My mom.

My TV show.

My life.

I am Ruby Rivera now. I still can't believe it. The thought gives me a surge of confidence like nothing I've ever felt before. For the past four years, I've channeled Ruby almost every time I was scared or anxious or unsure of what to say. And that's always gotten me through stuff. But now I don't have to channel her. I *am* her.

I feel like I could tackle anything. Do anything. Speak to anyone.

I quickly stuff the lamp under my shirt, doing my best to hide it. Then I take a deep breath and stride fearlessly out of the prop room.

Ruby Rivera can have middle school and the snobby Ellas and our cramped faculty housing apartment. I'm about to experience life as a star.

ALL THE TOPPINGS

I didn't get a very good look at the apartment when I first came in, because I was too eager to get to a bathroom and call Skylar. But now that I've had a chance to walk around, all I can say is this:

I've died and gone to heaven.

The place is small and cluttered, but it's cluttered with *books*. Seriously. Books everywhere. Stacked on the dining room table, covering the coffee table and end tables, lined up in giant towering shelves that make up an entire wall in the living room. I'm not sure my mom even *owns* a book. No, wait. That's not true. She has a bookshelf full of diet books in her office. And let's not forget the extra copies of my memoir—which I didn't write and refuse to even read—that she keeps lying around just in case she needs to hand one out and completely embarrass me. What twelve-year-old has a memoir? Memoirs are supposed to be poignant and introspective and full of wrong turns and life lessons. The only wrong turn mentioned in my memoir is that hideous feathered dress I wore to an awards show once that was so poorly made, I actually shed feathers down the red carpet.

Skylar's mother is standing next to me, watching me carefully. "What's wrong?" she asks. "Are you still feeling ill?"

"So. Many. Books," I utter in amazement before I can even stop myself.

She scoffs and walks into the kitchen, yanking open a drawer and riffling through a pile of papers. "Yes, yes. Very funny. I know, I'll clean up tomorrow. I was planning on tidying up *today,* but someone decided to ditch school and run off to Burbank."

Oh, right. She's still mad at me.

Also, I need to be careful about what I say. I can't exactly let on that I'm not really her daughter.

"So what are you feeling like?" Skylar's mom asks, continuing to rummage through the drawer. She grabs two of the papers—which I now see are menus—and holds them up. "Chinese or pizza?"

My knees practically give out.

Did she seriously just say pizza?

I haven't eaten pizza since I was eight years old. Unless you count that time Esperanza, our housekeeper and cook, tried to make me this low-carb, low-fat pizza with a cauliflower crust and a sprinkling of nonfat ricotta cheese . . . which I don't. It was a sweet gesture, but it tasted like feet.

"Uh . . . ," I say, trying to keep my voice steady so I don't give myself away. I'm sure Skylar eats pizza all the time. I'm sure her voice doesn't get all shaky and her legs don't get all wobbly at just the mention of the word.

"Or would you rather cook?" Skylar's mom asks.

Cook? Skylar knows how to cook? I can barely boil water. "No, no. Pizza sounds good," I reply quickly.

Skylar's mom returns one of the menus to the drawer, pulls her phone out of her pocket, and punches in a number. I watch her with the same fascination as a scientist watching a species of rare monkeys in the jungle.

"Yes, hello. I'd like to order a large pizza. Half with tomato and cheese, the other half with—" Skylar's mom pulls the phone away from her ear. "What do you want on your half?"

My half.

I get an entire *half* to myself?

My mind starts to spin with possibilities.

"Um . . . everything."

She gives me a strange look. "Everything?"

"Yeah," I reply, because it's true. I want *everything*. Any possible thing you could put on a pizza, I want.

"Even anchovies?" she asks, scrunching up her nose.

"What are those?"

"Tiny salty fish."

My stomach swoops. "Okay, everything *except* anchovies."

She nods and relays this back to the person on the other end of the phone. Then she recites her credit card number and hangs up. That's it. Done. A quick phone call and there's an entire pizza on its way to us right now.

This is the best life ever!

"Relax," Skylar's mom says, clearly misinterpreting my excited body language as nervousness. "I'm not mad at you anymore."

I sit down in a nearby chair and try to look comfortable. But it's honestly hard to focus on *anything* apart from the incoming pizza. So instead, I stand up again and browse the titles of the books on the shelf.

Skylar's mom has excellent taste! She's got all my favorites. *Pride and Prejudice, The Book Thief, Jane Eyre, To Kill a Mockingbird, The Outsiders*. Even a few titles I've never heard of. In the center of the next shelf, there's a glass plaque with an inscription on it that reads "Dr. Rebecca Welshman—English Literature Professor of the Year—Amherst College."

I can't believe I'm actually under the same roof with someone who *teaches* books. Someone who reads and analyzes stories for a living. Someone who . . .

I freeze.

Someone who hasn't made a sound in a very long time. I can feel Skylar's mom—Dr. Rebecca Welshman—staring at the back of my head. Did I mess up already? Did I say the wrong thing? But I didn't say anything!

I slowly spin around to see her watching me with the most baffled look on her face. "What are you doing?" she asks.

"Uh, nothing," I say.

I'm not sure what I did, but I know it was wrong. I should have asked Skylar on the phone what she normally does in the evenings. How she normally acts around her mother. What do they talk about? I'm suddenly realizing just how small this place really is. There's kind of nowhere to hide. At least back at home in the mansion, I can pretty much disappear the moment I walk through the door.

Rebecca sighs like she's giving in to some silent argument and plucks a book from a giant bag she brought in from the car.

I venture down the one hallway of the apartment in search of Skylar's bedroom. Apart from the bathroom, there are only two other doors. The first one is open and I can tell from the large bed and the books stacked up everywhere that it must be Rebecca's room. So I head for the other door and open it.

"GAHHHH!" I let out a shriek of horror as soon as I see what's inside. Skylar's mom comes running down the hallway, probably thinking I'm being kidnapped.

"What?" she asks. "What's wrong?"

But I can't speak. I can't form words. Every inch of this bedroom is covered in *my* face. Skylar has the entire Ruby Rivera collection. The bedspread, the pillowcases, the curtains, the rug. There's even a trash can with my smiling mug on it.

I didn't even know they'd *made* a trash can!

I remember when my mom told me they were going to start merchandising and putting my face on all sorts of stuff, but I've never actually seen it all in one place before. It's horrifying.

"What's wrong?" Skylar's mom repeats, peering into

the room. I turn to watch her reaction, but she just looks confused.

Of course. This kind of obsession with a celebrity is totally normal for her.

"Uh, nothing. I . . . thought I saw a mouse. But it was just a weird shadow."

She touches her hand to her chest. "Geez, Skylar. Don't scare me like that."

"Sorry," I say, and slowly back away from the room, shutting the door behind me. I'm definitely not going in *there* until it's absolutely necessary.

We both return to the living room. I take an uneasy seat on the couch, wondering what I'm supposed to do until the pizza arrives. Rebecca grabs a remote between two stacks of books on the coffee table and turns on the TV. "Keep it low, please. I have some reading to finish for class tomorrow."

I turn to the TV to see what she's put on and stifle a groan. It's a rerun of *Ruby of the Lamp*.

Ugh.

I really don't want to watch this. Especially not *this* episode. It's the one where I accidentally made my notes disappear with an incantation gone wrong and then I couldn't study for the big History of the Jinn exam. Miles saved the day by letting me borrow *his* notes, and we studied together.

I want to shut it off, but I force myself to watch. I don't want Skylar's mom to get suspicious. If this is what Skylar does in the evenings, then I suppose this is what

I should do, too. But after hearing myself recite cheesy lines for more than ten minutes, I can't take it anymore. Thankfully, I'm saved by the doorbell and I jump out of my seat. "I'll get it!"

I open the door to find an angel standing on the welcome mat. He's dressed in a red uniform with a red cap that reads "Pizza Heaven."

The smell of the food immediately wafts into the apartment, filling my nostrils and sending my stomach into high-speed spin mode.

"One large pizza, half cheese and tomato, half everything minus anchovies." He pulls the pizza out of a red vinyl bag, holds it out to me, and I can't help but think, *Yes, you really* are *sent from heaven.*

I take the box and carry it over to the table. Rebecca tips the driver, heads into the kitchen, and returns with paper plates, napkins, and cans of real soda with real sugar in it.

I stare at the box for a long time, just studying the grooves of the cardboard and the red lettering, and enjoying the smell. Oh my gosh, that smell. I'll remember it until the day I die.

"What are you waiting for?" Skylar's mom says. "I'm starving!"

Slowly and ceremoniously, I open the lid. A tiny gasp escapes my lips as I gaze upon the steaming hot, cheesy deliciousness that lies in front of me.

Maybe this vacation from my life will only last a few days, but I don't care. It's already officially the best vacation ever.

ALL THE CLOTHES

Skylar

"We're almost home," Eva Rivera says to me as she reaches across the giant SUV and pats my knee. This car is massive. Like it was meant to hold an entire classroom full of kids, not just Ruby and her mother. And her mom honestly looks pretty silly driving the thing. She's so tiny and the car is huge. It's like an elf getting behind the wheel of a tank.

A bolt of electricity travels through me as Eva turns onto a narrow road and starts driving up a windy hill. I can't believe I'm going to see Ruby Rivera's house! I'm going to sleep in her bed! Oh my gosh! That is like a million times better than sleeping in the *Ruby of the Lamp* sheet set.

Five minutes later, Eva pulls into the driveway of the largest, most amazing house I've ever seen. There are some big houses in Amherst, but this puts all of them to shame. I don't think you can even call it a house. Mansion would be more accurate. Or *palace*.

Eva pulls into a five-car garage, and I don't even wait for her to kill the engine before I'm clicking off my seat belt, jumping out of the passenger seat, and racing to the door. I stop with my hand on the knob, though, because it suddenly occurs to me that it's kind of rude to just barge into someone else's house. But then I remember that it's supposed to be *my* house.

I push open the door and tumble inside, my jaw nearly dropping to the floor.

I'm dreaming. I have to be dreaming. Either that or I've died and gone to heaven. This is the kind of kitchen featured in magazines. It's vast and open, with a tall ceiling, gray granite countertops, cream-colored cabinets, and a massive stove. It has like ten burners on it! The things I could cook in this kitchen are boggling my mind. I could make a feast in here!

A small chirping sound interrupts my thoughts. Eva responds to it like a dog responding to a whistle. "Oh!" She rummages through her bag for her phone. "That's the agency calling to talk about your contract for next season. The Channel is stalling, for some reason. I'm trying to get to the bottom of it." She finds the phone and nods toward the hallway leading off from the kitchen. "Why don't you go up to your room and rest? I'll have Esperanza make you some dinner."

"Okay," I say, trying to sound casual and not like my head is going to explode from the excitement of seeing Ruby Rivera's bedroom. I wander out of the kitchen into a massive foyer with not *one* grand, curving staircase, but *two* grand, curving staircases. Wow! I can't imagine living in a house with two staircases right next to each other. Is one for going up and the other for going down? How am I supposed to know which is which?

I choose the staircase on the left. With each step, I take in the impressive view of the giant foyer below: the crystal chandeliers hanging from the ceiling, the glittering marble floors. It's like I'm in a museum!

I continue down the hallway until I find a bedroom that I assume is Ruby's, based on the giant pink letters on the wall that spell out "Ruby."

The room is *massive*. Bigger than all the rooms in our Irvine apartment . . . combined! It's decorated in soft pinks and greens and has a huge canopy bed in the center, the kind you see in old movies about people who live in castles. And . . .

NO. WAY.

Is that the closet?

I rush across the room and through a door leading to a whole other room!

This can't possibly be a closet. It has *aisles*. Like a supermarket. And it's filled with more designer labels than South Coast Plaza! Everything is organized by color, so it feels like stepping into a rainbow. I excitedly run through each of the *five* aisles of clothes and then stop when I reach the end because my feet can't move. I can barely even breathe. There is a literal *wall* of shoes in front of me. As in floor to ceiling, left to right, every square inch covered with shoes.

I sit down in front of the wall and just stare at it in awe. I can't believe this is Ruby's life. I can't believe she has the audacity to *complain* about any of this. She's the luckiest girl in the world! She totally has it made.

Honestly, if this were my life, I don't think I'd ever leave this closet. I'd just try on clothes all day. If only the Ellas could see me now. How jealous would they be?

I don't know how long I sit there, just gaping at the wall of shoes, but eventually a beeping sound yanks me out of my reverie. I pull Ruby's phone out of my pocket and let out a screech when I see that Berrin James has actually texted me back! Or he texted Ruby back, anyway.

Hey girl. Just heading into the studio to record the solo album. Can't WAIT!

Solo album? Why is Berrin James recording an album without the rest of Summer Crush? They're not breaking up, are they? No, that would never happen. They're like the most successful boy band ever. Besides, I would definitely have heard about that. Maybe it's just a side project.

I bite my lip, trying to decide what to write back. The problem is I have no idea what Ruby Rivera and Berrin James talk about. So I just go with:

Have fun!

Which I admit is totally lame, but a moment later, Berrin texts back a smiley face and a music note and writes:

See you at the Tween Choice Awards on Saturday!

I squeal and hug the phone to my chest. A supermarket-size closet? A wall of shoes? Text messages from superstars? The Tween Choice Awards?

As I fall onto my back and stare up at the ceiling, all I can think is *How on earth will I ever be able to give this back on Sunday?*

JUNKIEST, SUGARIEST, CARBIEST

The first thing I do when I wake up on Friday morning is check my surroundings: Small bedroom. Small bed. My face on every surface.

It wasn't just a dream. The magic didn't wear off in the middle of the night.

"WOO-HOO!" I squeal, sitting up.

The last time I set foot in a real school was on my eighth birthday. At Clear Creek Elementary School in Dallas. Of course, I didn't realize it would be my last day of school until I came home that afternoon to discover that Mom had made the decision to move us to Hollywood to pursue my acting career.

If only I knew then what I know now, I might have put up a fight. I might have wrapped my arms and legs around one of the pillars on our front porch and never let go.

We left the very next day, and I've been homeschooled ever since, first by Mom and then, eventually, by tutors on the set of *Ruby of the Lamp*.

The truth is I miss being in a classroom. I miss being

surrounded by people my own age. I remember having friends back in elementary school. I remember playing and joking around during recess. I remember *enjoying* my life.

And that's exactly what I intend to do today. Enjoy every minute of my limited time in this life.

I push back the covers and jump out of bed. I admit it was pretty weird sleeping in sheets with my own face on them, but it was better than sleeping in that stuffy mansion, waiting for Mom to wake me up with the measuring tape.

I walk over to Skylar's closet and open the door. It's pretty tiny, but I don't care. I don't need much. Just the comfiest thing I can find. For once in my life, I'm not going to fuss over an outfit. I'm not going to worry about makeup or face masks or moisturizing cream. In fact, I may not even brush my hair!

This is what being normal is all about. Dressing however you want with *no* consequences!

Geez, I think as I riffle through Skylar's wardrobe selection. This girl has *no* sense of style. I remove a hanger with a black chiffon leopard-print skirt and nearly gag. "Eww," I whisper, and quickly put it back.

I eventually find a pair of sweatpants in a drawer and pull them on with a faded gray T-shirt and a soft, ratty hoodie.

Ahhhh. This is bliss. I feel like I'm ready for bed.

I quickly brush my teeth and head into the kitchen to find something for breakfast. Last night's pizza was so delicious, and now I can't wait to see what these people have in their pantry. I'm going to eat the junkiest, sugariest, carbiest breakfast I can find.

Skylar's mother is already up, dressed, and sitting at the kitchen table, typing on a laptop. She's surrounded by open books. The sight of it brings me so much joy, I nearly run up to her and hug her.

"Morning!" Rebecca says cheerily.

"Morning," I respond, inching my way over to the table to try to get a look at what she's working on.

"Sorry I went to sleep so early last night," she says, still typing away on her laptop. "I was beat. What did you do?"

I shrug and tilt my head in an attempt to read the title of the open book in front of her. "Just read a little and then went to sleep."

The keyboard stops clacking and a shocked silence fills the room.

I wince.

Did I say something wrong?

"You . . . *read*?" Rebecca asks, and I peer at her. Her face is deathly still.

"Um . . . ," I stall, wondering if I should try to backpedal. She looks like I just told her I murdered the neighbor. "A little. Yeah."

And then, just as soon as the reaction came, it's gone. She clears her throat and goes back to typing, but I can tell there's something less focused about it now. Like she's just going through the motions. I steal a peek at her screen and notice she's just typed a string of nonsense across the bottom of her Word document.

"What did you read?" she asks. It sounds casual, but there's a heaviness in her voice. As though the fate of the free world rests on my answer.

"Um . . ." Once again, I have no idea what to say. I know I just screwed something up. Upset the balance of this relationship. The truth is, I snuck a copy of *Little Women* into Skylar's room last night, but somehow I feel like that's not the right thing to say. I glance around the small apartment for help. What does Skylar normally read? Comic books? Magazines? Ruby Rivera fan sites? I say the first lie that pops into my head. "Um . . . just some celebrity magazines."

I watch Rebecca's reaction carefully. Her shoulders sag. "Oh," she replies. "Right. Of course. More Ruby Rivera news, I presume."

I swallow hard. "Yup," I say. "You know me. It's all Ruby all the time. She's soooo . . ."

A hundred words fill my head at once.

Fake.

Pathetic.

Cowardly.

"Awesome!" I finally finish, giving two thumbs up. I feel ridiculous, but Rebecca seems to relax a bit. Then, as though coming out of a trace, she notices what she's been typing. She starts backspacing in a frenzy, deleting the lines of gibberish from the page.

I have no idea what just happened, but I'm grateful to feel the air in the room settle. That was really strange.

I continue into the kitchen and start searching through the cabinets. When I find the pantry, I let out a yip of glee. "Yes! You have sugary cereal!"

Rebecca shoots me another strange look. Apparently, I really need to stop talking. Thankfully, though, she goes back to typing.

I grab a box of Lucky Charms, dump a heap of it into a bowl, and drench it with milk. It looks so delicious, I nearly just bring the bowl to my mouth and gobble it up like a dog. But I'm pretty sure that will cause more suspicion from Skylar's mother, so I grab a spoon and sit down at the table.

I shovel a heaping marshmallowy bite into my mouth and try not to moan aloud. My whole body tingles as soon as the sugar touches my tongue. It's the most amazing thing I've ever tasted. The crunch of the frosted cereal combined with the sweet flavor of the marshmallows . . . *YUMMMMM!*

I think about poor Skylar, sitting at my kitchen counter right now, suffering through one of my mom's disgusting flaxseed-and-spinach protein smoothies. Let's see how glamorous she thinks my life is after gagging down one of *those*.

This silence here is pretty awesome, too. The only sound is me chomping and Rebecca's typing. I've never really been in a room this quiet before. There's always some kind of noise in our house. Mom yapping on the phone to Lesley or the show's producers, or yelling at someone from publicity about a photo spread in a magazine she disapproves of. The TV blaring with the latest celebrity news.

"So," I say, between bites of sugary goodness. "What are you working on?"

Rebecca doesn't look up. "An article I was asked to write for *English Literary History*. It's an academic journal."

Wow. That sounds important.

"What's it about?"

Rebecca glances up at me and studies my face for a moment. I take another crunchy bite of cereal. "It's a comparison of modern horror novels with *Frankenstein* by Mary Shelley."

"Oh! I love that book!"

Rebecca stops typing again and rips her glasses from her face. She glares at me with that same expression I saw yesterday in the car on the way back from the Xoom! Studios lot. "What are you doing, Skylar?" she asks, a clear edge to her voice.

My spoon clanks down into my cereal bowl. Whoa. Where did all this hostility come from? We were having such a nice moment.

I open my mouth to respond, but Rebecca lets out a heavy sigh and closes her laptop. She stuffs it into a nearby satchel along with all the books on the table. "You better finish up. We're leaving in ten minutes and you're not dressed yet."

I glance down at my outfit. "I'm wearing this."

Rebecca looks confused, and I worry she's going to respond the way my mother would and *demand* I go and change, otherwise what will people think? What will the gossip magazines write if you're accidentally photographed by paparazzi?

But she doesn't. She just shrugs and says, "Okay."

After she leaves the room, I slurp up the excess sweetened milk from my bowl, drop the dish in the sink, and dart back to Skylar's room. I pick up her backpack and let out a small squeal thinking about all that awaits me today. Lockers and classrooms and those little desks that are attached to the chairs. Science experiments and math equations scribbled on chalkboards and discussing works of literature at great length.

So. Much. FUN!

I grab Skylar's phone and slip it into a side pocket of the backpack. Then I hoist the bag onto my back, loving the way the straps feel as they settle on my shoulders.

Ten minutes later, I'm back in the passenger seat of Rebecca's car as we drive in silence. The whole way, I'm staring out the window, giddily watching the streets.

"How about some music?" she says, turning on the radio. I immediately hear my own whiny voice flood out of the speakers, singing, "Wishing on a star won't get you very far. What you need, baby, is a genie like me."

"Ugh," I say, reaching for the volume knob to turn it down. "Not that. Anything but that."

Rebecca looks baffled. "But you always listen to Ruby on the way to school."

"Oh," I say, biting my lip. "Right. Well, I was just, you know, in the mood for something different."

"How about some Summer Crush?" Rebecca suggests. She stops at a red light and begins flipping through the playlists on her phone.

Summer Crush? Ruby Rivera? Yuck! Skylar has dreadful taste in music.

I know for a fact that not even Summer Crush listens to Summer Crush. In fact, they're breaking up, but no one knows that yet. Berrin James told me in secret.

"Or no music is fine with me," I say.

The light turns green, Rebecca shrugs, and returns her phone to the cup holder. "Okay."

When she pulls into the parking lot of the school, I can hardly contain my excitement.

"Try to stay *in* school today," Rebecca says.

I open the door. "Oh, that won't be a problem. Bye, Rebecca—I mean, *Mom*."

She flashes me another strange look and then just shakes her head like she'll never understand twelve-year-old girls. "Bye, sweetie."

I step out of the car onto the curb and just stand there, feeling what it feels like not to have people pointing cameras at my face and screaming my name. I can just be me . . . or, rather, *her*.

No paparazzi. No press. No risk of my picture showing up all over the internet tomorrow.

I take a deep breath, reveling in the sensation of anonymity. I stare up at the large gray stone building in front of me. White letters are affixed over the door.

FAIRVIEW MIDDLE SCHOOL

A beaming smile spreads across my face. This is going to be the best day of my life.

INVISIBLE ARM FAT

Skylar

This is going to be the best day of my life!

I wake up before sunrise because I'm just way too excited to sleep. Last night I spent over an hour exploring Ruby's house. It's officially the coolest house ever. It has everything. I mean *everything*. A pool. A hot tub. A sauna. A dance studio. A gym. Even a small movie theater with gigantic leather seats that recline and an old-fashioned popcorn machine.

And today I actually get to *be* Ruby! As in *star* in her show! I can't believe it!

I know I had my brief moment with Ryder Vance yesterday, but that doesn't count. That's when I still thought I was Skylar. Weak, shy, hiccupping little Skylar. Now I'm *Ruby*. Now I have confidence and self-assurance and talent. I'm going to *rock* that kiss scene. And any other scene they throw at me.

I jump out of bed and immediately run into the massive closet. For the next twenty minutes, I try on tons of outfits. It's so much fun. It's like being at the mall without having your mother follow you around, squinting at all the price tags and going, "Uh, why don't we look for something a little less pricey."

When I finally find the *perfect* outfit—a blue-and-pink sequined dress and gold boots—I stand in front of the three-way full-length mirrors and stare at my reflection from all sides. I still can't believe what I see. Ruby Rivera. *The* Ruby Rivera. She's right there, and she's me.

"Good morning!" Eva says, entering the closet.

I turn toward her and strike a pose like I'm on the red carpet. "What do you think?"

Her eyebrows shoot up. I can't tell if it's a look of approval or disapproval. "Lovely," she says flatly. "Now take it off."

I feel myself deflate. "What? Why? It's so cute."

"Because it's Friday," she says, like this is supposed to mean something to me. And when I don't automatically get what she's referring to, she sighs and adds, "Measuring day."

Measuring day?

Eva opens a drawer just to the left of the mirrors and pulls out a long red measuring tape. Then, with her toe, she slides out a scale from under a rack of clothes. "Come on. We don't have all day. Off with the clothes. Onto the scale."

Reluctantly, I pull off the boots and peel off the dress. I step onto the scale and watch Eva's reaction. Her face is impossible to read. But she makes a "hmmm" sound as she types something into her phone. Then she proceeds to wrap the measuring tape around my waist, followed by my hips, then each arm and each thigh. When she goes for my chest, I shrink back and cover myself with my hands. "What are you doing?" I screech.

"Measuring your bust."

I break out into giggles. "My *bust*?" Saying the word aloud makes me laugh even harder.

Eva looks at me like I've gone insane. "Yes. We need to get updated measurements to the costume department every week so they can stay on top of your wardrobe. You're still a growing girl, remember?"

I release my hands and let Eva wrap the measuring tape around the top of my undershirt.

"Although," she adds under her breath, "I wish you were gro ving more upward than *outward*."

My gaze flicks to her. Was that an insult about Ruby's body? No. She can't possibly think Ruby is fat. Ruby's body is beautiful! I spent about twenty minutes staring at it in the mirror last night. She's graceful and slender and is just starting to get curves in all the right places.

She releases the tape and types something else into her phone. When I turn back to the mirror, I suddenly don't feel as confident as I did only a few minutes ago. "Are we done?" I ask quietly.

She shoots me another strange look and then wraps the measuring tape around my wrist. My *wrist*! Why on earth would anyone care how big Ruby's wrists are?

After she's logged her data, she turns to look at me. She reminds me of a doctor about to give bad news. "Well, Ruby. I don't know how you've managed to do it, but you've gained another pound and your waist has grown an inch."

My mouth drops open and I stare at her in amazement. She misinterprets my reaction. "I know. I'm as shocked as you are. So I'm going to ask Stan to cut another hundred calories from your daily meals on set."

My stomach groans in response. Last night's dinner was pitiful: a tasteless piece of fish and steamed spinach. I left the table starving and wishing I could just cook something myself. But I get the feeling Ruby doesn't spend much time in the kitchen.

Eva grabs a yellow dress from a nearby rack and tosses it to me. "Wear this to set today. It hides your arm fat better." Then she turns and walks out of the closet.

Arm fat?

I gaze back at the three-way reflection, lift up one of Ruby's arms, and give it a shake. If there's any fat on this arm, you would need a microscope to see it.

Still, I pull the dress over my head.

After I force down the most disgusting smoothie I've ever tasted, Eva rushes me out the garage door and into the SUV.

"Are you ready for today?" she asks as she pulls onto the street.

"Absolutely!" I chirp.

"So you rehearsed scenes five, seven, nine, fifteen, and twenty in the script last night?"

Uh-oh.

The script! Ruby told me to read it and memorize the

lines and I totally forgot! I can't get to that studio and not be prepared! Ruby is counting on me to help her out. Plus, I definitely don't want to get yelled at by that Barry guy again.

"Of course," I say, trying to sound convincing. "But maybe I should review them again, just in case. Do you have the script?"

Eva flashes me a suspicious look as she steers the giant SUV down the winding hill. With her eyes still on the road, she reaches into her massive black bag in the back-seat and pulls out a thick stack of paper that's been bound together by little brass fasteners.

On the front cover, in a crisp black font, it reads:

```
              Ruby of the Lamp
    Episode 4.22 — "Hope Is in the Stars"
```

Butterflies start to flap inside my stomach. This is it. The final script for the final episode of season 4! I'm going to find out what happens before anyone else! I've never read a real script, let alone one from my all-time favorite TV show!

Excitedly, I flip to the first page. But my eyes instantly cross when I see that it's not written like anything I've ever read before. It looks nothing like a book, which I suppose is a good thing since I hate reading books. The text is always too close together. I look at those giant, dense paragraphs full of words and I just want to give up. Can't the author just say what they want to say with fewer words and make it easier on the rest of us? That's why I've always preferred TV. You don't have to *read* what everyone is doing. You just watch and listen.

I flip through a few pages of the script, trying to figure out how the formatting works. It looks like a character's action is written all the way across the page, while their dialogue is written in the center of the page, which is nice because it leaves lots of empty white space on the sides.

But then there are these weird words that I don't understand. Things like "INT" and "EXT."

While Eva is distracted by the road, I do a quick Google search and discover that INT stands for "interior," meaning the scene takes place inside, and EXT stands for "exterior."

Oh, that makes sense.

I flip back to the first page and start reading.

IRVINE BARBIE

Okay, why is everyone staring at me?

The moment I walk through the front doors of Fairview Middle School, it's like I'm suddenly back in my own body. It may as well be a red-carpet premiere and not a school hallway. All that's missing is the annoying photographers.

Click.

Nope, there's the annoying photographer. Someone just whipped out their phone and took a picture of me! Why are they taking pictures of Skylar? She's not famous, is she?

"Hey, *Belchman!*" someone calls out, and I'm not sure why I turn around, because it's not like someone is talking to me. Skylar's last name is Welshman, not Belchman. But I do turn around. And that's when I see a pack of boys laughing uncontrollably, slapping each other on the back, and giving each other high fives.

I continue down the hallway, searching for locker number 792, reciting in my head the combination Skylar gave me.

One, fifteen, twenty-nine.

But as I keep walking, more and more people are turning to look at me. Some even seem to be whispering to each other behind their hands, so I can't make out what they're saying.

What's going on?

And then it hits me.

Oh my gosh! I can't believe I didn't think of it before.

We've switched back!

The magic must have worn off, and I'm no longer in Skylar's body. I must be back in my own body. They must recognize me and are wondering what Ruby Rivera is doing walking down their school hallway.

I spot a girls' bathroom up ahead and start to run. But running only seems to make people whisper more, and laugh louder.

I finally make it to the bathroom and push the door open. Inside, three very pretty girls are gathered around the mirror. There's a ton of makeup spread out across the counter, like someone's bag exploded.

"Nooooo," one of them is saying. "You're doing it *wrong*. I saw it on a YouTube video."

When I enter, they all stop and turn to look at me at the exact same time, like they're doing some choreographed dance routine.

"Hi," I say breathlessly, pushing past them to get to the mirror.

One of them—the tallest and blondest—makes a scoffing noise that sounds like she's choking on an unchewed piece of meat. She's super skinny, and with her miniskirt and high heels (High heels? In middle school? Seriously?) she kind of looks like a Barbie doll.

"Uhhhh . . . ," she says, elongating the sound. "No offense, but what do you think you're doing?"

"I'm sorry. I just need to check someth—"

But I stop cold when I see that I was wrong. It's not me staring back from the mirror. It's still Skylar. Which makes absolutely no sense. Why would they be taking pictures of her? Why would they be staring at her?

"You just need to check what?" Barbie asks. "That you forgot to take off your pajamas?"

The other two girls snicker like this is the funniest thing they've ever heard.

"Seriously," says the other blonde, who's dressed nearly identical to the first. "Did I miss the email that it was wear-your-pajamas-to-school day?"

The third one—a lonely brunette in a blond sandwich— giggles and adds, "Yeah, we clearly missed the email that said you should wear your pajamas to school."

All three of them crack up and I glance down at my outfit in confusion. Sure, it's not as dressy as what the three of them are wearing, but they look like they're going to a club, not to school. School is supposed to be casual and laid-back, isn't it? "What's wrong with what I'm wearing?" I ask.

Barbie stops laughing and her expression turns serious. She takes a step toward me and bows her head, like she's about to tell me a secret. "The boys are already talking about it."

I squint. "Talking about what *I'm* wearing?"

She nods and gives me a pitying look. But I just shrug and brush it off. Whatever. I don't know any of these people. I don't care what they think. I'm comfortable. I'm happy. I turn on the faucet and start to wash my hands.

Blond Barbie scowls. She does *not* seem happy that I've just turned my back on her. "Did you hear me?" she asks. "People are saying you live on the streets."

I can see her reflection in the mirror. She's got her arms crossed and she's pursing her lips like she's waiting for me to cry or freak out or something.

Geez, what is with this girl?

It's like she gets a kick out of being mean to people.

And that's when the realization hits me.

"Oh! You're the Ellas!" I say excitedly, like a sleuth solving a big mystery. "Skylar told me—" But I stop when I remember that *I'm* Skylar. Which means I've just lamely referred to myself in the third person. I clear my throat. "I mean, I've heard about you guys."

The three girls stare at me with slightly baffled expressions, like I've just beamed down from the mother ship. "What are you talking about?" the tall one says. She's clearly the leader, because every time she speaks, the other two turn and watch her like she's about to reveal the secrets of the universe.

"Let me guess," I say, ignoring her question. "You must be Daniella."

Her startled expression lets me know that I'm right. I turn to the next one, the other blonde. "And you are . . ." I rack my brain, trying to remember the three names Skylar gave me. "Ariella . . . Anabella . . . No! Isabella!"

The girl I've just identified turns to Daniella as if to say *What did I miss?* But Daniella just goes on staring at me. I swing my finger to the last girl, the brunette. "Which makes you Gabriella!"

I beam, feeling pretty proud of myself, especially when I take in their completely flabbergasted looks. Finally, Daniella seems to regain her composure. She gives her hair a toss. "*Okaaaaay.* Now if you'll excuse us, we're kind of busy here."

She pushes her way back to the sink, giving me a not-so-subtle shove as she passes. The other two girls follow, until I'm edged away from the mirror and practically hugging the paper-towel dispenser.

Okay, I'm starting to understand why Skylar warned me about these girls. They clearly think they're better than everyone else.

I grab a paper towel—which is easy since I'm already hugging the dispenser—and wipe my hands, all the while trying to come up with a strategy. Skylar and I agreed we would help each other out. And these girls are obviously giving her trouble. She seemed really anxious when she talked about them. She told me to "be careful." But I still don't know why.

Maybe Skylar just doesn't know how to handle girls like this.

I certainly do. I spent the last four years on the set of a hit TV show. Trust me, you don't know mean girls until you've met *Hollywood* mean girls. I can definitely handle a couple of middle schoolers.

And that's when an idea comes to me.

Didn't Skylar say something about not having any friends? About not being able to talk to people? While I, on the other hand, have no trouble talking to anyone.

And that's exactly why *I* have to make friends for her!

I'll show her that middle school isn't as hard as she thinks it is. Compared to Hollywood politics, befriending people like the Ellas is a piece of cake. You just have to find the right angle, speak the right language, know your audience.

I take a step back and study the Ellas for a moment. The three of them are gathered around the mirror. Isabella and Gabriella are staring at Daniella, who's holding a liquid eyeliner pen in one hand. "This is how you do it," she's saying. "Watch me." She closes one eye and leans toward the mirror.

And suddenly, I know exactly what to do. I know how to help Skylar out of her friendless rut.

She is *so* lucky she has me.

RESURRECTING AUNT CLARENCE

Skylar

I'm so absorbed in the story of the season finale, I don't even realize we've arrived at the studio until Eva parks the car. The script is awesome! The ending is awesome. The dialogue is awesome. There's just one teensy problem.

It's filled with plot flaws and inconsistencies!

For example, on page four, it says that Miles is going to visit his great-aunt Clarence this weekend. But Aunt Clarence died from a mysterious genie disease in season 2. And then on page seventeen, it says Ruby is going to the Jinn Academy library to research the genie named Balthazar, who was with her mother the night she disappeared. Which would be fine if in season 3, episode 5, they didn't explicitly say that Ruby's mom was with her old friend Jenika that night. I mean, seriously, do these people not keep notes somewhere?

They really are lucky they have me. *Ruby* is lucky she has me. Otherwise she would say these lines and make a huge fool of herself in front of all her fans. I definitely need to tell someone about this.

When we arrive at the studio lot, a tall, skinny guy

guides me to the hair-and-makeup trailer while Eva runs off, saying something about going to talk to Barry again about the kiss scene.

Just the mention of the word "kiss" makes my stomach clench. But I assure myself that it'll be fine. Better than fine. It'll be great! Because I'm not kissing Ryder as myself. I'm kissing him as Ruby! And Ruby is bound to be an amazing kisser. She's amazing at everything! And most important, *Ruby* doesn't hiccup when she's nervous.

Ruby's phone rings as soon as I sit down in one of the makeup chairs. I pull it out and see that it's a call from someone named Lesley. She called three times last night, but I decided it's probably best that I not answer any of Ruby's calls while I'm in her body. It just doesn't feel right. (Text messages to members of Summer Crush are obviously exempt from this rule.) But honestly, I'm afraid I'll say the wrong thing and mess up something big in her life. So I silence the call and place the phone back in my bag. Whatever it is, Ruby can deal with it on Sunday. I mean, what could possibly be so urgent it can't wait a few days?

An hour later, I've been completely transformed. My hair has been styled, my makeup has been expertly applied, and I'm back in that skirt/top/belt combination from yesterday. I now look like the Ruby I know from the show. Just seeing the change in the mirror makes me giddy. As I step out of the hair-and-makeup trailer, Eva snaps a photo of me and I give her my best Ruby Rivera pose.

"Nice!" she commends as she taps away on her phone.

"Look! It's her! It's Ruby Rivera!" comes a squeaky voice from behind me. I turn to see a group of five girls around my age, huddled close together, glancing my way and pointing.

"She's looking!" one of them says, and they all pretend they weren't just staring at me.

I feel a rush of excitement. *My first fans!* I remember how Ruby Rivera reacted to me when I walked into the prop room. She looked terrified. Well, I'm *not* going to act like that. I push my shoulders back, paint on my best Ruby Rivera smile, and walk over to them. They grow very quiet as I approach.

"Hi, guys!" I say brightly. "I'm Ruby."

One of them starts giggling nervously. "We know."

"Are you on a tour of the studio?" I ask.

"We're extras," one of them replies. "For the diner scene."

"Oh, right!" I exclaim. "Extras! That's awesome!"

They seem a little confused by my excitement, so I try to take it down a notch. "I mean, that's cool. What are your names?"

"I'm Stacia," says the first.

"Gwen," says the second.

"Josie."

"Jordan."

"Claire."

I nod around the circle as each of them introduces herself. "Okay," I say with an exaggerated sigh. "I'll try to remember all that."

The five girls laugh like this is the funniest thing they've ever heard. I beam back at them. This is incredible! It's just like being the head of the Ellas. Except better, because I could go anywhere in the world and get this reaction! Daniella is only powerful within the walls of Fairview Middle School. If she were to set foot in any other school, she'd be a nobody. But not me. Not Ruby. I'm somebody no matter where I go!

"What's it like being the star of your own show?" the one named Josie asks, and the other four immediately nod like this is the most important question to ever be asked.

"It's awesome," I say. "Obviously."

They all laugh again. Having people laugh at you because they actually think you're funny—not because you accidentally hiccupped/burped onstage and the most popular girls in school made a video of it that went viral—is the best feeling in the world.

"And what's Ryder like?" Gwen asks.

"Dreamy," I confirm, causing them all to swoon a little.

"Is it true you're going to kiss him today?" Jordan asks.

I nod, raising my eyebrows a bit. "Yes. And I'm kind of nervous."

"Oh, don't be!" Claire says. "You'll be amazing. You always are."

I grin. "Thank you. That's so sweet."

I could easily talk to these girls all day, but eventually that tall, skinny guy with the clipboard—Russ, I think—appears and says, "They're waiting for you on set. Are you ready?"

I give my little fan club a "What are you going to do?" shrug. "Sorry, guys. I guess I have to go."

"That's okay!" Stacia says. "We understand."

"How about you all come and hang out in my trailer later?" I suggest, and then I watch all of their faces light up like I've just told them they've won the lottery.

"That would be so cool!" says Claire.

"We're totally there!" chimes in Gwen.

"Great!" I give them a thumbs-up and follow Russ toward the soundstage.

Making friends as Ruby Rivera is the easiest thing in the world. Everyone just *wants* to hang out with you. Unlike when I'm Skylar and everyone acts like I have the plague.

According to the call sheet, the first scene we're shooting today is scene 5. It takes place in Chaz's Diner—a local hangout for the Jinn Academy students. Ruby and Miles have just gotten home from their trip to the Sahara Desert to find Ruby's mom, and their first stop is the diner because they're both famished. That scene certainly won't require any *acting* on my part. I *am* famished.

As Russ and I walk, I quickly review the scene, trying to commit my dialogue to memory. Fortunately, I don't say much in this scene. I just eat a big juicy cheeseburger and nod with my mouth full as Miles yammers on and on about how he has to visit Aunt Clarence next weekend and how Aunt Clarence is old and senile and always accidentally turns her cats into inanimate objects. Which reminds me . . .

"So, Russ," I say casually as we walk. "I love the scene we're shooting. It's really funny."

He smiles, but it looks fake. "Yes, it is."

"But I have a slight problem with one of the lines."

Russ stops walking so suddenly, I nearly slam into his back. He spins around and pushes his glasses up on his nose. "What?" He looks terrified. "What's wrong?"

"Nothing!" I say, sensing I've overstepped my bounds. "The whole thing is hilarious. It's just that Miles mentions visiting Aunt Clarence, but Aunt Clarence died in the second season."

Russ stares blankly at me.

"Remember?" I say, trying to jog his memory. "Miles had to go to Aunt Clarence's funeral and he was going to miss the big holiday pageant? So then Ruby tried to clone him with an ancient cloning spell, but the clone ended up clucking like a chicken?"

Russ is silent for a long time before he finally replies. "Well, maybe Aunt Clarence was brought back to life."

I squint at him like he's lost his mind. "What? No, that's impossible. Genies can't bring people back from the dead. Remember, Ruby finds that out in season one, episode sixteen, when she accidentally killed Headmistress Mancha's pet hamster and tried to resurrect it." I snort out a laugh. "That was a funny one."

Russ stands very still. I know he's thinking hard about something, but I have no idea what it is. And I can't help but notice the look of panic in his eyes.

"Don't worry. It's easy to fix. I'll just tell Barry that—"

"Please don't tell Barry," he rushes to say. "Just let it go."

I bite my lip, confused. "But the fans will notice."

"The fans won't notice."

I fight not to roll my eyes and say *I'm a fan, and I noticed instantly*. "The real fans will."

Russ starts breathing heavily. He looks genuinely scared. "Look, just promise me you won't tell Barry."

"Tell Barry what?" a booming voice says, startling us both. I know, before I turn around, that Barry is going to be standing there.

And I'm right. He has his hand buried in a giant bag of potato chips, and there are crumbs around his mouth. He's chewing languidly, like a cow.

Russ turns a strange shade of red as he flounders for something to say. "Uh . . . um . . . nothing. Ruby was just—"

"I was just saying"—I interrupt—"that I found some inconsistencies in the script that I thought you might want to know about."

Barry stops chewing. In fact, for a second, it almost looks like he's choking. "Excuse me?"

For a moment, I consider backing down. Maybe Russ is right. Maybe I shouldn't say anything. But then I think about the promise I made to Ruby yesterday. I promised I wouldn't let her down.

I stand up straighter and flip to scene 5 in my script. "Right here," I say, trying to ignore the death stare Barry is giving me and the weird squeaking noise Russ is making. I point to Miles's line.

"Great Aunt Clarence died in the second season. Miles went to her funeral."

I watch with my heart in my throat as Barry's narrowed eyes scan the open page. He looks from me to the script. "*You* noticed this?" he asks.

I nod, although I'm wondering if I should lie and pin the blame on someone else. Barry does *not* look happy right now.

He crumples the now-empty potato-chip bag in his hand like he's strangling the thing to death. Then, with a rough voice that makes me regret ever opening my mouth, he grabs me by the elbow and starts to guide me toward the soundstage. "Come with me."

Helplessly, I glance back at Russ just in time to see the "I told you so" look on his face.

"Makeup, huh?" I say, balling up my paper towel and tossing it into the trash. "I know a lot about makeup."

The Ellas don't respond, but I swear I catch an eye roll from Daniella in the mirror.

I ignore it. "Maybe I could help you."

Daniella scoffs at this, which causes the other two to chuckle, too. Like I've made some big joke. "Yeah," Daniella sneers. "Like *you* could help *us* with makeup." Then she turns her attention back to the mirror, closing one eye and priming her eyeliner pen.

"You're doing it wrong," I say flatly.

Danielle looks put out. "What are you still doing here?"

"You're trying to do cat eye, right?" I ask.

Daniella doesn't respond, but I catch the most imperceptible nod from Gabriella, the shy brunette.

I squeeze between them and pluck the eyeliner pen right out of Daniella's hand. "You need to apply the mascara first." I search the mess on the counter until I find a tube of mascara. I brush it onto my upper eyelashes. "It's a common mistake," I tell them. "So don't feel bad. You see, if you apply the mascara first, it gives you a nice little flick in the corner. Then you use that as an arrow to guide the liner." I close my right eye and run the eyeliner pen in a smooth line from the top of my lid, up the side, creating the perfect cat-eye swoop.

I turn and show Daniella, closing and opening my eye. "See?"

She looks shocked. "How did you learn that?"

I smile. "From Cami, my makeup artist."

"What?" Isabella asks.

I immediately catch my mistake. "Uh . . . I mean, my makeup artist *friend*. She works in Hollywood. She teaches me all sorts of tricks."

"Like what?" Gabriella asks. She seems to bubble with excitement until a stern look from Daniella causes her to shrivel.

"Like what?" Daniella asks with an impatient sigh.

I fight back the grin that's threatening to give me away. *It's working!*

"Well," I say, clearing my throat as I scan the makeup items on the counter. I find blush and a bottle of foundation and pick them up. "Here's a cool trick. If you put the blush on *before* the foundation, it makes your cheeks look like they're glowing from the inside. It's much more natural. And no risk of that whole pink-cheeked clown look."

Daniella's mouth falls open. She closes it a second later.

"Want me to show you?" I offer.

She shrugs. "Whatever."

I take that as a yes. I carefully dip a brush into the

181

blush compact and move toward Daniella's face. She leans back and points to Gabriella. "Do it on her."

"Okay." I redirect my brush to Gabriella and get to work. I've been watching Cami do this on my own face for four years. The movements come easy to me. Once I'm done, Gabriella looks at herself in the mirror and beams. Her cheeks have just the right amount of color. She looks like she's blushing from a compliment.

"Not bad, right?" I ask Daniella, who studies Gabriella's face with what appears to be detached interest.

"It's *okay*," she says, but I can tell she's impressed.

"Well," I say, setting down my tools and brushing the blush residue from my hands. "If you want more tips, you know where to find me."

And with that, I swivel on my heels and turn toward the door. When I get back into the hallway, I'm careful not to let the door close all the way so I can listen in through the crack.

"That was kind of amazing," Isabella is saying. "Look how good Gabriella's cheeks look!"

Daniella doesn't agree or disagree. She just mumbles something that sounds like "Let me try that. Give me the blush."

I smile and ease the bathroom door shut.

My work here is done.

WRITER SCHOOL

....

Skylar

My heart is pounding as I follow behind Barry through the soundstage and down a long, scary hallway. It takes me a moment to realize it's the same hallway I came down yesterday when I was running from that security guard.

Barry stops at a door marked "Writers' Room." He opens it to reveal a long conference table with ten chairs. Except none of them are filled. A group of people are gathered around a laptop in the front of the room, all pointing and laughing at something on the screen. When they see Barry, they all freeze. One of the men shuts the laptop and everyone scurries to their seats.

"What's so funny?" Barry asks, although from the tone of his voice, I don't think he actually wants to know. Still, he saunters over to the closed laptop, opens it, and presses a key. Whatever the group was looking at suddenly appears on a giant projector screen in the center of the room. The guy who shut the laptop holds his hands over his heart, like he's about to pass out.

On the screen is a video with the title "Barry's Breakdowns."

Barry cocks a single furry eyebrow. "Interesting." The room is deathly silent as the video plays. It's exactly as the title suggests. A collection of scenes, set to music, in which Barry Berkowitz is having some kind of tantrum. He's either yelling at someone, throwing script pages into the air, or just seething quietly, his face turning almost purple. There's even a scene where he's angrily stuffing a powdered doughnut into his face while white powder sprays everywhere. This scene is slowed way down so it looks like the powder from the doughnut is gracefully falling snow.

I bite my lip to keep from laughing. I can actually *feel* the tension in the room. I wait for Barry to explode. And from the way the writers are all sitting stiff-backed and ramrod-straight in their chairs, I'm guessing they're waiting for the same thing.

But it never comes.

Instead, Barry stops the video and *calmly* says, "While you so-called writers"—he actually makes air quotes with his fingers—"were playing movie editor, this clever young girl was finding plot flaws in the season finale script."

Clever? Did he just say "clever"? Clever is good, right?

He nudges me with his elbow. "Tell them what you told me, Ruby."

I clear my throat and try to speak in an unwavering voice. "Miles's great-aunt Clarence died in season two."

"Season *two*," Barry snaps, spit flying from his lips

and landing in little tiny puddles on the table. "Who's in charge of consistency issues?"

One nervous-looking guy raises his hand.

Barry shoots him a look and I wonder if he's going to fire him on the spot.

"Well, congratulations, Rick. You've just been out-smarted by a *child*."

Rick bows his head, looking ashamed.

Barry turns to me, his voice surprisingly gentle when he speaks. "Did you find any other problems with the script?"

"Um," I say anxiously. Every single pair of eyes in the room is on me. "Actually, on page seventeen it says that Ruby is researching a genie named Balthazar—"

"We've never used the name Balthazar on the show," one of the female writers interrupts, obviously thinking I was going to point out that *this* character was dead, too.

"Technically, no," I say. "But you had a Baltha*zan* in season one."

All the writers look to each other, clearly trying to figure out if anyone remembers this.

"It was a small part," I explain quickly. "He didn't even speak. Rogue Raymond hired him for a day to sort through a pile of dirt that was brought to the junkyard, remember? Raymond thought he might find gold in the dirt, but he didn't."

The writers stop looking at each other and turn their gazes back to me with stupefied expressions.

"But that's not the problem," I go on. "The problem is that Ruby is researching Balthazar because he was supposedly with her mother the night she disappeared. But in season three, episode five, Ruby learned that her mother was with an old friend named Jenika."

More stunned silence. Barry gives me a pat on the back and lets out a deep guffaw. "It's a good thing *someone* is paying attention around here! Maybe I should hand over your jobs to a bunch of twelve-year-olds."

"Okay," one of the male writers says, "we'll just change Balthazar to Jenika and be done with it."

Barry looks to me, waiting for my reaction to this idea.

"Actually, you can't," I say, wincing slightly.

The writer who just spoke gives me an annoyed look. "And why not?"

"Because Jenika changed her name and moved to Greece. Ruby already tried to track her down in season three, episode eight, and it led to another dead end."

Barry tosses his hands up in frustration. "Why isn't any of this in the series bible?"

Rick jumps out of his seat and grabs a thick white binder from a shelf in the corner and starts thumbing through the pages. "I'm sorry," he mutters. "I guess I missed a few episodes."

Barry rolls his eyes. "You think?"

"Maybe," a writer in a plaid shirt puts in, "Jenika is the one who put Ruby's mom in the lamp in the first place?"

I immediately shake my head. "Nope. Ruby's mom

told her in the dream that the genie who put her in the lamp was a man."

"Is this *really* that important?" Plaid Shirt writer asks. "Are kids really going to care?"

"Of course they'll care!" I shout. Then I quickly recoil and tell myself to calm down. "I mean, I know my fans. They *care*. And you've been stringing them along for four seasons with this mother story line. You need to give them something. You can't keep them waiting another four seasons. They *need* to find out what happened to Ruby's mom! They're getting tired of all these dead ends! They want answers!" I've gotten myself all worked up again, but I don't care. These writers need to hear this. They need to hear what the fans *really* think.

"Fine," Plaid Shirt writer says, challenging me. "How would *you* fix it?"

I feel a rush of heat to my cheeks. This is it. This is my chance. How many nights did Leah and I stay up late brainstorming ideas for how Ruby could finally be reunited with her mother? How many times did we sit around dreaming about being able to give the writers of this show a piece of our minds? And now that's exactly what I'm going to do.

I take a deep breath, pull out one of the empty chairs, and sit down. "Well," I begin importantly, "let me tell you what *I* think should happen."

CRUSHING THE CRUSH

It takes me a few minutes, but I finally manage to locate my locker and dial in the combination. I yank up on the lever, but the locker doesn't open. Did I remember it wrong? Maybe I should have written it down. Or maybe there's some special way to open a locker that I don't know about. I've never actually *opened* a locker before. We have lockers on set, but they're all fake. The locks don't really lock. All I have to do is pretend to turn the dial and then lift the lever.

I feel myself starting to get flustered as I stare down the blue metal door.

"I will conquer you," I tell the lock.

I'm the star of the most popular kids' show on TV; I can open a stupid locker!

I take a deep breath, calming myself down, and try again.

I'm just turning the knob to 15 when I hear a voice behind me say, "You're doing it wrong."

I turn to see a skinny boy with shaggy blond hair

squinting at me like I'm from another planet. And I guess I might as well be. It's called Planet Hollywood.

"You have to turn it the opposite way on each number," he says. "And you have to pass the first number once before you get to the second."

Huh?

He must see the confusion on my face because he says, "Haven't you done this every day for the past month?"

"Uh," I say, trying to find a reasonable explanation, "I guess I just forgot."

He nods like he gets it. "One of those mornings, huh?"

"You have no idea."

He grins eagerly back at me, and suddenly I feel a little weak in the knees. This boy is really cute. And he's looking at me like he's . . . like he's . . .

The realization hits me like a truck.

He totally has a crush on me! Or, rather, on Skylar.

It's so obvious. It's written all over his face. What do I do? Flirt with him? Ask him out? Kiss him right here in front of everyone?

The truth is, I have no idea what normal twelve-year-olds do when they have a crush on someone. Not that my mom would *ever* let me date anyone. It would ruin that perfect wholesome image she's worked so hard to build over the past four years.

"So, do you want me to help you?" the boy asks apprehensively.

"Help me?" I repeat. "With what?"

He looks nervous. "With the locker."

Duh.

I got so wrapped up in the whole crush revelation, I completely forgot about the stupid locker. I scoot aside. "Yes, please."

He steps up to the locker and clears his throat loudly. "So, um, what's your combination?"

"One, fifteen, twenty-nine," I tell him, and then watch as he turns the dial to 1, then *reverses* direction, spinning it the other way, all the way past the 1, until he gets to the 15. Then he reverses again and finishes off on the 29. I hear a faint click and he pulls up on the lever, opening the door wide and then gesturing grandly, like he's presenting a gift to the queen.

I let out a grateful sigh. "Thanks!"

"No problem." His gaze darts anxiously up and down the hallway, like he's a spy running from an enemy agent and he only has five seconds until he's located. "I was . . . just . . . um . . . wondering something." He runs his fingers through his hair, causing the ends to stick up a little. "Were you planning on going to the dance tomorrow night?"

Skylar never mentioned a *dance*! I guess she wasn't planning on going. But I certainly *am*. There's no way I'm missing a *real* school dance.

"Yes!" I blurt out. "I'm totally going!"

And there's that smile again. It's so adorable, I want to pinch his cheeks. Obviously, I don't do that, though.

He shifts his weight from foot to foot, looking nervous again. "Oh, great. Well, I was kind of wondering if—"

But his words are cut off when a group of boys walks by—the same obnoxious ones who called me Belchman earlier—and one of them bumps roughly into me. I stumble forward, crash right into the cute shaggy-haired boy, and for a brief, embarrassing moment, we're . . . like . . . *hugging*.

I hastily jump back as I watch his face turn a deep shade of red. He looks about as mortified as I feel.

"Sorry about that!" I rush to say.

"Don't worry about it. Those guys are jerks."

But I'm still so embarrassed. "Well," I say, glancing anxiously around. "We should probably get to class, right?"

"Oh . . . yeah. Right."

He suddenly looks devastated. Like I've just told him I ran over his dog. Did I miss something?

I clear my throat and point to my locker. "So, thanks so much for your help, um . . ." I mean to say his name at the end of the sentence, but I soon realize I don't actually know it. And it's not like I can *ask*. If this boy has a crush on Skylar, she obviously knows him. But now I'm just stuck hanging here in the middle of the sentence. I can't back out. I can't pretend I *wasn't* going to say his name. It's already obvious that I was!

I search my mental notes, trying to remember if Skylar mentioned a cute boy.

But I really don't think she did.

"You don't remember my name," he says, looking extremely hurt.

Crud.

"Of course I do!" I say quickly. "It's . . . it's . . ." But I have no idea where I'm going with this. It's not like I'm going to be able to guess his name randomly out of all the names in the English language. "What does it start with?"

His shoulders slump. "E."

"Edward!" I yell, a bit too loudly.

He seems to shrivel up even more. "No."

"Edgar?"

"Ethan," he says, apparently growing tired of the game.

"Ethan! Right. That was totally going to be my next guess."

"Sure, whatever," he mumbles. "See you later." Then he turns and walks down the hallway, looking dejected.

"Bye, Ethan!" I call out brightly.

He lifts his hand in a weak wave but doesn't turn around. I feel a stab of guilt in my chest. I think about running after him and apologizing again, but just then, the loudest, most obnoxious shrill sound rings out across the entire hallway, making me jump.

What on earth was that?

Was it some kind of fire alarm? Do we need to evacuate the building or something?

"Come on," a deep voice says behind me. "First-period bell has rung. Time to get to class." I turn around to see a large forbidding-looking man wearing a name tag that says "Principal Keene."

"That was the *bell*?" I ask in disbelief.

"Yes," he replies gruffly. "Which means you're late."

"You know," I begin wisely, "you should really think about changing that to something more soothing and melodic. That sound is very distressing."

The principal glares down at me like I'm a bug he wants to crush under his shoe. "You know what's even more distressing? Detention. Now get to class."

I quickly spin on my heels, racing down the hallway. I have no idea *where* Skylar's first-period class is, but I'm smart enough not to hang around *that* guy any longer.

HAPPY MEALS
....

Skylar

As I leave the writers' room, I feel like I'm walking on air. Floating in space. Dancing on clouds. The writers of *Ruby of the Lamp* are going to use my idea for resolving the Ruby/mother story line. *My* idea! They loved it! And they're going to incorporate it into the next season! We sat around for over an hour just hashing out the details and brainstorming possibilities. It was so much fun!

Barry looked really impressed, too. He sat down next to me and listened intently as I laid out my plan: First, Ruby and Miles find a lead to the woman who was with Ruby's mother the night she disappeared. Then they track her down in Greece and she gives them another lead to where the lamp holding Ruby's mom prisoner might be. Ruby and Miles keep following leads on the lamp until it brings them all the way back to Rogue Raymond's Junkyard! That's when they discover that the lamp from Ruby's dream has been right under their noses the entire time!

It's been buried under a pile of rubbish in the junk-yard!

"Bravo!" Barry said after I finished. "All great stories

end where they began. Back home. It's *The Wizard of Oz.* Ruby slippers." Then he guffawed and pointed at me. "*Ruby* slippers!"

I could tell from the looks of the writers in the room that they'd never seen Barry so jovial before.

"Well done, Ruby," Barry says as we walk back down the hallway. "It's nice to see you taking such an interest in the show." Then he actually puts his arm around my shoulders!

I beam up at him. "Thanks!"

I can't believe this is happening. I wish I could tell Leah. After all, she and I had the idea about the lamp being in Rogue Raymond's Junkyard two seasons ago. Of course, I can't. She'll never believe I'm actually Ruby Rivera.

Although I might have a better idea.

But it looks like it'll have to wait, because when we get back to the center of the soundstage, the set of Chaz's Diner is already lit up and buzzing with people. The five extras I met outside are seated at a few of the booths with plates of food in front of them. They all smile and wave at me and I quickly wave back.

"You ready to rock these last few scenes of the episode?" Barry asks me.

"Absolutely!" I say.

Barry puts his hand up for me to high-five, and I do. He lets out a chuckle and I can't help but laugh, too. It's like he's suddenly a whole different person.

Russ scurries over and leads me onto the set. He sits

me down on one side of a booth. Cami immediately rushes over and starts dusting my face with powder. "Um, am I hallucinating, or did Barry just give you a high five?" Cami asks in disbelief.

I nod, feeling smug. "That he did."

Cami looks impressed. "What did you do? Save the human species from going extinct?"

I giggle. "No. Just a little script rewriting. No biggie."

"Nicely done," Cami commends me, and then scurries off set.

As Gina comes over to fluff my hair, I'm feeling pretty darn proud of myself. I'm already acing this day and it's barely even started. I knew I was cut out for this life. I just knew it.

"Places, please!" Russ calls out over a loudspeaker.

Just then, Ryder Vance strolls onto the set and slides into the booth across from me. Suddenly, all my confidence seems to melt into a gooey puddle by my feet.

He flicks his chin in a casual little nod and says, "What's up, Rubes?"

I want to reach across the table and touch his beautiful perfect hair, but I command myself to get it together. Play it cool.

You are not Skylar anymore. You are Ruby Rivera.

I try to imitate his informal nod, but it feels more like my face is twitching. "What's up yourself?"

He flashes me a teasing grin. "Do you think you can kiss me today without fainting?"

No! I think with a silent shriek. But I force myself to shrug and say, "I'll give it a try."

A moment later, someone walks on set carrying two juicy giant cheeseburgers on plates and sets them down in front of us. My stomach growls in appreciation. I am *so* hungry and that looks *so* delicious! It's the most amazing burger I've ever seen. It looks like it belongs in a commercial. The bun is perfectly toasted and covered in sesame seeds. The lettuce is green and crisp, the tomato a flawless shade of red. The cheese curves effortlessly around the edge of the patty. It almost doesn't even look real.

I give the burger a small poke, confirming that it is, in fact, real and not a prop, and let out a sigh of happiness. Finally, some real food.

I quickly review the scene in my head. It's mostly Miles talking while I comically stuff my face with burger and say things like "Mmm-hmm," "Mmm?" and "Mmmm . . . this is so good."

I giggled when I read that part in the script. Ruby is always stuffing her face on the show. It's a running joke. Miles will be trying to have a serious conversation with her and her mouth will be full of French fries or s'mores or cupcake.

"Are you ready?" Russ asks.

I glance down at the giant cheeseburger in front of me. "More than ever!"

Russ shoots me a funny look but doesn't reply. He just backs away and yells, "Quiet on set!"

Miles leans forward, ready to say his first line to me. I pick up the burger, inhaling its deliciousness, and prepare myself to take a bite.

Life doesn't get much better than this, does it?

"And, action!"

GIVING UP THE KETCHUP

I arrive late to Skylar's Language Arts class. Mostly because I don't have the faintest clue where it is. When I finally burst through the door, I'm so relieved to have found it, I collapse into the only empty seat, failing to notice that pretty much everyone is staring at me, including the teacher, a short, frumpy man whose clothes are so wrinkled, it looks like he slept in them last night. He clears his throat and says, "Skylar, how nice of you to join us. I assume you're late because you were working so hard on your oral presentation that you lost track of time?"

The oral presentation! That's right!

I got so sidetracked with locker doors and cute boys and Irvine Barbie that I nearly forgot. I jump up from my seat. "Absolutely. I'm ready."

He gestures toward the front of the room and I stroll confidently down the aisle between desks, taking my place before the students. They all watch me with expectant gazes, probably searching for signs of nerves and jitters. But not me. I've performed in sold-out stadiums in

Japan. I've presented awards in front of an auditorium full of A-list celebrities. *This*—a room full of half-awake twelve-year-olds—this is nothing.

I flash a bright smile to the class and then to the teacher, whose arms are folded across his chest like he's just waiting for me to mess up.

Maybe Skylar messes up. Maybe Skylar gets up here and stammers and fidgets and hiccups. But I'm not Skylar. I'm Ruby Rivera. And I've got this in the bag.

I clear my throat, lower my voice to a deep register, and begin in a smooth farmer's accent, " 'I was only foolin', George. I don't want no ketchup. I wouldn't eat no ketchup if it was right here beside me.' " I return to my normal voice and continue, "That was a quote from Lennie, one of the two protagonists from *Of Mice and Men*. Because of Lennie's simpleminded condition, he's not able to take care of George, but that doesn't mean he can't be a good *friend* to George. And the way Lennie views friendship is through ketchup. Does that make him any less of a friend to George than George is to him? That's the question I'm going to explore in my presentation."

For the next five minutes, I speak passionately about the book, about the characters, and about the author, John Steinbeck. I even compare this novel to the rest of his body of work. The class is like putty in my hands. They lean forward, mouths agape, eyes wide, drinking in every word. And it fuels me. My passion for the book fuels me. Being in this building of learning fuels me.

This is not a script I've memorized. This is not a cheesy

line from an episode of *Ruby of the Lamp*. This is my heart speaking. I just talk and they listen.

"So, in conclusion," I say, "we do what we can for those we care about. We bring to the friendship whatever we are capable of bringing. We *help* each other. No matter what. No matter the price. No matter how much ketchup it might cost us. Thank you."

The classroom erupts in applause and I take a little bow. I turn to the teacher, but he's just standing there, his hand frozen against the side of his face. He's staring at me as though he can't believe what he just heard.

And that's when I know that I've done my job for the day.

Just like Lennie helps George and vice versa, I've helped Skylar. There's no way she's not passing this class.

I just hope she's doing the same for me.

NOT-SO-HAPPY MEALS

Skylar

So apparently, you don't actually *eat* when you're acting. You take bites, you chew, you talk with your mouth full so it looks real, and then after someone yells "Cut!" you spit the half-chewed food into a bucket by your feet, which is hidden from the camera.

At least, that's what Ruby does when she's acting.

I didn't even notice the bucket when I sat down because it was concealed under the bench. But now it's filled with disgusting lumps of half-chewed cheeseburger.

So gross.

Every time Barry calls "Action!" I'm supposed to glance down at the big juicy cheeseburger in front of me, sigh about how hungry I am, take a huge bite, chew, and spit it out before I can swallow it. Then someone arrives with another delicious, untouched cheeseburger and we do it all again.

It's such a tease!

By the time the scene is finished, I'm so hungry from *almost* swallowing I feel like my stomach is caving in on itself.

There's also a giant food table set up on the sound-stage, with chips and cookies and doughnuts and little sandwiches with the crusts cut off. But I'm not allowed to have any of *that,* either. Instead, between scenes, I have to watch as the crew gathers around the table and stuffs their faces while I munch on a bag of celery Eva gave me.

I continue to remind myself that this is fine. I'm fine. It's a small price to pay to be Ruby Rivera. And so far, I'm proving to be *really* good at it. After the diner scene, we moved on to a scene in Ruby's dorm room, where I'm supposed to break down and cry about how frustrated I am that I can't find a single lead about my mother.

And I nail it! I even get real tears to come! I don't know how I do it. I just say the lines, I think about how frustrated *I* am that Ruby's mother hasn't yet been found, and the tears start flowing. It's the most amazing experience. It's like I just be*come* Ruby. Not Ruby Rivera. But Ruby of the Lamp. The character. The person I've spent the past four years laughing and crying with. Once I found her inside me, the emotions just come easy.

When Barry yells "Cut!" I can tell he looks impressed. Everyone looks impressed. And a little surprised, too. Like they weren't expecting me to do it that well. As I wipe my eyes, I glance over to the bank of monitors and see Eva giving me a beaming, proud smile.

By the time we break for lunch at one o'clock, almost *everyone* on set has come up to me to tell me how well I'm doing. Not to brag or anything, but I'm pretty dang good at this. Who cares if I'm starving! I saved the show from embarrassing plot holes *and* I rocked one of the biggest emotional scenes of the season. I mean, it's almost like I'm better at being Ruby than, well . . . Ruby! Which I guess shouldn't surprise me after hearing her complain so much about her life. She has no idea how good she has it.

Lunch smells amazing. It's being catered by a local taqueria, and the snack table transforms into a scrumptious buffet filled with platters of cheesy enchiladas, fajita meat, steaming-hot churros, and even a make-your-own-nachos bar!

I run for the stack of plates and grab one, ready to cover every square inch of it with greasy Mexican food. But the moment I reach for the serving spoon on the enchiladas, Eva steps between me and the table with a stern look on her face. "What do you think you're doing?"

I look between her and the food. "Eating lunch?"

She sighs, grabs the empty plate from my hand, and hands me a Tupperware. "Here's your lunch."

"Oh," I say, slightly disappointed. "Right. Thanks."

I suppose it makes sense that I would get a special meal. I am the star of the show and everything. I open the Tupperware to find a single grilled chicken breast, a hard-boiled egg, and three apple slices.

My shoulders slump.

"WHAT IS THAT?" Eva screeches, causing me to jump. When I look up, she's glaring at my Tupperware as though I've opened it to reveal live worms.

I feel a bit of relief at her reaction. I knew there must be some mistake. It's clearly missing *something*.

"I told Stan at Craft Services no more fruit. Especially not after those measurements this morning." Eva grabs the apple slices right out of the Tupperware and tosses them in the nearest trash can.

The comment stings. And once again, I want to say something. Not for myself, but for Ruby. I don't know why Eva insists that Ruby is in any way less than beautiful. Her body looked terrific to me in the mirror this morning. But then I see the look on Eva's face as she stalks back from the trash can and I lose my nerve.

I carry my Tupperware outside the soundstage, where the entire cast and crew are seated at long tables, chowing down on their Mexican food.

I find an empty seat across from Ryder and slide in, my stomach still doing a little lurch just from the sight of him. The novelty of being this close to him still hasn't worn off. I don't think it ever will. I mean, he's *Ryder Vance,* for crying out loud! And I'm about to have lunch with him!

Ryder looks surprised to see me, one eyebrow arching. "Look who decided to eat out here with the rest of us mere mortals."

"What?" I ask, confused by the sarcasm in his tone.

"You never eat with us," he says. "You always eat in your trailer."

"She does?" I ask, and then quickly correct myself. "I mean, I do?"

Ryder scoffs. "Whatever."

Well, no wonder she complains about having no friends. She needs to get out of her trailer and talk to people!

"Hey, Ruby," Ryder says, and I look up just in time to watch as Ryder takes a giant, messy, gooey, cheesy bite of his hot sauce–drenched burrito. Red sauce dribbles down his chin as he chews slowly, murmuring "Mmmm" over and over, like he's doing a food commercial. "This is so good," he says with his mouth full, so it actually sounds more like "Thuh ih so gooh."

Is he teasing me?

Is he making fun of the fact that he gets to eat that and I have to eat *this*?

I glance down at my plate of chicken breast, cut off a small piece, and pop it in my mouth. *Ugh.* What is wrong with this chicken? It tastes like someone ran it through the deflavorizer. It needs some serious seasoning. Like some garlic, and cumin, maybe a little coriander. I grab for the saltshaker on the table and start dumping it onto the chicken by the boatload.

Ryder raises an eyebrow at me. "You sure you want to do that? Salt makes you look bloated, remember?"

Okay, now I *know* he's teasing me. Because no one would tell Ruby Rivera she looks bloated. This must be what Ryder and Ruby do. Tease each other. Ruby did say that Ryder felt like a brother to her.

I roll my eyes. "You're so hilarious."

He stares at me with an odd expression. "And you're

acting weird." He pulls his phone out of his pocket and starts scrolling the screen.

I cut off another piece of chicken and rub it around in the grains of salt on my plate. "What are you doing?" I ask Ryder, trying to sound conversational.

He doesn't look up from the screen. "Just checking to see how my *twelve million* followers are doing."

The way he pronounces "twelve million," he sounds like a game show host comparing scores at the end of a bonus round.

"Wow, twelve million," I say, honestly impressed. Ruby only has eleven million.

He flashes me a goading grin as he sucks hot sauce off one of his fingers with a *sluuuurp!* "That's right. Twelve million. How are your *eleven* million doing?"

I stare at him in disbelief. He's totally putting Ruby down. Just because he has an extra million followers? *Pshh.* She's the star of the show. He's just her sidekick. But his comment does remind me of the idea I had earlier.

I turn on Ruby's phone, turn the camera to video selfie mode, and press record. Holding the phone out in front of me, I smile, wave, and in my best Ruby voice say, "Hi, everyone! I want to give a shout-out to one of my biggest fans, Leah Perini, in Amherst, Massachusetts. Hi, Leah! I've seen some of the awesome comments you've left and I wanted to say thanks for watching! Bye!"

I press stop on the recording and post the video to Ruby's feed. That should make Leah's entire year. In fact,

I wouldn't be surprised if I could hear her scream all the way from Massachusetts.

As I continue to choke down bites of chicken, I scroll through the rest of Ruby's feed and notice a new picture has been posted this morning. I click on it, immediately recognizing it as the one Eva snapped after I had my hair and makeup done. She must have posted it shortly after.

Does Eva post all of Ruby's pictures?

I feel a small twinge of disappointment. I always thought it was Ruby writing those cute captions on the photos, but maybe it was her mother all this time. I suppose that makes sense, though. Ruby is really busy being Ruby. She has lines to memorize, scenes to shoot, albums to record, red carpets to walk. She probably doesn't have time to manage social media on top of all that.

I scroll through some of the comments people have left on the new picture.

SO ADORABLE!
Ruby, you're the cutest!
Can't wait for the new episode!
When are you and Ryder going to get together???

I glance up at Ryder, who's shoveling the last of his burrito into his mouth while his eyes are glued to his screen. He washes the bite down with soda and then lets out a large burp that rivals even the sound I made onstage the other day.

"Ten minutes," comes a voice, and I glance up to see

Russ standing next to our table holding his clipboard. "Scene twenty is up in ten minutes."

I feel my stomach start to do somersaults. Scene 20? That's the kiss scene! Oh my gosh, it's happening. Ryder and I are going to kiss. My first kiss is going to be with Ryder Vance! I better go brush my teeth. I better go check my reflection in the mirror. I better go—

"Well," Ryder interrupts my thoughts, flashing me a wink. "I better go load up on those garlicky onions from the fajita bar." Then he blows me a kiss, laughs, and walks away from the table.

I try to laugh, too, because I know he's joking.

He's totally joking.

Right?

THE QUEEN OF MIDDLE SCHOOL

I'd just like to say for the record that I, Ruby Rivera, was *made* for middle school. I am on *fire*.

Oral exam in Language Arts? Aced.

Pop quiz in American History? Please, I took three Civil War courses on the Learning Space this year alone. I could have *written* that quiz.

Gym class? C'mon. You call that a workout? That gym teacher has clearly never met Tyler, my personal trainer. I barely broke a sweat.

I even found Ethan's contact information in Skylar's phone and sent him a message, apologizing again for the whole name mix-up thing. I followed it with like seventeen emojis to try to get my point across.

He wrote back with a single smiley face. I took it as a good sign.

Middle school is everything I thought it would be and more. I raise my hand in every class with every question, and the teachers are überimpressed by everything I say.

Seriously, Skylar is going to come back to her life and not even recognize it, that's how much I'm helping her.

By the time I head to the cafeteria for lunch, I feel like I'm walking on clouds. No, strutting. I'm strutting on clouds.

I stand in the doorway of the noisy cafeteria and take in all the sights and sounds. Almost all the tables are filled with kids eating, talking, laughing. They're all radiating energy and excitement. They're all just being . . . *kids*. Something I never get to do. Lunch breaks on set are always awkward and weird. For starters, I can't eat what everyone else is eating. Plus, there's no one else there my age, unless you count Ryder, but I'd rather gouge my eyes out with a fork than sit next to *him* at lunch. Of course, there's always extras hanging around. The show needs random kid actors to fill in the hallway scenes and classrooms. But I learned a long time ago *never* to trust the extras. They *pretend* to be your friend, but they always want something from you: a regular part on the show, an introduction to a big-shot music producer, anything to give them a leg up in this town. Which is why I usually eat alone in my trailer. It's just easier.

But now I have a chance to actually hang out with kids my own age. Mingle. Talk. Make friends!

There's a line forming outside the kitchen, and I hurry over and join it. When I reach the front, I scan the various food options: some kind of suspicious-looking pasta and a rubbery grilled chicken sandwich. "What are you having?" the woman behind the counter asks. She's old and crusty looking, and her hair is tucked up under a hairnet. She looks about as happy to be working at a middle school cafeteria as I am to be working on a kids' TV show.

I stand on my tiptoes, attempting to glance behind her. "Don't you have like nachos back there or something?"

She barks out a laugh. "Nachos? No."

"Well, could you make me some?" I ask. "I mean, all you need is cheese and chips."

The lady rolls her eyes. "Pasta or chicken."

I frown. "Pasta, I guess."

With my plate of "pasta," I weave through the tables in the cafeteria, trying to find an empty seat. Somehow there doesn't appear to be one anywhere. My only options seem to be eating alone or asking someone to scoot over.

I start to walk toward the closest table when out of the corner of my eye, I spot a glimmer of shiny blond hair. My head whips to the side and there they are. The Ellas. Sitting at a table by themselves.

I switch direction and head straight toward them, placing my plate down on the table and beginning to slide onto the bench. But suddenly an arm juts out in front of me, stopping me.

"Um, no offense, but what do you think you're doing?" The voice (and arm) belongs to Daniella.

I glance down at my plate of pasta. "Having lunch."

She gives her head one firm shake. "Sorry, no room. You'll have to find another place to sit."

"But," I begin to argue, ready to point out that there are tons of seats open.

"We reserved this table," Daniella says, "And unless your name ends in -ella, you can't sit here."

I look to Isabella and Gabriella, but neither one will meet my eye. They're both staring down at their barely touched plates of pasta.

Okay, so befriending the Ellas is going to be *slightly* harder than I thought. But I am not discouraged. I *will* prove to Skylar that I can make it in middle school. That she has been blowing this whole thing out of proportion.

I glance down at my own pasta—watching the red sauce start to congeal with the sprinkles of off-color cheese—and suddenly another idea comes to me.

I bound back up, grab my plate, and in an extra-bubbly tone say, "No problem! I totally understand. This is your table. I get it. That makes perfect sense."

Daniella looks slightly surprised by my response, but she quickly hides it, flashing me a curt smile before turning back to her friends and resuming her conversation.

I bring my plate to the dishwashing area, my brilliant plan brewing in my mind. You don't need a name that ends in -ella to sit at that table. You just need a little creativity and ingenuity.

I put my tray on the conveyor belt. Then I pull Skylar's phone out of my backpack and download the Ding Dong Delivery app. The writers on the show use it when they have to stay late to finish writing an episode. They deliver food from local restaurants right to your door. Of course, I've never been able to try it before because they don't deliver rabbit food.

I quickly set up an account, putting in the school's address as the delivery location and Skylar's emergency credit card number in the payment field. I know Rebecca got mad at Skylar for using the card to buy her Xoom! Studios tour ticket, but that was different. This is a *real* emergency. I'm saving Skylar's social status at this school. Which means, I'm basically saving her *life*. And if that's not an emergency, I don't know what is.

"Congratulations!" the screen says. "You are now ready to place your first Ding Dong Delivery order!"

I search the app for Mexican restaurants, quickly finding one that serves nachos. I add three orders with all the toppings to my cart. Then I press order, and I'm done! It's so easy. It even shows me a little progress bar of how long it will take for my Ding Dong driver (Chester, four point seven stars) to get to the restaurant, pick up my food, and deliver it right here to the school.

That is too cool. You can order anything you want and they just *bring* it to you. Who cares what Ruby can do on that stupid show—*this* is the real magic.

While I wait, I wander into the school's library and check out a copy of *Life of Pi*. I quickly find where I left off and start to read, keeping my eyes on the app's progress bar. When my driver is "Nearing the destination," I dash out the front doors of the school to meet him.

"I've never delivered to a student before," he tells me.

I chuckle. "Well, if you were to taste what they're trying to pass off as food in there, you'd understand."

He rolls his eyes. "Middle school? Yeah, I remember that. Rough times."

Oh my gosh, I'm bonding with a stranger. And he's

not squinting at me, trying to figure out why I look so familiar and then, five seconds later, asking for my autograph because his little sister/niece/cousin/daughter is my biggest fan. We're just two regular people, chatting about food and middle school.

He says goodbye and I give him a five-star rating in the app.

I carry the bag with my three *giant* containers of nachos back into the cafeteria and head straight for the Ellas' table.

Time to put on an award-winning performance.

As I near the table, I put on my best "panicked" face. It's easy. It's the look I'm supposed to get every time I try to find a lead about my mother on the show and it doesn't work out.

"Oh my gosh!" I say, collapsing onto one of the benches. I place the brown paper bag on the table with a plop, knowing they can smell the delicious cheese and tangy salsa. "I ordered *way* too many nachos! Can you guys please help me finish these?"

I notice Gabriella's eyes light up at the word "nachos." And even Isabella looks like she's mildly interested, but Daniella adamantly shakes her head. "No. We don't want any nachos. And what did I tell you about—"

But I ignore her and swing my feet over the bench, making myself comfortable as I pull the first container of nachos out of the bag and pop open the lid. I grab a chip loaded with toppings and steer it into my mouth. The explosion of flavor and gooey cheese hits my tongue. I chew slowly, stopping only to moan a little, the same way Ryder does whenever he eats in front of me. "Mmm . . . these are *soooo* good."

I notice Gabriella hasn't taken her eyes off the nacho container since I opened it.

I pop another chip into my mouth. "Are you sure you guys don't want any?"

"Yes," Daniella says, but it's too late. Isabella is already lunging for the nachos. Gabriella quickly follows. And before long, both of them are crunching in delight right along with me.

"Good, right?" I ask, and they both nod ardently.

"So good," Isabella mumbles with her mouth full, causing both me and Gabriella to laugh.

Daniella glares at me.

"Oh, sorry!" I say, removing the second container of nachos and taking off the lid. "We've been hogging them. Here you go. All for you." I slide the container so it's sitting right in front of her. For a moment, she's silent, just glowering at the nachos. Gabriella, Isabella, and I all watch her in silence, waiting to see what she'll do.

She can either stand up in disgust and walk away, or she can dive in. Because really, those are the only two options. There's no way she can just sit there and stare at the nachos without eating them.

Daniella slowly reaches out and breaks off a tiny tip of one of the chips. She dips it daintily in some of the melted cheese and brings it to her mouth.

I try not to let the victory show on my face and quickly

move on to the next phase of my plan. "So I thought of another celebrity makeup tip, if you guys are interested."

Daniella doesn't answer. Instead, she grabs another chip—this one loaded with toppings—and pretends to look uninterested.

"What?" Isabella asks.

I lean forward like I'm about to tell them something top-secret. Isabella and Gabriella lean forward, too, but Daniella stays put. I cover the side of my mouth with my hand and whisper, "Egg yolk."

Isabella scrunches up her nose. "What?"

I nod. "You put it on your skin for like five minutes and then wash it off. It works wonders with breakouts."

"No way!" Gabriella says, and I notice Daniella glance uneasily between her two followers, who are both watching me with extreme interest.

"Yes way," I insist. "My makeup artist friend says all the celebrities do it. Especially the ones with really bad acne, like"—I glance over both shoulders, pretending to check for eavesdroppers—"Carey Divine."

Isabella's jaw drops. "What? Carey Divine has acne?"

"Yup. Her makeup artist spends hours covering it up before she goes on set. And her hair's not real. Extensions."

"How do you know this?" Daniella asks dubiously.

I flash the Ellas a conspiratorial smile. "Oh, the things I know would make your head spin."

GARLICKY PUNCH IN THE FACE

Skylar

He *wasn't* joking. The stench hits me the moment Ryder steps onto the set of the Jinn Academy hallway. He smells like he just rolled around in a giant vat of onions and garlic. His breath *reeks*.

"Whoa, Ryder," Cami says, waving her hand in front of her face like she's trying to clear the air of a bad fart. "What have you been eating?"

He smirks. "Just a little lunch."

"Do you need a breath mint?" She asks all nasally, like she's breathing through her mouth.

Ryder glances at me and grins. "Nope. I'm good."

"Places!" Russ calls out, and Ryder and I resume our positions from yesterday. I stand with my back to the lockers and Ryder leans in with one hand behind my head.

"*H-h-h-hiiii,*" he murmurs, blowing out as much breath as he can.

The odor hits me like a garlicky punch in the face. Oh gosh, it's awful. *Awful.* I immediately feel my gag reflex kick in.

The reaction must show because Ryder chuckles. "*What's* the matter?" he says, breathing heavily.

I cough and choke and turn my head away from him to avoid suffocating from the stench.

"Ruby!" Barry calls out from behind the monitors. "What's with that face? You're supposed to be in *love* with this person. Not repulsed by him."

I school my expression.

"Okay, people, let's do this!" Barry calls out. "Camera speeds! And, action!"

Ryder's expression instantly transforms. He's no longer that taunting, teasing boy he was at lunch. Now he's sweet, adorable, tender Miles, Ruby's best friend. Ruby's *crush*. And seeing that shift immediately reminds me what I'm supposed to be doing. I try to relax.

Pretend you're in love with him, I tell myself. *No, you* are *in love with him.*

I think about every time I've seen his face in a magazine. Every time I've paused an episode of *Ruby of the Lamp* on a close-up of those gorgeous eyes. And now he's here. Those eyes are right in front of me, finally staring back at me.

I just need to not breathe through my nose.

"I just wanted to say," Ryder says, his voice gentle and compassionate, "that we'll find her. I promise. I'm not giving up and neither should you."

And then it happens. He leans toward me. His eyes sink closed. His lips drift toward mine, as though they're floating all on their own, separate from his body. And suddenly the smell doesn't matter. Because I can't breathe anyway. All the oxygen in the room vanishes in a tiny explosion of light. The world slows down, time seems to disappear, until all that's left in the entire universe is this moment. And as his lips lightly brush mine, all I can think is *I am the luckiest person in the world*.

CINDERELLA ENDS WITH ELLA

"No offense, but we need to find you something to wear to the dance tomorrow night."

Daniella links her arm through mine and guides me into a store. We're at the South Coast Plaza mall in Costa Mesa. The Ellas invited me to come shopping with them after school and, after Rebecca told me it was okay, I, of course, said yes. It took a little while for the Ellas to warm up to me—especially Daniella—but I loaded them up with makeup tips and celebrity gossip at lunch and made them a list of all the places in LA where the members of Summer Crush hang out, so they seem to have granted me temporary access into their group.

Which is just another indication that I am totally rocking this middle school life. I've aced presentations and tests and gym class. I've even managed to make friends! All in one day!

And honestly, I'm not really sure why Skylar seemed so scared of the Ellas. Despite some of the not-so-nice things they say (always proceeded by "no offense"), they're really not that bad. After dealing with the sharks of Hollywood, these girls are nothing more than harmless little guppies.

"Yeah," Isabella says as she riffles through a rack of dresses. "No offense, but you could totally use some new clothes."

"Oh, I agree," I say wholeheartedly. Especially if I'm going to go to that school dance for Skylar tomorrow night. I've seen her closet. Nothing in there will suffice.

"What about this?" Gabriella holds up a hanger with a sparkly orange dress on it, and I fight not to cringe. She and Skylar would get along great. They have the exact same horrible taste in clothes.

Daniella, on the other hand, does nothing to conceal her dislike. "No offense, Gabriella, but that dress is hideous."

"Are you trying to get her to look like a sparkly pumpkin?" Isabella asks.

Daniella chuckles and I chuckle, too, because it seems like the right thing to do, but then I see the look of hurt flash on Gabriella's face and I quickly stop giggling.

"This one," Daniella says, plucking a blue dress from the rack with the same decisiveness I've seen on Sierra, the show's costume designer. She shoves the hanger into my hand and points toward the dressing room. "Try it on."

I do. And it's perfect. It's absolutely perfect. I stand in front of the dressing room mirror and do a spin. The pale blue fabric brings out Skylar's eyes, and the fitted waist makes her look much curvier than she really is. Daniella could totally be a costume designer when she grows up.

When I come out of the dressing room, the Ellas actually applaud.

"Yes," Daniella says. "One hundred percent *yes*."

"Perfection," says Isabella.

Gabriella nods. "One hundred percent perfection."

"I'm going to get it!" I proclaim, and then return to the dressing room to change back into my school clothes. After removing the dress, I check the price tag. It costs six hundred dollars. I guess that's a normal price for a dress. I honestly have no idea how much dresses cost. I didn't buy any of the clothes in my closet. They were all either gifted to me by designers or Mom bought them for me.

I realize I'm going to have to use Skylar's emergency credit card again, but I don't think Rebecca will mind. I'll just explain to her later that I really needed a dress for the dance.

After I've paid and the cashier has put the dress and the receipt in a bag, the Ellas and I continue to walk laps around the mall, and all the while, they gossip about people at school. They talk about what everyone wore this week, and who they saw flirting with who in the hallway. The whole time, I can't help thinking, *So this is what normal twelve-year-olds do on a Friday afternoon*. They don't shoot promo videos for the upcoming season finale of their hit show. They don't sit around their trailer discussing plans for a sold-out concert tour. They go to the mall. They talk about clothes and makeup and boys. They just *hang*.

We grab frozen yogurts and I load mine up with about fifteen toppings, everything from sprinkles to cookie crumbles to gummy bears. There's so much delicious stuff in my cup, I literally have to dig through it with my spoon to reach the vanilla-strawberry-swirl yogurt underneath.

We find a table near the merry-go-round in the Carousel Court and sit to eat. When we're all finished, Daniella takes out her phone and snaps a dozen photos of us. Some are selfies. Some are candids of me laughing. Some are posed—all of us smiling or looking fierce.

I let out a contented sigh as I glance around the Carousel Court, admiring it the way a tourist would admire an ancient cathedral in Europe. The high ceilings, the bright lights, the bustle of people just going about their everyday, *normal* lives.

I know I'm technically doing all this for Skylar—making friends and proving to her that middle school can be *fun*—but in this very moment, *I* feel happy. And for the first time in a long time, I feel like I'm part of something. Like I actually *belong* somewhere.

I tip my head back and stare up at the second floor of the mall. And that's when my blissful state comes crashing to a halt. I let out a terrified shriek as my gaze lands upon a *ginormous* picture of my face.

My *real* face.

Hanging from the rafters are three huge banners advertising the upcoming autograph session with Ruby Rivera. After everything that happened today, I forgot all about that. That's my deadline. That's when Skylar and I are supposed to meet up and change back. It's a cold, harsh reminder that my time here is limited.

My whole body deflates. Like a balloon someone is slowly letting the air out of. On Sunday, I'll be that girl again. I feel like Cinderella at the ball, staring at that clock, knowing that when it strikes midnight, it will all be over. The magic will be gone.

The Ellas all look up to see what I'm shrieking at and Daniella lets out a groan. "I can't *believe* people actually line up to see Ruby Rivera. She is so incredibly *lame*."

"Totally," Isabella chimes in. "She has no talent."

"No talent," Gabriella echoes, nodding way too enthusiastically.

I wait for one of them to quickly add "No offense," but it never comes. Because why would it? They don't know they're actually insulting me to my face. Not that I care. I mean, I pretty much agree with them. Ruby Rivera *is* lame.

"I'm not sure why you even like her," Daniella says, and it takes a moment for me to realize she's talking to me.

Oh, yeah, I remember. *Skylar is obsessed with Ruby Rivera.*

"Well," I begin, wondering how exactly I should proceed from here. "I mean, she's not *that* bad, right?"

Daniella scrunches up her face like she's just smelled bad fish. "She can't sing. She can't act. And she dresses like she's eight. Carey Divine is way more talented than she is."

"She is not!" I snap without thinking, and then quickly regret it. All three Ellas are staring at me like I just admitted I grow potatoes out of my ears. "I mean," I say, trying to keep my voice casual, "don't you think Carey Divine is a little fake?"

"Ruby Rivera is fake," Daniella says.

"Y-y-yeah," I stammer. "But maybe that's just because she's being controlled like a puppet. Maybe she's not allowed to do anything she wants to do or wear anything she wants to wear. Maybe if she actually got to *be* herself, you'd like her!"

The Ellas all exchange nervous glances and I realize I need to change the subject ASAP. "Hey," I say, standing up. "Let's go to Sephora and I'll show you some more makeup tricks."

For a long time, I'm the only one standing. The Ellas are still sitting there, studying me warily. Then, thankfully, Daniella rises from her seat and tosses her empty cup into a nearby trash can.

"Cool," she says nonchalantly. "I could use some new makeup. Let's go."

And just like that, the other two Ellas follow suit, as if the last two minutes never even happened.

Skylar

"That was the most romantic thing I've ever seen!" Stacia says as she lets out a dramatic sigh.

"So romantic!" Gwen echoes.

I'm in my trailer with the extras from today's shoot. I'm sitting on the couch in the living room, and each of them—Stacia, Gwen, Claire, Josie, and Jordan—are sitting facing me. Like I'm the queen of the court and they're all just hanging on my next word. I'm not going to lie. It's a pretty fantastic feeling.

"What did it feel like?" Claire asks.

"Amazing," I gush, and they all giggle. "I mean, when his lips touched mine, I felt like my feet weren't even on the ground."

Sighs of jealousy spread through the group. I don't tell them about the garlicky onion breath, because I don't want to spoil their illusion. Plus, I can barely even remember that now. All I remember is the butterflies. I realize I've never been kissed before, so I'm not exactly an authority on the subject, but I think I can safely say that Ryder is the best kisser in the world.

Unfortunately, we only did one take. That was apparently part of Eva's negotiation. As soon as Barry yelled "Cut!" and I came crashing back down to earth, I immediately prepared myself to do it again. But then Barry called out, "Perfect! Moving on!" And I felt myself wilt with disappointment.

"That is totally going to win for Most Romantic Moment at next year's Tween Choice Awards," vows Jordan.

"Speaking of which," Gwen says, bouncing up and down on the leather recliner chair. "Isn't this year's awards tomorrow? Are you excited?"

"What are you going to wear?" Stacia asks.

I still can't believe I'm going to get to go to an actual awards show. Dress up in a fancy gown, walk the red carpet, be interviewed by magazines!

"Carey Divine better not win Best Actress *again*," Claire says.

I let out an involuntary snort. I just can't help it. Especially after what Ruby told me in the prop room yesterday, about how they only *pretend* to be friends.

"What?" Josie asks, looking from me to the other girls with a curious eyebrow raised. "What was that about?"

I wave the question away. "Oh, nothing. Never mind."

"No, tell us," Stacia urges. "Please. Did you and Carey have a fight?"

I struggle not to roll my eyes. "No."

"Then why did you react like that?" Jordan asks.

"Yeah," Claire says. "Aren't you guys like best friends?"

I bite my lip, wondering whether I should tell them

what Ruby told me. I mean, why not? We're all friends now. And they seem like really nice girls. Plus, I just can't wait to see the looks on their faces when I drop this gold nugget of gossip.

"Well, actually," I begin, glancing around the room, like I'm checking for hidden cameras.

As if on cue, all five of them lean forward, their eyes wide with anticipation.

I lean forward, too, looking into each of their eyes before whispering, "Can you guys keep a secret?"

A MEMBER OF THE CLUB

"See!" I say, stepping back from Daniella and tilting my head to admire my work. "You can use a light shade of lip gloss to create a really cool eye shadow look!"

Daniella reaches for the stand-up mirror on the makeup counter at Sephora and stares at her reflection. "I love it!" she exclaims. "It's so shimmery!"

I smile. "Exactly."

"That is so cool," Isabella gushes.

"So cool," Gabriella echoes.

Isabella turns back to Daniella. "Ethan is going to be so sorry he snubbed you when he sees you looking like that."

I immediately perk up when I hear the name Ethan. Is Isabella talking about the *same* Ethan? The one who helped me with my locker this morning? The one who clearly has a crush on Skylar?

Daniella's expression sours. "He didn't *snub* me, Isabella. I turned *him* down."

Isabella's face goes white as a sheet as she quickly tries to backpedal. "Totally. That's what I meant. No offense!"

"Isabella," Daniella says with a sigh. "You can't say 'no offense' *after* you've offended someone. You have to say it *before*."

I want to step in and argue that this logic makes no sense whatsoever, but I'm smart enough to keep my mouth shut and stay out of it.

"Sorry," Isabella rushes to say.

"Ethan asked you to the dance?" I ask casually, pretending to be absorbed in an eye shadow palette display.

"Yes," she whispers, like it's a really big secret. "But I said no. The poor thing was devastated."

"And now he's going to fall all over himself when he sees you tomorrow night," Isabella adds.

Daniella examines her reflection in the oval-shaped mirror again. "Well, that's just mean, Isabella. The guy's heart is already broken."

Isabella seems to shrink in on herself, looking chastised. Meanwhile, my head is reeling with all this new information.

"So," I begin, still trying to piece everything together. "You *don't* like him?"

Daniella scrunches up her nose. "No way. Absolutely not."

I feel a wave of relief. If Daniella liked Ethan, that could definitely make things complicated. Now Skylar is totally free to dance with Ethan tomorrow night. And by Skylar, obviously I mean *me*! I can't wait to see the look on Ethan's face when he sees me in my new dress. It makes me giddy just thinking about it.

I'm so relieved not to be going to the stupid Tween Choice Awards. I hate walking that red carpet, answering the same lame questions from interviewers over and over.

"Who are you wearing tonight?"

"Can you tell us any secrets about the season finale?"

"When are you and Ryder Vance going to get together in real life?"

Just once, I would like to give the real answers to those stupid questions.

"I'm wearing whoever my mother told me to wear, because she treats me like a two-year-old and doesn't trust me to pick out my own clothes."

"No, I can't tell you anything about the episode because my mother and I signed a confidentiality agreement and if I do, the Xoom! Channel will sue us for about a million dollars."

"Ryder and I will get together in real life when the moon falls out of the sky and hits me on the head so hard that I forget what an obnoxious, self-centered, numb brain he is."

But no. I have to smile politely and give the cheesy pre-scripted answers my mother writes out for me.

Not this time, though. This time that's all Skylar. Instead, I'll just be a normal girl dancing with a normal boy, having the time of her life.

"OMG," Daniella says after she's handed over a credit card to the woman at the counter and purchased the lip gloss. "I can't wait for tomorrow night. You're totally coming with us, right?"

It takes me a moment to come out of my reverie and realize that Daniella is talking to me.

"Me?" I ask, surprised. "You want *me* to go to the dance with you guys? Like, in the same car?"

Daniella chuckles. "Skylar, you're soooo hilarious. Of course we want you to go with us. You're like one of us now!"

I look between Gabriella and Isabella, who are both nodding enthusiastically. "Absolutely," echoes Isabella.

I'm about to open my mouth to tell them *Yes! Of course I'll come with you!* when a flash of suspicion makes me pause.

I mean, I know I said it would be easy to make friends in middle school, but was that *too* easy?

Suddenly, my warning radar is going off, telling me not to trust them. That there might be something else going on here.

But then I quickly push the thought away, chastising myself for being so skeptical and jaded. This isn't the set of a hit TV show. These aren't cutthroat child actresses trying to get their big break. These are just normal girls trying to be nice, welcoming me into their group. I need to seriously chill out.

This is exactly what I wanted. For me . . . and for Skylar.

"Okay," I tell them with a confident nod. "Count me in."

As we stride out of the Sephora, shoulder to shoulder,

I feel lighter than I've felt in a long time. In one day, I've managed to completely transform Skylar's life.

"Wait a minute," I say, stopping and turning to each of my new friends. "Does this mean I have to change my name to Skyella?"

Then all three girls break into fits of laughter like this is the funniest thing they've ever heard.

MEAN TWEEN DRAMA MACHINE

Skylar

And that's a wrap! I've done it! I've finished filming the season finale of *Ruby of the Lamp*. It's "in the can," as they say in Hollywood. (I just learned that phrase today, by the way.)

After Barry called "Cut!" on the final take of the final scene, everyone exploded in applause. Cami, Gina, Sierra, Russ, Eva, the extras . . . even Barry joined in. I felt so overwhelmed by all the attention and praise, I didn't know what to do. So I started bowing, the way an actor would at the end of a play. That made everyone laugh and clap harder. So I kept bowing and curtsying theatrically, until finally Ryder murmured out of the corner of his mouth, "Okay, show-off. I think that's enough."

Then I stopped.

As Eva drives us home from the set, I can't help feeling elated and proud. Like I've accomplished something huge. I don't think I've ever felt this way before. I mean, sure, I've accomplished things in my life—acing school projects, learning to cook the perfect steak, finally beating Leah at Frisbee golf. But this feels special. Important.

Like I'm changing lives or something. And in a way, I am. When the fans of the show see that kiss, they'll be forever altered. I know *I* am!

Eva must sense my giddiness, because she pats my leg affectionately and says, "You did wonderful today, baby."

I grin back at her. "Thanks!"

"It's so nice to see you having so much fun in your job."

Eva's comment makes me kind of angry. Why doesn't Ruby have fun in her job? Why doesn't she appreciate what she has? She's so lucky to live this life. She completely takes it for granted.

"Mom," I say hesitantly. I'm not sure I should say what I'm about to say, but I feel like I have to leave some part of me behind. I can't leave this life on Sunday without telling Eva how I feel. She works so hard for Ruby. She puts so much effort into her career. She deserves to feel appreciated.

"Yeah?" Eva says, keeping her eyes on the road.

"I just wanted to say I'm sorry if I've been acting a little . . . I don't know . . . out of it lately."

Eva glances at me quickly, confusion in her eyes. "What do you mean?"

"I just mean, I *do* love my job. I do have fun. I'm sorry if I don't always show it or say it. But I'm so grateful for everything you've done for me."

When Eva looks at me again, I know I've said the right thing. There are tears shining in her eyes. "Oh, Ruby," she says, beaming. "You have no idea how happy it makes me to hear you say that. I know I can be hard on you sometimes, but it's only because I care about you and your career."

I place my hand atop hers on the gearshift. "I know."

Eva takes a deep breath and focuses back on the road. The energy in the car feels so different than it did yesterday. I feel like I've fixed something. Realigned something that's been out of sync for a long time. Ruby couldn't stop complaining about her mother in that prop room, but her mother isn't that bad. They just needed to *talk* to each other.

When we arrive home thirty minutes later, Eva collapses into one of the couches in the formal living room and sighs dramatically. "Wow. What a day! I am *exhausted*!" She reaches into her bag and pulls out what looks like another script from the show, except much thicker. The *Ruby of the Lamp* script I read this morning was only about thirty pages. This one looks to be at least a hundred.

"Ruby," Eva says, kicking off her shoes and tossing the script on the coffee table. "Will you put this in my office?"

I nod and curiously pick up the script. On the cover page, blocking the title, is a pink Post-it note that says:

Ruby would be perfect for this!
—L

L? Who's L? And what would Ruby be perfect for?
I lift up the Post-it note and read the title.

Mean Tween Drama Machine
By Darrel Davis

I glance back at Eva, who has her eyes closed and her legs stretched out on the couch. "What is this?"

She snorts. "What do you think? Another desperate producer trying to get you to star in their new movie."

Ruby has actually never been in a real movie before. Last year she did that TV movie with Carey Divine, *Lemonade Stand-Off,* but never like a movie-theater film. For a while there were rumors that they were going to do a *Ruby of the Lamp* movie, but they died out about a year ago.

"Have you read it?" I ask, eagerly flipping through the first few pages.

Eva's eyes stay closed as she responds with a sigh. "It's garbage. Just like the rest of them."

My eyes nearly bug out of my head. *The rest of them?*

I try to keep my voice conversational. "So . . . um . . . like . . . how many?"

Eva opens one eye to study me. "What does it matter how many? None of them are good enough. Remember, you only get one shot at a movie career at this age. We can't afford to blow it on some cheesy tween comedy. We're holding out for something epic. A big-budget franchise or some massive young adult novel adaptation. That's the stuff that really skyrockets your career."

I peer down at the script in my hand again and reread the title. *Mean Tween Drama Machine*. That definitely does sound cheesy.

I nod. "Right. I guess that makes sense."

"So will you put it in my office with the others?"

"Sure." I clutch the script to my chest and wander down the hall until I find the one room I didn't explore last night—because the door was shut and I could hear Eva talking on the phone inside. I open the door and am struck with the same startling reaction I had to the rest of this amazing house.

Eva's office is gorgeous. With dark wood furniture, floor-to-ceiling windows, and built-in bookshelves that cover an entire wall. The shelves are filled with scripts from every single episode of *Ruby of the Lamp,* all the way back to season 1, and what looks like a collection of trophies. I approach the shelves to get a closer look, and that's when I realize . . .

Oh my gosh!

These aren't trophies. They're *awards*. Every single award Ruby has ever won! There are Tween Choice Awards and Billboard Music Awards and platinum records in a frame. There's even the Emmy *Ruby of the Lamp* won last year for Outstanding Children's Program.

I knew Ruby had won a ton of awards, but seeing them all here in front of me is something else entirely.

I wander around the rest of the office until I locate a giant stack of scripts in the corner that literally comes up to my waist. Wow! There have to be at least a hundred scripts here! Are these really *all* movies that Ruby has been asked to star in? And she's turned down every single one of them?

I flip through a few on top. Some of them definitely have cheesy titles, like *Woof!* and *Zap To It!* and *My Alien BFF*, but some have really interesting titles, like *Winter's Dawn* and *Answers to What If* and *Between Lost and Found*.

And suddenly, I'm struck with an amazing idea.

Checking that Eva is not lurking in the doorway, I grab a few of the scripts from the pile and scurry up the stairs, determined to continue my quest to improve the life of Ruby Rivera.

DADTIME

· ·

Daniella's mom drops me off at the UC–Irvine faculty housing complex. I find the key to the apartment in Skylar's backpack and let myself in. Rebecca must still be at work, because the place is empty.

Excited to finally be alone with all these books, I drop Skylar's backpack on the floor, walk over to the bookshelves, and slowly run my fingers across the cracked spines. I love how they all feel so worn and read. Like someone has devoured the pages so many times, the stories are now a part of them.

I'm just searching for a title to read when Skylar's phone rings, startling me. For a moment, I'm terrified that it's Skylar calling to tell me she wants her life back now. She can't wait until Sunday. She's having a rotten time, Barry barked at her, Ryder's a jerk, my mom is intolerable, and she hates my life with a passion. Of course she does. Because my life stinks.

What if I just don't answer the phone? What if I hide out in her apartment and refuse to give her life back to her? What's she going to do? Call the police? Tell them her body has been hijacked by a TV star? They'll think she's crazy. They'll never believe her.

But when I look at the phone, I see that it's a video call from "Dad" and my stomach swoops a little.

Should I answer it? Is it my place to answer a call from Skylar's father?

I bite my lip, feeling torn. I've never seen that name on my caller ID before. My own dad left before he even knew my name.

I press answer.

A man's face suddenly fills the screen, and even without the caller ID I can immediately tell that it's Skylar's father. He's got the same pale skin as her, the same soft blue eyes, the same straw-colored hair. Even the same wide nose.

"Hi, kiddo," he says. "How are you? How was school? Gosh, it's good to see you. I've missed you!"

For a long moment, I'm speechless. I can't even breathe. His voice. It's so gentle. So kind. So . . . *loving*. And the way he looks at me through the phone, it's . . .

Well, it's like no one has ever looked at me before.

"Sky," he prompts after a few seconds of awkward silence. "Are you okay? Did the video freeze?"

I blink and pull myself back into reality. "No. Sorry. I'm here."

He smiles the most amazing, kindhearted smile. "How was your day?"

How was your day?

Such a casual, simple question. Like he asks it every

single day. Like it's totally normal for a dad to call up his daughter and ask her about her day. I don't know long I've dreamed of having my father ask me that very same question. Wherever he is. *Who*ever he is.

I feel a pinch in my chest. "Good," I manage to say, but it comes out more like a croak. "I mean . . . great!"

His smile broadens. As if that were even possible. "Good to hear! So, are you finally making some friends?"

I think about the afternoon I just had with the Ellas. "Yes. A few."

"And how was your Language Arts presentation? I know you told me you were worried about it."

"It went great! I totally aced it. The teacher was really impressed."

The man beams with pride. "Terrific! You should tell your mom that. She's been worried about you in that class."

I nod. "I will."

"Look, I'm sorry I can't talk very long today. I've got to run back to campus. I just wanted to say hi."

"Oh," I say awkwardly. "Right. Hi."

Skylar's dad laughs. Then he glances at something I can't see. "Oh, crud. I gotta go. I'll try you tomorrow. Have a good weekend!"

And then, just like that, he's gone. His face vanished, replaced by a cold, dark screen. I instinctively reach toward it, as though I could actually reach through the phone and bring him back. As though I actually had magic genie summoning powers.

As though he were actually *my* dad.

Which, of course, he's not.

I don't get to feel this strange stirring in my stomach at the memory of his smile. I don't get to miss him already. I don't even *know* him. He thinks I'm someone else. Someone with a nice, simple, normal life.

Someone with a father.

I stare at the darkened screen for a long time. I don't often let myself think about my own dad. What's there to think about? I've never seen a single picture of him. Mom says he left the moment she found out she was pregnant. That's what kind of a father *he* was. Not the kind who video chats with his daughter just to say hi and ask about her day.

When I was a kid, I used to think about him all the time. I used to wonder what he looked like. Did he have my eyes, my nose, my freakishly long fingers? I used to fantasize about him coming back. Walking through the door of our small two-bedroom house in Dallas, with his arms full of gifts and his mouth full of apologies. In my mind, he always had a valid excuse. Something to explain away the years of neglect and invisibility.

"I was on the first manned mission to Mars!"

"I was kidnapped by pirates and held prisoner!"

"I got amnesia and couldn't remember where we lived!"

But then I got older. We moved to LA. I got the job on *Ruby of the Lamp*. My face was broadcast all over the world. And he still didn't show up. That's when I started to realize that he never would.

That's when I stopped letting myself think about him.

Because it was bad enough to play a girl on a fictional TV show whose father died and whose mother has been trapped inside a genie lamp for the past decade. I didn't need to come home every day to a similar reality.

But today, something stirs in me. A longing I haven't felt in a long time.

I search Skylar's phone until I find a picture of her father. Then I run into the bathroom and stare at Skylar's reflection in the mirror. *My* reflection for at least one more day. I hold the phone up to the mirror, lining up the screen so that our faces are side by side.

A father.

And his daughter.

Then, for the first time in many years, I allow myself to dream. To wish. To hope. To wonder.

KABOOM!

....

Skylar

The alarm on Ruby's phone goes off at five a.m. on Saturday and at first I think it's a mistake. That is, until Eva shows up a minute later, dressed in a pair of neon-yellow workout pants and a matching sports bra.

"C'mon. Ruby. Time to get up. Tyler is already downstairs in the gym."

It's still dark outside the window but she flips on the overhead lamps, shocking me awake. I blink wearily, still trying to make sense of what's happening.

I roll over and try to go back to sleep, but a second later the covers are literally ripped off me. "Don't start with this, Ruby. We don't have time. We already have to cut Kaboom! short today because of your eight a.m. call time at the photo shoot."

Kaboom? Photo shoot? What is she talking about?

I sit up and rub my eyes, certain that when I'm finished, she'll have disappeared back into the depths of my mind, where I'm certain this bad dream is taking place.

It works.

When I pull my fists away from my eyes, she's gone.

I sigh in relief, collapse back against the pillow, and pull the covers back up. But then, a second later, she emerges from Ruby's mall closet with an armful of clothes and tosses them on the bed. "RUBY!" she screams, causing me to jolt back up to sitting.

"What?" I ask, exasperated.

She looks at me like I'm supposed to know exactly why she's yelling at me. "GET. UP. You're not missing Kaboom! again today. I didn't wake you up for it yesterday because of the whole fainting thing, but you're fine now."

Eva stalks over to the speakers on Ruby's desk and presses a few buttons. A second later, music blares into the room, causing my heart to skip about seven beats.

> *"Get up! Stand up! Rise up! We're*
> *living out louuuud!*
> *Wake up! Face up! Way up! You can't*
> *keep us doooown!"*

It takes me a moment to recognize the song. It's "Living Out Loud," from Ruby's second album. Normally, it's my favorite, but today, I just want to hurl the pillow at the speakers and yell "SHUT UP!"

"Make it stop!" I scream, covering my ears.

But Eva just stands there, arms crossed. "Come over here and stop it yourself," she replies, but she has to yell to be heard over the music.

Is this how Eva gets Ruby out of bed in the morning? By blasting her own music at her?

"Everybody gather round! This is the
  sound
That your dreams will all come true to.
Everybody feel the beat! Get off your
  seat!
We're about to break all the ru-ules."

I blow out a breath and push the covers off. "Okay, okay. I'm getting up."

The music is still blaring. It's so loud, it's physically hurting my ears. I race over to the desk to shut off the song but trip along the way, nearly landing on my face. Thankfully, I manage to catch myself on the desk chair. I look back to see what I've tripped over and my gaze lands on the stack of scripts on the floor. Although, now they're more of a scattered pile than a neat stack.

Oh, right. That's why I'm so tired.

I stayed up almost all night, reading, trying to find a movie that Ruby could possibly star in. Some of the scripts were awful—just like Eva said—but some were actually pretty good. There was one in particular I liked about a twelve-year-old girl hacker who stumbles upon a giant corporate conspiracy.

I think I'm getting the hang of this script-reading thing. It's so much better than reading a book. You can actually finish a whole story in less than an hour, as opposed to a book, which takes like weeks. Well, it takes weeks for me. My mom finishes a book in a day.

I finally reach the desk and shut off the song. The silence is blissful.

"What's all this?" Eva asks, glancing down at the kicked-over pile of screenplays.

I bite my lip. "Nothing. I just needed some help falling asleep."

She gives me a quizzical look before evidently deciding to let it go. "Okay. Get dressed. I'll meet you downstairs in five minutes."

I still have no idea what's going on. I glance down at the pile of clothes she tossed on the bed earlier, noticing a pair of shorts and a sports bra in the mix. Wait a minute—this is all exercise gear.

I peer at the time on the phone to make sure I'm not just imagining this.

Nope. It really is five-thirty in the morning.

And that's when the realization hits me like a ton of bricks.

She wants me to *work out*?

BRUNCH BUFFET FOR ONE

Do you hear that?

Listen. Listen closely.

It's the sound of nothingness.

Nothing to do and nowhere to be. No alarms, no crack-of-dawn Kaboom! workouts, no mothers nagging me to get up, do my hair, wear something "cute" and "respectable." No photo shoots. No recording sessions. No interviews.

Nothing.

When I open my eyes and check the phone, it's eleven in the morning. I can't remember a time I slept this late. It feels amazing. My body feels rested. My mind is empty. For once in my life, my morning is not a chaotic circus of clothes and shoes and diets and exercise and scheduling and voice lessons.

I lie there for a good twenty minutes and *no one* comes in to bug me. When I finally do get up, I don't even bother to change my clothes or brush my teeth or even look in the mirror. I just wander out into the living room in my pajamas, morning breath and all. The apartment is empty. I find a note on the counter from Rebecca. It says she's gone to campus for a while and she'll be home around two o'clock. Which means I have the place to myself for three whole hours.

I can't even tell you how amazing that feels.

A whole house to myself? With nothing to do and no one to boss me around?

This is the best Saturday ever!

I get a bowl and pour myself more of that delicious sugary cereal, but just as I'm dumping in way too much milk, I get a better idea. I open the Ding Dong Delivery app and find a place that delivers breakfast—which is technically *brunch* now—and order practically everything on the menu. Pancakes, an omelet, bacon (extra crispy), toast, chocolate chip waffles, and an extra-large chocolate milk. Excited, I shut off the phone and am about to pour the cereal and milk down the drain when I think, *Why waste it?*

There's no reason I can't have cereal, too!

So I stand in the kitchen and happily shovel spoonfuls of crunchy deliciousness into my mouth as I watch the little Ding Dong Delivery avatar move down the progress bar from "Heading to the restaurant" to "Picking up your delivery" and finally to "On the way!"

When my food arrives, I transfer every dish to its own plate, throwing the containers down the trash chute in the hallway. Then I spread the food out on the coffee table like a giant buffet. I turn on the TV and navigate to the History channel. There's a special on about the French Revolution.

I take a deep breath, inhaling the scents of pancakes

and crisp bacon, before digging in with all my might. I eat and eat until I can't eat any more. There's still tons of food left, but I'm stuffed.

Then I lie back on the couch, resting my hands on my full belly, and watch TV until I slip into a beautiful food coma and fall asleep.

Two hours later, I'm awoken by a hand shaking me. "Skylar?"

"Mmm?" I murmur dreamily. Still in total bliss over my perfect Saturday morning.

"Where did all this food come from?"

My eyes flash open and I see Rebecca standing there, eyeing my half-eaten plates of food. "Um . . . um . . . ," I stammer, before remembering Rebecca saying something about Skylar liking to cook. "I made it?"

"Well, I assumed *that*," Rebecca says, thankfully buying it, "but why so *much* food. It looks like you cooked enough to feed a whole village."

"Oh," I say, biting my lip. "That."

I have no idea what to tell her. I can't very well say that I've been on a carb-free, sugar-free, taste-free diet for the past four years and now I'm making up for lost time. So I just say the first thing that pops into my mind. "I thought you'd be hungry when you got home."

It's definitely the right thing to say. Rebecca's face brightens almost instantly. "That's so nice of you, sweetie! And you're right. I'm famished." She sits down next to me on the couch, grabs the fork, and starts eating with the same enthusiasm I did.

I chuckle. "Rough morning?"

She nods, covering her mouth as she speaks and chews at the same time. "My in-box was flooded with emails from students." She swallows and wipes her mouth. "All complaining about their paper grades. I'm sorry, though, if you fail to properly analyze the book, I can't give you a good grade. I don't think these kids are used to working hard. They all took Literature Through the Ages freshman year, which is a joke of a class taught by a professor who sleeps through all his lectures and gives As for correctly spelling the author's name." She scoops more hash browns onto her fork but then sets the fork down. "I'm sorry, sweetie. I'm probably boring you. I'm sure you don't want to hear about all this university drama."

I sit up straighter. I hadn't even noticed I'd been leaning on my knees, hanging on every word she said. "What? No. Of course I want to hear about it."

And it's the truth. This woman lives and breathes books. I can't think of anything more interesting than that.

She gives me a dubious look and laughs. "Since when?"

"Since . . ." I hesitate, not wanting to make a wrong step, but I really want her to keep talking. "Since now."

She shakes her head and continues eating. "Well, anyway. I didn't give in to any of them. I told them all they could rewrite the paper if they wanted and try for a better grade. I mean, I've read better analyses of *1984* from high schoolers."

"*1984*?" I say, perking up. "That book blew my mind. Like . . ." I mimic an explosion near my head. "*Kaboo—*"

But I never get to finish my sound effect because Rebecca is staring at me like she's never met me before. I drop my hands to my lap and close my mouth.

"Are you mocking me?" she asks, hurt suddenly filling her eyes.

"No!" I rush to say. "Not at all. I really did like . . ." And suddenly, something clicks in my mind. Something that's been bugging me ever since I magically poofed into this body.

Mr. Katz's reaction in Language Arts class. Rebecca's strange expression yesterday morning when I tried to talk to her about *Frankenstein* and her even stranger expression now. The giant bookshelf in the living room and the complete lack of books in Skylar's room.

It hits me all at once.

Skylar hates to read.

Rebecca Welshman is a renowned professor of literature and her daughter doesn't read. It's the saddest thing I've ever heard. I can't even imagine how frustrating it must be for Rebecca to have a daughter who doesn't share her passion.

Then again, I don't share my mother's passion, either.

But that's totally different! My mom is passionate about awards shows and best dressed lists and how many times my picture appears in the latest issue of *Star Beat*. Rebecca Welshman is passionate about something that matters. Books! Reading! Great works of literature! And Skylar has no clue how cool that is.

I look back at Rebecca, who's finished off the hash

browns and has moved on to the pancakes. I can still see the lingering hurt in her eyes. The result of thinking her daughter doesn't care about anything that's important to her.

And I make a decision.

"Mom," I say.

She looks over at me as she takes a bite of syrupy, buttery pancake. "Yah?" she says with her mouth full.

"What are you doing the rest of the day?"

"I have to stop by the university library to check out a few books for class next week, but other than that, not much. Why?"

I shake out my stiff leg and wrinkled pajama bottoms. "I thought we could spend the day together."

Rebecca smiles. "That would be great. What do you want to do?"

"I want to see where you work."

She stops chewing and stares at me, completely dumbfounded. "What?"

"Show me everything. The university. The library. Your office. Wherever you spend your time. I want a full tour of your life."

She looks like she's about to argue or question my motives or both. So before she can do any of that, I stand up, step around her, grab one more piece of toast, and head down the hallway to get dressed.

DEATH BY CARDIO

....

Skylar

I have never worked so hard in my entire life. That was worse than ten gym classes combined! By the end of the forty-five-minute Kaboom! workout, I am completely drenched in sweat, panting like a dog, and I feel like I might collapse.

Oh, wait.

I *am* collapsing.

Here I go. Down. Down. Down. Now I'm on the floor. I might think the Riveras' state-of-the-art gym was impressive if I weren't on my back right now.

What on earth was that?

That wasn't a workout. That was an execution method. And Tyler, Ruby and Eva's personal trainer, is the executioner. I can't believe Eva actually *pays* him for this. He should be put in jail for the stuff he just made us do. Fifty push-ups, followed by twenty jump knee tucks, followed by fifty burpees? I didn't even know what a burpee was before this morning. But now I know all too well. It's probably a form of torture in some countries.

You would think, given that I'm in Ruby's body and

Ruby seems to do this every day, that I would have been able to handle it. But apparently, fitness is about a lot more than just muscle. Because I certainly *didn't* handle it.

I think I'm just going to lie here for the rest of the day. Not by choice, but by necessity. I don't think my legs work anymore. And I'm fairly certain if I attempt to stand up, I'll probably barf.

But it becomes apparent that spending my Saturday on this gym floor is not going to be an option when Eva says, "C'mon Ruby. Stop being dramatic. We need to be at the photo shoot in an hour. Get up."

I can barely breathe and she wants me to be *photographed* right now? Is she crazy? If I don't get a giant doughnut for breakfast after this, I'm going to stage a formal protest.

THE SUPERPOWER OF MOMS

"And what's this one about?" I ask, plucking a copy of *Pride and Prejudice,* by Jane Austen, from Rebecca's office shelf.

Of course, I know what it's about. It's one of my favorites. But Skylar hasn't read it, so I have to pretend. Plus, I just like listening to Rebecca describe the books. She has a way of talking about the stories that makes me feel alive inside. And it obviously makes her feel alive inside, too, judging by the way her eyes sparkle as she speaks. And she doesn't just describe what happens, like she's reading straight off the back of the book. She dives into the complexities of the plot, the internal conflicts of each character, the way it fits into the time period during which it was written. I swear I could listen to her describe books all day. And I pretty much have been. Ever since we got to her office, I've just been walking around her bookshelves, picking titles at random, and asking her about them.

She tilts her head and studies me from her chair behind the desk. I can tell she's been enjoying our afternoon together, but that air of suspicion hasn't vanished from her face since we left the apartment. "Skylar, what are you doing?"

I turn the book around and run my fingertips over the illustration of Elizabeth Bennet on the cover. She was a girl who never let anyone tell her what to do. Not society, not Lady Catherine de Bourgh, and certainly not her mother.

I could learn a few things from Lizzie Bennet. I don't have half the guts she has.

"I just want to know more about what you do all day."

"I get that," Rebecca says, leaning forward in her desk chair. "I'm just wondering *why* all of a sudden you've taken such an interest in my job. You never have before."

I'm about to apologize on behalf of Skylar, when Rebecca says, "Is this about Dad?"

I blink in surprise. "Dad?"

It's the first time Rebecca has brought him up. And apart from our brief conversation on FaceTime yesterday, I don't know much about him. I remember Skylar telling me that her parents are getting a divorce. She seemed upset about it in the prop room. But it's really not my place to get involved.

"No," I tell her. "Why would this be about him?"

Rebecca shrugs. "I don't know. I thought maybe with Dad being so far away, you might be feeling a bit lonely and wanting to spend some extra time with me. And don't get me wrong. I love it. I love you pretending to be interested in my work and all these books, but you don't have to do that. You don't have to pretend just to hang out with me. We can hang out and *not* talk about books."

I shake my head adamantly. "No. I really do *want* to know." And then, for good measure, I add, "And yes, I do miss Dad. A lot, but . . ."

My voice breaks and I can't even finish the sentence. Because it's in that moment I realize the statement is true. Truer than I ever knew.

I miss my dad.

Even though I don't even know him.

I've never admitted it to anyone, but every time I stand in front of a camera, a thought flickers through my mind for just a moment. The thought that maybe he'll see this. That maybe somewhere out there, wherever he is, whatever he's doing, he'll see his daughter on a screen and wonder how I am.

I know it's stupid. I know he's not doing that. I know he left more than twelve years ago, and if there was ever a chance he might come back or even reach out, it would have happened by now. And yet, I still find myself thinking about it every time someone yells "Action!" Maybe it's the one thing that's gotten me through the past four years.

I haven't even realized I started crying until Rebecca is beside me, holding out a tissue. I sniffle and take it, wiping my eyes and feeling ridiculous. "Sorry," I say, trying to laugh.

Rebecca puts her arms around me and pulls me into a hug. "I miss him, too, sweetie."

I know she's talking about someone else. Someone I don't miss and don't love and barely even know. And yet it still feels good to hear her say that. To feel her wrap her arms tightly around me. To feel her run her fingers down my hair.

It's not even my body she's squeezing. It's not even my hair she's touching. It's not even my mom.

And yet, she still makes me feel like everything will be okay.

Like the world is safe.

I guess that's just what moms do. No matter who they belong to.

DOUGHNUT DISAPPOINTMENT

Skylar

I don't get a giant doughnut. I get another flaxseed protein smoothie with exactly one quarter of a banana and two—count them, *two*—strawberries. It tastes like cement. Not that I know what cement tastes like, but I imagine it tastes a lot like this.

Afterward, we get into the car and Eva drives us to a huge rusty warehouse in the middle of downtown Los Angeles. The outside looks like the kind of place kidnappers take their victims. But the inside is completely different. The giant, open space has been transformed into a magnificent photography studio. There's a huge white backdrop that's been set up in the middle with about a zillion lights pointed at it. On the far wall is a table full of delicious-looking food. A woman in a chef's hat is standing in front of an omelet station.

Mmm. Omelets . . .

But before I can even get a chance to *smell* the food, I'm whisked into a curtained-off section of the warehouse, where another woman introduces herself to us as Michaela, my stylist.

Eva shakes her hand and immediately starts talking in her usual bossy voice. "For the new album, we want something a tad more mature than the last album but that still says 'fragile little girl' . . . "

Eva keeps talking, but I don't hear a word. I'm too busy dissecting her first sentence.

New album?

Ruby Rivera has a new album coming out? Why don't I know about this? Have they been keeping it a secret? Is it already finished? Will I get to hear it?

I try to listen in on Eva and Michaela's conversation in hopes of picking up some more information, but they're not talking about the album at all. They're discussing which clothes I should wear for the cover. Then, for the next forty-five minutes, I feel like a Barbie doll as they dress me in a million different combinations and argue over *every* little thing: the length of the dresses, the cut of the sleeves, the dip of the collars, the color of the head-bands, boots vs. flats, necklace vs. choker, belt vs. no belt. Everything Michaela suggests, Eva vetoes. I'm not sure why there even *is* a stylist when Eva ends up making all the decisions.

Finally, after what feels like forever, five complete out-fits are selected and I'm dressed in the first one. It's a cute blue-and-white sundress with a yellow belt. Even though I agree with Michaela that it's a little on the "safe" side, I don't dare tell Eva.

Next, my hair and makeup are done. That takes a full two hours. And then *finally,* I'm ready to actually take the photos. This is something I'm quickly learning about celebrity life. Nearly half of the time is spent *preparing* to be a celebrity, and the other half is spent *being* the celebrity.

The photographer's name is Jules, and she is super funky. She's dressed in baggy black pants, a cropped shirt, and a trucker hat that she keeps tilted to one side.

"So, Ruby!" she says, talking rapidly and clapping her hands. "We're going to have fun today. Yeah? Fun? We're going to have it?"

I nod. "Yes!"

"Good. Good. Good. Okay, so first things first. Music?"

"Um . . . yes? I like music."

She laughs like I've made a big joke. "LOL. Winky emoji. Good one. What *kind* of music do you want to listen to?"

Oh! Duh!

Well, obviously I want to listen to Ruby Rivera! I mean, if anything is going to help me channel her for this photo shoot, that would be it.

"Do you, um, by chance, happen to have the *new* album?" I ask hesitantly.

Jules looks at me like I'm speaking another language. "Whose new album?"

I glance uneasily between Jules and Eva. "Um . . . mine?"

Eva gives me a confused look. "Why?"

I fidget with the hem of my dress. "I just thought listening to it would help me get into the right mood for the cover photos."

Jules blinks like she's waking up from a dream. "Oh! Right! Yes. Good idea. Clap. Clap. Clap. High five."

I reach up to give her a high five before realizing she's only *saying* high five. She's not actually offering one. She turns and yells at an assistant to get the music ready.

"Are you sure that's what you want to listen to?" Eva asks.

Why is everyone so shocked that I want to listen to my own music? What does Ruby usually listen to during photo shoots?

You know what? It doesn't even matter what Ruby listens to. She's not here. *I'm* here. And I choose to listen to my favorite artist. "Yes, I'm sure," I say with authority.

Eva shrugs. "Okay, sweetie. I just ask because last time you were in the studio you said you never wanted to hear any of those songs again for the rest of your life."

I snort. That sounds just like Ruby. She's so ungrateful for what she has.

I flash Eva a confident smile. "Well, I changed my mind."

She beams back at me. "Great! I personally *love* the new album, and I think your fans are going to—"

But I don't hear the rest of what she says, because just then, the most amazing song in the history of music comes on over the warehouse speakers.

SURPRISE DINNER DATE

We spend the rest of the afternoon walking around UC–Irvine. It's a beautiful campus, with modern brick-and-glass buildings, tree-lined sidewalks, and students milling around, talking about everything from politics to literature to architecture.

The libraries are my favorite part of the tour. They actually have more than one! They have a whole library devoted entirely to science, another one devoted to law, and another to film. And, of course, the regular library, which houses all the great works of literature. Rebecca spends extra time in there, walking me through the fiction section, telling me stories about hiding in the stacks of her elementary school library during PE. That was before anyone figured out how brilliant she was and skipped her ahead two grades.

Two grades! Skylar's mom is basically a genius!

As we walk through campus and Rebecca points out each building and tells me what people study inside, I can't help but picture myself at one of these places someday. If I were a normal kid, at a normal school, I could be here in six years. This could be my home. I could be one of those students.

And who knows? Maybe I will be. Maybe Skylar and I will never figure out how to reverse the magic. Maybe I'll get to live this life forever and go to middle school, and high school, and college. Maybe I'll actually get to decide what happens in my life.

Or maybe on Monday morning, I'll wake up and find myself back in that mansion that I paid for. Maybe I'll poof back into Ruby Rivera and be stuck doing what everyone tells me to do for the rest of my life.

When we're finally tired and starving again, Rebecca takes me to one of the university cafeterias. It reminds me a little of the commissary on the Xoom! lot, with various stations offering everything from burgers to salads to stir-fry. Not that I've ever been able to *eat* in the Xoom! commissary, but we once shot a scene in there after they closed. It was the episode where Ruby and Miles sneak into the middle school down the street from the Jinn Academy and have to pretend to be normal kids.

Strangely enough, that's kind of how I've felt the past two days. Like I'm sneaking into someone's life and pretending to belong there.

"What looks good?" Rebecca says as we stand in the middle of the cafeteria.

I scan my options before finally deciding on a massive burger from the grill. Rebecca joins me there, and we order and bring our trays to the dining area.

We're just looking for a seat when I hear a voice call out, "Hey! Over here!"

My instincts immediately kick in, and without thinking, I turn and try to cover my face with my tray to avoid being photographed. Until, a second later, I realize how ridiculous I look. I'm not Ruby anymore. I don't have to hide every time someone calls out to me.

Besides, the person wasn't even calling to me. It turns out they were calling to Rebecca, which makes sense. She's the one who's known around here.

"What are you doing?" Rebecca asks me, and I realize I'm still holding my tray up, hiding my face behind my massive cheeseburger. I try to play it off by pretending to scratch my nose with my upper arm.

"Nothing," I mutter.

She nods to the man who's standing up, waving us over. "That's a fellow professor from the literature department. Do you mind if we sit with him?"

I shrug. "No."

I don't mind at all. In fact, all I can think about as we walk over there is how much I hope they talk about books so I can eavesdrop.

"Hi, Clint," Rebecca says as we approach the booth. "This is my daughter, Skylar. Skylar, this is Clint."

He flashes me a *huge* smile and sticks out his hand. I'm still holding my tray, though, which it takes him a second to realize, and then he quickly lowers his hand and rubs his palm against his jeans. He almost looks *nervous* for some reason.

"Hi," I say pleasantly. "Nice to meet you." I glance down at the table, searching for a place to put my tray, but the entire surface is covered in papers and open books, which Clint doesn't seem to notice.

Rebecca directs her gaze to the cluttered table as well, clearly hoping to bring it to his attention. But he's too busy smiling at us. Rebecca clears her throat and nudges her chin toward the table.

Clint finally gets the hint and looks down, jumping into action. "Oh gosh. I'm sorry. I forgot, I . . ." But I can't hear the rest of the sentence, because he mumbles it under his breath as he hurriedly clears space on the table.

I look over at Rebecca and she's biting her lip to conceal a smile.

Did I miss something?

We sit down and I immediately go to work on my burger. It's way too big and messy to eat with my hands, so I carve into it with a fork and knife.

"So you're the famous 'To a Skylark,'" Clint says.

"Huh?" I ask, my mouth full of meat.

Rebecca laughs and nudges me with her elbow. "I told him about the Shelley poem you're named after."

I smile and nod. "Oh, right." Of course Skylar would be named after something cool like an old poem. That's what happens when your parents are both professors. You get cool names that mean something. My mom named me after her favorite precious gemstone.

"Your mom told me you're going to your first middle school dance tonight," Clint says. It sounds like he's fishing for something to get me talking. A conversation starter. Well, if he is, then he just caught the big one, because the reminder of tonight's dance makes me positively giddy. I nod. "Yup."

"Are you going with a date?" Clint asks.

I shake my head. "Nope, just some new friends."

Rebecca visibly perks up at this. "Friends? What friends?"

I shrug. "The same girls I went to the mall with yesterday."

Rebecca's face lights up like a Christmas tree. She looks so proud, and I feel a swell of satisfaction. Not only have I improved Skylar's relationship with her mother, I've managed to make her mother smile like that.

"Great!" Clint says. "That should be fun. Maybe they'll play some Ruby Rivera songs."

I choke on my food.

Gosh, I hope not, I think as I cough up the burger that's lodged in my throat.

Rebecca pats me on the back. "Slow down, sweetie."

"Your mom tells me you're a huge fan," Clint explains.

I swallow my bite and wash it down with a sip of Coke. "Yes. Huge fan."

"My niece loves her, too," Clint says. "Watches every episode of her show and can't stop talking about her. She's about your age."

I nod *and* take another bite of burger, and that's when I see it. It's so fast, I almost miss it.

A fleeting look.

A secret glance when they think I'm not looking.

A mutual smile.

It's the exact same look I saw on that boy Ethan's face when he grinned at me in the hallway yesterday.

I look up at Rebecca and she's suddenly super focused on her own burger, like it's the most important thing in the world. But I notice that her face is a shade redder than it was a second ago and her knee is bouncing up and down under the table like she's had too much sugar.

I cast my gaze to my plate, my mind spinning as this entire situation suddenly becomes very clear.

Skylar's mom has a *crush*!

ROARING FOR THE CAMERA

Skylar

The song is bouncy. It's energetic. It's perfection.

After a short upbeat intro, Ruby's voice comes in.

> *"So you say you wanna be a star.*
> *Don't you know, baby, you already are.*
> *So you say you wanna be the queen.*
> *Look around, you already rule the*
> *scene."*

Oh my gosh. Oh my gosh. Oh my gosh! I love it so much! It's so amazing! I immediately start jumping around and moving to the beat. I don't even care that my legs are sore from the workout this morning. I just can't *help* but dance.

Jules leaps into action and starts taking my picture.

"This is great!" she calls. "Own it! Do it! Love it! Dance it! Be it!"

"Turn it up!" I call out, and the music gets even louder, until I can't even hear my own thoughts. I'm consumed by Ruby's voice. Ruby's words.

"You don't need a si-ign,
'Cause you already shi-ine.
There's no straighter li-ine,
This is by des-ign.
Don't you know?
Don't you know?
Don't you knooow?"

By the second chorus, I already know the words and am singing along at the top of my lungs.

"You are a star!" Jules shouts over the music.

"This is the best song ever!" I shout back.

"Okay, now give me some goofiness!" she says, and I cross my eyes and stick out my tongue. She laughs and snaps a hundred photos, the lights around me flashing with each click.

"Now pretend that someone has just said the sweetest thing in the world to you."

I giggle and make an "awwww" face as I cross my hands over my heart.

"YES!" Jules enthuses. "Now show me serious. You're a teacher who's angry at her students."

I twist my mouth into a grimace and glare toward the camera, channeling Mr. Katz after he found out I didn't read that stupid *Of Mice and Men* book. Who cares about that book now! I'm Ruby Rivera! I'm a superstar! Just like the song says, I already shine!

"That's perfect!" Jules shouts, clicking furiously.

A moment later, the song comes to an end and the next

one begins. This one is a ballad. And I'm grateful, because I was starting to get a little winded from all the upbeat dancing and posing. I can already tell I love this ballad. It seems to be about going back to where you're from, returning to your roots.

> "I've traveled this world near and far,
> But I'll never forget what's in my heart.
> I've seen everything there is to see,
> But I'll never forget what makes me,
>   me.
> No matter where you roam,
> There's really no place like home."

There's a sadness in Ruby's voice that I'm not sure I've ever heard in any of her other songs before. Or maybe I'm simply hearing it for the first time because I know her a little better now. The words themselves are more sweet than sad, but it's like she just can't help it. The sorrow seeps in. It shapes the words, making them much more melancholy than I'm sure the songwriter intended.

I wonder if Ruby was thinking about her father when she sang this. The one she said she doesn't know.

"Okay, good. This is good," Jules says, watching my reaction carefully. "Let's bring it down, down, down. Let's do sad and pensive. Let's do frowny face. You're missing someone a lot."

As soon as the words are out of her mouth, I think about my dad, how far away he is, living on a completely different coast. I think about the divorce and how quickly it all happened. One minute they were sitting me down, telling me they were going to separate, and the next, Mom was packing our stuff for California. What's going to happen after this year is over? Will we ever all live in the same house again?

Mom keeps telling me that this move is temporary. That we'll be back in Amherst before I know it. But what if that's a lie? What if she loves her job here and wants to stay?

What if . . .

"AMAZING!" the photographer shrills, interrupting my thoughts. "Yes! Ruby, you are a natural! Love the tears!"

Tears?

I quickly run my fingertip under my eyes and it comes back wet. I didn't even realize I'd been crying. The makeup artist hurries over to touch up my face and I apologize to her for messing it up.

"Don't be!" she whispers to me. "You're doing so great. Your mom was just saying she's never seen you so into a photo shoot before. Keep it up!"

As the photographer switches out cameras, I steal a peek at Eva, who's watching from the sidelines, beaming at me. She gives me a thumbs-up and I smile back at her. It feels kind of amazing knowing someone is proud of you. I know Mom loves me and everything, but lately it seems like I'm just disappointing her. I know she'd never say it aloud, but I can tell. She hates that I watch TV.

She hates that I don't read. She hates that I'm not more like her.

And watching Eva beam at me like I'm her pride and joy lifts my heart and makes me feel lighter somehow, despite my totally sore and stiff muscles. I mean, I know she's not my mother, but she's someone's mother. And she thinks *I'm* doing a good job.

The photographer returns with a new camera just as the ballad comes to an end and another loud, upbeat song comes on.

"Okay, Ruby," Jules says, hoisting up her camera. "Let's try *fierce*! You're a lioness protecting her cubs!"

I immediately brush off my former melancholy and let the rhythm of the song take me over. I let out a giant roar as I claw the air. The photographer clicks her camera like crazy. Then someone turns on a wind machine and my hair starts blowing wildly. It tickles my face and I start laughing.

"Yes! Yes! Yes!" the photographer calls out, getting excited. "Heart face! More of that."

I fight to push the hair from my eyes, laughing the whole time.

Click! Click! Click!

Thirty minutes and nine incredibly awesome songs later, the album comes to an end and Mom and I gather around Jules's laptop as she swipes through the photos. With each picture, I stare at Ruby's gorgeous dark hair and golden skin and vibrant smile and I still can't get over the fact that it's me. I mean, *me* inside. I'm wearing those clothes. I'm inside that skin. I'm smiling that smile.

"These are incredible, Ruby," Jules says, clicking her track pad. "Even better than your last album. Your fans are going to love them."

"Yes," I whisper in awe as each photo flies by on the screen. "I'm pretty sure they will."

Jules stops on a picture of me looking forlorn and pensive. It was clearly taken when the ballad was playing, when I was thinking about Mom and Dad and how much I miss home. The picture is beautiful, yet sad. Like a bittersweet heartbreak.

Jules turns to look at Eva with a raised eyebrow.

Eva nods knowingly. "That's it. That's the fragile little girl I was looking for."

And just like that, Ruby has a new album cover.

STRANGLING THE STEERING WHEEL

As we drive home from campus, my mind should be on the dance. The Ellas are picking me up in an hour and I need to figure out what to do with Skylar's hair. But right now the dance is about the furthest thing from my mind. I've been subtly trying to get Rebecca to talk about Clint the whole car ride home.

I say things like "So, that meal was interesting," and "So, that was a surprise, seeing one of your colleagues there," and even "So, Clint was nice." But she doesn't seem to get the hint, or if she does, she's trying to avoid the topic. She just gives me one-sentence answers like "Yes, it was," and "Yes, he is."

By the time we pull into the parking lot of the faculty housing, I'm so frustrated by her evasive answers that I finally just blurt out, "Do you have a crush on Clint?"

Rebecca nearly slams into a parked car. Thankfully, she hits the brakes just in time and manages to calmly pull into an empty spot, but I can see my question has unnerved her. When she puts the car in park, her hands are gripping the steering wheel tightly.

"Um . . . ," she says, not looking at me. She's looking at a dirt spot on the windshield, like she's wondering where that came from and how long it's been there. "Where did you get that idea?"

I shrug. "It's pretty obvious."

Her head whips toward me. "It is?"

I giggle. "Yes, Rebec—I mean, *Mom*. You two were flirting like teenagers."

Her face reddens and she looks down at her lap. "No we weren't."

"You totally were," I counter, and then when I see the smile crack on her face, I add, "He likes you, too, you know?"

For an instant, her grin broadens, but it disappears almost as quickly. "Oh, well, it's nothing. Clint is . . . We're just friends."

Rebecca is doing a horrible job of lying. It's obvious she likes this guy.

"Has he asked you out?"

Her face reddens again. "No. Of course not. He knows I'm going through a div . . ."

Divorce.

That's what Rebecca was going to say, but she couldn't seem to finish the word. Like she was afraid of it. Like it was a bomb about to go off.

And that's when I realize why Rebecca is acting so cagey. She thinks this is going to upset me. Or, rather, Skylar. She's trying to protect Skylar's feelings. And in that moment, my affection for her balloons to the size of this car.

I'm not sure my mother has ever put my feelings first. I don't think she's ever once thought of how *I* would feel before making a decision or speaking her mind. That's pretty obvious every time she tells me I need to trim another inch off my waist or insists I change because my current outfit makes my hips look fat.

Or basically every decision that's been made for me in the past four years.

Skylar's mother cares about her daughter.

My mother cares about her daughter's image.

Skylar's mother wants her daughter to be happy.

My mother wants her daughter to be rich so she can continue buying herself Tiffany diamonds.

Skylar's mother cares more about her daughter's feelings than her own.

My mother just doesn't.

"Mom," I say.

"Mmm?" She turns and faces me, but I keep my gaze trained out the windshield. For some reason I can't look at her when I say this. Maybe it's because I know Skylar won't approve. But that's only because Skylar doesn't appreciate what she has. She doesn't realize that her mom is hurting, too, and she wants to be happy. She *deserves* to be happy.

One day Skylar will thank me for this.

"You should go out with Clint," I say quietly.

There's silence on the other side of the car, and I can't bear to look. I don't want to see her expression. Will she be shocked? Hurt? Confused?

When she speaks, I can hear there's a little of all three. "What?"

I bite my lip. "If he's asked you out, and you're just saying no because of me, then don't. You should go out with him."

"B-b-but," she stammers, clearly not expecting this. "But what about . . ." Her voice trails off again. I have no idea what she was going to say next. I don't think she quite knew, either.

I take her hand. It feels warm. It feels inviting. Like a mom's hand is supposed to. "You should do what makes you happy."

Skylar

By the time we get back to the mansion, I'm completely exhausted. After the photo shoot, I had to film promos for the season finale. I had to stand in front of a camera for two hours saying, "You're watching the Xoom! Channel! Now stay tuned for the season finale of *Ruby of the Lamp*!" over and over again. You would think one time would be enough, but it wasn't. The producer handling the promos wanted every different combination of enunciations.

"You're watching the *Xoom!* Channel!"

"You're *watching* the Xoom! Channel!"

"You're watching the Xoom! *Channel*!"

All I really want to do is veg out in front of the TV for the rest of the night, but as soon as we walk through the door, Eva says, "The limo is picking us up in an hour for the Tween Choice Awards."

On a normal day, the words "limo" and "Tween Choice Awards" would cause me to get all sorts of giddy and excited. But after that torturous workout and the photo shoot and the promos, I can barely stand up, let alone prance down a red carpet.

As Eva riffles through dress options, I sit on a sateen bench in the middle of the closet and scroll through Ruby's feed on my phone. I'm trying to pull strength from the thousands of likes and comments. All these people are waiting to see Ruby at that awards show tonight. I can't let them down. But somehow, and for some reason I can't even begin to fathom, I find myself wandering over to my own profile. The old and boring Skylar Welshman.

But the picture I see on the top of the feed completely takes me by surprise. Apparently, I'm not the old and boring Skylar Welshman. I'm some new and exciting Skylar Welshman. One who hangs out with . . .

The Ellas?

I squint at the picture, certain I must be seeing things. But nope. There *I* am, sitting and laughing with none other than Daniella, Isabella, and Gabriella. In fact, if I didn't know any better, judging from this picture, I would say the four of us were best friends. The pictures were actually posted on Daniella's feed, but Skylar Welshman is tagged and the location is pinned as South Coast Plaza.

What on earth is going on over there? How has Ruby managed to become friends with the Ellas in less than two days? Is this some kind of mean joke? Are they playing a prank on her? That's the only rational explanation. But what if she doesn't realize it? What if she has no idea? I need to warn her!

My throat constricts as I hastily open a text message and type in my number.

"What about this one?" Eva says, holding up a shimmery purple gown.

"Great," I mutter absently as I type.

Why are you hanging out with the Ellas?

As I wait for a response, I tap my fingers anxiously on the side of the phone. Ruby texts back a moment later.

They're actually not as bad as you think. They invited me to go to the dance with them tonight

It's a trap. It has to be. The Ellas don't just *invite* random people to hang out with them. They're luring her in, making her feel safe, and then they're going to pounce! They're going to completely humiliate her (me!) again. I cannot let this happen! I quickly type back:

BAD idea. You don't know the Ellas like I do. You shouldn't trust them

A few seconds later, she replies. I feel my heart start to race.

Don't worry! I've got this under control. Have fun at the Tween Choice Awards!

She doesn't get it. I want to tell her about the burping video. She needs to see it to fully understand what she's getting herself into. But . . . I just can't. It's too embarrassing. Ruby Rivera can't know just how pathetic I am. Plus, typing it out, explaining it all, will only force *me* to rehash it. And I just can't bring myself to do that. Not when I'm about to get into a limo to go to the Tween Choice Awards! This is one of the most exciting nights of my life. I can't let anything ruin it.

So I force myself to turn off the screen and put away the phone, vowing not to waste another second thinking about the life of Skylar Welshman.

As soon as we get inside the apartment, I dive into the task of transforming Skylar for the dance. Admittedly, I don't have a lot to work with here. Skylar's mom doesn't seem to keep one beauty product in the house. I'd kill for a single tube of lip gloss or even a curling iron. But there's no time to run out and buy anything. I'm going to have to improvise.

After showering, I blow-dry my hair. There are no round brushes in the bathroom, so I have to make do with a regular one. But I still manage to get a nice wave going by wrapping the ends of Skylar's hair around the brush and blasting it with heat. I also flip my head upside down and blow-dry the roots from underneath, which gives them some lift.

Next, I go to work on Skylar's face. I search the bathroom and kitchen for supplies, collecting an old toothbrush, a tub of Vaseline, a coffee filter, an overly ripe avocado, and a carton of raspberries.

First, I mash up the avocado and apply it to Skylar's cheeks, chin, and forehead like a face mask. Cami often does this to my skin when she wants it to have a little extra glow. While the mask sits, I dab a little bit of Vaseline onto my fingertip and rub it into Skylar's blond lashes. Then I use the old toothbrush to comb it through. The effect is immediate. The Vaseline darkens Skylar's lashes, while the toothbrush gives them length and fullness. Cami once did this for me on the episode where Miles and Ruby went camping in the woods and stumbled across a tribe of leprechauns. Because my character was supposed to have been camping for three days, my face couldn't look made-up, so Cami used a bunch of beauty hacks.

I scrape off the avocado mask with a wet washcloth, immediately noticing the new shimmer of Skylar's skin. Then I use the coffee filter to blot the oiliness around her T-zone.

Next, I squeeze a few of the raspberries between my fingers until my fingertips are stained pink. Then I rub them across my lips and dab at my cheeks. The pop of color is perfect. Not too bright. Just subtle enough to make a difference. Finally, I zip up the fabulous new dress I bought for Skylar and give a quick twirl in front of the mirror.

When I study my finished product in the mirror, I'm feeling really proud of myself. It's not a TV-show-worthy transformation, but it's definitely an improvement. Skylar looks great. Her skin is glowing, her cheeks are rosy, her eyes are bright, and her hair falls in soft waves around her shoulders.

When I emerge from the bathroom, I stand in front of

Rebecca—who is seated in her usual reading chair—and strike a red carpet–worthy pose. Skylar's mom looks up from her reading and flashes me a smile. "You look nice," she says, and then dips her head back to her book.

Nice? I think, feeling a little stung. All that work and the only response I get is "nice"?

What about the new dress? What about the hair? What about Skylar's glowing cheeks? Maybe she just can't see my handiwork because the light is too low. I take a step toward her and duck my head down so it falls into the beam of her reading light. "What do you think?" I ask, batting my eyelashes.

Skylar's mom squints, like she's a doctor examining a patient.

"Do you notice anything different?" I prompt.

"Hmmm," she says, turning her head this way and that. "No. Did you do something different?"

I can't help feeling just a twinge of disappointment. How could she not notice? Skylar looks so much better than she did only an hour ago. My own mother would have noticed the changes right away. She would have been applauding me for my ingenuity and creativity.

In fact, she would have been in that bathroom and kitchen with me, whipping out ingredients like a crazed chef on a cooking show, saying things like "Oh, I read on a beauty vlog that coconut oil works really well as a moisturizer!"

And in that one instant, as I'm standing in front of Skylar's mom, all decked out in my dress and homemade beauty products, and she's staring back at me with a blank, confused expression, I kind of, sort of miss my mom.

I know it sounds crazy. I mean, she's basically been the bane of my existence for the past four years, but she's still my mom. And I know she would be proud of me right now.

You can always tell when my mom is proud. Like after I've nailed a particularly dramatic or poignant scene in the show. Or when I step out of the recording booth after belting out an incredibly high note in a song. She gets this really bright beaming smile on her face. It's like it completely takes her over.

"Never mind," I mumble, and Skylar's mom goes back to her book.

I bend my head to get a glimpse at the title. "What are you reading?"

She sticks her finger between the pages to mark her place and then flips it closed. *Jane Eyre.*

"For work?" I ask.

"No. I just like to pick it up from time to time. It's one of my favorites."

Warmth travels through me and I can't help but smile. Who cares if Rebecca doesn't notice a little Vaseline on my eyelashes or a little curl in my hair? I mean, she's reading Charlotte Brontë for *fun*. She's still pretty awesome.

The doorbell rings and I give a giddy little leap. I open the door to find all three Ellas standing there, looking fantastic in their sparkly dresses, with their made-up faces and white-toothed smiles.

"You look so *fab*," Daniella says. "Love the hair."

I beam at the compliment but then try to play it cool with a shrug. "Thanks."

"Bye . . . Mom," I call back to Rebecca.

"Bye, sweetie!" she calls from her reading chair. "Have fun!"

As I shut the door behind me and follow the Ellas down the stairs to the parking lot, I momentarily flash back to the text Skylar sent earlier.

You don't know the Ellas like I do. You shouldn't trust them

But I think it's *her* who doesn't really know *them*. Not like I know them. We're friends now. There's absolutely nothing to be worried about.

This is going to be a night to remember.

THE FROZEN YOGURT CODE

Skylar

I can't believe it! I am on my way to the Tween Choice Awards in a *limo*. Yes, an actual limo. I've never been in a limo before. It has everything! A TV, a killer stereo system, a bar stocked with sodas and yummy snacks. It even has Wi-Fi!

As we drive to the theater, I can't stop touching things. I turn the TV on and off. Then the radio. Then I open the sunroof and close it.

"Ruby!" Eva scolds from the seat next to me. "Will you quit it? I have a headache the size of Texas."

I shrink back in my seat and stifle a yawn. "Sorry."

"I don't think this Bowl Diet is working. I'm feeling faint all the time," Eva complains, pinching a layer of skin on her upper arm. "Ryder's mom told me about this amazing new thing called the Taste Patch. You basically stick this patch on your tongue and it makes every piece of food you eat taste horrible."

I squint at her, trying to gauge whether she's serious, but I honestly can't tell. "Why would you want food to taste bad?" I ask.

"So you don't eat it!" she snaps. "Obviously."

"Oh. Right. Obviously," I reply, even though this still makes no sense to me whatsoever. Thankfully, I'm saved from having to hear more about the Taste Patch when Ruby's phone rings and I pull it out of my tiny clutch. It's that Lesley person again. I'm about to ignore her when Eva glances at the screen and sits up straighter.

"It's Lesley! Pick it up! She could be calling about the contract negotiations. Wait, why is she calling you?" And before I can respond, she rips the phone from my grasp and answers the call.

"Lesley, it's Eva. Were you trying to get ahold of me?" She pauses and listens. "Uh-huh . . . Well, what's taking so long? . . . Uh-huh . . . You've got to be kidding me. Those slimeballs! What do they think they're— Oh? What for? . . . Well, yes, I know you're Ruby's agent, but I'm Ruby's manager."

So that's *who Lesley is! She's Ruby's agent!*

"Okay, hold on." Eva passes me the phone. "She wants to talk to you."

My eyes widen in alarm. "Me? Why?"

Eva shrugs. "Something about a new frozen yogurt place she found on Melrose. Although I can't imagine why. She knows you can't have frozen yogurt."

I shakily take the phone and press it to my ear. "Hello?"

"Ruby!" comes a screechy voice. "What do think you're doing?"

I glance around the interior of the huge car. "Riding in a limo to the Tween Choice Awards?"

She sighs. "I mean by not picking up yesterday. I told you I couldn't hold them off any longer."

Out of the corner of my eye, I can see Eva staring intensely at me.

"Uh . . . ," I hesitate. "I'm sorry. Things have been a little crazy."

Lesley huffs into the phone. "Okay, look. This is important. I need an answer right this second."

An answer? About what? This doesn't sound like it has anything to do with fro-yo. Oh gosh, I can't be making important decisions about Ruby's life! Maybe if I could just tell Lesley to hang on and call Ruby on the other line and—

"Are you doing the fifth season or not?" Lesley asks bluntly.

My thoughts come screeching to a halt.

WHAT?

"Of *Ruby of the Lamp*?" I clarify.

Lesley sounds like she's choking on something. "Yes, of course! What did you think I was talking about? *American* freaking *Idol*?"

I don't get it. Why on earth would Ruby not do the fifth season? I've read the script. It ends on a total cliffhanger! Plus, I helped Barry and the writers figure out a way to reunite Ruby with her mother. If Ruby doesn't do another season, we'll never get to see it!

Obviously, there's been some kind of mix-up. Obviously, I don't have the full picture. *Obviously,* Ruby is planning to do the next season. She wouldn't just leave her fans hanging like that.

"Look, I know your mom is right there," Lesley says quietly. "I told her I wanted to talk to you about frozen yogurt, so let's just say this. If you *want* to do season five, say 'rainbow sprinkles.' But if you want to turn it down, say 'coconut flakes.'"

There's silence on the other end, and even though it's through a phone, it still feels heavy and thick. And then there's Eva, still staring at me like the world is ending outside this car and the woman on the other end of the phone is giving us directions to the safety shelter.

I'm doing the right thing, I tell myself.

Ruby would want it this way.

The fans would want it this way.

I can't let down the fans.

"Ummm, I think you should go with the . . . ," I begin in a shaky voice. ". . . rainbow sprinkles."

There's another long pause on the phone. This one feels more like surprise than anything else. "Are you sure?" Lesley finally asks.

"Yes." I say.

"Are you really sure?"

Gosh, why is she acting like I'm agreeing to lock Ruby in jail and throw away the key? It's just another season of the show. A very popular and successful show, I might add. That brings joy to many kids—including me.

I glance at Eva out of the corner of my eye. "Yes. Definitely sprinkles."

Lesley sighs. "Okay, I'll let the Channel know. Put your mom back on."

I hand the phone back to Eva, and she gabs to Lesley the rest of the ride.

When the limo pulls to a stop, Eva motions for me to get out and mouths, "I'll meet you inside." I nod and open the door. But as soon as I step outside, thoughts of the show and the phone call instantly vanish as I'm blinded by a thousand flashes of light.

THE MIDDLE SCHOOL STAND-AROUND

My stomach is doing backflips as we walk down the long, empty hall toward the gym. I can hear music playing in the distance, and I start to get giddy at the thought of my first school dance. What will it be like? Will there be fancy decorations and a live band and a table full of yummy appetizers? Will everyone be dancing and jumping around and having the time of their lives?

We reach the doorway and I stop in my tracks, certain the Ellas must have led me to the wrong place. This doesn't look anything like I'd imagined. This doesn't even look like a dance.

There are *no* decorations.

There is *no* food table.

There is *no* band.

In fact, there's not even a DJ. It's just some older guy—who looks like someone's dad—standing in the corner, scrolling through an iPod hooked up to the speaker system.

And *no one* is dancing.

Okay, that's not true. A few people are dancing. But

they're all teachers. I spot the PE teacher attempting to do some kind of sad excuse for a pop-and-lock move.

The "dance floor"—if you can even call it that—is just a wide rectangular section in the middle of the gym that's only recognizable by the kids milling around the edges. They're all clustered in small groups, talking in hushed voices and glancing furtively around at the other groups like a bunch of little spies. What is going on? Have these people never seen a movie about a school dance? Don't they know you're supposed to like . . . you know . . . dance? It's in the title of the event!

Otherwise, why not just call it a middle school stand-around?

I glance to the Ellas to see if they're just as shocked by this development as I am, but they seem like they expected as much. They beeline to a spot next to the bleachers, form a tight little circle, and immediately start talking about what everyone is wearing.

I run over to join them. "Um, you guys, why is no one dancing?" I ask, interrupting Daniella's breakdown of what some girl named Andrea is wearing, like Daniella is a fashion commentator on the red carpet.

The three girls shoot me an odd look. "That's just what you do," Daniella says.

"Yeah, it's like a rule," Isabella adds.

I look to Gabriella, hoping for more of an explanation, but she just shrugs and repeats, "Yeah, it's basically like a rule."

Does that girl ever have an original thought?

Then they all go back to their discussion on clothing. But I can't participate. Not only do I not care about dissecting the wardrobe of every single girl in this room, I came here to dance!

Who cares what the rule is? Maybe no one is dancing because everyone's too afraid to be first. Maybe they just need someone to show them it's okay. Someone brave enough to get this party started.

I glance around the gym until my gaze lands on Ethan. He's huddled with a group of his own friends on the other side of the room, talking and laughing. He looks really cute in khaki pants, a button-down shirt, and still-wet hair. I don't know what it is, but why are boys infinitely cuter when they dress up? It doesn't take much. A nicer shirt, a shower, pants that don't have holes in them. But it makes a world of difference. I feel a sizzle of electricity travel through me at the thought of what I'm about to do.

This is my chance to fully redeem myself after what happened in the hallway yesterday. This is my chance to redeem *Skylar*. He clearly has a crush on her and I totally devastated him when I didn't remember his name.

I peer back at Daniella, thinking about what she said at the mall yesterday, about turning him down. She swore she didn't like him. She even made a face at the mention of his name, which means he's totally fair game for anyone else.

While the Ellas are still fully engaged in the creation of their own version of the Best- and Worst-Dressed Lists,

I turn and walk purposefully across the gym. I can feel people's eyes on me. I know they're wondering what I'm doing, breaking away from my little group, defying the rules of the middle school stand-around.

Ethan's back is to me, so he can't see me. But all the guys around him immediately fall quiet when I approach. I tap him on the shoulder and he turns around, looking genuinely surprised to see me. He gives me a quick once-over and I see a small smile make its way onto his face.

He likes the dress.

"Hey, *Ethan*." I emphasize his name, so he knows that I remembered it this time.

"Hey, Skylar," he replies, unable to look me in the eye.

I gesture to the dance floor. "Do you want to dance?"

For a moment, he looks panicked, like I've just asked him to rob a bank. "But no one else is dancing," he says nervously.

I shrug. "So?"

That seems to stump him. "Oh." Then he gives his damp hair a small flick and says, "Okay, I guess."

As we walk into the middle of the gym, once again I can feel every pair of eyes in the room on me. They're watching us. Waiting to see what we'll do. I'm not sure why this is such a big deal. We're going to *dance*. Because this is a dance.

Except just as we reach the center of the giant space, the current upbeat song comes to an end and a slow ballad starts playing.

A chorus of giggles echoes throughout the room and I fight not to roll my eyes. Seriously, middle schoolers are kind of immature. It's a *slow song*. Not a wedding march.

Ethan looks to me with his eyebrows raised, as if to ask *What now?*

To answer him, I place my hands on his shoulders and start gently rocking to the beat. He clears his throat and nervously places his hands on my hips. Then we're swaying together. I have to say, it feels super awkward. Ethan is so stiff, and all these people goggling us is clearly not helping.

Just ignore them, I tell myself, and focus on Ethan. I rack my brain for something to talk about—a conversation starter—but all I can come up with is "Thanks again for your help with my locker yesterday."

He grins sheepishly. "No problem."

And then we fall silent again.

"Um . . ." I pause, thinking of something to say. "How was your day?"

He nods. "Good. I just went to lacrosse practice."

"Oh, you play lacrosse? That's so cool!"

He squints. "I thought you knew I played lacrosse. We had a whole conversation about it last week at your locker."

I suddenly feel foolish. "Oh, right. Sorry, I just forgot for a minute."

He tilts his head and studies me, like he's trying to piece together the final clues of a big mystery. "You've been acting kind of . . . strange lately."

I pretend I have no idea what he's talking about. "Strange? How?"

He shrugs with one shoulder. "I don't know. Just . . . different."

I let out a soft chuckle as I realize he might be the only person who's noticed. I mean, apart from the strange looks I've been getting from Skylar's mom. But in terms of the people Skylar goes to school with, Ethan seems to be the only one who's picked up on the fact that I'm different. As in *not* her.

"Thank you," I say with a sigh.

Ethan's forehead crinkles in confusion. "For what?"

"For noticing. You seem to be the only one who has."

He looks down at our feet. "I notice you every day."

I feel my face flush with heat. A boy has never said anything like that to me in real life.

"Really?" I ask, feeling something start to glow inside me.

Maybe it's just my imagination, but I swear I feel Ethan scoot just the tiniest bit closer to me. "Yeah. I mean, I don't know how a guy *wouldn't* notice you. Ever since you moved here, I don't know, I kind of can't stop thinking about you."

Suddenly, all the air that was trapped inside my lungs whooshes out. My chest squeezes painfully, and a deep, profound sadness washes over me.

He's not professing these things to *me*. He's not even talking to me.

He's talking to Skylar. He's talking *about* Skylar.

This isn't my life. This is *her* life. I'm still just living on borrowed time. I'm still just trespassing on private property. Somewhere I shouldn't be. No matter what I do to improve Skylar's life—get her a good grade in Language Arts, make friends with the Ellas, bond with her mother, dance with a boy—I eventually have to give this all back. Because it doesn't belong to me.

That wasn't *my* Language Arts grade.

Rebecca isn't *my* mother.

Those aren't *my* friends.

I quickly glance over at where the Ellas are still standing, but I notice they've stopped talking to each other and are now staring at Ethan and me. Actually, staring might be the wrong word—*glaring* is more like it. In fact, they look so furious, I'm momentarily distracted from my self-pity party.

What is their problem? Are they angry that I actually decided to dance at a dance? Or are they just annoyed that I walked away from them?

"Are you okay?" Ethan asks, bringing my attention back to him.

"Yeah," I say quickly. "Sorry. It just looked like my friends were mad at me for some reason."

"Your *friends*?" Ethan asks incredulously.

"Yes. Why do you sound so surprised?"

"Do you not remember what they did to you?"

A bolt of fear travels through me.

You don't know the Ellas like I do. You shouldn't trust them.

Is that what Skylar was warning me about? Did the Ellas do something horrible to her? I want to ask Ethan what it was, but I also know that will make me sound crazy. If it was bad enough for *him* to remember, then *I* should remember, too.

I try to laugh it off. "Oh, it wasn't that bad."

He looks like he just bit into a rotten egg. "Not that bad? Are you kidding?"

"I mean . . ." I try to backpedal. "Forgive and forget, right?"

He cringes. "Okay. But I'm not sure I could forgive that. I know it's not my business who you're friends with or who you hang out with, but I wouldn't trust Daniella if I were you. She's . . . I don't know . . . she seems kind of unstable."

Unstable?

Is he just saying these things because he's mad she turned him down? Is he just bitter?

"She's not that bad," I say again, trying to play the whole thing off with a laugh, although inside I'm still dying to know what happened between Skylar and the Ellas.

Ethan shrugs. "Okay. If you say so, but I've never liked that girl. Ever since elementary school, she's always given me a bad vibe."

"Then why did you ask her to the dance?" I ask.

Ethan's hands immediately fall from my hips and I worry I've gone too far. Hit a sore spot. I should have just kept my mouth shut. He looks really mad now. So mad, he can't even speak.

"What?" he finally sputters out.

"Daniella said you asked her to the dance and she turned you down."

His eyes go wide. "I never asked her to the dance! She asked *me* to the dance and I turned *her* down."

Now it's my turn to fall speechless. I struggle to remember our conversation at the mall yesterday. I could have sworn she said she was the one who said no to him. What is going on here?

I glance back at Daniella and she's still watching us, her arms crossed over her chest, her eyes narrowed. Something bitter coats the back of my throat. It takes me a minute to figure out what it is, and once I do, I know this night is about to take a very sour turn.

It's dread.

ROCKING THE RED CARPET

Skylar

For a moment, I can't move. I can't even blink. I'm frozen on the edge of the red carpet, taking in the unbelievable scene in front of me. Lights. Cameras. Celebrities.

Everywhere!

Everywhere I look there's another superstar. Another famous face from some famous TV show. I spot Summer Crush doing an interview with a reporter from TMZ, and Berrin James actually turns and *waves* at me! Which I suppose shouldn't really surprise me. After all, we are text buddies now. But I'm still far too stunned to wave back. In fact, I'm far too stunned to do much of anything. For a long time, I just stand there with my mouth hanging open, still unable to process any of this.

Then about a hundred people start calling my name at once.

"Ruby! Ruby! Over here! Ruby! Look this way! Ruby! Who are you wearing?"

I blink out of my trance and suddenly remember where I am. *Who* I am. I'm Ruby Rivera! And Ruby Rivera doesn't stand on a red carpet like a deer trapped in head-lights; she *works* the red carpet. She flounces and flirts and poses.

I snap to it and do my best impression of Ruby on the red carpet. I've seen enough videos of her in action. I know exactly what to do. I put one hand on my hip, turn, and smile. The cameras go crazy. Flash! Flash! Flash! People continue to call my name, and it spurs me on. I start sashaying my hips and tilting my chin this way and that. I have no idea what I'm doing, but the crowd seems to love it. They're laughing and clapping and more photographers are running down the red carpet and positioning themselves in front of me to get a good shot.

Before I even realize what I'm doing, I've broken into a series of dance moves taken straight out of the opening theme song of *Ruby of the Lamp*. The photographers laugh and snap away, and by the time I make it to the center of the red carpet, where all the interviewers are stationed, I'm tired and pretty breathless.

"Well, that was something," says a young blond man dressed in a blue suit. He thrusts a microphone in my face and says, "Hi, I'm BJ Bauman from *Tell It Like It Is*."

"Oh, I love that YouTube channel!"

BJ looks shocked. "You know it?"

"Yes!" I exclaim. "I watch it all the time. You guys have the best updates on Rub . . ." I clear my throat. "On *me*!"

BJ chuckles uneasily. "Right. Great. Well, glad to hear that you like keeping up on . . . celebrity news. Are you excited to be at the Tween Choice Awards tonight?"

I beam. "I am *so* excited. I mean, look at all these celebrities! It's like I've died and gone to heaven."

BJ looks positively enchanted. He's clearly loving my responses. "It's certainly nice to see someone of your level of fame and success still getting excited about seeing your favorite artists. Do you think you have a good chance of winning tonight?"

I know how I'm supposed to answer this question. I've seen Ruby do it a hundred times. I tilt my head and say, "Honestly, BJ. It's just such an honor to be nominated."

BJ grins back. "It certainly is. Good luck tonight, Ruby."

"Thanks!" I step away, continuing down the red carpet toward the entrance of the theater up ahead.

Not to toot my own horn or anything, but I am *amazing* at this. For the next ten minutes, I practically float down the red carpet, taking interview after interview with TV stations, bloggers, vloggers, and magazines. Three days ago, this very situation would have terrified me. But not today. Not now. Not wearing Ruby's clothes, with Ruby's hair and Ruby's skin.

As Ruby, I feel like I can do anything.

And trust me, *everyone* wants to talk to me. It's like walking down the hallway of middle school and everyone knows your name and everyone wants to be your best friend. Except like a zillion times better. Because this is like being popular all over the world.

And the fans! They're everywhere! And they're all screaming my name. Okay, well, technically it's Ruby's name, but whatever. They're going crazy. There are so many of them, and they're so excited, they have to be fenced in behind these metal barriers. Which, when you think about it, is a little strange. *People* have to be barricaded from other people? I mean, Ruby *is* just a human being, like everyone else.

"Ruby! Over here!" another interviewer calls, and I happily step over to him and assume my interviewing position, which I've gotten really good at as well. One hand propped on hip, shoulder angled toward the camera, gentle hair toss.

"Hi, Ruby. I'm Chad Darcy from *The Celebrity Spot!*"

I nearly choke. "*Celebrity Spot*? Like THE *Celebrity Spot*?"

He laughs, clearly thinking I'm joking. *The Celebrity Spot* is the biggest celebrity gossip blog out there! They have all the exclusive breaking news, which they call a "Star Snoop!" And that's how it feels. Like someone has been snooping around the celebrities' lives, picking up all the insider information. I have no idea where they get all their juicy tidbits, but they always seem to be way ahead of the rest of the blogs and celebrity news channels. I think they must have spies all over Hollywood.

"So who do you think is going to win Best Actress tonight?" Chad asks.

I finally manage to regain my composure and answer the question with the same poise and diplomacy as the last one. "Oh, I have no idea. I mean, everyone in the group is so talented. It's such an honor to even be nominated."

"What about Carey Divine?" Chad goes on, raising

his eyebrows. "Do you think she'll nab the award for the fourth year in a row, or does someone else have a chance?"

Just the mention of Carey's name makes my stomach turn. She better not win *again*. But of course I can't say this. Ruby already told me they're *supposed* to be best friends. And even though I don't agree with it, I can't ruin the illusion that Ruby has worked so hard to maintain. Plus, she might be watching right now, so I need to play it cool and act the way she would act. I flash another polite smile and say, "Carey is very talented. And as my best friend, if she wins, I'll be really happy for her."

Even as I say the words, inside I feel like barfing all over Chad's shiny black shoes. But I keep my smile light and professional. I'm actually pretty proud of my answer. It's totally something Ruby would say.

"Really?" Chad asks, looking genuinely surprised, like he doesn't quite believe me. "You'd really be happy for her if she stole the title away from you for the fourth year in a row?"

I flinch. What kind of a question was that? It almost seems like he's trying to *imply* something. Plus, there's something about the way he's looking at me that kind of unnerves me. As though he's not just posing a question, but watching my reaction carefully. Like a scientist watching a test tube, waiting for it to explode with fizzy green goo.

I stretch my smile even wider until it physically hurts. "Yes. Really. Carey is my best friend."

"Hmm," Chad says, sounding confused. "Because here

at *The Celebrity Spot,* we've just announced a very interesting Star Snoop!"

A knot forms in my stomach. What is going on? What is he talking about? What Star Snoop!? I feel my smile start to falter and I remind myself to stay calm. Think about what Ruby would do. She wouldn't let her anxiety show.

"What's that?" I ask breezily.

Someone steps out from behind a camera and hands Chad an iPad with a news article on it. He shows it to me and I can feel the camera zooming in on my face. Literally. The cameraman actually takes a step forward, getting so close to my face, it's like he's trying to focus on each individual eyelash.

As I read the headline of the article, the knot in my stomach quickly turns into a gnarled, tangled mess. I fight to keep my face neutral, my smile painted on, but it's nearly impossible.

The cameraman zooms in even closer, and suddenly I can't breathe. My vision starts to cloud over. I blink rapidly, trying to clear it, but it just keeps getting fuzzier.

"So what do you have to say about this?" Chad prompts, like he's poking at a wound, trying to see if he can get me to cry. But I won't cry. Of course I won't cry. I'm Ruby Rivera! I've never seen Ruby Rivera cry during an interview.

Then again, I've also never seen Ruby Rivera run off the red carpet like the bogeyman is chasing her.

And yet that's exactly what I do.

I was right. This dance *did* just need two people to kick it off. By the time the slow song has come to an end, there are at least ten more couples on the "dance floor." The next song is another fast song, and Ethan immediately starts bouncing and swaying and jumping around to the rhythm. His dancing is so completely nonsensical, it makes me laugh.

Yes, laughing. Laughing is good, I try to tell myself.

As more and more people start to dance, it becomes harder and harder to keep my eye on the Ellas. They're still huddled together on the sidelines, and for a second, I swear I see Daniella whip out her phone and Isabella and Gabriella gather around it, peering over her shoulder at the screen, but then a swarm of middle school boys comes bobbing and jumping onto the dance floor, blocking my view.

Ethan does some impressive slide-hip-jut move, and I vow to keep all my focus on him. Who cares what the Ellas are doing? Who cares that Daniella was practically trying to murder me with her eyes just a second ago? It doesn't mean anything. That might be how she looks at everyone.

By the time we leave the dance floor, there are so many bodies crammed together, we have to push our way through. I silently congratulate myself for being the one to finally get this party started. Now, *this* is a dance!

Ethan and I find a watercooler set up next to the bleachers and we guzzle down three cups each. I'm desperate to ask Ethan what this awful thing is that the Ellas did to Skylar, but I know I can't. I know it will only give me away as the intruder that I am. So instead I say, "How long have you played lacrosse?" hoping it's a safe question that Skylar hasn't asked him before.

It seems to be. He shrugs. "About two years. Since I was ten. I'm hoping to make varsity in high school."

"That's cool."

"How about you? How long have you been . . ." But his voice trails off when he obviously can't think of Skylar's version of lacrosse. He laughs. "Sorry . . . what are you into? I feel bad that I've never asked."

I laugh, too, as I rack my brain for an answer. What *are* Skylar's hobbies? I mean, besides me—Ruby Rivera. I know she hates to read, and judging from the look on her PE teacher's face when I climbed that rope yesterday, I'm guessing she's not very athletic, but she's got to be good at something.

"Um," I begin, struggling to figure out how I'm going to finish this sentence. "Well, I really like . . ." And then I remember the brunch buffet I scarfed down this morning and how I told Skylar's mom that I'd cooked it all. That's right! Skylar likes to cook. But I personally know nothing about cooking so I just say, "Food."

Ethan laughs. "Okay. What kind of food?"

"Everything!" I exclaim. "Pancakes and waffles and burritos and pizza and nachos and . . ." I trail off when I realize that I'm doing it again. I'm slipping back into myself. I'm forgetting whose life this really is. Who this conversation really belongs to. I mean, maybe Skylar likes pizza and nachos, too, but that's not the point. The point is I cannot let myself fall for this guy. Not for real, anyway. Tomorrow afternoon, Skylar and I are switching back and that will be that. I'll never see him again. I have to do this for *her,* not for me. I have to pretend.

Except I'm sick and tired of pretending. I'm tired of playing a role. Acting like someone else. *Being* someone else. For once in my life, I want to do what *I* want to do. Say what *I* want to say. Be *me*.

But who is the real Ruby Rivera? That's the problem. She's definitely not the girl you see on TV. Or the girl the Xoom! Channel and my mother have made me out to be through strategic publicity campaigns and a carefully selected wardrobe. She's someone else.

And I have no idea who that is.

"And . . . ," Ethan prompts, and I realize he's still standing there waiting for me to tell him what other foods I like.

I shake my head sadly. "Never mind. Let's dance."

He doesn't seem to notice my sudden bout of melancholy. "Okay."

We both chuck our empty paper cups into the nearby trash can and head back to the dance floor. Another upbeat hip-hop song is playing, and I try to lose myself in the beat. But it doesn't take me long to realize that people aren't dancing with the same energy as they were before. They're all kind of lightly moving to the music, but their attentions are focused elsewhere.

On their phones.

Everyone seems to be either staring at their own phones or peering over a friend's shoulder at theirs. Laughter starts to trickle through the crowd, starting out as just a small tinkling of noise before quickly growing to a full-on roar.

"What's going on?" I ask Ethan over the music.

But he just shrugs and shakes his head. "No idea."

I do my best to try to block out the noise, but it becomes increasingly more difficult to do so. Especially when I notice that the attention of the room has shifted again. Now they're no longer looking at their phones.

They're looking straight at me.

MEAN MEME

Skylar

I stand in the stall of the bathroom, staring down at the screen of my phone in disbelief. My hands are trembling as I read the headline of the *Celebrity Spot* article again and again. But no matter how long I stare at them, the words on the screen don't change.

Ruby Rivera disses "BFF" Carey Divine

I scroll down farther, my palms sweating as lines of text seem to jump right off the screen and slap me in the face.

"She has no talent . . ."
"Our friendship is a sham . . ."
". . . all the Xoom! Channel's idea."
"I actually can't stand her . . ."
". . . thinks she soooo amazing."

The article claims *I* said these things about Carey. (Or rather, Ruby did.) They're even in direct quotes, like it was pulled from an interview. But Ruby would *never* say anything like that in an interview. She said so herself. She's always keeping the illusion of the friendship alive. And I certainly never said those things.

Although for some reason, they seem eerily familiar. . . .

I scroll farther down and suddenly my heart stops beating. My jaw drops and I use my fingertips to zoom in on a single line of text on the screen:

A source close to the actress says Ruby
divulged these things to her on the set of her hit
show, *Ruby of the Lamp.*

On the set of her hit show . . .

The bathroom stall starts to spin. The scene comes flooding back to me like a tidal wave.

I *did* say those things.

I remember now. The quotes are real. I said all that. *Word for word.* It was just yesterday, when I was sitting in my trailer with that group of extras. The girls I thought were my new friends.

"Can you guys keep a secret?" I asked.

They all leaned in, their eyes wide and glinting.

"We're not really friends," I whispered, to which they all gasped in delight.

"What?" Stacia asked.

"Our friendship is a sham. It was all the Xoom! Channel's idea."

"To pretend to be BFFs?" Claire asked, looking scandalized.

"Yup. They thought it would help the TV movie we starred in together. But I actually can't stand her. She has no talent, but she thinks she's soooo amazing."

"I can't believe it!" Gwen declared.

I sat back and crossed my arms, loving all of the attention. "Well, it's totally true. But you can't tell anyone."

"We won't," Jordan swore, glancing around the trailer at each of the girls in turn. "Your secret's safe with us."

I stumble backward and sit down on the toilet seat. I feel light-headed. I feel like I might faint. I stick my head between my knees and take deep breaths.

HUUUGHHUUP!

Those girls. They betrayed me. Or at least, one of them did. But which one? It's impossible to tell. They all seemed super intrigued by what I was saying. And does it really matter which one? The damage is done. The big secret is out. And it's all my fault.

It's like one of them snuck out of my trailer and wrote down everything I said. Or rather . . .

I let out a low whimper.

It's like they *recorded* everything I said.

HUUUGHHUUP!

Oh gosh, I'm going to be sick. I spin around and thrust open the toilet lid. I try to retch but nothing comes out. No surprise there. Eva barely let me eat anything today. She was worried about my stomach bulging on the red carpet.

I fall onto my knees and lean back against the bathroom stall as big fat tears start to well up in my eyes.

HUUUGHHUUP!

What am I going to do? Ruby is going to kill me. No, *Eva* is going to—

"RUBY?" I jump when I hear her voice, followed by the click-clacking of high heels on the tile floor. "Ruby? I know you're in here. Helga from Xoom! publicity said you ran off the red carpet and came straight here."

I hold my breath, hoping that maybe she'll just go away. But then I notice my beautiful silk gown is spilling out underneath the door of the stall. Eva must notice it at the same moment, because she comes stalking toward me and bangs on the door.

"Open up. Now."

She knows. I can hear it in her voice.

I crawl over to the door and flip the lock. The door flies open a second later and Eva glares at me. "What do you think you're doing? Get off the filthy floor! You're going to soil your gown!"

I pull myself to my feet, keeping my phone clutched in my hand.

"It's all over the news," Eva says, spinning me around and brusquely brushing off the back of my dress. "It's already trending."

"WHAT?" I screech.

"Well, what do you expect?" Eva grabs me by the arm, guides me over to the sink, and scrutinizes my makeup, which has been totally ruined by the crying.

I can't believe this is happening. I was just trying to make friends! I was just trying to impress those girls. I wanted to feel, for one second, what it felt like to be popular and liked and the center of attention. And now it's turned into this giant *trending* mess!

HUUUGHHUUP!

"Ruby!" Eva scolds. "Get ahold of yourself."

I close my mouth and hold my breath, willing myself not to hiccup again. Eva reaches into her bag, pulls out a bundle of emergency makeup, and goes to work on my face. Meanwhile, I open Twitter on my phone and let out a gasp when I see the hashtag #RubyvsCarey at the top of the Now Trending list.

I click the hashtag and start scrolling through the various tweets, my heart pounding harder and harder with each horrible comment I read. Almost all of them are directed at Ruby.

Or rather, at *me*.

@RubyRivera after you learn how to sing, maybe then you can start dissing people for having no talent.
@RubyRivera I never believed that BFF act for a second. You're not that good an actress.
@RubyRivera Why don't you go back to Texas and leave Hollywood to the real celebrities?

"Ruby!" Eva hisses. "Stop crying. I'm trying to fix your makeup."

I didn't even realize I'd started crying again. I sniffle

and try to keep my tears under control. But I can't help it. Every time my gaze scans another hurtful tweet, the shock and pain is so strong, so deep, I feel like I might drown in it.

How could people say those things about me? About Ruby? She's the greatest. She's the most talented actress and singer in the world.

Eva finishes up my face and stuffs all the makeup back in the bag. She looks calmer now. More in control of her emotions. I wish I could say the same for myself.

"How did this happen, Ruby?" she asks, sounding composed and diplomatic. "How did you *let* this happen?"

I think about telling her the truth—that I spilled everything in that trailer—but I know she'll just get angrier and I'm not sure I can take angrier right now. So I just shrug, hiccup, and say, "I don't know."

Eva closes her eyes for a moment, as though she's trying to summon strength from deep within. "Okay, we can't let this affect us right now. We have an awards show to get through."

"WHAT?" I screech again. "You mean I still have to go out there?"

"Of course you have to go out there," Eva snaps. "If you leave now, everyone will know how much this is affecting you."

But it is *affecting me!* I want to scream at her. It's affecting me because I now realize I can't escape it. The betrayal. The humiliation. I thought I'd be safe from that in this world. I thought if I just left middle school, I wouldn't be the loser I've always been. But it turns out I still am. It turns out my mistakes follow me wherever I go. And in that way, this is almost worse than the Ellas turning my hiccup into a viral video. Worse than everyone laughing at me in the hallway and calling me Skylar Belchman. Worse than anything! Because I did it to me *and* Ruby. I ruined both of us.

HUUUGHHUUP!

HUUUGHHUUP!

HUUUGHHUUP!

"RUBY!" Eva screams, startling me and I jump. But apparently, it's enough to scare away the hiccups, at least for now.

All I want to do is run home and put my head under the covers. Hide inside Ruby's giant bedroom and not come out until this is all over. But apparently, that's not an option. Not for Ruby Rivera. And so not for me, either.

"C'mon," Eva says, straightening out my dress and giving my hair a final fluff. "Put on your game face and let's go."

I follow Eva toward the door of the bathroom and I notice how fast her expression changes the moment we step back into the theater lobby. It's like someone has hit a switch.

I try to mimic her transformation, but I can feel all the eyes on me, staring at me, judging me. Celebrities, photographers, producers. Everyone. I know what they're all thinking. They're thinking about that hashtag. They're thinking the exact same things those mean tweeters wrote.

My phone buzzes and I pull it out to see a text from Ryder.

Nice going, Ruby. Way to ruin it for all of us.

I'm starting to think Ryder Vance is a not a very nice person.

"Smile!" Eva says brightly as she pulls out her phone and points it toward me. "Tween Choice Awards!" she trills, snapping photos of me in my amazing designer gown and flawless makeup and perfectly styled hair.

I take a deep breath and smile, trying to draw out the last remaining shreds of Ruby Rivera inside me. Trying to tap into the seemingly infinite well of Ruby inspiration that I've always had access to. That has helped me through some of the toughest moments of my life.

But now the well is empty.

And so is my smile.

STATUS DOWNGRADE

The girls' bathroom in the middle school gym reeks, but I don't care. It's the only place where I can be alone. I need to be alone. I need to figure out how this happened.

And by *this,* I mean the picture I'm currently staring at on the screen of my phone. It was posted on Daniella's feed ten minutes ago.

It's a picture of Skylar. Or rather, of me *being* Skylar.

Or rather, of me *failing* at being Skylar.

Because that's exactly how I feel right now. Like a big fat failure. Like I've totally messed up. Skylar trusted me with everything. And I let her down. I've made her the laughingstock of the entire school.

I try to take deep breaths as I stare at the photo.

I recognize the setting. It was taken at the mall yesterday. Daniella snapped it when we were all hanging out in the Carousel Court, eating our frozen yogurts. I can see the carousel in the background, and in my hand, I'm holding my frozen yogurt cup. When the picture was taken, I was doubled over, laughing at something one of the other girls had said.

Except now, in *this* picture, I'm not laughing.

I'm throwing up.

And there's a giant pile of vomit on the table in front of me.

And the caption reads:

Looks like Belchman has been upgraded to Barfman.

The picture has already gone viral. Okay, so not like celebrity viral, but like middle school viral. Two hundred people have already liked it and fifty people have already commented. But this is way worse than celebrity viral. This is worse than those mean comments that people post online about Ruby Rivera. Because those are strangers. They don't know me. They just presume to know me. I'm just an easy target to direct their hate at. I can easily brush off those comments. But not this. This is personal. These are people Skylar goes to school with, has to see on a daily basis, has to sit next to in Language Arts class. This is a direct attack against her.

Oh, who am I kidding? This is a direct attack against *me*. I was the one at the mall. I was the one who trusted the Ellas even though Skylar warned me not to. Even though I *should* have known better. I deal with this kind of stuff every day, and yet I ignored my instincts. Because I was the one so determined to prove something. Prove that I could do this. That I could be a normal kid, go to a normal school, make friends with anyone.

And look where that's gotten me!

Tears sting my eyes. It's not fair. The picture isn't even real! They clearly Photoshopped it with one of those horrible photo-editing apps. They made something fun and innocent look like something horrible and embarrassing. They turned one of my triumphant moments—a fun-filled day out with new friends—into a nightmare.

How could they do that?

Why would they do that?

Is it because I danced with Ethan? But that doesn't make any sense. Daniella swore she didn't like Ethan. She swore she turned him down.

But then I remember what Ethan said on the dance floor: *"I turned her down."*

Is that true? Was Daniella just *saying* she didn't like him to cover her own wounded pride? Well, how on earth was I supposed to know that?

If Daniella is going to lie about liking a boy, then she can't get angry at me for asking him to dance!

I reread the caption of the photo again. I don't think I noticed it the first time because I was too distracted by the fake contents of the photo, but now something is bugging me.

Looks like Belchman has been upgraded to Barfman.

What is this Belchman reference? Skylar's last name is Welshman. Why are people calling her Belchman? With a flick of my fingertip, I scan back through Daniella's feed, stopping when I reach a video. It's not long. Just a few seconds, but it's been set to play over and over again on an endless loop.

It has over six hundred views.

In the video, Skylar is standing on the stage in the middle school auditorium. She looks like she's about to say something, but instead, she lets out a huge, booming, earth-shattering burp.

Except it's not a burp.

It's one of her super-loud hiccups. I remember them from the prop room. I remember how they seemed to shake her entire body. Just like in this video. My gaze drifts to the caption and my body turns cold.

Welshman or Belchman?

And suddenly I realize this was about more than just Ethan. This was about a group of very mean girls doing a very mean thing. Daniella wasn't ever really my friend. She didn't invite me to the mall or to the dance because she *liked* me. This whole thing was a trap.

The Ellas were pretending.

The way so many people in Hollywood pretend.

The way Carey Divine and I have been pretending for the past year.

Which is why I, of all people, should have recognized a fake friendship. But I didn't. I was too blinded by what I *wanted* this world to be. I couldn't see it for what it really was. I couldn't see the truth.

More tears spring to my eyes. Except this time they

326

well up. This time, they fall. I try to swat them away, but it's no use. They're coming too fast. Too relentlessly. As I glance at my reflection in the mirror, I see the same girl I met in that prop room just a few days ago. The girl who cried on the floor in front of me. I thought she was a super-stalker fan. But no.

She was just this.

A girl being picked on at school.

A girl being bullied.

The word sinks to the pit of my stomach like a rock. *Bullied.* Skylar tried to tell me. She tried to reach out to me in that prop room, but she couldn't bring herself to admit it. Or I couldn't bring myself to listen. I was so convinced that her life was perfect. Or at the very least, better than mine. I was so convinced that she didn't know what she had.

But it was *me* who didn't know what she had. It was *me* who needed convincing. And now I know. Now this horrible sick feeling in my stomach is all I need to understand what it's like to really be her. To be that girl who doesn't fit in at school. Who is teased mercilessly by her peers. Now I know.

It's awful.

It's sickening.

It feels like the walls are caving in on you.

It feels like you can't breathe.

I can't breathe!

No wonder she wanted to be me. No wonder she wanted to be *anyone* but her. She wanted an escape. Just like I do right now. I'm desperate to get out of here. Run from these crumbling walls and never look back.

But that's not what I do.

Instead, I turn. I run into the stall. I kneel down in front of the toilet, and I throw up.

This time, for real.

FAKE STAR

· ·

Skylar

Don't look. Just stop looking. Turn off your phone and put it away.

But I can't! I can't stop. It's like driving past a car crash. You want to look away. It's horrible and terrifying and awful, but you just can't help keeping your face glued to the window.

That's how I feel right now. Like I'm driving past a car crash. Except *I'm* the car crash. And I can't stop reading all the horrible tweets people are writing.

I've already missed half of the Tween Choice Awards. They've already announced the award for "Best Almost-Kiss," "Best Dog Costar," and "Best Flash Mob Scene," and I've barely heard any of it. My first Tween Choice Awards ever and I'm missing it! Because I'm so distracted by these hurtful things people are saying.

I had no idea how many people out there absolutely *hate* Ruby Rivera. And now *me*! It's like this one error in judgment has brought them all out of the woodwork. Like they were cockroaches lurking in the darkness, just waiting for me to screw up so they could *finally* share how they really feel.

And some of the tweets don't even have anything to do with the Carey Divine scandal. Some of them are just plain mean.

@RubyRivera When are you going to get it through your skull that no one on this planet thinks you're cool
@RubyRivera Your face looks like someone ran over it with a tractor

What is this person even talking about? Ruby has a gorgeous face. Why are people so cruel?

I close Twitter and click over to the picture Eva posted after we stepped out of the bathroom. Even though my smile is completely fake and devoid of any happiness, I look pretty. My makeup is great. My hair is perfect. My dress is sparkling. And the picture already has over fifty thousand likes! I quickly scroll through the comments, my spirits lifting with each one.

I still love you, Ruby Rivera!
Don't listen to anything anyone says about you.
You are a goddess.
You are the best, Ruby! I <3 you to the moon and back!

I smile. See? People still love me. The true fans will never be shaken.

But then I scroll a little farther down and my blood turns ice-cold in my veins.

I thought you were a role model, Ruby.
Turns out you're just a snob. #Unfollowed
Who do you think you are, dissing Carey Divine?
She is so much more talented than you!
I hope they cancel your stupid show.

Cancel the show? Would they really do that? *Could* they really do that? Have I actually ruined more than just Ruby's career? Have I ruined Ryder's career and Barry's career and all those people who work on the show?

Oh gosh, I can't breathe.

I can't stop thinking about the barrage of negative comments people have posted about such a sweet and innocent picture. What is the matter with them? Don't they realize that Ruby has feelings like any normal human being? That *I* have feelings? Do they not think Ruby will see these comments? Or maybe they *hope* she will. Maybe there are people out there who are just that mean.

"Ruby!" Eva hisses from the seat next to me. "What are you doing?" She quickly grabs the phone from me and stuffs it into her purse.

I sit numbly in my seat, staring at the stage only three rows in front of me. That's how famous Ruby Rivera is. She's been seated in the *third* row at the Tween Choice

Awards. And yet I can't seem to focus on anything that's happening. I think Summer Crush is accepting an award. I can hear Berrin James's voice coming from somewhere, but it's like I can't really hear it. It blends into a buzzing sound that seems to have taken over my brain.

Eva must notice my near-comatose state, because she puts a gentle hand on my knee and whispers, "Don't worry about it, sweetie. This will all blow over."

"Those comments," I whisper back numbly. Thankfully, no one can hear me over the raucous applause and cheers that Summer Crush is getting as they walk off the stage. "They were so horrible."

Eva just chuckles. "There are always going to be hateful comments, honey. That's the nature of the game. Don't worry. The publicity team is already hard at work deleting them all."

What?

My head whips in her direction so fast, the room starts to spin. "Deleting them?" I repeat a little too loud.

Eva shushes me and points to the stage, where Ryder Vance is standing at the mic, saying something about the award he's so excited to present.

Ruby's publicity team deletes all the negative comments on her pictures.

I always thought there were no bad comments posted about her because everyone simply loved her. But that's not the reality at all. There are people out there who have nothing better to do than to write awful things.

It doesn't make any sense.

What did Ruby ever do to any of these people, except entertain them. And sing for them? And give up her childhood for them? No wonder she wanted my life so badly. A little shade from the Ellas is nothing compared to what Ruby deals with on a daily basis.

It's like the whole world is a pack of mean girls to her. The whole world bullies her.

And yet every day she gets up, she goes to work, she films, she records, she performs, she dances.

She smiles.

I feel sick to my stomach at the thought of all of those smiles. Every interview I've ever watched. Every picture I've ever downloaded to my phone. Every bright and shiny smile she's ever flashed at a camera.

They were all masks.

They were all covering something underneath. Something I'm only starting to see. Feel. *Know*.

Suddenly, the room erupts in wild applause, interrupting my thoughts and finally cutting through the buzzing in my head. I glance up at the stage and Ryder is staring right at me, clapping his hands and beaming at me. I glance around and notice that everyone in the whole theater is looking at me.

"Ruby!" Eva calls out over the cheers. "That's you! He called your name! You won! You finally won! Get up there!"

Huh?

I'm so confused. I'm so disoriented.

I feel Eva pushing at my back. "Go!" she says.

Suddenly, there's a man in front of me with a camera hoisted onto his shoulder. It's pointed right at my face.

"Smile," Eva whispers to me. It sounds like a threat.

Dazedly, I rise to my feet and walk down the aisle toward the stage. But I can't feel a single thing. Not happiness. Not elation. Not even shock. All the sensation in my body is gone. I mount the steps and someone thrusts a gold statue into my hand. I stare down at it in a complete fog. On the bottom there's a plaque that reads:

"Best Actress"

Ruby finally won.

I won.

And yet, even as I dig deep down, searching for some kind of emotion, some kind of reaction, the only thing I can bring myself to feel is loss.

REGRET . . . WITH A SIDE OF RICE

The next morning, I refuse to get out of bed. I refuse to do anything, including look at Skylar's phone. For one, I don't want to see that picture again. It's already ingrained in my mind. I barely slept at all last night because every time I closed my eyes, I could see the image. The Photoshopped image of me barfing all over the South Coast Plaza table.

And also, I refuse to look at Skylar's phone because I don't want to see all the missed calls I've undoubtedly gotten from her. She has to have seen the image. I know she checks her own feed because that's the reason she even texted me in the first place yesterday to warn me about the Ellas. She saw me tagged in one of Daniella's photos. And now she'll be calling to tell me she told me so. She told me to watch out for them and I didn't listen.

I'm sure Ethan has texted, too. I didn't even say goodbye last night. I just left.

Finally, at lunchtime, Rebecca lures me out of bed with the promise of Chinese takeout. When I drag myself into the living room, the food has already arrived and Rebecca has arranged it on the coffee table. It smells delicious. I drop down onto the couch, grab a plate and some chopsticks, and start stuffing my face.

Rebecca sits down in her usual reading chair and studies me, like she's trying to decide whether or not to say something that's on her mind. "Are you sure you don't want to talk about last night?"

I look away from her, unable to meet her eye as I swallow down a lump of sesame chicken. "Mmm-hmm."

She's been trying to get me to talk to her about what happened at the dance ever since I called her from the bathroom and asked her to come pick me up. As soon as I got in the car, she could tell something was wrong. If my tearstained cheeks didn't give me away, my total silence the entire way home probably did. But I refused to talk about it. I wanted to. I really did. I could think of no better person to open up to than Rebecca. Kind, warmhearted, understanding Rebecca. But then I remembered the look on her face at the cafeteria when I told her I was going to the dance with my "new friends." She looked like she had just won the daughter lottery. I couldn't bear to burst her bubble and tell her I'd already messed it up. That my "new friends" turned out to be the girls who have been bullying Skylar for who knows how long. I couldn't bear to see that disappointment on Rebecca's face.

Or maybe it was my *own* disappointment I just couldn't bear.

"I know what will cheer you up," Rebecca says, picking up the TV remote. She scrolls through the list of recorded shows on the DVR until she gets to the one that says *Tween Choice Awards,* and pushes play.

I sigh. I really don't want to watch this. I really don't want to see what an amazing time Skylar had last night living my life. It'll just remind me of how *horrible* my night went and how dreadfully I let her down. The opening music of the awards show starts and the deep voice of the announcer booms, "Live from the Red Carpet in Hollywood, California. Welcome to the Annual Tween Choice Awards!"

I grab the remote and push pause. "Maybe later," I mumble.

"Okay," Rebecca says nervously, and when I glance over at her, I notice that she's not eating. Instead, she's just sitting there, fidgeting with the ends of her fingernails. I also notice, for the first time, that she looks different. Her hair is not tied back in a ponytail, but instead is flowing loose and long over her shoulders. I never even realized how long it is. Or what a pretty shade of strawberry blond it is. Her face is still clean of makeup, but it looks freshly washed and moisturized. And even her clothes are different. Normally, she just wears basic blacks and grays but today, she has a pop of color. Her shirt is *pink*. Not like a bright pink. More of a pale, almost peachy pink. But still pink.

"Why aren't you eating?" I ask suspiciously.

She straightens up a bit, looking anxious. "Well, actually, that's something I wanted to talk to you about." She clears her throat." I was thinking about our conversation yesterday in the car . . . after we got back from campus, and I thought maybe . . . well, you might be right."

I swallow the lump of fried rice in my mouth. "About what?"

"About going out with Clint."

She stops and watches my reaction carefully. Like she's expecting me to jump up and flip the table in a fit of rage. I nod for her to continue.

"The truth is he *did* ask me out"—she fights to hide a smile—"a few times, actually, but I've always said no. Because your father and I . . . well, we're still working out the logistics of the divorce and I was worried about you and . . ." Her voice trails off, like she's afraid to even finish.

"And . . . ," I prompt, feeling my spirits lift for the first time today.

"And, well, you said I should do what makes me happy and you're right. So I called him last night while you were at the dance and we're supposed to have lunch today." She says this last part fast, like she's just trying to get it over with. "But I can cancel. If you—"

"No!" I practically yell. I set my plate down on the coffee table and leap off the couch. "You should go! I'm happy for you! You're going to have so much fun."

She gives me an uneasy look. "Are you sure?"

I nod. "Absolutely." One of us should have some fun around here, and it's certainly not going to be me.

She smiles. "Okay, good. But if you need me, just call or text. I'll have my ringer on the whole time and—"

I roll my eyes playfully. "Mom, I'll be fine. Go. Have fun."

She sighs, like a huge burden has just been lifted from her shoulders. Then she stands, flashes me another warm smile, grabs her bag from the kitchen table, and heads out the door.

I turn back to my Chinese food and the paused recording of last night's Tween Choice Awards. I guess I have nothing better to do than watch Skylar prance around, having the time of her life on the red carpet. I pop another piece of sesame chicken into my mouth, grab the remote, and press play.

Skylar

The next morning, there are about thirty people packed inside Ruby's living room. All of them have been brought in to "deal" with the celebrity scandal.

That's what Eva has been calling it. A celebrity scandal. Ruby trusted me with her life, her career, her body, and this is what I've done with it. I've ruined everything.

There are people from the Xoom! publicity team, people from the Xoom! legal team, studio executives, Ruby's agent, Ruby's personal lawyer, even some guy named Peter, who I believe is some kind of money manager. They're all milling around, throwing out suggestions, talking on phones, typing into laptops. It looks like a war zone. And apparently it is, because according to all the celebrity blogs and news sites, I've declared war on poor Carey Divine.

And, of course, Carey is playing the victim in all this. She actually spoke to *The Celebrity Spot* after the awards show last night and told them how much it saddens her to see her BFF unnecessarily lash out like this.

Now everyone is trying to come up with the right

"angle" to go to the press with. An excuse that will "restore" Ruby's perfect angelic wholesome image. I've heard every ridiculous suggestion from "she was poisoned by the on-set caterer and not acting like herself," to "Ruby Rivera's evil twin, who she was separated from at birth, took her place."

After that one, I left the room.

I've been hiding out in Eva's office ever since, reading screenplays from the pile. All the movies Eva rejected for her daughter. I don't know what it is, but somehow, reading these screenplays calms my nerves. I can still hear the voices from the war zone down the hall, but getting lost in these stories is keeping my pulse at a semi-normal level. It's funny. I've always watched my mom disappear into books after she's had a bad day or after she used to have bad fights with my dad. The books were like her friends. Her confidants. The things she could turn to when the rest of the world seemed to be closing in on her. I never understood that. And maybe that's because I never liked books.

But these aren't books. They're screenplays. They're totally different. They're not full of pages and pages of daunting words. They're full of action and emotional cues and entertaining dialogue. They get straight to the point, instead of wandering around it for countless chapters.

And yet, they seem to have the same effect on me as the books do on my mom. Each time I turn the final page of one, I immediately reach for another. It's like I crave their comfort. I love meeting all these new characters, watching them go on wild adventures, frantically turning the pages to see how they're going to get out of all that trouble they seem to get themselves into.

But mostly, I love how I can hide inside these worlds. Even the cheesy ones. I never realized how easy it is to hide inside stories. When I'm in the middle of one of the screenplays, it's like all that other noise disappears. The war zone in the other room doesn't even exist.

But that's not the only reason I'm hiding in this office. It's not just the war zone out there. It's the war zone in my head. It's the guilt and the shame and the regret. They've been following me around ever since I ran off that red carpet. No matter where I go or what I do, I can't seem to shake those emotions.

And also, I'm hiding from Ruby's phone.

After I bumbled through the world's shortest acceptance speech ever last night, I insisted to Eva that we go straight home, even though we'd been invited to countless after-parties and celebrations around town. As soon as we got back, I hid Ruby's phone in the back of the mall closet, and I haven't looked at it since. For one, I can't bear to see any more of those hateful comments. But more than that, I can't bear to see my phone number on the caller ID. I know Ruby has probably been calling and calling. There's no way she hasn't heard the news. There's no way she doesn't know. And now she's probably trying to get ahold of me so she can yell at me for ruining her life. For messing up *everything*.

I just don't think I can take that right now.

I don't think I can take her anger and disappointment on top of Eva's, on top of the Channel's, on top of my own.

"Ruby?" A voice interrupts my thoughts. I look up from the script that's open on my lap and see Lesley standing in the doorway. I just met her and already I like her more than any of the others. She has a kindness in her eyes. Even though she talks faster than anyone I've ever met, there's a gentleness about her. In fact, when she came to the house this morning, she was the only one who didn't look mad at me. She looked more like she felt sorry for me.

"Yeah?" I say.

Lesley walks over and sits down next to me. Without a word, she peeks at the title page of the script in my lap and lets out a chuckle. "Ah, yes. The killer tween robots from outer space. I remember that one."

"It's better than it sounds. The dialogue is funny. Although the middle needs some work."

Lesley nods. "Most of them do." She pauses and studies me for a second. "Since when are *you* interested in reading scripts?"

I shrug. "I like the stories. And they're easier to read than books."

She furrows her brow. "I thought you loved books. I never see you without one."

I don't know what to say to that. Of course, she's talking about the real Ruby. Not this fake imposter version that I am. "Screenplays are more fun. They're like getting to *read* a movie. I can see it all happening in my head."

Lesley smiles. "Barry told me how you saved the final episode from those giant plot flaws the writers missed. And then you came up with a bunch of amazing ideas for next season?"

I bite my lip, remembering. That *was* pretty awesome. "Yeah."

"I was surprised to hear it," she admits. "You've never really taken that much interest in the show. But it sounds like your ideas were really good. Maybe you have a future as a screenwriter."

I let out a small laugh, because it feels like she's joking. But when I glance over at her, she looks completely serious. I have no idea how to respond to that, though. I don't know if Ruby has any interest in becoming a screenwriter. Somehow I doubt it. So I decide to change the subject. "How's it going out there?" I ask, jutting my chin toward the door.

She gives me what I think is supposed to be an encouraging smile. "Good. I think we finally have a strategy."

I raise my eyebrows. "What is it?"

"We're going to announce the fifth season of *Ruby of the Lamp. The Celebrity Spot* is on their way over to film an exclusive interview with you about it. We think it will rally enough excitement from the fans to drown out the other stuff. And if not, the Channel is prepared to move forward with *Lemonade Stand-Off Two*."

I frown. "There's a sequel to *Lemonade Stand-Off*?"

She laughs. "There will be, if there needs to be. The Xoom! folks think if you and Carey sign up to do another

TV movie together, it will prove that the whole thing is water under the bridge."

"Is it?" I ask. "Water under the bridge?"

She smiles kindly. "It will be. Eventually. Just let the adults handle it."

Lesley reaches out to smooth the wrinkle that is obviously forming between my eyes. It's this small action that tells me that she and Ruby must have a special kind of bond. It immediately makes me feel closer to her, even though I technically just met her this morning.

Lesley leans her head back against the wall with a sigh. "I always thought that this business was too much pressure for a kid. I've seen too many child celebrities fall apart under the weight of it. But audiences are just obsessed with young stars, so the networks and studios keep making shows and movies for them. If it were up to me, children wouldn't be allowed in Hollywood at all."

This takes me by surprise. "But you *work* in Hollywood."

She nods. "Exactly. That's how I know." Then, after a long stretch of silence, she groans and rises to her feet. "C'mon. Let's get you dressed. *The Celebrity Spot* will be here in an hour."

SALT IN THE WOUND

This isn't happening.

This is NOT happening.

I stare in bewilderment at the TV screen as Chad Darcy of *The Celebrity Spot* shoves an iPad into Skylar's hands. Meanwhile, across the screen, they've posted their breaking news Star Snoop! headline:

Ruby Rivera disses "BFF" Carey Divine

"What did you do?" I shout at the screen. At Skylar. At *myself*.

But, obviously, Skylar-Ruby doesn't answer. In fact, she doesn't do much of anything. She seems frozen to the spot, her eyes wide as she takes in the headline.

"So, what do you have to say about this?" Chad asks with a sneer. I hate when they do that. When they jab at you like they're poking at an open wound. *Here. Does this hurt? How about now? What if I pour salt in it and then push on it?*

Skylar looks like she's about to start crying right there on the red carpet.

"Don't do it," I command her. "Do NOT cry."

Thankfully, she listens. She doesn't cry. I almost breathe out a sigh of relief. That is until I watch in horror at what Skylar does next. She bolts. The cameraman swings the camera toward her, zooming in to follow her as she literally books it down the red carpet like an Olympic sprinter. Although, she's hardly an Olympic sprinter in that ridiculous dress my mother most definitely picked out for her.

"Well," Chad is saying after the camera focuses back on him. "That was interesting. If you want more on our Ruby/Carey Star Snoop!, be sure to log on to our website, or follow us on Twitter for up-to-the-second celebrity news and—"

I punch the pause button on the remote, freezing obnoxious Chad with his obnoxious mouth open. I run back into Skylar's room and yank open her desk drawer, where I hid her phone. I swipe it on, cringing as I wait for all the notifications to pop up. Missed calls from Skylar. But the screen is blank.

That's odd.

Is there a chance she hasn't seen the photo Daniella posted?

Not that it matters. I might have messed up royally last night, but it appears Skylar has messed up even more. I navigate to the *Celebrity Spot* website and scroll through the feed until I find information on the story. I don't have to go far. It's the third post down.

UPDATE on Ruby/Carey Feud

My stomach seems to drop to my knees. This isn't good. They've already upgraded it to a "feud." That means Carey has retaliated. That means it's full-on war now. My house is probably buzzing with publicists and executives trying to figure out the best way to spin this.

How did this even start? I quickly scan the article, but the answer is somewhat unclear. It seems as though Skylar spilled the beans to someone about my make-believe friendship with Carey and *that* person sold their story to *The Celebrity Spot*. But who would Skylar have told? And when? She's barely even been in my life for a full weekend. When would she have had time to blab all this to someone?

I click over to my feed—Ruby Rivera's feed. The one I barely even look at. Mom manages all my social media. She posts all the pictures and writes all the captions. And then, of course, there's the entire team of publicists that sits around deleting all the negative comments. Apparently, it's a full-time job.

I cringe when I see my follower count. It's dropped by over a hundred thousand people.

That's bad. That's *very* bad.

But even as I sit there, scrolling through the comments left on the most recent post, there's this little nagging voice in the back of my head that keeps asking, *Why do you care?*

And it kind of has a point. Who cares if I lose a *million* followers? I don't care about that life. I don't care about that whole Hollywood world anymore.

At least, I shouldn't.

I'm just about to close the app and vow not to look at it again, when something appears at the top of Ruby Rivera's feed. It's a brand-new post. A video. It has the iconic *Celebrity Spot* logo in the bottom corner, meaning it's a repost from their account. And the caption reads:

Hey you guys! Check out my BIG EXCITING NEWS!

Curiously, warily, I press play.

And that's when my entire life explodes before my very eyes. Because apparently, in the three days that Skylar has been living in my body, she's not only managed to ruin my career, she's also managed to ruin my life.

"Hi, everyone! Ruby Rivera here! And I'm ecstatic to bring you this exclusive *Celebrity Spot* Star Snoop! For you die-hard fans of my show, it's time to get excited, because it's official! I am returning for a fifth season of *Ruby of the Lamp!*"

BRAVING THE PHONE

··

Skylar

I take a deep breath.

Do it, Skylar. Just do it. It's easy. Turn it on.

I stand in the middle of Ruby's closet, clutching her phone in my hands. I've just finished filming the exclusive Star Snoop! with the people from *The Celebrity Spot* (there's a sentence I never thought I'd ever say in my life), and now it's time to face the music. Time to face Ruby Rivera.

I swipe on the phone and wait, convinced that any minute, the phone is going to light up and explode with alerts of text messages and missed calls. It does. But shockingly, none of them are from my number. None of them are from Ruby.

How is that possible?

The news is everywhere!

Has she not seen the news? Has she not turned on a TV or opened a web browser or a social media app?

What on earth has she been doing?

I open my feed—Skylar Welshman—and scroll through to see if Ruby has posted anything from yesterday or today, but she hasn't. The latest picture on the feed is the one she was tagged in from her trip to the mall with the Ellas.

That's weird.

I click on posts that Skylar Welshman has been tagged in and the first thing on the list is a video posted late last night from Leah. Curiously, I click on it and my heart squeezes as I see my best friend's face fill the screen.

"OMG! OMG!" she's saying into the camera. "I can't believe it! Ruby Rivera did a shout-out to me in one of her videos. THE Ruby Rivera! Star of *Ruby of the Lamp*! Skylar, did you see it? Did you see? Everyone go to her feed now and watch it! She actually names me by name and thanks me for being a fan!" Then she opens her mouth and literally screams for three seconds straight.

A smile makes its way across my face. The first one in hours. In all the chaos of yesterday, I completely forgot that I'd posted that video for Leah. I rewind the video and let it play again, watching how happy she is. At least I was able to make *one* person happy in all this.

I pause the video while she's midscream. She looks jubilant. She looks radiant. She looks *exactly* how I would have looked if Ruby Rivera had posted a video about me. Before all this happened. Before I messed everything up.

In this very moment, I miss Leah more than I've ever missed her. But even more than that, I miss who *I* was when I was her best friend. Just her best friend.

Not a celebrity.

Not the most famous twelve-year-old in the country.

Not the star of a hit show.

Just a girl.

Just a fan.

I close the video and continue scrolling through the posts. But I don't get very far. Because the next picture is one posted by Daniella. And as soon as I see it, all the blood in my veins turns to ice.

Bile starts to rise in my throat. I swallow hard to keep it down. My eyes desperately try to take in all the information at once. The picture, the caption, the likes, the comments, the . . .

Vomit?

Is that seriously vomit?

The Ellas actually took a picture of Ruby throwing up?

Of course not, a voice inside of me says. *Since when do the Ellas ever post anything real?*

I can't *believe* Ruby let this happen. I can't believe she trusted them after I warned her not to. I can't believe she's actually managed to make my life *worse* than it already was.

With shaking fingers, I click on the Phone app and start to dial my own phone number—ready to give Ruby a piece of my mind—but before I can even get past the area code, the phone starts ringing in my hand with an incoming video call.

It's Ruby.

THE APOLOGY STANDOFF

"What did you do?" I roar as soon as my face appears on the screen.

Skylar's all made-up from the interview she just filmed, but her mascara is slightly smeared, as though she's been crying.

"Me?" she screeches back. "What about you?"

I cringe. So she *does* know. But I don't care. I'm too mad to deal with her tiny little problems right now. I need to deal with my massively huge *big* problems. "We're not talking about me. We're talking about you. You started a feud with Carey Divine and then agreed to star in another season of the show? That was *not* your decision to make! You had no right to do that!"

She looks confused. "Wait, you mean you don't *want* to do another season?"

"No!" I say, throwing my free hand in the air. "I was going to quit!"

"Well, how was I supposed to know that?"

"Didn't you hear a single word I said in the prop

room? I hate everything about my life. I was going to quit and—"

"So why didn't you?" she interrupts me, her brows pinched together.

Her question pokes holes in my resolve . . . and my anger. I start to deflate. Then, as if she can sense my hesitation, she asks, "Were you *really* going to quit?"

I close my eyes for just a moment. I let out a breath. I hear the answer deep within me. Like the far-off voice of some far-off person I've always *wanted* to be but never have had the courage to become. The kind of person who's brave enough to tell her mother how she's really feeling, to put her foot down, to take control of her own life. To speak her mind.

No.

That's the real answer to Skylar's question. I was never going to build up the guts to talk to my mother. I was never going to be that person. But what about now? Could I stand up to my mom and tell her the truth? Or would I just cave again?

"Well," Skylar prompts, leaning in to the camera as though she's trying to see right through me. "Were you?"

And maybe she *can* see right through me. Maybe living a few days in my skin has given her some sort of insight into the pathetic coward I really am.

"It doesn't matter," I snap impatiently. "You had no right to sign on to another season of that stupid show without my permission."

"It's not a stupid show," Skylar defends. "It's an amazing show, and if you quit, you're going to let down millions of fans."

"You mean I'm going to let down *you*? If I don't do the show, *you'll* be disappointed."

She snorts at this. "Trust me, you've already let me down. I've seen Daniella's picture. Didn't you listen to anything *I* said? About *not* trusting the Ellas? You were just supposed to go in there and get a good grade for me in Language Arts. You weren't supposed to make my life worse than it already was! I could have done that all on my own."

Her words punch me in the stomach. Because they're true. They're right. That's exactly what I was supposed to do. Make her life better, not worse. And I truly thought I *was*. I thought middle school would be easy.

But it turns out it's not. It's really, really not.

It's freaking hard.

I'm sorry, I want to say. But all that seems to come out is anger. "You mean like *you* making *my* life better?" I growl. "*You* were just supposed to film one stupid episode, kiss one stupid boy. And you couldn't even manage to do *that* without messing it up."

Skylar goes very quiet. Every few seconds, her body shudders quietly with another bout of hiccups. They look so strange coming out of *my* mouth. For a moment, I wonder if she's going to apologize. She looks like she's going to apologize. If she apologizes, I will, too. I know it. I'll break down and cry and tell her how sorry I am. How right she was about everything. How hard her life really is.

But she doesn't apologize. Instead, her eyes squint as she stares intently into the camera, like she's looking for something. "Wait, where's my mom? It's Sunday. She never leaves the house on Sunday. She always stays home to catch up on her reading."

I glance behind me at the empty living room and the empty reading chair that must have caught her attention. "Uh . . . she's out," I say vaguely.

Her forehead crinkles. "Out? Where?"

"Actually," I say, trying to brighten my voice, "she's on a date."

Skylar makes a strange strangled kind of sound. "A date?" Then her voice fills with eagerness. "Oh my gosh! Is my dad there? Did he fly out from Amherst to surprise her?"

I cringe, knowing she's not going to like what I'm about to say. "Not exactly."

"What do you mean?"

The truth is going to break her heart. But it's for the best. "She's on a date with Clint."

Now she just looks confused again. "Who's Clint?"

I perk up, hoping my enthusiasm will rub off on her. "Oh, he's this really cute guy from her work. He's another professor in the literature department. Totally nice. And sweet. And he has this major crush on her. You should see them together. They're like teenagers. After I saw them flirting at the university cafeteria, I told your mom she should totally go out with him and—"

"YOU DID WHAT?" she thunders.

I wince. "You would have done the same thing if you had seen how happy she looked."

"No I wouldn't!" she vows, and I can see the angry tears pooling in her eyes. "How could you betray me like that? And my dad! You've ruined everything!"

"No," I rush to tell her. "I didn't. I swear she really looked happy. Happier than I've ever seen her."

Skylar scoffs, looking away from the camera like she can't even meet my eye.

"I know she wanted to go," I tell her. "She just needed me . . . *you* to be okay with it."

"Well, I'm *not* okay with it."

"Why not?" I press.

She throws her free hand in the air. "Because my parents might have gotten back together. But if she goes off and falls in love with someone else, then—"

"Skylar," I say in a gentle voice. "I don't think they're getting back together."

"What do you know?" she snaps. "You've known her for three days. I've known her my whole life."

"Maybe that's the problem."

"What is that supposed to mean?"

"I just mean—" I begin to say, but she doesn't let me finish.

Her anger seems to boil over until it's spewing from her mouth in the most hurtful words. The kind you can't take back. "You just don't know what it's like to have a dad. So you don't know what it's like to lose one."

I swallow hard, heat rushing to my face and tears rushing to my eyes. I can't believe she just said that to me. "And *you*," I seethe, "are so obsessed with what you want, you're completely blind to what anyone else wants."

Her eyes narrow at me. I can tell her breathing has gone completely wonky. She sounds like she's breathing through a mask. For a moment, she just glares at me, and I'm afraid she's going to say something even worse than the dad remark. What could possibly be worse than the dad remark?

But she doesn't.

Instead, she says exactly what I'm thinking at the exact moment I'm thinking it. "I want to change back."

FAN NO MORE

....

Skylar

It's settled. Our original plan is moving forward as scheduled. I'm going to South Coast Plaza for my autograph session at four o'clock, and Ruby is going to meet me. I'll bring the lamp and we'll sneak off somewhere, make the wish to change back, and presto. This nightmare will all be over. I'll be back in my old life by dinnertime.

When Ruby and I sign off from our video call, we're both so angry, we can barely look at each other. We both just say a terse "goodbye," keeping our gazes trained anywhere but into the cameras, and end the call.

I can't believe what she did! The whole catastrophe with the Ellas is one thing, but telling my mom she could go on a *date*? That is crossing the line. That is so much worse than anything I did! So what if I got her into a little hot water with Carey Divine, or signed her up to do another season of the show. None of those things are permanent. The Carey feud will probably blow over, and I'm sure she can still back out of the show. Or even if she can't, she can suffer through one more season.

But what she did to me is *personal*. She messed with my family. My whole life.

I'm so mad, I toss the phone across Ruby's bedroom. I expect to see and hear it shatter with some kind of satisfying cracking noise, but it doesn't. It just bounces harmlessly off the soft white carpet and skids to a halt.

Whatever.

I can fix this. As soon as I'm back in my old body, I'll talk to my mom. I'll set the record straight. I'll tell her I'm not ready for her to date yet. I'll tell her *she's* not ready to date yet. I'll make her see the truth. I'll cry if I have to. But I'll make sure she never sees that Clint guy again.

Ruby's words come streaming back into my mind.

"And you are so obsessed with what you want, you're completely blind to what anyone else wants."

For a moment, a small part of me wonders if she's right. Have I been blind to something my mother wanted this whole time? Have I been only thinking about myself?

No. Of course she's not right. She's wrong. About everything! She doesn't know anything about it. She's never met my dad. She's never seen my parents when they were happy. And they *were* happy. And they *will* be happy again. As soon as we get back to Amherst, they'll work things out. They'll realize how much they've missed each other and how ridiculous they've been and get back together. But that's never going to happen if Mom is out there dating every random guy she meets.

"Ruby!" Eva calls from the stairs. "We're leaving in twenty minutes! You better be ready."

"Oh, I'm ready," I reply quietly through gritted teeth.

I carefully pack the genie lamp into my bag and change into the outfit Eva has picked out for me for the signing. Then I head into the bathroom to attempt to fix my makeup. It's pretty hopeless. I've completely ruined it with all my crying and angry yelling. No matter. Cami is still here from the *Celebrity Spot* interview. I'm sure she'll fix it before we leave.

I stare at Ruby's reflection in the mirror and take a deep breath. Just a few days ago this reflection brought me so much hope and excitement and giddiness. Just a few days ago I would have killed to have gotten a phone call from Ruby Rivera. But a lot can change in a few days. Now seeing her face in the mirror makes me want to scream.

HUUUGHHUUP!

Relax, I tell myself. Soon this will all be over. Soon I'll be back in my own skin. My own room. My own bed. And the first thing I'm doing when I get there is stripping my room of every piece of Ruby memorabilia I can find. I'm done with Ruby Rivera. Forever.

Soon this face will be nothing more than a distant memory.

A REAL EMERGENCY

When Rebecca gets home from her date, I'm waiting for her in the living room, dressed and ready to go. Ready to get my life back. But her date clearly didn't go well, because she closes the front door with a *bang* and scowls at me.

I want to ask her about it. I want to console her, but there's no time. The autographing session at the mall started five minutes ago and I need to get there. I need to put an end to this. That girl ruined my life. I can't stand for her to be in my skin for a second longer than she has to.

"Mom," I begin rationally. "I'm sorry if your date didn't go well and I want to hear about it, but you promised to take me to the mall to see Ruby Rivera and we're already late, so can we talk about it in the car?"

She squints at me as though I'm speaking another language. "What?"

"The autograph session at South Coast Plaza?" I prompt. "Ruby Rivera is there right now. You promised to take me."

"You think I'm going to take you to the *mall* after what you've done?"

I gape back at her, completely confused. What is she talking about?

She brandishes her phone toward me. "I just got a call from the credit card company."

Uh-oh.

"Did you really use your *emergency* card to buy a six-hundred-dollar dress?" The way she emphasizes "emergency" tells me she doesn't have the same definition of the word as I do.

I wince. "Is that not okay?"

Clearly, that was the wrong thing to say, because she throws her hands in the air. "Of course it's not okay! My first car didn't cost that much!"

"Really?" I reply stupidly. "How is that even possible?"

That doesn't help.

"That card is supposed to be for emergencies only. Not for buying six-hundred-dollar dresses. And then there are two charges for something called Ding Dong Delivery?"

I perk up. "Oh, well, actually that *was* an emergency. The food in the cafeteria at school was completely inedible, so I had to improvise."

Rebecca clearly isn't convinced. She's fuming. "I don't know what's going on with you, Skylar, but I don't like the person you're becoming."

"Neither do I," I mumble under my breath. And that's the problem.

"Excuse me?" Rebecca asks.

"Nothing." Geez, she's really mad. Like even more mad than when Skylar ditched school to go to Burbank. Or maybe this is the same mad. It's just been compounded on top of the other mad.

"Mom," I say, trying to smooth things over. I'm running out of time. I know how these mall signings work. She's in, she signs, and she's out. If I don't get there in time, we'll miss our window. "I'm really sorry about the dress. Look, I'll return it when we get to the mall!" The idea is so inspired that I dash out of the room that instant and run to get the dress from Skylar's room. "I still have the receipt!" I say when I return, holding up the piece of paper proudly.

Rebecca lets out a scornful laugh as she collapses into her reading chair. "Oh, you're returning the dress, all right."

I stare blankly at her. Why is she sitting down? We have to *goooo*.

"Just not today," she says. "There's no way I'm taking you to the mall after this. There's no way I'm rewarding you for this behavior. I'm sorry to say it, but you're grounded, Skylar."

SMILE, SIGN, REPEAT

....

Skylar

Ugh.

Don't these people have anything better to do than stand in line on a Sunday afternoon waiting to get a twelve-year-old's autograph? This line is ridiculous. I'm sitting in the Carousel Court, next to the merry-go-round, and there are people lined up all the way around the courtyard, down the hallway, and out the door of the mall! I can't see from here, but I think the line might wrap around the building.

Ruby Rivera is just . . . a person.

I admit that three days ago I totally would have been one of those people lined up, but not anymore. I am so done with Ruby Rivera.

Being her.

And obsessing over her.

However, I will say it's a good thing I spent that summer between fifth and sixth grades practicing her autograph over and over again. That's really coming in handy today. By the one hundredth bright-eyed, toothy-smiled kid who comes through the line, I've practically become a professional autographer.

Although my hand is starting to cramp.

I kind of feel bad for the fans, though. Apart from the fact that they've been completely deluded into thinking Ruby is this amazing person—which she is *not*—they barely even get a chance to talk to her (or, rather, me). There's a mean man named Nolan from the Xoom! Channel whose sole job is to keep the line moving. Not to mention the three scary-looking security guards who are standing around me like they're protecting a castle from invasion. What do they expect people to do? Storm the table with cannons?

Lots of the fans want to take pictures with me, but mean Nolan won't allow that. Although a few manage to snap some selfies while I'm signing. I barely have enough time to say hello to each fan as they come to the table. A Xoom! staff member slides a *Ruby of the Lamp* postcard in front of me, I sign it, another staff member hands it to the fan, and the process starts all over again. Look up, smile, look down, sign. Look up, smile, look down, sign. I feel like a robot on an assembly line.

I take a quick break to massage my throbbing hand and check the time on my phone. The autographing session is almost over. Where is Ruby? I keep craning my neck to see if I can spot her in the line, but so far she's nowhere to be seen.

She better be here. This lamp is burning a hole in my bag. She better not decide she wants to hijack my life and continue to make horrible decisions on my behalf that she has no business making. Because two can play at that game. I'll stand up in this chair and announce to everyone that Ruby and Ryder are now officially dating. I'll agree to do *ten* more seasons of *Ruby of the Lamp*.

"C'mon, Ruby," Mean Nolan says. "We gotta keep this line moving."

I sigh, pick up my Sharpie again, and go back to work. But not before stealing one more glance at the hordes of people waiting for an autograph.

And that's when I see her.

She's standing toward the end of the line, holding shopping bags and dressed in jeans and a T-shirt. I blink hard, trying to refocus my eyes, because I'm dead certain all of this smiling and signing has done something to my vision and I'm not seeing correctly.

But nope. There's no mistaking. It's her.

Not Ruby.

But Gabriella!

I glance around to try to locate the two other Ellas, but they're nowhere to be seen. Gabriella is here alone. It's so strange seeing her by herself. Until now, I thought the three of them were physically attached to each other.

What is she doing here?

"Ruby?" I look up to see Nolan gesturing toward the postcard in front of me and I snap back to attention.

"Oh, sorry." I sign and then look up to smile at the next fan in line.

With each postcard that passes across the table, I can

see Gabriella moving closer and closer to the front of the line. My heart starts to pound and my palms start to sweat. Just like they always do when I'm around the Ellas.

She's here to make fun of me. I just know it. She knows I'm not really Ruby. She knows I'm Skylar and she's here to crack one of her mean jokes that starts with, "No offense, but . . ."

Relax, I tell myself. *She doesn't know.*

But what if she's here to make fun of *Ruby*? What if she gets to the front of the line and then announces to the entire mall that Ruby's music stinks and Ruby is totally lame and—

"Oh my gosh! I'm so excited to meet you! I've been waiting for this day for months. Oh my gosh! I can't believe it's really you." I startle at the sound of a high-pitched girl's voice, and I look up to see Gabriella standing right in front of me, bouncing around like she has springs in her shoes. When our eyes meet, her face transforms into a huge beaming smile. Bigger than I've ever seen anyone smile. Definitely bigger than I've ever seen *Gabriella* smile. She always looks so miserable and depressed. Like someone has literally drawn frown lines on her face.

"Hi!" she says to me, waving so wildly, I'm afraid her wrist might snap.

"Uh . . . hi," I manage to say, but for the most part, I'm utterly speechless. She doesn't look *anything* like the girl from my school. In fact, she looks a lot like . . .

Well, a lot like me. *Skylar.*

Or, at least, how I used to be. Before I learned the truth about who Ruby Rivera really is.

"Ruby," Mean Nolan reminds me again. "Let's keep it moving."

But I can't. I'm sorry. This is too big a mystery not to be solved. "Hold on," I tell Nolan, and glance back at Gabriella. She starts bouncing again.

"So," I say uneasily. "You're a fan?"

She nods way too many times. "Yes. Yes. Yes. I'm your biggest fan. I have both your albums and I know all the lyrics to all your songs and—"

"*My* songs?" I confirm, still thinking this is a huge joke.

She nods again. "Yes. My favorite is 'Living Out Loud,' and—"

"That's my favorite!" I exclaim before I can stop myself.

And then Gabriella does the one thing I never in a million years thought I'd see an Ella do. She *squeals*. Like a chipmunk. "Really? We have the same favorite? That's so cool!"

What is happening right now?

This is definitely not the same miserable girl who follows Daniella and Isabella around and parrots everything they say.

"Ruby," Nolan says, this time more sternly. But I'm barely even listening. I lean forward eagerly. "Do you watch the show?" I ask.

She does a little dance. "Of course! I've seen every episode."

"What's your favorite?"

"Definitely season two, episode fourteen. It's called . . ."

" 'Bottle Shock'!" we both say at once, and then break out into giggles.

"Oh my gosh!" she exclaims. "That part where you convinced Miles that you were trapped inside the body of the frog . . ."

"And then he starts carrying the frog around in his pocket and talking to it and sleeping with it in a box next to his bed!"

"That was the best. I laughed so hard, I almost peed my pants!"

"Me too!" I exclaim, and for a moment, I nearly forget who I am and who Gabriella thinks I am and how mad at Ruby I am. For a moment, I forget everything that's happened in the past few days and I'm myself again. My old self. The one who used to curl up on the basement couch with Leah and watch old *Ruby of the Lamp* episodes until we fell asleep. The one who decorated her entire room with Ruby's face. The one who would have done anything to be here today.

But then I remember.

Then it all comes flooding back to me. The shame I felt when I ran from the red carpet. The pure agony of picturing my mother out on a date with another man. The Photoshopped picture of me throwing up on a table not far from this very spot.

A picture that *Gabriella* is partly responsible for.

I clear my throat and bend my head to sign the post-card. "Thanks for coming," I say politely as the staff member hands the postcard to Gabriella and Nolan gives her a gentle nudge.

"Oh," she says, her face visibly deflating. "Right. Okay. Thanks so much! It was so nice meeting you!" And then she's ushered away.

I sign a few more postcards, politely smiling at the fans as they're herded past the table. The line is finally dying down, but there's still no hint of Ruby. I'm beginning to lose hope. I'm beginning to think she changed her mind. I'm beginning to think I'll be stuck in this life forever.

And that's when I hear the commotion coming from the mall entrance. My three security guards instantly perk up and one of them rushes toward the noise.

"This is an emergency!" someone yells. "I have to see her! You have to let me through!"

I instantly recognize the voice. After all, I've lived with it my entire life.

I DON'T KNOW YOU, BUT I DO

Sneaking out of the house wasn't easy. Rebecca was watching me like a hawk. Like she *knew* I would do it. I had to wait until she used the bathroom before I darted out the front door and ran through the entire housing complex to the road. I didn't have time to take a public bus. I'd already Googled the bus route and it would have taken me forty-five minutes to get to South Coast Plaza. I needed something faster and more direct. So I used Skylar's credit card again to pay for a car service.

I know, I know. It's the very thing that got me grounded in the first place, but this time it really *was* an emergency. I'm sure if I had been able to explain it to Rebecca, she would have understood.

I'm sorry, Rebecca. But I'm not really your daughter. I'm an imposter. Your real daughter is trapped in my body and I'm trapped in hers. So you see, it's a bit of a messy situation.

Yeah, that would have gone over *really* well.

Well, whatever. Skylar can explain it however she wants when she gets back. It's not my problem anymore.

The driver got me here in record time. Now there's only one thing that stands in the way of me getting my life back. And it's a *big* thing. It's a six-foot-five giant security guard who looks like he belongs outside a medieval castle instead of the entrance to a mall.

"I'm sorry," the hulking guard says, putting a massive hand on my shoulder. "The signing is over."

"No, you don't understand. You have to let me through."

"I don't *have* to do anything," he says in a menacing tone.

"Please!" I beg, "Ruby and I are *friends*. She's expecting me."

He actually rolls his eyes at this. "Yeah, like I've never heard *that* before."

"But this time it's true!"

"Please remove yourself from the premises or I'll do it for you."

My shoulders slouch. This is pointless. This muscle head is never going to let me through. For a moment, I consider dodging under his armpit and making a run for it. I'd probably be able to reach the signing table before they can catch me. But then I think about the last person who did that. The one who chased me around the food court, claiming to be my BFF. It didn't end well for her.

I'm just about to turn around and admit my defeat when I see someone out of the corner of my eye and my spirits lift.

It's my mom. She's standing off to the side of the

autographing area, tapping something into her phone. I feel tears of joy welling up at just the sight of her. I didn't realize how much I missed her until right this second. But that fleeting glimpse of her wavy brown hair and red-painted lips and towering high heels—it does something to me. It lights up something inside me.

I don't care how awful she can be—how controlling or demanding or clueless—she's still the woman who raised me all on her own. Who took care of me after my dead-beat dad left her alone and pregnant and broke. She's still my mom, and moms are forever.

"Mom!" I call out desperately, but of course she doesn't turn. Why would she? *Her* daughter is not standing in the doorway to the mall being blocked by a giant. *Her* daughter is inside the mall, signing autographs for her legions of fans.

At least, that's what she thinks.

But if I could just get her attention—just get her to look at me—I don't know, I guess I'm convinced that maybe somehow she'll recognize me. That she'll know her own daughter. Not by the color of my hair or skin or the sound of my voice. But by me. The person inside. We have a connection, right? Sure, we don't always get along, but for twelve years it's just been her and me. That's got to count for something.

"EVA!" I shout, and that seems to really anger the security guard. He starts to roughly spin me around and push me out the door.

"No!" I scream. I duck and turn and just manage to

slip through his grasp. I run straight to my mom. I grab her by the shoulders and I force her to face me.

"Eva. Please look at me."

At first, she's startled by being manhandled by a random twelve-year-old girl, and her shocked expression makes me think she's about to yell at me, shake me loose, call for help. But then our eyes catch. Our gazes lock. And for just a moment, she looks at me. Like really looks at me.

Confusion clouds her face. Her eyes squint like she's trying to see me through a filter. I know she knows. I can feel it. She can feel it. She recognizes me. And yet, she can't figure out *how* she recognizes me.

"Ru—" she begins to say, but stops herself. Because it's crazy. Because I'm not Ruby. I look nothing like Ruby. She glances back toward the table where her daughter is sitting, staring at us, watching this whole thing go down with a mix of fascination and helplessness.

I want to scream "YES! Mom! It's me! It's Ruby! I'm trapped inside here!" but I don't get the chance. Because just then, the spell is broken. The giant security guard grabs me and literally lifts me off my feet, dragging me toward the entrance to the mall. I twist my body until I can see my mom again. She's staring dazedly at the ground where I was just standing, like she's trying to figure out what happened.

The security guard sets me down on the sidewalk, straightening his shirt and giving me a cold, warning stare. "If you try to come in here again, I'll call the police. Do you understand?"

I nod, tears of frustration filling my eyes. She saw me. She knew me.

It's no use. I can't get in there. I can't get close to Skylar. I'll never get my mother back. I'll never get my life back.

Just then, the phone in my pocket dings. I pull it out, fully expecting to see a very angry text from Rebecca, demanding to know where I am. But it's not from Rebecca. It's from Skylar.

Meet me in the dressing room of the Gap in
2 minutes

SPICING THINGS UP!

Skylar

I've discovered that being a celebrity is a lot like being a prisoner. You're escorted everywhere you go. There are guards surrounding you at all times. And when you ask to use the bathroom, you're regarded with suspicion. As though you're really planning some elaborate escape.

Of course, I *am* planning an elaborate escape, but that's beside the point.

I can't believe Ruby lives like this. Never being able to do normal things like go to the mall, go to a restaurant, go to the bathroom, without the fear of being swarmed.

"We've cleared a restroom for you inside Bloomingdale's," Mean Nolan tells me. "Lawrence will escort you." He nods to one of the burly security guards, who walks over to stand by my side like he's afraid I'll try to bolt.

Of course, I *am* planning on bolting, but that's also beside the point.

"I'm fine going by myself," I tell Nolan, trying to sound casual.

Nolan glances around the Carousel Court at the hordes

of fans still hanging around, trying to snap a photo. "I don't think that would be very wise."

And so I guess I'm stuck with Lawrence. We walk silently, side by side through the crowd. He uses his big, burly arms to literally hold people back. All the while, they're screaming, "RUBY! RUBY! RUBY!"

I close my eyes for a moment, trying to drown out the sound. I just want out. I just want some peace and quiet. I just want to walk through the mall without needing a stupid escort.

Lawrence and I enter the Bloomingdale's and I quickly glance around, searching for an escape route. Thankfully, there are many places to hide inside a department store. But first I need a distraction.

I saw this in an episode of *Ruby of the Lamp* once. On one of her trips to look for her mother, Ruby was captured by evil Genie Hunters, who wanted to chain her to a lamp and use her as a wish-granting slave. Her only hope of an escape was when they were transporting her back to their lair and had to pass through a busy marketplace. It wasn't exactly a department store, but it was close enough. Ruby kicked over a table full of spices, sending a plume of paprika, cumin, and turmeric into the air. Everyone was blinded by the spice cloud, and by the time they all stopped coughing, sneezing, and waving curry powder from their faces, Ruby was gone.

I don't have any spices to use, but I might have something better.

Just as we're passing the Chanel counter, I make my

move. I pretend to trip and stumble, crashing into the counter. I reach out my arm and sweep ten bottles of sample perfumes onto the ground. The bottles smash and the noxious scent hits me immediately. Perfumes mixing together, invading my nostrils, stinging my eyes. A commotion instantly ensues. People are running over from all directions to help. Lawrence doubles over, coughing, and I don't waste a second.

I turn and run, ducking behind a nearby shoe display. Lawrence, realizing I'm gone, spins desperately in a circle, his eyes scanning the various makeup counters. He makes a split decision, heading farther into the department store. I take the opportunity to run in the other direction. Out the way we came, back through the mall, and straight into the Gap.

I find an open dressing room and slam the door closed behind me. I turn around and let out a yelp when I see that someone is already inside this dressing room. Someone who looks exactly like me.

"It's about time," Ruby says with her hands on her hips. "Now, where is that lamp?"

THE FACES IN THE MIRROR

Skylar and I stand side by side in front of the dressing room mirror. She's me and I'm her. She is in my body and I'm in hers. But not for long. Soon, I will be her again.

Ruby Rivera.

I feel a catch in my throat. Is that what I want? To return to that life? Those long days on set, those cheesy lines, those horrible clothes that are so not me? Being told what to do and what to say every single day?

But it's not like I can stay here. In Skylar's body. I can't continue to live a life that's not mine.

I guess neither life really feels like mine.

"Okay," Skylar says, taking the lamp from her bag. It seems to shimmer under the fluorescent lights of the dressing room. "Last time we were both holding it when we made the wish."

She grasps it with both hands and positions it so it's right between us. I can feel it there. Like it's radiating some kind of mystical energy. Like it's calling to me somehow. Inviting me to touch it.

Make the wish, Ruby.

Change yourself back.

I dare you.

"Ruby," Skylar coaxes, giving the lamp a nudge.

"Right. Sorry."

I swallow, staring down the golden object in Skylar's hands. One week ago, this thing was just a prop in a prop room. Now it represents so much more. A choice. A crossroads. A divide between worlds.

I glance up and stare at my old face. The face that appears on the cover of a million albums and on a million shower curtains and pillowcases and hand towels and trash cans.

Then I stare at my current face. Skylar's face. A face that can walk right out of here and be nobody. And also be *anybody.*

"Grab the lamp," Skylar says, waking me from my reverie. "C'mon. We're going to run out of time. The entire mall is probably out there looking for me . . . or you . . . or whatever."

She's right. We're running out of time. *I'm* running out of time.

I need to make a decision. I need to stop pretending. I need to give Skylar her life back. I may not know what to do with my own, but I can't keep hijacking hers.

Slowly, I reach out and grab the lamp. My skin hums at the touch of it.

"On the count of three," Skylar says in a voice I've

never heard from her before. She sounds like a girl who knows what she wants. I wish I could say the same about me.

"One, two, three," she counts us off, and then in one, unified voice we say, "I wish we could change back."

Skylar

I close my eyes. I wait for the earth to shake, the walls to quiver, the universe to tremble. I wait for the lamp to pull me out of this body and place me back into my old one. I wait to feel like myself again.

And then, as I wait, I wonder if I ever will. Feel like myself, that is.

I wonder what myself is *supposed* to feel like.

When I walked into that prop room on Thursday, I had such a clear picture of who I was and what I wanted.

I wanted to be more like Ruby.

I wanted to be less like Skylar.

I wanted . . .

To escape.

To escape middle school. To escape my parents' rocky relationship. To escape the Ellas. To escape myself.

But isn't that exactly what I'm doing now? Trying to escape again? Trying to run away from an epic mistake that *I* made?

So really, what's changed?

"Nothing's happening." A voice breaks into my

thoughts, causing my eyes to flutter open. I stare into the dressing room mirror. I lift my hand and wave it in front of my face. In the mirror, the reflection of Ruby Rivera does the same. Which means I'm still trapped inside her.

It didn't work.

"Why didn't it work?" Ruby asks. There's a strange quality to her voice. She doesn't sound angry or panicked or even desperate. She sounds almost . . . relieved.

And I *feel* almost relieved.

But why? Why would I feel relieved? I can't stay here. I can't be her forever. I'm not good at it. I ruined everything for her. And yet, I'm not good at living my own life, either, so where exactly does that leave me?

Stuck.

"I don't know," I reply calmly, staring down at the lamp. We're both holding it. We both said the words. It should work.

Then again, what the heck do I know about how genie lamps work? All I know about genie magic comes from a kids' show.

"Is there something else we should be doing?" Ruby asks.

I shrug. "Should we try it again?"

She shrugs, too. "It can't hurt."

"Concentrate really hard," I instruct her. I can't believe I'm actually giving Ruby Rivera orders. I can't believe she's actually taking them.

"Okay," she replies.

I clutch the lamp tighter in my hand. I feel Ruby's

grasp tighten as well. I watch her eyes close in the mirror. I squeeze mine shut. I concentrate hard on my wish. What I want more than anything. But my mind can't seem to focus. It's like it just empties out. Goes blank. A white screen.

"I wish we could change back," we both say at the same time.

But again, nothing happens. When I open my eyes, I'm still Ruby Rivera. And she's still Skylar Welshman. My hair is still dark and hers is still light. My eyes are still brown and hers are still blue. I still look like a TV star and she still looks like an average kid.

I still have this longing in my heart that I can't make sense of. Like a question that's calling out to me that I don't have the answer to.

And then, from somewhere far away, like a voice at the end of a long tunnel, another question is called out to me.

"RUBY? ARE YOU IN HERE?"

It's Eva.

Ruby and I both reply at once, "Yes."

But it's still me they've come for.

THE HIDDEN TRUTH

After my mom comes to take Skylar away, I sit in the dressing room for what feels like centuries. I can't bring myself to leave. I can't bring myself to go out there. Because what is out there waiting for me?

A middle school full of kids ready to laugh at me?

A mother ready to yell at me?

A life that's not mine?

But I know I can't hide in here forever. That's what I've been doing my whole life. Hiding. Pretending. *Acting*. And I don't just mean on the show.

When I step out of the dressing room, the Gap is quiet. The mall is closing soon, and the stores are emptying out. There are only a few shoppers still wandering around, riffling through shelves of tank tops, shirts, and jeans.

I walk out to the parking lot of the mall and sit down on a bench. I pull Skylar's phone out of my pocket and prepare to call a car to take me home. Skylar's mom is going to be livid. But I'll just have to deal with it. I'll have to take the heat.

"Skylar?" a familiar voice startles me.

I look up and do a double take when I see a tall, slender girl with long dark hair standing in front of me. She would look familiar if it weren't for the way she was dressed. I'm used to seeing her in miniskirts, designer tops, and high heels. Today she's wearing jeans, a T-shirt, and sneakers.

"Gabriella?" I ask, squinting up into the sun that's setting behind her, casting a sort of angelic glow around her head.

"Hi," she says, and she sounds nervous. "Are you here to see Ruby? I know you're a fan."

I nod. "I was, yeah." It's the truth. Just not the whole truth. But she doesn't need to know the whole truth. Besides, I need to be careful what I say to her. Anything and everything could be delivered back to the Ellas and used as ammunition. I learned my lesson there. Don't trust the Ellas. Not even the shyer, dark-haired one who never seemed to fit in.

"Me too," she says quietly, and then for a moment, we just stare at each other. It's awkward.

She takes a breath that seems to shudder through her. "Look," she says, biting her lip. "I'm glad I ran into you. I wanted to apologize for what Daniella did last night. It was so mean."

"For what *Daniella* did?" I repeat incredulously, almost angrily. "You're saying you had nothing to do with it?"

"No!" she rushes to say. "I mean, yes. I don't know." She's rambling now, making very little sense. "I knew

Daniella was setting you up when she invited you to the mall, and then to the dance. I knew she was going to do something bad, but I didn't know what it was."

So I was right, I think miserably. *It* was *a trap.*

"I'm not sure she even knew what it was until she saw you dancing with Ethan, and I guess she sort of freaked out. That's when she decided to Photoshop the picture. But I swear, it wasn't my idea. I didn't want to do it."

"Did you tell her that? Did you try to talk her out of it?"

Her gaze drops to the ground, like she's ashamed to even look at me. "No."

I cross my arms over my chest. "Well, thanks a lot."

She's silent for a long time, and just when I think she's scurried away, I hear the smallest, quietest sob. When I glance up again, Gabriella is crying into her hands.

I feel a twinge of annoyance at her tears. I'm the one who should be crying. Not her. But I can't help but feel curious, too. "Why are *you* crying?"

She wipes her nose. "I'm so sorry. I should have said something. I should have told her not to do it. I should have warned you before it all got out of hand. But I don't know, whenever I'm around those two, I just become this other person. This cowardly person. I can't say anything that's on my mind. I'm too afraid."

I shake my head, confounded. "Then why are you even friends with them?"

Gabriella starts bawling again and then plops down on the bench next to me. I instinctively scoot farther away from her. When she finally gets ahold of herself, she whimpers, "I didn't want to be. I never wanted to be."

"What?"

She swallows and sniffles. "I moved here two years ago. In the middle of fifth grade. I was new, too. I know how hard it can be. I was so desperate to make friends. And Daniella and Isabella were so popular. Everyone wanted to hang out with them. But they were like this little exclusive club and no one was allowed to even talk to them. They ruled the school. Even back then. Then, a few days after I'd started school, they came up to me on the playground. They asked me if my name was really Gabriella. I remember how they pronounced it. Gabri*ella*. Like the last four letters were the most important letters in the world. I was so shocked they were even talking to me, I just nodded. They turned to each other and this look passed between them. I can't explain it. It was like they were sharing a silent secret.

"Then they turned back to me and said I should hang out with them. I was so happy that someone was actually talking to me. But that was before I realized how awful they are. How horrible they treat people. It's like their one goal in life is to make other people feel bad about themselves. I think it makes *them* feel good. They come off as so confident and mature. But they're really not. They're like the exact opposite. And they're so mean. To me, to each other, to everyone. Once I figured it out, it was too late. I couldn't leave. Or . . ." She stops, wiping her nose again. "I guess I was *afraid* to leave." She lets out a huge sigh, like she's setting down a massive boulder that she's been carrying around for years. "I'm sure you don't get it, but—"

"I get it," I interrupt. "I *so* get it."

Everything she said is ringing in my ears, like the loudest alarm clock ever.

How long did it take me to figure out that I hated Hollywood? Hated being famous? Hated my life? Hated that stupid TV show? A few days? A few hours? And yet how long have I kept quiet about it?

Four. Years.

Gabriella and I are exactly the same.

Too afraid to speak up. Too afraid to walk away from something we know is all wrong for us. Too afraid of what will happen if we tell the truth.

Gabriella looks over at me, her face tearstained, her nose running. She looks *nothing* like the girl I met in that bathroom on Friday morning.

I guess everyone is hiding something. Even possibly a whole other person.

"You do?" she asks, sounding hopeful. "You get it?"

"I do," I tell her. "I know exactly how you feel."

A small smile makes its way onto her face.

"And," I go on, hearing the hope form in my own voice as well, "I know exactly how you can fix it."

Her smile instantly fades, replaced with dread. "How?"

I take a deep breath, letting the words flow from deep within me. From that place where truth lives. From that place where truth hides. "You need to tell them how you feel. You need to stand up for yourself. You need to speak your mind. If you don't do it now, you could be trapped forever."

And as the words tumble out of my mouth, I know they don't only apply to her.

They apply to all of us.

But mostly, they apply to me.

WHAT MOMS DO

Skylar

What happens now? I have no idea. Ruby and I were so sure the wish would work, we didn't even come up with a plan B. And then Eva came and whisked me away and we had no chance to talk about it or make plans or even try to figure out why it didn't work.

Eva and Nolan guide me out of the mall and into the parking lot. I'm just getting into Eva's SUV when I see my mother. She's getting out of her car. She looks angry and worried at the same time. The sight of her steals my breath away. I can literally feel it being sucked out of my lungs. And I suddenly find myself wondering if I'll ever be able to breathe normally without her again.

Why does it feel like I haven't seen her in months, when it's really only been a few days? Maybe because the hope of ever seeing her again is so slim now.

She doesn't look like herself. Her hair isn't tied back into its usual ponytail; it's falling loose around her shoulders. And she's wearing *pink*. I didn't even know she owned anything pink.

She looks beautiful.

I always knew she was, but I'm not sure I ever really saw it until right this second. Despite the sour expression on her face, she's the most beautiful person in the world to me. She's the *only* person in the world to me.

Except she hasn't come here for me. She's come here looking for Ruby.

From the outside of the SUV, Nolan closes the door with a firm shove, giving me a scowl. He's not happy about my disappearing act. No one is. I'm pretty much in huge trouble now.

After he walks away, I scan the parking lot until I see her again. She's walking briskly toward the entrance to the mall, pointing the key fob over her shoulder to lock the car as she goes.

"Mom," I whisper longingly into the glass.

"What?" Eva snaps, jabbing the start button in the car.

I blink and turn to flash her a hurried smile. "Nothing," I mutter.

She sighs. "Look, Ruby. I'm sorry. I'm just . . . I don't know what's gotten into you. You've been acting so strange lately. At first I thought it was great. You seemed to finally be getting back into your job and the show. But now, with all these little stunts you've been pulling, it's like you're an entirely different person. I don't even know who you are anymore."

"I'm sorry," I tell her, because there's nothing else to say. And because it's true. I *am* sorry. Sorry this happened to me and to Ruby and to Eva and to my mother. Sorry the lamp didn't work and now I'm trapped inside this body. Sorry I even made the wish to begin with.

Eva puts the car in gear and turns the stereo up loud. As we pull out of the parking lot, I'm able to steal one last glance at my mother—my real mother—just before she disappears through the entrance of the mall. I want to roll down the window and shout out to her that I miss her and that I love her. I want to tell her that she can date whoever she wants. I don't care. I want to tell her about all the screenplays I read—the good ones and the bad ones. I want to dissect their stories with her the way she dissects stories with her students. I want her to bring me library books I probably won't read and babble endlessly about feminism and corporate agendas and Jane Austen. I want to eat pizza with her in the living room while I watch TV and she reads in her special chair. I want all this and I fear I will never, ever have it again.

"I don't know who I am anymore, either," I tell Eva, but honestly, I'm not sure she heard me over the music.

All I know is that I miss my mom. Miss her so badly, it hurts deep in my chest. I want to talk to her. No, I *need* to talk to her. I need her to tell me it's going to be okay. She's the only person in the world who can make me feel better right now. Because she's the only person in the world who will ever be my mom.

And that's what moms do.

THE WRONG EVERYTHING

Rebecca lectures me the entire way back to the apartment. I stay quiet. Because there's nothing more to say. I can't argue with her. I *did* sneak out after she grounded me. I *did* betray her trust.

And it turns out, I did it all for nothing.

I'm still here.

And Skylar is still there.

We're like passengers on the wrong ships, heading in the wrong directions, with no way to turn around and go back.

But my mom recognized me. I know she did. Even if she doesn't realize she did. And somehow, that gives me hope.

When we get back to the apartment, Rebecca sits down at her laptop, mumbling something about catching up on emails. I skulk down the hallway to Skylar's room, passing Rebecca's bedroom on the way. The door is half ajar, and I stop and peer inside. I haven't been in Rebecca's room since I arrived here. There was never a reason to go in. Plus, it seems kind of strange, wandering into the bedroom of someone else's mother. It's like sleeping in someone else's pajamas. Sure, they're comfy and soft and worn in, but they're not yours, and you'll never be able to get a good night's sleep in them.

And yet now, something seems to be calling to me from inside the room. A warmth, an energy, a sense of security. And I suddenly find myself thinking about the Dallas house. About how I used to hide in my mom's closet when I was scared or had a bad dream, or a bad day at school. I would run into her tiny closet and burrow myself under her hanging clothes. Her clothes were simpler. The fabrics cheaper. The labels less flashy. But they smelled like her. And that smell always seemed to envelop me like a warm blanket. It always seemed to chase all the bad feelings away.

Checking to make sure Rebecca is still busy with her emails, I push open her bedroom door and make my way to the closet. It's small, like my mother's used to be. And almost all the clothes are the same three colors—black, white, and gray. I crawl under a rack of shirts and sit with my back against the wall. I take deep breaths, inhaling the scent. But it's all wrong. It doesn't envelop me like a warm blanket; it only reminds me of how far away I am, which just makes me feel colder.

I never thought I'd ever miss my mom's ridiculously high heels, or overly flashy dresses, or hundreds of skirts that still have the price tags on them because she buys more stuff than anyone could ever wear in a lifetime.

I never thought I'd long to see any of that again.

I never thought I'd miss her the way I miss her right now. Seeing her in that mall, knowing that she saw me—the real me—it makes my heart ache with longing.

It makes tears well in my eyes.

It makes me want to give anything—*do* anything—to have her back. To talk to her. To just hear her voice again.

DREAM A LITTLE DREAM

Skylar

It takes me a long time to find the episode I'm looking for. The shelves full of *Ruby of the Lamp* scripts in Eva's office seem endless. Four seasons of wonderful stories. Four years of me on the edge of my seat, waiting to find out what happens next. That's how long I've been in love with Ruby Rivera. Four years.

Because she gave me something to aspire to.

She gave me someone to root for when I couldn't root for myself.

She gave me somewhere to escape to.

When my parents were fighting, when my mom packed up boxes, when the Ellas were mean, when it seemed like I'd never survive another day of middle school, the Jinn Academy was always there waiting for me. Ruby and Miles and Headmistress Mancha and Rogue Raymond and everyone on the show were like my second family. They kept me safe. They drowned out the noise.

When I finally locate the script I'm looking for, I pull it off the shelf and run my fingertips over the title page.

I carry the script upstairs and head in the direction of Ruby's room. Except I don't go in. I don't even stop walking when I reach the door. Instead, I go to the end of the hall, to Eva's massive bedroom. I know she's not in there. She's downstairs, pacing the living room on her phone, still trying to sort out the last details of the scandal.

I push the door open and tiptoe through the bedroom. When I reach the closet—which is even bigger than Ruby's—I climb under a rack of designer dresses and pull my knees up to my chest.

There's something so inviting about a mom's closet, even if it's not your own mother's. It's safe and quiet and warm. Hidden away from the rest of the world. But as soon as I settle down, I feel the wrongness about it. The shoes are too tall. The clothes are too sparkly. The smells are too foreign.

All at once, it comes back to me. Seeing my mom through the window of the SUV. Wanting so badly to call out to her. Knowing that she wouldn't even recognize me if I did.

And suddenly, I know what I want. I want my old life back. My old room. My old clothes. My eyes. My skin. My hair.

I want it all because it comes with *her*.

I can handle the Ellas. I can handle the divorce. If I can

handle being a celebrity for three days, then I can handle anything.

My throat starts to sting from the tears I know are coming. I try to keep them at bay by flipping open the script I brought with me. I've seen this episode a million times. I know every line by heart, but there's something soothing about *seeing* those words on the page, reading them, letting them sink into my mind and wash over me like a warm, gentle wave. Maybe this is what my mom loves so much about books.

My mom always told me the joy of reading is being able to put yourself into the story, being able to *change* the story with your own experiences. I never understood that until now. Maybe I just never found the right thing to read.

I flip to the final scene of the episode. My favorite scene of the entire show.

INT. RUBY'S DORM ROOM—NIGHT
Ruby wakes up gasping for air, the dream still vivid in her mind.

RUBY
Mom? Was that really you?

There is no answer. But Ruby knows. She saw her. She was there.
Ruby starts to cry.

RUBY

Mom! I know it was you. I saw you.
I thought you were dead. But now I
know you're still out there. Still
alive. I will find you. I promise.
Even if I have to spend the rest of
my life looking, I will find you. I
will get back to you.

Ruby lies down, closing her eyes. Just before
she falls asleep, she hears a voice. Is it
another dream? Or something else?

RUBY'S MOM

I'll be waiting.

PHONE HOME

....

I pull out Skylar's phone.
I'm just going to call and hang up.
I dial my mother's number.
I just want to hear her voice.
I press the phone to my ear.
I just want to tell her I love her.

Skylar

I pull out Ruby's phone.
I'm just going to call and hang up.
I dial my mother's number.
I just want to hear her voice.
I press the phone to my ear.
I just want to tell her I love her.

COLLISION

· ·

The room starts to shake.

Skylar

The earth starts to tremble.

The world is breaking apart.

Skylar

And coming back together.

A voice answers the phone. "Hello?"

Skylar

"Mom?"

THE OTHER ROOM

Skylar

"What are you doing?"

The voice on the other end of the call is all wrong. No, it's not wrong. It's right. It's very, very right.

But I don't understand.

"Why are you calling from the other room?" it asks.

"The other room?" I repeat. Bewildered, I glance around the tiny closet. At the T-shirts and jeans and comfortable shoes.

"Why don't you just come out here and talk to me?" the voice on the phone says.

"Come out where?"

She laughs. A beautiful carefree laugh. "To the living room, silly lark. What's going on with you?"

Lark?

To a Skylark.

I drop the phone and run. The world is a blur. The room is a blur. The hallway is a blur. The living room is a blur. And then . . .

Everything slams into focus.

And all I see is her face.

Her face.

"Mom!" I scream, and wrap my arms around her.

WISH GRANTING 101

The phone slips from my grasp. I can hear a voice coming from the tiny speaker. It sounds so small and far away.

"Ruby? Ruby? Are you there? What's going on?"

I scramble to grab the phone, and that's when I see it. My hand.

My hand. My skin. My fingernails. My . . . everything.

I glance around the closet. It's so big, I could do cartwheels across it. I almost do.

It happened. I don't know how it happened, but it happened. I'm back. I'm here.

"Ruby?"

I pick up the phone. I bring it to my ear. My heart is pounding. "Mom?"

"Yes?" She sounds worried. She sounds winded. "Are you all right?"

"Eva Rivera?" I ask, because I can't bring myself to believe it. It's her voice. It's her closet. And yet I have to be sure.

She laughs a nervous little laugh. "What other mom would it be? Where are you?"

"In your closet," I tell her.

"What are you doing in"—she opens the door, she walks in, she stands in front of me, hands on hips, lips pursed in confusion—"my closet?"

I climb out from under her dresses and run to her. I practically bowl her over as I leap into her arms. "Mom! It's you! It's really you!" I know she doesn't like to hug. She doesn't want to wrinkle whatever expensive outfit she has on. But I don't care. I squeeze her tighter than I've ever squeezed her before.

Her hands remain limp at her sides, like she doesn't know what to do with them. But I keep hugging her. I don't let go. I show her how it works.

This is what mothers and daughters do, Mom.

Somehow she must understand, because eventually her arms lift and she circles them around me. "Sweetie," she says gently, tenderly. "What's wrong? Is everything okay?"

I pull back and look at her. Tears are streaming down my face, but I don't wipe them away. She has to see them. I have to show them. I can't hide them any longer. "No, Mom. It's not. It's not okay."

Her brows pinch together, like she's going to scold me. But she doesn't scold me. She sits down on the small sateen bench in the center of the closet and pats the space next to her. "Come here. Talk to me. You know you can always tell me anything."

She's said that to me a thousand times, but I've never believed her.

Now I know I have no choice. I have to believe her.

Because I have to tell her everything.

THE JUST-RIGHT CHAIR

Skylar

I tell her everything.

Everything I haven't been able to tell her before. That I have no friends here. That middle school is hard. That the divorce is breaking my heart. That I miss Dad and Leah and the Amherst house.

But most of all, I tell her that I want her to be happy. And if going out with Clint is what will make her happy, then so be it. I'll deal with it. If she likes him, then I'll figure out a way to like him, too.

Mom listens with tears sparkling in her eyes. When I finish, she reaches out and pulls me onto her lap. Onto her special reading chair. I'm too big to be on her lap. And the chair isn't meant for two people. But it doesn't matter. It feels just right.

I cry into her shoulder and she strokes my hair.

She tells me it'll all be okay.

And I believe her.

Mom doesn't yell. She doesn't rant. She doesn't throw anything. She just listens to everything I have to say. About hating the show. About never wanting to be on TV in the first place. About wanting to go to school and learn things and go to college and learn more things. About being hungry all the time. About how this life was never my choice. It was hers. And I don't want it anymore.

"I'm done," I tell her. I'm sobbing now, but I can't stop talking. I have to get it all out. I can't keep it inside any longer. "I'm sorry if that makes you sad. Or angry. Or disappointed in me. I'm sorry if that means we'll have no money after this. Or if—"

"Shhh." Mom stops me, putting her arm around my shoulders and pulling me close to her. "Ruby. Ruby. Ruby."

My name—my real name—it sounds so melodic on her lips. It sounds like a song. A song I want to play on repeat for the rest of my life.

"Don't worry about any of that." She chuckles. "You're

way too young to worry about money. That's why you have me."

"But," I begin to argue, thinking about the phone call I heard between Mom and our money manager, Peter, in my trailer. It was the whole reason I lost my nerve to tell her I wanted to quit.

"What do you mean there's not enough? I thought you said we were fine. I thought you said not to worry about it."

"What about that conversation you had with Peter?" I ask. "Didn't he tell you there wasn't enough money?"

Mom's brow furrows, like she's trying to remember what I'm talking about. Then her eyes flash with recognition. "Oh! The call about the investors?"

"Investors?" I ask, confused.

"Peter has been working on getting some investors together to finance a hotel. We're one of them. But he's having trouble finding the rest."

My face pinches in confusion. "Huh?"

Mom laughs and squeezes me tighter against her. "Ruby, this is adult stuff. Adult problems. You're only twelve. You shouldn't even be thinking about all of that. And trust me, money is the last thing we have to worry about."

"So . . . ," I say, trying to wrap my head around everything. "We're not going to go broke if I quit the show?"

Mom tips her head back and laughs. "Of course not. Do you think I've been squandering every penny you make? I always promised myself I would never let us be poor again. That's why I hired Peter to help me make smart decisions. I've been saving. Investing. Making some really great choices. Just in case you decided you didn't want to do this anymore."

I blink, unable to fathom what I'm hearing. "What?"

Eva's face softens. "Ruby, I thought you liked this life. I thought this is what you wanted. That's why I've busted my butt for the past four years to make it happen for you. That's why I've pushed you to wear the right clothes and look the right way and say the right things. Because I thought you loved this job. And I wanted to make sure you could do it for as long as you wanted. Because I wanted you to be happy. I never knew you were so miserable."

I bow my head, feeling foolish. She never knew because I never told her. I never told anyone. I just grinned and bore it. On every red carpet. In every photo shoot. In every costume fitting. In every recording session. On every stage.

"If you hated it so much, why didn't you just tell me?" she asks.

I sniffle. "I guess I was afraid of how you would react."

Mom pulls back and looks me in the eye. And that's when I see it. Something familiar. Something comforting and compassionate and loving.

Something I've been searching for, for a long time.

Maybe it's always been there. Maybe I didn't look close enough to see it. Or maybe she didn't do her best to show it.

Either way, now we both know it's there.

FADE-OUT

....

Skylar

Three months later . . .

"And, action!" I call out from behind the camera. I watch on the small viewfinder as the scene I wrote unfolds. It's exactly how I scripted it.

EXT. DESERTED WOODS—DAY
Clarissa scurries out from behind a tree. She looks left, looks right, and then starts to dig. A moment later, she unearths a gorgeous sapphire RING. She holds it up to the light.

CLARISSA
Ah, yes. This will do very nicely.

Just then, Hans and Theresa appear, startling Clarissa.

                    HANS

        Okay, Clarissa. Game's up.

        Hand it over.

Clarissa slides the ring onto her finger.

                  CLARISSA

        Never.

                  THERESA

        Don't make us take it from you.

Clarissa starts to laugh. A dark, evil laugh.

                    HANS

        What's so funny?

                  CLARISSA

        The fact that you think you can

        catch me.

And then Clarissa is off, vanishing into the
trees.

    "And, cut!" I call, glancing up from the viewfinder.
"That was amazing!"
    Gabriella rushes over with her makeup bag. "I
got chills!"

I grin. "Me too!"

We're behind Fairview Middle School, where there's a small patch of trees that we're using as our "forest" set. We're shooting my very first short film. I wrote it as my first project for the film club. As soon as Gabriella found out I was shooting it, she offered to be my makeup artist and hairstylist. She's really good. She's also surprisingly nice, now that she doesn't hang out with the Ellas anymore. Actually, the Ellas aren't really the Ellas anymore. Once Gabriella left, it didn't really make sense for them to be called the Ellas any longer. Now they're just Daniella and Isabella, two best friends who mostly keep to themselves. I think they lost some of their power when they lost their third member . . . and their cool name.

Ethan also wanted to be in the movie. He's playing Hans. My friend Leah is playing Theresa. She flew out from Amherst during Winter Break just to be in the film. When I told her I was making it, she said she wouldn't miss starring in my debut for all the world. Ethan and Leah run over from the trees and peer over my shoulder.

"Can you play it back?" Ethan asks.

"Sure." I tap the menu button on the new digital camera my dad bought me when I went home to Amherst for Thanksgiving. It shoots video and takes amazing photographs.

The scene replays and I get chills all over again. When it's finished, Ethan does a cute little fist pump. "Oh yeah. That was awesome. Up top!" He puts his hand up, and Gabriella, Leah, and I each give him a high five.

416

I like Ethan. He's funny and nice. And after Ruby told me he had a crush on me . . . well, at first I didn't believe her, but then we started to hang out more. I'm not sure why I never really noticed him before. Maybe because I was too distracted worrying about the Ellas, I failed to see what was right in front of me.

"C'mon, costar, you too," Ethan says, turning toward the girl running over to us from the trees. He keeps his hand in the air, and Ruby comes up to high-five it.

After *much* begging, she agreed to play Clarissa. I can't *wait* to see the reaction of everyone at school when we premiere the movie and they all see I got Ruby Rivera to be in my first-ever film. Although it'll be nothing compared to the reaction I got from Gabriella and Leah when they found out. I told them Ruby and I had met when I went on a tour of the Xoom! Studios lot, which isn't *technically* a lie.

Ruby turns to me. "So, *director,* how was it?"

"Perfect!" I exclaim, bouncing on my toes. "Absolutely perfect! You're such a star."

She rolls her eyes at me. "Don't be so dramatic."

I throw my arm around her shoulders. "Thanks for coming out of retirement to be in my movie."

She grins back at me. "I wouldn't have come out of retirement for anyone else. Not even Barry Barktastic Barkface."

"I know," I say, giving her a mournful look. "I still can't believe you won't be on the show next season. It's going to be so sad to watch."

Thankfully, since Ruby and her mother had never actually signed the new contract, Lesley was able to get her out of doing the fifth season of *Ruby of the Lamp*. Ruby told me all about it when we met for lunch in Beverly Hills a few weeks ago. Yes, I have lunch in Beverly Hills with Ruby Rivera now. That's how cool I am. But in all seriousness, it turns out we actually have a lot in common. Something we never realized until we literally spent a few days in each other's shoes.

"It'll be fine," Ruby assures me for what must be the hundredth time. "The show will go on. Ryder will take over as lead, and they'll cast some new up-and-coming tween actress to be his love interest."

"Poor girl," I say, and Ruby and I both start laughing.

"Look on the bright side," Ruby says. "Soon you'll have a brand-new face to decorate the walls of your room with."

I shake my head. I know she's teasing me. The truth is, I took down all my Ruby Rivera decorations a few months ago. Now I'm having fun filling my walls with photographs I've taken with my new camera. Like of me and Gabriella hanging out at the mall, Leah in her first big drama club role, Ethan in his lacrosse uniform, and me and Dad with the massive Thanksgiving feast we cooked together.

You know, stuff from my *own* life.

After filming a few more scenes, we pack up the equipment and head back to the school. Eva is waiting for Ruby in her SUV out front. She's become a lot more relaxed lately about Ruby's life. Which is why she seems to be okay with Ruby hanging out with a regular girl from the suburbs like me.

"Mom and I are going for Mexican," Ruby tells me. "Want to come?"

"Wait, you got your mom to eat Mexican food?"

Ruby frowns. "Not really. She's on something called the Baby Food Diet. She brings her own jars of baby food with her everywhere. It's totally embarrassing. But at least she lets *me* eat whatever I want now."

I giggle at the thought of Eva eating out of tiny baby food jars.

"So, are you in?" Ruby asks.

I shake my head. "I can't. Sorry. I'm late for script club with my mom."

Mom and I recently started our own version of a book club. Except instead of books, Mom brings home screenplays from the UC–Irvine film library. We read them together and then watch the movie and analyze the plot, the characters, even the set design! It's really fun. We've done everything from classics to Pixar movies. Plus, it's nice to have something that's just ours. Mine and Mom's.

Even though I told her I didn't mind, Mom decided not to continue to date Clint. She swears it's not just for me, but for her, too. She says she's not ready. She needs more time.

I still have no idea what's going to happen at the end

of the school year. Maybe we'll move back to Amherst. Maybe Mom will get a full-time job at UC–Irvine and we'll stay here. Either way, I know it'll all work out.

"We should get together this weekend," I suggest to Ruby.

She nods. "Totally! But we'll have to do Sunday. My mom has an audition on Saturday."

My mouth falls open. "She does? For what?"

Ruby giggles. "The host for some new reality make-over show."

I burst out laughing. "She'd be perfect for that!"

"I know, right? I really hope she gets it. It'll give her something to do. Plus, I can do my homeschooling while she's on set."

I bite my lip, trying to build up the courage to ask the question that's been burning a hole in my mind for the past few months. "Do you think you'll ever go back to acting? Some of those scripts I read in your mom's office were actually pretty good."

Ruby glances up at the sky as if she'll find the answer to my question there. Then she shrugs. "Maybe one day. But for now, I'm just really loving sleeping in."

I nod. "It is pretty nice."

"I feel like I have four years of sleep to make up for." She laughs and then stops, an idea suddenly lighting up her face. "How about this? I'll make you a deal."

I'm immediately suspicious. "This deal doesn't happen to involve any magic lamps, does it?"

She chuckles. "No! Here's the deal: when you shoot your first full-length feature film, I promise to star in it."

A huge smile breaks onto my face. I thrust my hand out to Ruby. "Deal."

We shake hands, and I can feel the large sapphire ring still on her finger from the scene we just filmed.

Then, a second later, the ground starts to tremble violently beneath our feet. I stare wide-eyed at Ruby. She stares wide-eyed back at me. And just as quickly as it started, the trembling stops.

"Whoa," Gabriella says, running up to us. "Did you feel that earthquake?"

I quickly glance down at my hands, checking to make sure they're still mine. I peer over at Ruby, who's doing the exact same thing. I let out a sigh of relief.

I'm still me. And she's still her.

"I think that was my very first earthquake," I say.

Gabriella laughs. "Pretty scary, huh?"

Ruby and I share a look. And then, at the exact same moment, we both say, "You have no idea."

ACKNOWLEDGMENTS

This book was so much fun to write, from the first page to the last. But like any book, it couldn't have been done without the help of some tremendous people. Thank you to Wendy Loggia and Audrey Ingerson at Delacorte Press for falling for Ruby and Skylar as hard as I did and for your boundless editing wisdom. Thank you to Jim McCarthy for continuing to be the best agent a writer could ask for (and for coming up with the *perfect* title for this seemingly untitle-able book). Thank you again to Leslie Mechanic for creating, hands down, the cutest cover I've ever had the privilege of seeing my name on. And to Kathy Dunn and everyone at Delacorte/Random House Children's Books for your amazing work getting my books into the hands of young readers.

I interviewed a *ton* of middle schoolers during the process of brainstorming and writing this book. I was sworn to secrecy, but you know who you are. Thank you for sharing your secrets and experiences with me.

As always, thanks to my family—Michael, Laura, Terra, and my brand-new brother-in-law, Pier. Welcome to this crazy family, fratello! And of course, my undying love and gratitude goes to Charlie, who never seems to tire of hearing about my endless plot problems. Or if he does, he's a better actor than Ruby.

But the biggest thanks *always* goes to my readers, especially the tweens. You have captured my heart with your enthusiasm, your letters, your Instagram photos, and your smiles. Just knowing you're all out there, reading these words, makes me feel like the luckiest person in the world. Remember, there's no better you than you. Trust me.